They called us a Firm.
We called ourselves an
EMPIRE.

To Mum & Dad I know you always did your best

& my wife Suzanne

The Krays Not Guilty Your Honour

'It's a Dog eat Dog world, always has been,
and sadly… always will be.'

Joseph Henry Gaines

"So they call me a villain, a psychopath, a cold-blooded killer! All I ever did was look out for my own, protect my family ... No one else was there to fucking look out for us, so what! If I cut a few mugs, so what if a few ears had to be sliced off, so what if I shot a few bullets, that's just the way things are where we're from...whatever happens tomorrow morning in court, one thing is fucking certain, they'll remember me...they'll remember the name Ronnie Kray!"

Ronnie Kray-Brixton Prison.

INTRO 5
CHAPTER ONE BACK ON THE MANOR 7
CHAPTER TWO MARBELLA & MURDER 16
CHAPTER THREE CHEERS AND TEAR'S 40
CHAPTER FOUR THE ONLY GOOD COPPER'S, A DEAD UN! 54
CHAPTER FIVE ANOTHER DAY AT THE BAILEY 77
CHAPTER SIX BUSINESS & BULLETS 126
CHAPTER SEVEN ON THE HUNT 156
CHAPTER EIGHT ANOTHER DAY IN LONDON 178
CHAPTER NINE THEM & US 205
CHAPTER TEN LOYALTIES 236
CHAPTER ELEVEN IT'S ONLY BUSINESS 257
CHAPTER TWELVE ERE WE GO AGAIN 271

Intro

28th of February 1969.
Outside court number one at the Old Bailey, Central Criminal Court London.

"It's pandemonium! Outside the courts, Ronnie Kray accompanied by his two brothers Reg and Charles, has just left the court acquitted on all charges. The three men were picked up by a cream coloured Rolls Royce and driven back onto the streets of London. All around me everyone is looking at each other in utter confusion, everyone is in shock. This case, the longest in British Judicial history has caused utter chaos in the streets that surround the Old Bailey. After two murders and one suspected murder, and three further murders since their arrest, the notorious Kray Firm has again walked away free from all charges!"

BBC reporter Russell Taylor a senior crime reporter working for BBC radio was suddenly barged from his position on the steps. Taylor turned to see that his colleagues and the crowd were rushing frantically towards the side entrance of the Bailey as news broke that one of the Kray Firm was making his exit. Taylor forced his way to the front of the crowd by using his status as a BBC reporter just in time to see Freddie Foreman exit the building; Foreman punched the air in victory as he bustled his way through the crowd.

"Mr. Foreman!"

"Mr. Foreman! Russell Taylor from BBC news, Do you have a statement?"

"Mr. Foreman, Mr Foreman!"

"Can we have a statement please?"

Russell Taylor sensing from his years of journalism that the jubilant Foreman was not going to say a word, swiftly found some room and ordered his film crew to film him with Foreman in the background.

"Behind me now making his way to a car is Freddie Foreman, long-time associate of the Kray Gang, Foreman has been found not guilty on all counts."

Then suddenly another forceful surge of the crowd interrupted the filming, Taylor turned to see his colleagues from the press turning their attention to Detective Superintendent Read, who was flanked by two burly policemen and was leaving the courts.

After countless pleas from the crowd, Reid stopped on the steps.

"Detective, what are your thoughts?"

"Was this a miscarriage of justice, Detective?"

Read held his hands up to the crowd as if trying to calm the bedlam.
"Please! Please there will be an official statement from the police at an appropriate time."
"Do you have any links to the murder of Dixon?"
"Will there be any further charges?"
"I have no comment at this time."
Russell Taylor again forced his way to the front of the crowd where he blocked the Detectives' path.
"Are the Krays untouchable now Dectective?" He asked.
Detective Superintendent Leonard ("Nipper") Read. Suddenly stopped in his tracks; he gazed up at the old wily face of Taylor angered by his remark.
"I shall rephrase the question Inspector."
"Are the Krays above the law?" Asked Taylor now more quietly.
Read tilted his head in frustration.
"No one is above the law! Not one single individual or group, it is the laws that bind us as a civilisation. We have a system, a very old and trusted system. It is not perfect, but that is justice, we put our faith and prayers into it and in the end it always wins."
"Was today a victory for you Inspector?"
"Like I said before Mr. Taylor there will be an official statement at a later date, but I will add that as long as I continue to serve in her Majesties Police force I shall not cease to apprehend and convict the culprits who commit murder or threaten the public's safety with violence and intimidation."
"There we have the words of Chief Inspector Read." Replied Russell Taylor as he turned towards his TV crew.
"Today's events are sure to be a landmark in London's History, only a few months ago we heard how the Kray gang were finished from their life of crime. In the words of Detective Superintendent Leonard ("Nipper") Read, he said on the day of their arrest that London was now a safer place, and now on the 28th of February 1969, that same gang has walked away from the Old Bailey as free men. Have we witnessed justice here today? ... Or have we witnessed the blackest day in British judicial history? And possibly the greatest travesty to ever take place inside a British court! ...... This is Russell Taylor for the BBC, outside the Old Bailey Court."

Not Guilty Your Honour
Chapter one

'Back on the Manor'

As the cream coloured Rolls Royce turned into the Mile End Road it seemed as if the whole of the East-End of London had heard the news, shopkeepers had left their shops to stand cheering at the roadside and people had stopped their cars and were like wise clapping and cheering.
As the car turned left into Vallance Road where their mother Violet lived, the press and the Kray's friends and family were all gathered outside the house waiting for them to arrive.
Ronnie was first to get out of the car followed by Reg and their elder brother Charlie, Ronnie looked poker faced as he walked towards his mother, who had rushed to greet him at the front door while Reg looked much more jubilant with Charlie, as they punched the air in signs of victory as they stopped to shake the hands and hug their neighbours and friends.
Ronnie wrapped his arms affectionately around his mother and only allowed himself a slight smile before he turned looking agitated towards his brothers.
"Reg!" he called out as he nodded in the direction of his mother, almost like an order for his brother to hurry up.
Both Reg and Charlie embraced their mother before they both disappeared into the house.

Once inside the house Ronnie threw off his jacket and greeted his Father Charlie sr with a Firm handshake and a slight business like smile.
“Reggie! Get hold of Tony and Chris and tell them I want a meeting.” Ronnie snapped at his brother referring to the Lambrianou brothers.
“I would think they would want some time with their family Ron.” Charlie added, as he knew that Reggie would only pass the chore over to him.
“Well, let them have some time with them, then tell them to get round here.” Ronnie snapped as he made is way upstairs to the room that he so often used as his office.
Charlie turned in a frustrated way to his brother Reg who was now seated and being poured a cup of tea by his mother.
“Don’t he ever fucking stop! This morning we was all looking at getting lifed-off, Tony and Chris will want some time by themselves, they got family Reg.”
“Just call em Charlie! We got a lot of things that need saying,” Reg replied, as he made sure he had Ron a cup of tea before walking upstairs to join him.
Charlie sighed loudly as his mother gently patted his head and he leaned over to pick up the phone.
“Is Tony there?” he asked.
“Tony speaking, who’s that, is that you Charlie.”
“Yeah it’s me.”
“Fucking hell Charlie its bedlam out here, there must be a hundred fucking reporters outside.”
“Same ere mate.”
“Just had to fight our way in the door, they took a right fucking liberty with us at the Bailey. They said you and the twins weren’t leaving till all the fuss outside had died down, they tried to make us wait but Chris said bollocks and we forced our way out.”
“Listen Tony, Ronnie wants a meet tonight.”
“What is he fucking joking? We’ve been with him every day for the last few months; we wanna spend a bit a time with our families.”
“Well just pop your head in some time later, just for ten minutes all right, let’s not fucking wind him up.”
“Charlie I’ll be there, but I don’t know if Chris will alright.”
“Alright Tone see ya later mate.”
With that Charlie hung up the phone and began to make his way upstairs, but before he could get to the stairs Johnny Walsh an old time associate of the family, who was standing by the outside door to make sure that none of the reporters knocked, opened the door and ushered Charlie over.
“Charlie I’ve just seen Jimmy from Islington pulling up.”
“Bring him in.” Charlie replied encouragingly.
“Charlie!”
“Alright Jimmy come in.” Charlie replied as he saw his friend.

"Had to come over and shake your hands mate, were all over the fucking moon!"
"Come upstairs Jim the twins are up there."
Charlie then turned back to Johnny Walsh and asked him to continue standing by the door.
"Keep an eye on them leeches John, don't want them driving Mum mad."
"Don't worry Chas."
Charlie then led Jimmy upstairs to the room where Reggie and Ron was, both the twins turned around at the same time as the door was opened and rose to their feet to greet there friend.
Jimmy Ryan was the youngest of four brothers based in Islington North London, they went back a long way with the Kray's, and they had their own feet in quite a few dealings, it was commonly known that the Ryan's from North London were not a Firm to mess around with.
Jimmy threw an arm around Reggie as he shook Ronnie's hand.
"My brothers send their best Ron."
"How are they?" Ronnie replied quietly.
"Their good, still away but now all this has been sorted out we can start making plans for them to come home." replied Jimmy as he referred to his three elder brothers who on the arrest of the Kray Firm had left the country, just as a precaution in case they were going to be pulled in themselves or be called as witnesses at the trial.
"Do ya want a cup of tea Jim?" Reggie asked.
"No thanks Reg, I can't stay mate I only popped in to say congratulations and to pass on my brothers regards."
"Tell your brothers that we will take care of everything to get them back here safely, then we can sit down and get things back to how they used to be." Ronnie replied.
"Well let's just take things one at time Ron, there's gonna be a lot of eyes on all of us mate."
When Tony Lambrianou turned up at Vallance road and walked upstairs he was surprised to see that the twins had already amassed a large crowd. Tony walked over and hugged Ronnie then proceeded to have his hand shook by all the other men in the room, men like Trousers Johnny who got the name trousers because of the high waistline, 'gangster style' as he liked to wear them, then there was Slicem Sid from Hackney, Eddie Brenner from Mile End, and Dennis Smith also from Mile End,
Bill and Georgie Hayes from Hoxton and little Sammy Carpenter from Tooting which was south of the river.
Once all the greetings had taken place Reggie asked everyone to sit down. A bottle of scotch was passed round where everyone was urged to pour them

self's a drink. Ronnie waited for every ones glass to be filled before he rose from his seat with his glass in hand.
"Where's Chris Tony?" Ronnie asked.
"Couldn't get away Ron, mi Dads not to well."
Ronnie nodded slightly before he addressed his friends.
"Thanks for all coming, I wanted you all here so you could hear what me and Reg have got say with your own ears. Firstly I know there's a few of you here that have let us down while we've been away, but today is a new start, we are willing to forget all the crap that's gone on while we've been in the nick. Just as long as it ends now, at this meeting here. And all of you come back to work with us."
Suddenly the room burst out in mumblings of approval "always Ron." "Goes without saying Ron"
"Let me finish! You all had jobs to do and you've all fucked them up! When we went away we had interests in clubs, pubs, shops and gambling, you've lost the fucking lot. Most of the reasons we already know of, other reasons well find out, I want to know who, how and when of everything that's gone on in the manor, then I will tell how were gonna get it all back."
"And make no mistake about it, were gonna get everything back." Reggie added.
Billy Hayes suddenly got to his feet.
"Ron if you're talking about the snooker hall and spieler we had mate, there was fuck all we could do, that fucking Irish mob came at us from everywhere. There are four brothers and a thousand fucking cousins. They came into the game one night about fifteen handed with shooters, even if we were tooled up, we couldn't have done anything."
"Don't worry about that, we'll take care of them bastards." Reggie added.
"They must be crapping themselves now." remarked slicem Sid.
"That's one of the first things on our agenda when we get back." Ronnie replied.
"You going away Ron?" asked Georgie Hayes.
"Me, Reg and Charlie are gonna go away and get some sun, do a bit of sailing and have a few drinks. And while were away I'm gonna give you all a few little tasks to do, so when we come back everything will be ready for us to make our moves."
"So get all the boys back together and tell them we got a lot of work to do, and if any fucker thinks we're old news! Then you tell them, we're be paying them a visit real soon. Holidays over! We're back, and this time there be no fuck ups!" Reggie said as leaned back into his chair and took a large drag on his cigarette.
"What about Fred Ron? Do you want me to see him while you're away?" Tony Lambrianou asked referring to Freddie Foreman.

“Fred’s got his own plans, he’s our pal for life, but our paths go in different ways, I don’t want anyone seeing Fred or going into South London without speaking to me first.”
“That also goes with the west end, lets sort our own manor out first then me an Reg will see what’s about up the West End.”
After about an hour Ronnie asked everyone to leave except for the Hayes brothers Billy and George, and told the rest of them to meet them down the carpenter’s arms later that evening for a good old drink. Once every one had left, Ronnie sat the brothers down and spoke quietly to them,
“While we’re away I want you to get in touch with Jeff Samuels, tell him your speaking on my behalf and give him this grand.” Ronnie suddenly broke off speaking and rolled off a thousand pounds from a large wad of money he had in his inside suit pocket.
“I want you to tell him to go down the old speiler and clock everything that’s going on, tell him the grand is for him to play with. Tell him not to win, just play nice and slow, I want to know what time the paddy bastards get there? What time they leave? Who they’re with? How busy it is? Every fucking detail I want to know, barmaids, friends, associates, and who’s playing at the tables, do ya understand Bill? I want to know everything.”
Ronnie then motioned Reggie to get something from the drawer; Reggie pulled out another thousand pounds and brought it over to the table
“Here’s another thousand pounds, in two weeks’ time when you have all the information, we want you to come round here and see our Dad, he will give you a phone number where you are to drive out of town and call us. We’re tell you what to do then, don’t blow that grand cos you’re gonna need it when you call us, now remember Bill we want to know everything about these paddies. While Jeff is finding out about the game we want you and your brothers to get the addresses of all the bloody Irish fuckers, don’t let us down, you let us down before so do this for us now to the letter… and everything that’s gone on in the past will stay in the fucking past.”
Said Reggie as he fondly patted Billy on the cheek.
“It’s done Reg!” Georgie replied.
With that Ronnie got to his feet in a manner that immediately signalled that the meeting was over.
“I’m gonna have a wash!” Charlie said as left the room leaving Ronnie and Reg alone.
“Give Joey Pine a call before would ya Charlie, ask him if he can meet us down the Carpenters later.”
“I’ll do it now Ron.” Charlie replied as he left.
Ronnie then sat down with Reggie again.
“Do ya remember that kid, who came into Wandsworth for the stabbing, said he was a cousin of Joey’s?”

“Yeah, what about him?” Reggie asked.
“He told me once while we was on exercise that Joey Pine and his Firm had a bit of grief getting a license for a big boozer they had in Chelsea.”
“Yeah I remember now, Fred pulled some strings and got them the license.”
“We did more than that Reg we paid for it, four and half grand we give em.”
“Why didn’t you tell me about that?” Reggie asked.
“That don’t matter Reg, it was just something I did for Fred, you was down the choky when it happened.” Ronnie replied warmly as he instinctively looked over his shoulder and began to whisper in Reggie’s ear.
“Listen Reg, we are gonna be looked at by every fucking one under the sun, I want to use Joey’s Firm to take care of the paddies for us. There off the manor, no one will suspect it’s them. Joe’s got a good little Firm down there, they use all the blacks and the Gypo’s , give em fifty quid and their shoot anyone.” Ronnie added with a wry smile.
“Do those fuckers! While we’re all away on holiday.”
“That’s it Reg, while we’re away sitting on a beach getting sunburnt and pissed, those paddy bastards will get one in the nut.”
Reggie smiled broadly and shook his brother’s arm.
Later that night the Carpenters arms in Bethnal green, was packed to the rafters, outside there must have been fifty cars parked up and down the street. Outside the front door stood three big men who were stopping any of the public or reporters full of bravado from getting in , this was the Kray’s night and only friends or family were invited.
Once inside the door the bar was packed with one end of it roped off where the Kray’s family sat, Their Mum and Dad sat next to Charlie and his wife Dolly, while Reggie as usual was standing by the bar cracking open bottles of Champagne.
Ronnie sat at his usual table looking serious with a couple of up and coming film actors, while Tony Lambrianou, Eddie Brenner and Dennis Smith stood round him joking and larking around.
At the other end of the bar was Lennie Davids, a well-known singer who had lost his eye sight in a stone fight as a boy. Lennie was playing his heart out on the old piano and singing a lot of the old songs that the twins loved to hear.
Reggie passed Ronnie over a glass of Champagne and touched glasses with him.
“Here’s to us Ron!” Reggie said.
“And to our Mum.” Ronnie replied as he leaned over and tapped her glass.
“To the twins!” Tony Lambrianou shouted which started everyone off repeating it.
After a couple of hours of joyful celebrations one of Ronnie’s friends came over to him and whispered in his ear.
“Joey Pine’s just pulled up.” he said.

“Go out and meet him quick! And bring him in through the back and take him upstairs alright.”
“No problem.”
Ronnie then caught Reggie’s eye and motioned him to come over.
“Joey Pine’s here Reg, were see him upstairs.”
Reggie just nodded before immediately heading for the stairs while Ronnie excused himself politely from his company and mother.
“Bit a business Mum won’t be long.”
“Alright darling try not to be long.” she fondly replied as she caressed his cheek.
When Ronnie got upstairs and walked into the room they sometimes used for business meetings, he found that Joey Pine had already arrived and was busy congratulating his brother Reg.
“Ronnie.” he said warmly as he saw Ron turning to him.
“What a result!” he added.
Ronnie was carrying a bottle of champagne in one hand and three glasses in the other, he placed them down on the table before shaking Joey’s hand firmly, after which all three men sat down and Ronnie poured them all a glass each, as Reggie lit three cigarettes, one for each of them.
“We’re all over the moon for ya Ron.” Joey Pine replied as he toasted his drink.
Ronnie and Reg just nodded and smiled then Ronnie took a large drag on his cigarette before he pulled his chair very close to Joeys.
“Listen Joe, we got a big favour to ask you.”
“Yeah that sounds fucking ominous.” Joey joked
“No seriously Joe, its important mate.”
“Alright, what is it Ron?”
Ronnie glanced over quickly to his brother Reggie who in turn looked up at the door before moving his own chair closer to Joey’s so that now both brothers were sitting on either side of him with both of them having one hand on Joey’s chair.
“We need four paddies taken out.” Ronnie uttered with a tone like it meant nothing at all.
“Fuck me Ron that’s a big favour mate.” Joey frowned.
Reggie then put his hand on Joey’s arm as if to reassure him.
“We will have addresses, cars, haunts the whole run down on them.”
“Yeah Reg but four, two or three would be hard, but four would be nigh on impossible.” Joey sighed.
Ronnie then interrupted.
“Joey you owe us mate, we would do these bastards ourselves, but we got too much heat at the moment, this is very important to us.”

“Ronnie look, we’ll do it! But I don’t know if we can do four for ya , that means four different shooters and to be honest with ya I don’t know if I’ve got four men round me who I trust that much!”
Ronnie took another large drag on his cigarette.
“We know about the troubles you got with the Carters out of west London, we’re take care of that for you, you can keep the four and half grand you owe us and we will pay you another ten.”
“It’s not the money Ron, believe me it’s the numbers, four men is a real fucking problem, they’ve all got to be done on the same night otherwise there scatter underground and we’ll never find them.”
“The best thing would be to cop for them one at a time and take them all to the same place to do em, that’s how we would do it.” Reggie added.
Joey Pine relaxed back into his chair.
“Get me everything you know about em, and we’re promise we’re do our best.” Joey replied coldly.
Ronnie nodded and smiled broadly.
“Right Joe, me, Reg and Charlie are going abroad tomorrow, you’ll be contacted by Billy Hayes in about two weeks’ time. He’ll give you all their details, were gonna need the bastards done while were still abroad, see.”
Joey Pine just nodded.
“Before we go tomorrow I’m gonna go and pay Tommy Carter a visit.” Ronnie added refereeing to the Problems Joey Pine was having with the Carter family out of Notting hill.
“Ronnie we would deal with that fucking slag all day long, but he’s got that fucking old bill Brooker knocking around with him.”
“Fuck his old Bill slag” Reggie uttered angrily.
“We got something on him, he’ll listen to us alright I’ll give you my word he won’t ever stick his fucking nose into your business again.” added Ronnie.
“Alright Ron, Reg, we got a deal.” Joey answered as he got up and shook their hands.
Back downstairs the party was now going full swing, everyone was singing and in a great mood. When Ron and Reg got back the whole place wanted to shake their hand.
Reggie went round talking to everyone while Ronnie sat back down next to his mum.
Ronnie stayed for about an hour then turned to Tony Lambrianou.
“Tony, go get us a car I’m going for something to eat.”
Ronnie then motioned Reggie over.
“Reggie I’ve had enough of this I’m gonna go up the West End.”
“Do ya want me to come with ya?”

"Nah you stay with Mum I'm gonna go to Quaglinos for something to eat." Ronnie replied. "I'll see ya in the morning, we'll go and see Carter, and then we're go away." added Ronnie as he kissed his brothers cheek.
As Ronnie sat in the back of his Jaguar driving through the streets of the West End, he began to feel angered that over the last few months, while he had been imprisoned, his interest in the smoke had all been lost by his so called friends. Before his arrest he had a beautiful club in the heart of Soho, but it was now gone because the people he left to run it, spoiled the business and couldn't pay the rent.
"I'll get it all back." he grimaced "Every fucking thing and ten times more!"

Not Guilty Your Honour
Chapter two
'Marbella & Murder'

The next day in the Kray household was like the twins had never been away. Charlie snr sat in the kitchen like he did every morning sipping from a large cup of tea while he flicked through the horse racing pages, hopefully looking to find the days winners. While Violet Kray was busy cooking Ronnie and Reggie's Breakfast.
Ronnie was the first one down, and he wasted no time tucking into the bacon, eggs, sausages and toast that his mother had made him.
"Handsome, this is Mum." Ronnie added.
"How long you gonna be staying son?" Ronnie's Dad asked.
"You just leave him alone Charlie, they're my boys and they're staying just as long as they want."
"I wasn't saying it like that." Charlie snapped.
"It's alright mum, when we get back off holiday we're find a place."
"Well your under no pressure from us darling, I love having you back home." Violet added as she ran her hand affectionately over Ronnie's shoulder.
"Have you decided where you're going son?"

“A place called Marbella in Spain, I’ve been told it’s really beautiful there, lovely beaches great bars and there are a lot of opportunities there for people like us.”
“Can’t you give business a rest Ron, you’ve only been out a day love, why don’t you and your brothers just go and enjoy yourselves.”
“We will Mum but it can’t hurt looking can it” Ronnie replied smiling.
“That’s it son, you’ve always got to be on the lookout, never know what you might miss.” Ronnie’s Dad added.
“Hark at him over there!” Violet suddenly said while pointing at Ronnie’s Dad “The only thing you ever looked out for was the old bill, and what things did you ever miss, apart from the war.”
“I did my bit.”
“Yeah your bit of running.” Violet added warmly.
Charlie sighed loudly and buried his head back into his paper while snapping its pages so as to make a noise with it.
“That’s it Charlie Kray! You put your head back in that paper or you might MISS the next winner at Kempton.”
“What’s all this commotion?” Reggie asked as he walked into the kitchen to find Ronnie smiling warmly.
“Ya Dad’s talking about missing opportunities.” Violet smirked.
Reggie just grinned and sat down next to Ronnie.
“Alright Bruv, did you have a nice time up west?”
“Not bad.” Ronnie replied as he took a mouthful of toast “Not as good a time as you did, Tony told me you had half the girls from the Green sniffing round you all night.” Ronnie added looking disdainfully.
“What time we leaving Ron?” Reggie replied.
“In about an hour, Johnny Walsh is picking Charlie up and bringing him round here at ten, I’ve done my packing already.”
“Make us a cup a tea Mum.” Reggie replied.
“Just doing it now love,” she answered.
Johnny Walsh, the ex-Professional boxer stood six foot one inch, he was twenty nine years of age, fit, strong and good looking. He first met Ronnie about four years ago when a mutual friend introduced them, Johnny was boxing at the time and was unbeaten. Most people in the boxing world were touting Johnny as the next middleweight Champion. Ronnie always keen to stay involved with boxing, sort of sponsored Johnny by giving him little jobs to do. Nothing too risky, mainly errand jobs and paying him a few pounds a week. Everything was going well until Johnny got stabbed in a dance hall in the Elephant and Castle in South London. Johnny was stabbed three times and nearly died; the doctor remarked that if it hadn’t had been for his excellent fitness he wouldn’t be with us now. Johnny made a full recovery but it ended his boxing career and it impressed Ronnie immensely when Johnny took his

revenge on the fellas that stabbed him. Two men ended up blinded while the one who stabbed him ended up crippled. After that Johnny came to work full time for Ronnie. Johnny loved Ronnie, he would joke fully remark that Ronnie was a Knight and that he was his squire. Everything Ronnie wanted Johnny would do, and often without being asked. Other than Reggie and Charlie, Johnny was the closest Ronnie had to family.
Johnny Walsh had been knocking on Charlie Kray's door for about ten minutes when Charlie finally answered, all sleepy faced and obvious that he had just got out of bed.
"Johnny! Alright mate what time is it?" Charlie yawned.
"Bout half nine Chas, Ronnie asked me to pick you up and get ya round the house by ten."
"Tell him I'll see him later."
"He won't be happy Charlie, he wants to go into west London to see someone, then get to the airport by twelve, we ain't got much time mate."
"Ah Fuck, yeah I forgot about that, look tell him I will come out there in a couple of days."
"Don't do that to me Charlie."
"What?" Charlie snapped.
"Sticking me in the middle between you two, if you're not coming then pick the phone up and tell him yourself otherwise I'll get the bollocking."
"Alright John I'll phone him now come on come in."
Both John and Charlie walked into Charlie's house and into the posh looking living room; Johnny adjusted his tie in the mirror as Charlie picked up the phone.
"Hello."
"Is that you Charlie?" Reggie replied as he picked up the phone.
"Listen Reg I ain't gonna be able to make today mate."
"Don't fucking say that." Reggie interrupted.
"Reg!, I've been banged up for ten fucking months, give me a couple of days to spend at home with my family and I'll come out and meet ya."
"Charlie it's important."
"Well is this, Dolly will go through the fucking roof if just piss off now, for fuck sake Reg just give us a couple of days will ya."
"Ronnie won't like it, we got things we need doing."
"Reggie two days alright, two days and I'll be with you."
The conversation suddenly went silent and after a short pause Reggie answered,
"Two Days Chas, I'll square it with Ron, but two days only mate, don't let me down."
"Cheers Reg, have a nice time alright."
"I'll send someone round with the details of where we're be."

"Nice one, see ya in a couple of days."
"Alright see ya." replied Reg.
Back at Vallance road Ronnie was finishing off his packing when Reggie entered the room.
"Ronnie that was Charlie on the phone, he says he's a bit tied up and he's gonna see us out in Spain in a couple of days."
"What's he mean by that?" Ronnie snapped.
Reggie shrugged his shoulders.
"I guess it means he's tied up with his family."
"We're his fucking family!"
"Ronnie let him have a couple of days with his wife, he must have a lot of things he needs to talk to her about."
"Talk to her about what!, you know full well what we're doing here, what do you want to leave him here to get himself fucking banged up!"
"Ronnie two days ain't gonna make no difference." Reggie snapped, now himself getting angered at Ronnie's tone.
"What the fuck are we running here?" Ronnie snarled as he threw a tie on the bed he was folding.
"Tell me Reg, what the fuck is going on, what is all this bollocks, I got pals who only wanna get pissed, pals who can't get away for this reason or that reason, and brothers who want to spend time with their fucking wives."
Reggie stiffened at Ronnie's remark and Ronnie felt the anger and rage welling up in his twin brother, Ronnie knew that he should not have said wives especially not to Reg who was still sensitive over the suicide of his late wife Francis.
"I didn't mean that about you Reg." Ronnie said.
Reggie just stood silent for a moment.
"I told you what Charlie said Ron, if you want to argue about it and have a fucking row! Then you call him."
When Johnny Walsh returned the house he found Ronnie's cases already in the hall, without a second thought he loaded them into the boot of the Jaguar and returned back into the house where he found Ronnie sitting in the lounge with his Mum and Dad.
"I put the cases in the car Ron, is that all of em?"
"Reggie's got some, give him a shout will ya."
With that Reggie walked into the room.
"Give your cases to Johnny Reg; he'll put them in the car for ya." Ronnie said.
Ronnie and Reg kissed their Mum goodbye and shook their Father's hand before they left.
"Look after yourselves and come home safe." Violet called out as they both climbed into the back seat of the car.

Johnny was driving and he turned the car around and drove off in the direction of Whitechapel, when they reached The Mile End road they picked up Tony Lambrianou who was standing on a corner with a paper under his arm. Tony jumped into the car.
"All set for the trip Ron, I wish I was coming with you."
"Next time Tone, we need you here now mate, keep an eye on things while were gone."
"No Problem!" Tony sternly replied "Right what do ya want me to do today Ron?"
"Before we go away, we got to pay Tommy Carter a visit over Notting Hill."
"Carter!, nasty bit a work Ron , he's knocking about with a copper named Brooker, he carved a bird up while we was away, do you remember that kid who came in it was his Mum." Tony added.
Ronnie just nodded he didn't tell Tony at the time but the kid Tony was talking about spent a lot of time with Ronnie inside. In fact it was Ronnie that stopped the boy from informing to the police about Carter cutting his mum. The boy in question was a young lad aged twenty from Notting Hill West London called Shaun Larkin; his Mum was a local call girl and Shaun spent most of his youth keeping watch as his Mum worked the streets and clubs round that area. He told Ronnie that his Mum used to pay Carter money every week for protection and that it was the copper Brooker who would collect it, but one week she lied about how much work she had had and Brooker found this out as he had secretly recommended her to a couple of Northern coppers who were down in London on a few days break. The silly cow kept this hidden from Carter who then decided to put fifty odd stitches in her face as an example to all the other girls he collected from.
When the boy got arrested for holding up a local jeweller, the police knowing of his mother asked him to make a deal with them about Carter and the crooked copper Brooker. Everyone knew it was them who did it but the police had no proof. Brooker had been warned countless times about his association with the Carters but he was a cagey old fucker, who always knew how to worm his way out of tight situations.
When Shaun Larkin got remanded to Wandsworth prison he told Ronnie everything and asked Ronnie's advice on what to do, he was afraid that with him inside the Carters would kill his mum.
Ronnie told him that life is full of dangers and pitfalls but he should never grass to the old bill, Ronnie advised him to do his bird then when he's free he should go and take care of Carter himself, adding that if anyone ever laid a finger on his Mother then Ronnie would kill them stone dead.
Tommy Carter owned a big boozer in Ladbroke Grove; the Carters had a reputation for violence and were feared all over west London. Ronnie never liked them, he met them once down the Astor club in the West End but

refused to greet them as he despised their morals and the way they earned their money, they thought nothing of earning off of prostitution or setting someone up for their own benefit or to help out their copper pal Brooker.
Ronnie made Johnny Walsh pull the car up right outside the main window of the Carter's pub, and then himself Reggie and Tony walked in the door; the whole pub went quiet as they walked in.
Ronnie strolled up to the barmaid.
"I wanna see Tommy Carter!" he stated firmly.
"I'll see if he's in." she replied as she walked over to the corner of the bar and whispered to a very unkempt man who was reading a paper while sipping on a pint of Guinness.
"Brooker." Tony Lambrianou whispered to Ronnie.
Brooker put his drink down on the bar and began to walk over to the twins.
"Alright Ronnie, Reggie, you here to see Tommy are you?" he said as he greeted them,
Ronnie gazed Brooker up and down coldly, and ignored him by turning his attention back at the barmaid.
"Is he here love?" he asked her.
"Alright!" Brooker smirked "Now what you want a see Tom about?" he added.
Ronnie suddenly turned violently towards Brooker, Tony Lambrianou stiffened as he noticed the look on Ronnie's face, a look he had seen so many times before just as Ronnie was about to chin someone.
Reggie grabbed Ronnie's arm as if to calm him and make him think before he knocked out a policeman.
"We know who you are Brooker, I don't want to talk to ya and nor does my brother, do us all a favour and just piss off back to your paper before something happens we'll all regret." Reggie replied as he nudged himself in front of Ronnie.
Brooker took a step back and grinned.
"Ronnie and Reggie Kray!" he said loudly "Only been out a day, and still walking round like they own the fucking place." he added bravely.
"You PONCE!" Ronnie snapped as he reached for a glass off the bar only for Reg to quickly grab him.
"Let him go!" Brooker shouted at Reg "Let him go, go on you'll all be back in the nick by afternoon."
"Go on FUCK OFF!" Tony Lambrianou shouted angrily back at him and pushing him towards the corner.
Then just as things seemed to spiralling out of control Tommy Carter walked down from upstairs.
"Ronnie, Reg." he warmly shouted as he gave Brooker a cold look.

“Come upstairs come on.” he added as Brooker got the message and backed off and Tommy lifted up the bar and ushered them in.
Upstairs the pub was like a knocking shop there was blankets and fresh towels outside the rooms, the four men walked up to the third floor where Tommy Carter invited them into his office which was decorated so posh it was totally out of proportion to the rest of the shabby pub.
“You know my brother Jack.” Tommy said as he invited them in.
Jack got up from his chair and made sure they all got seated in front of Tommy’s huge wooden desk.
“What do I owe this pleasure?” Tommy Carter asked as he sat behind the desk raising his feet up on one end as if he didn’t have a care in the world.
Ronnie pulled out a cigarette and lit it before answering him.
“I’m here to tell you I’m working with Joey Pine.” Ronnie replied sternly.
Carter gazed quickly over to his brother and sighed.
“Then that means we’ve all got a problem then Ron.” he relaxingly said.
“NO! That means you got the fucking problem!” Ronnie snapped.
Tommy Carter pulled his feet off the table and now leaned across it with his hands open.
“Ron, me and the Pine’s got a lot of history, goes back a lot of years mate.”
“I don’t give a fuck how many years it goes back, I’m just here to tell you, and your fucking old bill obbo, that any more fucking about with the Pine’s and your fucking about with us!”
“Now hold up a minute,”
“No you fucking hold up Carter, and hear me out, we know every fucking thing there is to know about you, we know about ya pubs, your dealings with that piece of shit downstairs, your fucking brothels and we know about what you did to that bird Beryl.”
“What about that tart?” Carter asked with an arrogant smile.
Ronnie suddenly lunged across the table and grabbed Carter by the throat then pulled him around the desk and punched him straight in the face and splitting his lip.
Reggie almost as quick jumped up and clocked Jack carter with a beautiful punch knocking him out onto the floor.
“Ronnie!” Carter shouted in defence as Ronnie was now on top of him and Reggie had grabbed his arms leaving him wide open for whatever damage Ronnie wanted to do to his face.
“What about that tart!” Ronnie mouthed repeating what Carter said. “That poor women you put fifty stitches in her face, you fucking slag.” he added as he punched Carter hard in the face causing another cut to appear on his eye.
“It was me ya bastard that stopped her from nicking ya.” Ronnie shouted as he threw two more punches before getting up and kicking Carter forcefully in the balls.

“Take this as goodwill message! Come anywhere near my Firm or Joey’s, and I’ll kill ya stone fucking dead, you ponce!” shouted Ronnie just before he spat at Carter and once again decided to kick him in the balls while Tony picked up one end of Carters huge wooden desk and tipped it over on top of him.
Outside Johnny Walsh was growing concerned over the length of time it was taking; he had kept the engine running as usual, when he saw the twins coming out the pub he allowed himself a smile. Ronnie and Reg jumped in the back and Tony jumped in the front besides Johnny.
“Get us out of here.” Tony told him.
“Just like old times.” Tony said as he leaned over the his seat towards the twins smiling.
“Keep an ear to the ground about that ponce while were away would ya tone.” Reggie replied.
“Done!” Tony snapped, “I don’t think we’ll hear anything from him, he’s just West London, not interested in anything else.”
“Yeah, well his dangerous all the time he’s got that copper round him.” Ronnie replied.
Ronnie then told Johnny to pull up outside Notting Hill tube station.
“Tony I’ll let you out here, I’m gonna phone Jean McCarthy’s flat in two days’ time at seven in the evening, make sure your there to take the call alright.”
“I’ll be there Ron.”
“Alright mate keep an eye on things while were gone and phone Mum up every couple of days will ya, just to make sure she’s ok.”
“Ronnie, don’t you worry about a thing, go and have a great time!”
“What times our flight Ron?” Reggie asked when Tony had got out of the car and they had begun to drive off.
“Change of plan Reg, were taking the ferry and driving to Paris, we’ll catch a flight there.”
“Well I’m having a sleep then you know how I hate long drives.” Reggie replied.
By nightfall the twins were in Paris, Ronnie told John to find the nicest hotel and book them in while they would jump out of the car here and go and have a drink in a local bar. Johnny dropped them off and wrote down the name of the bar before he drove off to search for a hotel.
Once inside the bar Ronnie Reg walked over to the host, both twins were dressed immaculate as usual and they could not help notice everyone in the bar looking at them as they ordered there drinks. Ronnie ordered a large Vodka and tonic while Reggie asked for a cold beer. Within a few minutes of them standing by the bar a smart looking Parisian walked over
“Excuse moi are vou the Kray twins from London?” he asked them hesitantly.
Ronnie nodded his head in surprise.

"Are you a policeman?" he jokingly replied.
"Non!" the Frenchman answered "NON!" he added again now shaking his head " I would just want to shake hand." he warmly said in his broken English tone before turning to everyone in the bar, and in his native French obviously introduced Ronnie and Reg as the Kray twins to everyone in the fucking bar. Within seconds everyone was raising their glasses and coming over to shake their hands.
"I think I like Paris." Ronnie uttered to Reg.
Johnny Walsh had booked them into one of Paris's best hotels the Grand Metropolis right in the heart of the city and when he walked into the bar he couldn't believe his eyes when he saw every one round the twins.
That night the three Londoners had a great time in the bar and when they walked out they were all a bit pissed, the first man to approach them earlier that night was called Pierre and he had insisted that he would drive them back to their hotel as Johnny Walsh had left the jag there.
Reggie looked hesitant as he climbed into the back of the old Renault, as Pierre was obviously drunk as a sack.
"Ronnie I don't think this is a good idea." he laughed quietly
"Nor do I but we can't refuse him, he's just spent his weeks' pay on us, it might insult him."
"He can't fucking stand up." Reggie added as Pierre fell into the driver's seat. Then suddenly with a roar of the engine they was on the move, Pierre was all over the street bibbing everyone out of way.
"How far is this fucking hotel John?" Reggie shouted.
"How the fucking hell do I know." Johnny Walsh shouted back as he held onto the dash board.
"Pierre!" Reggie shouted "Pierre slow down for fuck sake your get us all killed." Reggie shouted at the smiling Frenchman.
"Don't worry nearly there!" Pierre shouted back at him.
Then suddenly the Renault swerved violently knocking Reg flying into Ron on the back seat as the car pulled into the drive of the hotel.
"Nearly missed it!" Pierre shouted laughing.
The old Renault raced up the drive and slammed on the brakes just in time before it hit a large marble column, the two doormen standing outside the hotel in there green overcoats and hats jumped swiftly out of the way.
As soon as the car was at a stop Reggie leapt from the car.
"Thank fuck for that!" he shouted as he turned to see both the doormen standing open mouthed, and in total confusion on whether to open the doors of the old banger or chase them of the premises.
Pierre nearly fell out of his door as he got out to open Ronnie's door, Ronnie got out laughing his head off as he had thoroughly enjoyed the ride.

Once they had said their farewell to Pierre and entered the hotel Ronnie ordered three coffees to be served to them in the hotels impressive lounge. Ronnie sat down in a quiet corner and grabbed Reggie and John's attention.
"Johnny I want you to get us on a flight to Spain tomorrow, go down the airport in the morning and book it will ya, I also want you to sort out with the hotel somewhere we can keep the jag garaged until we get back."
"No problem Ron, what time do you want the flights for?"
"Anytime in the afternoon John, I want to go up the Eiffel tower in the morning."
The next evening Ronnie, Reg and Johnny Walsh walked out the entrance of Malaga Airport and into a lovely warm evening. Reggie took off his coat as Johnny beckoned over a taxi driver and asked him to take them to a good hotel in Marbella. The taxi took them to a very posh hotel called Puerto Marbella, he told them it was where all the rich and famous stayed. That night they booked into their rooms then had a nice meal in the hotels French restaurant before they all went to sleep having an early night.
The next morning Ronnie woke Reggie up at about eight in the morning and told him he had sent Johnny out already to find a car to rent, and that they were to meet him downstairs for breakfast at nine. Reggie said he would see them downstairs and Ronnie left him telling him to hurry up. Ronnie walked down to the hotels swimming pool where he sat down on a chair; his mind was racing as he found it hard to relax. His mind was still angry over the last ten months he had spent in prison and how he had lost all of his business ventures because of it. He knew he would try and get it all back but he found it deeply frustrating that he was going to have to put all his time and effort into getting back into a position he was once already in.
Ronnie took out a fag and lit it as he leaned back and gazed up at the beautiful Spanish morning sun "I'm gonna them pay every fucking one of em." he whispered.
When Reggie walked downstairs for breakfast he saw that Ronnie and John were already seated having a cup of tea.
"Looks like a gorgeous day Ron."
"Well its Spain ain't it what did ya fucking expect snow!" Ronnie replied. Reggie looked at Ronnie twice in a sort of relaxed amazement, anyone who didn't know Ronnie would have thought he was being nasty, but Reg knew his twins ways too well, he pulled up a chair and ordered himself a cup of coffee from the waitress ignoring his brother's comment.
"Be nice to go down the beach today Ron, lay on the sand and ave a dip in the sea." Reggie added.
"Johnny got a car Reg, nice one."
"Yeah what did you get John?" Reggie asked.
"A Cadillac, one where the roof comes down."

"Yeah nice." Reggie said "Pull a few birds at the beach wont It." he added smiling at Johnny.
"Yeah, well we're leave the beach for now Reg, we got a few things to do first. Do ya remember Mario on the two's in Wandsworth?" Ronnie said referring to a guy who was in a cell on the second floor in Wandsworth Prison.
"Yeah the half Spanish fella what about him?"
"He lives out here in Marbella I got a couple of numbers he gave me , he told me about this place, he told me that Marbella was a land of opportunity. I remember him saying that if put enough money in the right hands we could control a lot of power over here."
"We're give him call then Ron."
"Already have Reg he's on his way now."
When Mario turned up Reggie couldn't believe it was the same guy, Mario in prison was always unshaven and had greasy unkempt hair, but the Mario who was walking over to his table now looked like a Hollywood film star. His dark curly hair had grown and was swept back, he was wearing a silk shirt unbuttoned half way down to reveal his chest, and silk trousers with brown sandals, he was smothered in jewellery and wore solid gold sunglasses.
"Ronnie you made It." he smiled as he hugged Reggie's twin.
"Reggie it's great to meet you again." he followed by shaking Reggie's hand.
"Come please, come, my family want to meet you all, my Father wishes to thank you Ron for looking after me while I was in Britain, come please, I have a car waiting outside."
Ronnie smiled warmly and motioned to Reg and John to get up from their seats.
They walked outside to find a huge Mercedes limousine with a thickly built Spaniard waiting by the side of it in anticipation of opening everyone's doors. Ronnie climbed in first followed by everyone else.
"It is so great to see you again Ronnie, I am going to show you all the best of life in Marbella." Mario said as he once again shook Ronnie's hand.
Reggie had undone his window and was busy leaning out it getting a lovely warm breeze onto his face; suddenly he was cheerfully surprised to see the limo pulling into a driveway. He saw a man run from what he could only explain as a sentry box and hurriedly open the gates.
The limo drove through them and Reggie saw a huge Villa more like a mansion come into view "Jesus is this yours?" he said to Mario.
"Welcome to the Delgado estate." Mario boasted.
"The what estate?" Reggie asked.
"The Delgado estate, that is my name Delgado, Mario Rodriguez Delgado." he added.

Once the car had come to a halt the men got out, they was greeted by Mario's brother Pedro and his mother Theresa. Mario introduced them and invited them in. the first thing Ronnie noticed were the ornamental shotguns hung on the wall of the huge entrance. He also noted the sound that his shoes made on the plush marble floor. Mario then led the twins into a large study like room, which led out to the back gardens and gave a great view of a massive swimming pool. In a corner Ronnie caught sight of a very impressive character sitting on the side of a huge ornamental desk talking on the telephone. Mario directed them to the desk where the gentleman swiftly ended his call and shuffled his silk jacket before holding out his hand to greet Ronnie.
"Senor Kray, welcome to my home." he warmly said as Ronnie noted how Firm the man's handshake was.
Mario then introduced the gentleman as his Father "My Father, Don Paco Delgado."
"I wish to thank you for looking after my son while he was in your country."
"My pleasure." Ronnie replied, "He's a good kid." he added.
Paco Ramirez Juan Delgado was every part a Spanish aristocrat, he came from a very old and established family with their roots firmly embedded into the Spanish political societies. It was said that the Delgado family actually fought against the Moors at the side of El Sid, they were the largest landowners on the Costa del Sol. They owned Businesses up and down the length of Spain but most of their wealth was centred around Marbella. Paco's brother, Mario's uncle was in fact the mayor of Marbella.
Mario and his Father invited Ronnie and Reg out onto the patio besides the pool where a lady asked them what refreshments they would like before they all sat down and began to talk.
"So what brings you to Marbella?" Paco began.
"We have come for a holiday; I suppose Mario has told you that we were all found not guilty."
"Yes my son has informed me, it was also on the news."
"On the news!" Reggie asked.
"Ce, it seems your country makes a habit of arresting innocent men." Paco replied pleasantly and glancing across at his son.
"I am going to try to persuade Ronnie to invest in some business out here Father." Mario said.
"It is a very good time to buy property in Espanola, General Franco is getting old, and he can't have much time left. When his time comes to leave this world then our country will once again fall into the hands of the monarchy, and let us say that under a more relaxed regime Espanola will blossom. International companies will find it more appealing to invest their hard earned cash."

“Our Mum would love a place like this.” Reggie added.
“Mario why don’t you take Senor Kray over to Pedro’s office?” Paco replied.
“My cousin Pedro has the largest realty office in Marbella; he has hundreds of properties for sale.” Mario added.
“I would enjoy that.” said Ronnie.
The twins stayed with Mario’s Father for about an hour before they left with Mario for Pedro’s office, Ronnie and Mario went in while Reg decided that him and Johnny would go down to the beach and go in some bars and catch up with Ronnie later at the hotel.
Mario introduced Ronnie to his cousin where they then looked at various properties, one of which really caught Ronnie’s eye, it was a ten bedroom villa that rested on the shores of the beach about two hundred yards from the exclusive Marbella yacht club. It had a giant swimming pool and landscape gardens both at the front and the rear, three reception rooms and eight bathrooms.
“How much is this one?” Ronnie asked.
“Ah you have fine taste senor.” Mario’s cousins replied as he began scribbling on a piece of paper.
“This would work out at fifty thousand pounds in your British currency.” he added.
“Would you like to see it Ron?”
“I would love to.” Ronnie replied to Mario.
When Reggie returned to the hotel in the early evening with Johnny Walsh, he found that Ronnie was already washed and ready to meet Mario, who was taking the three of them out to one of Marbella’s swankiest restaurants.
Ronnie seeing Reg from the corner of the bar waved him over angrily.
“Where the fuck ave you been all day?”
“What’s the fucking matter with you?” Reggie angrily replied.
“Mario’s picking us up in half an hour, look at the fucking state of you two.” Ronnie answered referring to them.
“You look like a fucking red rooster.” Ronnie added remarking at Johnny’s sunburn.
“I told him not to stay in sun all day.” Reggie laughed.
“Well hurry up Reg, go and get ready will ya.”
“What’s all the fuss Ron? Fuck Mario!” Reggie said.
“What’s all the fuss, can’t you see I’m grafting here, didn’t you see all the fucking dosh that fuck Mario’s got.”
Reggie then seemed to sober up and sent Johnny Walsh upstairs to wash before answering his brother.
“What’s the angle Ron?”
“Not sure yet bruv, but we just brought a ten bedroom villa off him.”
“WHAT!” Reggie snapped.

"Yeah gorgeous it is, Mum all love it."
"How much we paid for that?"
"Fifty grand but don't worry about it, were gonna do a deal with Mario."
Ronnie smiled
"What kind of deal Ron is gonna get us, that kind of wedge for a place down here?"
"His Father owns it, so he reckons he can sort us out a deal where we can pay him off when we want." Ronnie replied. "Go and get ready quick Reg, and then were have a chat, when ya come down."
Johnny Walsh was down in about fifteen minutes followed by Reg five minutes later; Mario had yet to turn up. Johnny Walsh got the message that Ronnie wanted to speak privately with his brother so he walked away and sat down at a table nearby.
"Listen Reg just follow my lead tonight, I ain't figured out an angle yet but I can smell the dosh round him."
Dallio's in the heart of Marbella was an Italian restaurant hugely based upon the swanky New York and Las Vegas dinner and dance establishments. Its décor was that of the nineteen twenties and its clientele were only the rich and famous. The owner and host was an Italian American called Tony Dallio, who had spent most of his life running one of the most successful eateries in Manhattan, New York. Dallio now in his sixties was a larger than life character and every night except Sundays which was his day off he would take to the stage in his restaurant and give a ten minute welcome and thank you routine, before introducing the cabaret acts.
As Mario and the twins sat down at the Delgado family table they were suddenly swamped by waiters, bringing them over fresh water, bread rolls and a bottle of finest champagne.
Mario sat in the middle of the twins and suggested to them that they try the steak, adding that it was the finest in all of Marbella. Ronnie agreed then made everyone laugh at the table when he ordered brown ale for his drink.
"They don't drink brown ale out ere Ron." Reggie laughed.
The meal was, as Mario suggested superb, they wolfed it down and ordered more champagne, Reggie noted how his brother kept filling Mario's glass.
"Ronnie you drink so fast." Mario cried.
"We been away for ten months, got a lot of catching up to do."
After the meal the waiters cleared the table and they turned their chairs towards the stage in anticipation of the cabaret.
On first came a young Latin women who sat down and began to sing an opera song from Madame Butterfly, Ronnie became totally entrenched by her beautiful voice, then one of Mario's playboy friends walked over to the table, ignorantly he pulled up a chair in between Reggie and Mario turning his back towards Reggie, Ronnie very sternly asked him to be quiet as his talking while

the young girl was singing was not a polite thing to do. Mario's friend shrugged off Ronnie's remark like he never heard it.
Then just as Ronnie was about to grab him by the scruff of his neck the beautiful singer ended her song, Ronnie jumped to his feet and led the applause followed by Reggie and Mario and the rest of the crowd. Out of the corner of his eye he glanced over to see that Mario's playboy friend was still seated fumbling about in a drunken way through his pockets searching for a light.
As soon as the applause stopped Ronnie leant over and tugged at the man's arm "I wanna see you about something in the toilet now." Ronnie ordered.
The drunken guy too stupid to realise Ronnie's anger duly got to his feet and even led the way, once inside Ronnie was pleased to see that they was alone.
"What do you want to see me for?" the man asked as he put a cigarette up to his mouth.
Ronnie took one quick glance towards the door as he heard it open and saw Reg coming in, then cracked him with a right handed punch that sent him flying into the basins and sending him into oblivion in the process.
Ronnie then calmly walked back to his table and finished his drink without sitting down and suggested to Mario that they move on to somewhere else.
The members only Piano Bar at Marbella's yacht club was a fashionable nightspot, Mario signed his three friends in, then they found a table downstairs, the club was full with beautiful and exotic women who were all obviously on the game, Ronnie and Reg didn't even give them a second glance while Johnny Walsh who was a ladies man couldn't keep his eyes off them.
"Did you like Dallio's Ron?" Mario asked.
"Not bad but we could do a lot better." Ronnie replied.
"Are yes I heard about your clubs, one day when I am back in London you must take me to them." Mario replied totally ignorant to the fact that the twins had lost all their interests in them.
Ronnie then pulled Mario closer.
"One of the reasons were out here is to look into the possibility of getting a club out here, maybe your realty geezer could help us out."
"Pedro would be your man Ron, in fact I know of a club right now that's just gone on the market."
"We're not interested in just any club, it's gotta be the best, we want to bring over all the acts from the states, people like Sinatra and Judy Garland, so we can't bring them to a dive Mario."
"No this club is perfect, it is a new complex called Puento Romano, it is owned by the Arabs they have spared no expense on its building."
"Sounds interesting Ron." Reggie added as he picked up on the conversation.
"Why don't you get involved Mario." Ronnie cunningly added.

"What, with you Ron?"
"Yeah, be our partner."
"The three of us could turn it into a great success, and anyway me and Ron ain't gonna be in Spain all the time are we? We're gonna need someone over here to keep an eye on it while were back in London." Reggie added.
"Sinatra would love it over here wouldn't he Reg." Ronnie said.
Mario took a sip of his drink and smiled.
"So what do ya say?" Ronnie enthusiastically insisted.
"I say it would be great!" Mario replied.
Ronnie then held out his hand and shook Mario's hand,
"The Kray's and Mario Delgado, the partnership!" Reggie said as he shook hands.
"Listen Mario this is what were gonna do." Ronnie added but now with much more authority. Reggie sat back and relaxed as he knew his brothers views on the importance of a handshake, Reggie smiled to himself as knew that Ronnie had netted his dinner, if you shake Ronnie Kray's hand and toast to a partnership then come flood, pestilence or the fucking end of the world you're on the firm.
"We're all have a third of the action each, you me and Reg, but you'll put up fifty percent of whatever needs to be put up for your third alright, me and Reggie are one so we will pull up the other fifty but we'll be in it thirds with ya that's only fair mate. Can't have you having fifty's and me and Reg twenty five each can we, I tell ya what we'll even call the place Mario's if ya want." Ronnie said now in his most convincing voice.
"Whatever Ronnie, tonight we make a marriage you me and Reg, together with equal shares."
Ronnie smiled then suddenly something struck his mind.
"Reg I gotta call Tony."
"Yeah fuck me, what time is it?"
"About twelve." Ronnie said looking at his watch.
"Mario excuse me I have to make an important call, talk to Reg while I'm away he'll tell ya all about the clubs we run back home." Replied Ronnie as he got to his feet.
Tony Lambrianou had been sitting round Jean McCarthy's house for three and a half hours, his mind was racing at why Ronnie had not called him on time and Jean McCarthy was going mad.
"Tony look love whoever was meant to call you at seven obviously isn't gonna call, its half ten now and I've been wanting to go out since nine."
"Jean! I'm sorry darling but I have to get this call and I can't leave here till I get it, go out if you want I'll lock up."
"What and leave you ere, and come back and find an house load."

Just as she finished her sentence the phone rang, Tony looked at jean to leave the room as he picked up the phone.
"Ronnie you alright!" Tony asked.
"Yeah why!"
"Got worried Ron when you never called at seven."
"Ah I got involved in something couldn't get away, listen you got a pen, go round and see Charlie first thing in the morning tell him to get his ass out here straight away, tell him to not to get fucking lazy and just jump on a flight at Heathrow, you drive him to an airport in France, he's got to fly to Malaga airport in Spain then get a cab to the Puerto Marbella hotel in Marbella."
"Yep got it Ron Puerto hotel in Marbella."
"Puerto Marbella hotel! And it's in Marbella."
"Puerto Marbella hotel in Marbella and fly to Malaga got it, its wrote down."
"How is everything tone?"
"Lotta spiel on the streets Ron, everyone's talking about ya."
"Like what? What they saying."
"Nothing bad Ron, well least not to me, just good wishes."
"You heard anything from Carter?"
"Not a fucking thing."
"Alright well keep your eye out on that one, listen I will call you at silly Bobs number ten days from today, at seven in the evening make sure you have Billy Hayes with you."
"No problem Ron, leave it to me."
For the next week Ronnie, Reggie, Mario and Johnny Walsh really enjoyed themselves, Ronnie spent almost all his time with Mario, they confirmed the sale of the villa for a knocked down price of forty grand, and viewed and agreed to buy the club that Mario had suggested. Reggie spent most of the time sunbathing and swimming with Johnny. Charlie arrived okay and Ronnie told him to take charge of the purchase of the villa.
Ronnie Kray also began getting closer to Mario's Father who looked at Ronnie as a good influence on his son, Ronnie found that quietly amusing. Mario's Father also found out about the guy that Ronnie knocked out at Dallio's and when Ronnie explained to him in a private one on one conversation that he found the man's manner rude and un gentlemanly in front of females, Mario's Father then opened up to Ronnie and told him that the man in Question was into taking drugs. And that he was pleased that Ronnie reacted in the way that he did because he had previously feared that his son could be influenced into drugs, he went on to add that it was a growing problem amongst the young sons and daughters of his friends and family. Ronnie reassured him that as long as Mario was his friend and partner he would make sure that none of Mario's friends would be able to talk him into taking any of that crap.

Paco and Ronnie's friendship seemed to grow day by day as Paco entrusted Ronnie with many stories about his son. He said that going into partnership with the club was the best thing that could happen to his son, as it would give him a responsibility.
The Regines night club in the Puento Romano complex was exactly what Ronnie had been after, it had a drive up entrance that was lined with palm trees where cars could drive right up to the entrance and stop by the two giant Roman like columns where a short walk on red carpet up a small flight of stairs accessed its entrance. Once inside the club it was decorated like a grand Roman spar, marble columns lined the walls, as you walked in you could see the dance floor down a small flight of stairs or walk upstairs to the VIP lounge that overlooked the dance floor and stage, it had kitchens for serving food, private car parking, everything that a an up market club needed, this place had it.
Ronnie wondered why the owners wanted to sell it so he discreetly enquired and quickly found out that a rich Arab sheik had built the club for his son, who subsequently got himself killed in a traffic accident. And that the grief stricken Sheik could no longer be associated with the club as it held so many memories of his son.
Ronnie and Mario agreed a price and Mario put down a small deposit with an agreement that the outstanding monies would be forwarded in ten days' time.
It was a cold and breezy morning when Jeff Samuels the Kray's old and trusted friend left the now named Hennessey's Snooker hall, just besides the Mile End underground train station. He gazed at his watch and wiped off the rain to see that it was quarter to six in the morning. He yawned out loud as he checked over his shoulders on his way to his car. He had just spent seven hours, losing one hundred pounds playing dice in the back room of the hall.
Samuels as he did every night for the last two weeks parked a bit up the road, he got into his car and sat quietly for about ten minutes till he saw Kieran Hennessey, the eldest of the brothers, lock up the hall and climb into the passenger seat of a Daimler car which had just turned up for him.
Samuels picked up a notebook and looked at his watch. Five to six Kieran Hennessey leaves club, gets in Daimler with one unknown person driving. He scribbled down.
Later that day the rain was now pouring down as Jeff Samuels now fresh from a few hour sleep and a change of clothes banged on the door of Georgie Hayes.
Jeff Samuels was always a very smart and quiet man, he had been friends with Ronnie for over fifteen years, but he never socialised with the Firm and was only ever seen when Ronnie required him for specific needs. Samuels was a man in his late fifties, he had a long career in the army and had seen action in both the Second World War and in Korea, he had no family, no ties, some of

the Firm who had met him called him the spy because of his manner and that Ronnie once let it slip that Samuels had been caught in Germany, during the war carrying out a very high level operation for the English government.
Once inside Georgie Hayes house he removed his rain soaked Mac and followed George into the living room.
"All right Jeff what you got for me?" George asked as Jeff pulled out a folder and laid it down on the coffee table.
"It was very busy down the club last night, I got in there at eleven PM, I stayed playing till five forty five AM, I saw Kieran Hennessey leave the premises, lock it and climb into a Daimler, at five fifty five AM,. I could not see the number plate as it was parked awkwardly and the weather was atrocious, though I am almost certain it was Gerry Hennessey his younger brother's car whose number I gave you before."
"That's great Jeff, you said it was busy anyone we know playing."
"Mostly the regulars, Jones, Travers, a few of the Smith Brothers came and left during the evening, the Greaves Mob from Walthamstow were there. A lot of money went over the table, I would give a good guess that it was in between three to four thousand pounds."
"What about the Hennessey's?"
"Kieran was there all night, Gerry was there between two and four, and jasper and mike came in together at three stayed for fifteen minutes, then left and never returned."
"Good work Jeff; I'll see ya in a couple of days then mate."
Later that same day Tony Lambrianou and Billy Hayes were sitting in Jean McCarthy's front room, at seven o'clock the phone rang, Tony picked it up.
"Ronnie that you?" Tony asked.
"Is Billy with ya?"
"Sitting next to me."
"Put him on."
"Hallo Ron How's everything?" Billy asked.
"Billy I want Tony to drive you round my old man's now, he will give you a number to call me on in one hour's time, don't call me from the manor, drive out at least ten miles and call that number from a call box do ya understand?"
"Understood, do it now."
The two men left, doing what Ronnie asked and drove out of East London in the direction of Essex where they found a nice phone box in a quiet country lane.
"That'll do Tone." Billy replied pointing out the box.
They sat in the car for ten minutes until the time was right to call, Ronnie picked up the phone after only one ring.
"That you Ron?" Billy asked.
"Listen very careful, have you got all the info on the paddies?"

"Got everything, addresses, girlfriends, and times, we got the lot."
"Good! Right I want you and Tony to go and see Joey P, over his pub in Chelsea, you know who I mean don't ya?"
"Yeah." Billy replied.
"Give him all the details you have on the paddies and tell him to do it two nights from now, and make sure that you, Tony and all the Firm are right off the plot in two night's time. Do you understand that, you gotta all have alibis that you're nowhere near the fucking East End alright, and get Tony to see Fred and tell him to make sure he's in company tomorrow?"
"Crystal clear mate, it's done."
"Call me on this number in three days' time."
"What time?"
"Seven." Ronnie replied as he hung up.
The next day in Spain, Ronnie, Reg and Charlie, were sitting round the hotel pool waiting for Mario to arrive, this was the day when they were supposed to sign the contracts and pay up the remainder of the monies for the club. Charlie was feeling a bit agitated, as he knew they never had the money on them or had even discussed it amongst themselves, every time he had raised the topic with Ronnie he was told to don't worry about it.
When Mario arrived he arrived with one of his Father's lawyers, they walked over to Ronnie's poolside table and the lawyer pulled out some papers from a brief case he had with them.
"What ya drinking Mario?" Ronnie asked calmly.
"I'll have a beer."
"Good idea." Ronnie said as he called over a waiter.
"Right I have the papers here for the signing of the club, is everything okay from your side Ron?"
"Everything's great!" Ronnie replied as he picked up the contract.
"Do you not want my lawyer to explain this Ronnie?" Mario asked as he saw Ronnie just sign it. "What's to discuss, were buying a club."
"Ok!" Mario replied.
The lawyer then reached into his case and pulled out another document "I have here instructions to our bank to forward your share of the cost to the owners bank, I trust you have made arrangements for your end, I am sorry senor Kray but I have not discussed this yet with Mario, will you be paying with cash or by letter of credit?"
"Cash!" Ronnie replied.
"Excellent, if you wish I could deliver it to the owners club when I see them in one hour."
Ronnie then stretched out his arms and pulled Mario closer.
"Bit of a small problem Mario." Ronnie whispered as he got up from his seat and then excused himself from the lawyer.

"Excuse me but I need to speak to my partner in private." he added as he put his arm round Mario and led him away to a small table.
"Mario we've got a small problem mate." Ronnie said sincerely.
"The fucking law have frozen our accounts back home because of the trial, had murders on the phone all morning with our lawyers, they have got to take off the freeze cos we all got not guilty's but there just being fucking slow mate."
"But Ronnie we have to pay this money today or I will lose my deposit and the club will go back on the market." Mario replied anxiously.
"Mario listen it's not a problem, but we don't want to ring Scotland Yard up and tell them we need the money for a club in Spain do we? There be all over the fucking place, look my lawyers told me it's only a matter of days then I'll get someone to fly out with it straight away."
"But we don't have a couple of days Ronnie, the meeting is in one hour, we will lose the club."
Ronnie leaned back in the chair and sighed as he held up his hands looking frustrated.
"Be a shame that Mario, especially after you've told everyone you're taking it over, well if they wanna be like that then we'll get another club."
"But Ronnie this is perfect for us and I would look like a fool if we pull out."
"What can I do?" Ronnie sighed.
Mario sighed out loud before Ronnie pulled him closer.
"Listen I know a way out, look me and you are partners see, well you front my end for a couple of days till I get my money sorted out, once I get all the shit straightened out back home I'll pay you back straight away. This way we can keep the club and be in there next week, and I'll tell ya what I'll get hold of Charlie right now, and get I'm to get on the phone to America and tell Frank Sinatra, to get his ass out here for the opening night, that's what we're do, we're make a fortune Mario, the best club in all a Spain."
Ronnie then smiled broadly and rustled Mario's hair.
"C'mon this ain't gonna be a problem between partners is it?" he added.
Mario smiled and nodded.
"Course not Ronnie, I will front it for you."
"That's my boy Mario; now then let's go buy a club."
Weather warnings had been issued on the news and papers throughout London, they warned of gale force winds and torrential rain. Most of Southeast London had been put on flood alert.
Tony Lambrianou along with George and Billy Hayes walked into Joey Pine's Pub looking like drowned rats after parking their car just across the street and having to run through the pouring rain. As the three men walked in most of the pub regulars recognised Tony and a silent atmosphere fell upon the establishment. Joey Pine was sitting next to the log fire with his brother Ted

and a couple of pals studying the horse racing in one of the daily papers. When he saw the boys, he immediately called them over.
“Alright boys, you alright, ya wanna drink?”
Greetings were made then Billy whispered that he needed a word in private, Joey asked his brother to take care of the drinks for Tony and George before disappearing upstairs with Billy.
“Spoke to Ron last night Joe, he asked me to give you all these details we have on the Hennessey’s.” Billy Hayes said as he sat down in Joe’s office.
Joe just nodded his head and quickly flicked through them
“Looks like you got everything here Bill.” he said.
“Everything Joe, all their addresses, times they usually get in, go out, where they drink, fuck, sleep, the lot mate.”
“How’s Ron, Bill?” Joey then asked as he put the papers back down.
“He’s good Joe; I gotta call him in a couple of days, he asked me to tell ya to do whatever you gotta do tomorrow night.” Billy replied as feigned ignorance all though he knew damn well what Pine was going to do, but in street codes it was not the right thing to say it out loud.
“Ok.” Joey remarked coolly.
“How’s the weather?” Joey added laughing as he nodded his head back in the direction of the window obviously trying to change the subject.
“Fucking raining!” Billy replied in a tone of voice and action that echoed Joey’s attempt to change the subject and to show that they were on the same wavelength.
Billy Hayes got to his feet and shook Billy’s hand.
“Make sure you’re not around tomorrow night Bill.” Joey whispered.
Billy smiled and nodded his head once in an action to say thank you and tapped Joey on the arm.
“Be lucky mate.” he replied as he walked back downstairs.
The next morning in Spain, the Kray brothers were once again sitting by the pool side, Reggie was swimming in the pool with Johnny, while Charlie was keeping an eye on Ronnie who could not relax. He walked up and down the length of the pool at least a dozen times.
“Come and sit down Ron, C’mon ave a drink.” Charlie said to him.
Ronnie pulled up a chair and sat down.
“I don’t fucking like being out here; I wish I was back home making sure there were no fuck ups.”
“Relax Ron, the boys ave got everything covered.”
“How can you fucking say that?” Ronnie replied violently.
Charlie lost for words held out his hands and then reached out his hand and rested it on Ronnie’s arm.
“Just relax Ron, ave a drink.”

"DON'T WANT A FUCKING DRINK!" Ronnie suddenly and very menacingly shouted at his brother as he swiped a glass of the table causing it to smash on the ground. Reggie saw what Ronnie did and quickly jumped out the pool.
"Just leave him Charlie, he'll be alright." Reggie said to his elder brother as they stood watching Ronnie walk off in the distance.
Later that day when Mario turned up for his meeting with Ronnie he was surprised to find only Reggie and Charlie.
"Where's Ronnie?"
"He doesn't feel very well today Mario, sit down and have a drink."
"But we had a meeting today, we were supposed to go over to the club, look I have the keys."
"You got the keys?" Reggie replied.
"Yes here." Mario said showing them.
"Triffic come on let's have a drink, toast our new club." Reg said smiling.
The next evening there was only one story grabbing the headlines on the six-o'clock news. Tony Lambrianou was sitting in his mother's house when the news started.
'Four dead in London's East End'. Was the headline.
Tony stiffened in his chair and sat forward as the report began.
'Four men of Irish origin were found dead in London's East End earlier today, their bodies were found in an abandoned car, on a side road of the dump in Stepney Green, each man had been shot once in the head, police have issued no official statement as yet but earlier today at the scene of the crime, one of the detectives from a local police station stated that it was obviously gang related'
"Fuck me!" Tony smiled as he took a sip from his tea just before another report began.
"I have with me here in the studio ex detective Jonathan Durose from Scotland yard, Detective Durose."
"It's Mr Durose now I'm retired."
"Sorry Mr Durose, you was a detective in the police force for fifty years have you ever seen such a unashamed gang killing as we have seen today."
"Well firstly I must say that the police have not issued any statements to establish that fact yet."
"Yes but you must agree that everything points to it being gang related."
"Yes I agree, due to the fact that each man was killed with one bullet to the head, and that they were all related, does steer me to believe that it was a rival gang or family who did this heinous crime."
"Is this the beginning of gang warfare in London Again?"
"I can't comment correctly on that as I have no proof."

"Yes but in your experience as a veteran detective would you suggest that this could be the beginning of retribution killings?"
"Once again it would be difficult for me to comment on the talk of revenge killings, as I am not privy to the case, but I will say that the area that these murders have taken place is a breeding ground for gangs."
"London's East End."
"Of course, we have seen in recent years gangs from that area taken to court where the prosecution cases have fell apart and disintegrated into thin air, there are certain parts in that area of London that have become impossible to police."
"In what way?"
"There are places in that area where no one will talk to the police. I do not want to get into naming individuals, but it is well known that certain gangs in the East End have now almost become beyond the law. No one for fear of their lives or their family's lives would bear witness against them."
"That's chilling." the reporter replied.
"It's terrifying!" added Durose.
"Are you saying to me that the Police force cannot offer people or be seen to offer certain people, protection in certain parts of London?"
Durose suddenly stiffened in his pose,
"No!, you misunderstood me, what I am saying is that people from the East End of London will not come forward as Police witnesses, I never said the police will not grant them protection."
"No! But you're saying that the peoples trust in our Police force is non-existent."
"Yes I suppose I am."
"Well thank you Mr Durose we will have to leave it at that point and I can only add that this must be worrying times for Mothers and Fathers, in the East End of London.....

Not Guilty Your Honour
Chapter Three
'Cheers and Tear's'

"Cheers" Ronnie cried as he raised a champagne glass against the glasses of Reggie, Charlie and Mario.
"To the club!" Reggie replied as the three men turned towards a photographer who was taking their picture on the red-carpeted entrance.
It had now been four days since the shootings back in London. George and Billy Hayes had flown out to Spain to meet the twins and filled Ronnie in with all the details of the Hennessey murders. The police back home had pulled in over thirty people for questioning but they still had no leads. Most of the Firm had been pulled in but everyone close had cast iron alibis, the law had paid the twin's mother a visit, and enquired as to where her sons were, but she said she didn't know where they were, and told the law to piss off.
Ronnie pulled Reggie away from the steps of the club as the midday heat was making him sweat; they walked inside and sat alone together in one of the clubs alcoves. Charlie went into the office with Mario and Johnny Walsh

together with the Hayes brothers who kept an eye on the Spanish painters to make sure they didn't slouch from their jobs.
Ronnie took a large gulp of a glass of iced water before he spoke to Reg.
"I'm thinking about going home Reg."
"When?"
"In a couple of days' time maybe."
"What about the opening night?" Reggie asked.
"That's not for a couple of weeks is it, we can come back for that, but we need to be back on the manor now mate." replied Ronnie as he took another mouthful of water.
"Ya know the laws gonna want to see us when we get back."
"Course I do, but there's fuck all they can do to us, we was out here."
"There try to put it down to us Ron, they know the paddy bastards took our club while we was inside."
"Fuck em!, got no proof , no witnesses , fuck all Reg."
"What ya wanna do about all this out ere then." added Reggie.
"We can leave Charlie out here, he can sort it all out with Mario, we got the villa now so he can bring his wife and kid over."
"You spoke to him about it?"
"Mentioned it briefly, told him there's gonna be a lotta rows back home, so it would be more of a benefit to us all if he took care of all this for us,"
"What he say to that?"
"He said yeah!"
"What about the dosh for the villa, Mario's been asking me for it Ron?"
"Has he, ain't said fuck all to me."
"He's been hinting Ron."
"Don't worry about it, I'll call I'm over now."
Ronnie then called over Billy Hayes and told him to fetch Mario, Mario appeared with Charlie about a minute later and they both sat down to join them.
"Mario, listen mate, me and Reg ave got to go home for a few days, gotta a bit of business that needs our attention."
"What about the opening night and all the arrangements?" replied Mario nervously.
"Don't worry about it, we're going to be back for that, and anyway Charlie's gonna stay here and take care of everything, now listen Mario I need a favour."
"Ok Ron." Mario asked.
"Now, you know the villas we're buying! Charlie gave the fella a grand as a good will gesture and deposit, but he ain't given us the keys yet."
"No he is waiting for the rest of the money from you."

"Ah now there's, where we got the problem Mario, we still got all that fucking agro back home, getting our hands on our own money, now if Charlie is gonna stay out here and look after things, he's gonna need somewhere to stay. It's fucking stupid staying in the hotel when we got our own place ain't it, I thought it would solve his problem if you got the keys for him."
"That could be a problem Ron."
"How can it be a fucking problem? The guys your cousin."
"Yes Ronnie but." Ronnie interrupted Mario in mid-sentence.
"Tell ya what were do." Ronnie said loudly as he grabbed Mario's arm
"Are the bank accounts open for the club yet Mario?" Ronnie then added although he knew full well they were.
"Yes they have been open for two days."
"Right, here's what were do. Tomorrow morning you and Charlie go down the place and use the club to get the villa, the clubs half ours anyway, we can use our share of the profits from here to pay off the house. Their stand for that as they got the club as collateral, then that way we can then go back home and sort out all our problems, and Charlie can get into the villa, take care of everything here, were come back in about ten days with everything sorted out. Where we will have the best party Marbella's ever fucking seen, and then crack on with the business."
Mario shrugged his shoulders and gave in.
"Ok Ronnie you go home and take care of your business, and me and Charlie will take care of everything out here."
"That's a boy Mario." Ronnie smiled just before turning to his brother Reg.
"This is what I love about him Reg." Ronnie said putting his hand on Mario's shoulder "He knows what it means to be a partner, whenever we need a favour he never lets us down does he?" he added.
"He's one of the best Ron." Reggie added as he also placed an arm on Mario's other shoulder.
The next day Ronnie, Reg, and Johnny Walsh flew into Heathrow, Billy and his brother George got flights to Paris so they could pick up the Ronnie's Jaguar at the hotel where he left it. As the twins walked through immigration and presented their passports they were detained immediately, and put in the holding cells till they could be questioned by detectives from Scotland Yard. Ronnie knew this would happen and he said this would be the best way as he didn't want the law coming round his Mother's house and putting her through any more stress.
Ronnie was the first to be called into an interview room where he saw two detectives that were familiar with him, Detective Bill Jones, who was a senior fit and verbal you up old school copper, who despised Ronnie. And Detective Bob Crawley who was about ten years younger and not as crooked as Jones, but he was just as ambitious.

Both coppers sat smoking cigarettes and they both smiled sarcastically as Ronnie sat down.
"Ronnie!" Jones drooled.
Ronnie picked up a packet of cigarettes and lit himself up one ignoring Jones's greeting.
"Now let's not go through all the shit Ron, you know why we're here, where was you on the night of the Hennessey's murders?"
"You see my passport ain't ya, you seen the fucking stamps in it."
"Yeah we've seen your passport." Detective Crawley added.
"But we wanna hear it from you Ronnie; see what you got to say?" Jones sternly said.
"See what I got to say." Ronnie replied angrily. "Here's what I got to say, BOLLOCKS! That's what I gotta fucking say, now fuck off back to you ya fucking stink hole."
With that Ronnie jumped up violently and walked over to the door and banged on it loud.
"Take me back to my fucking cell!" he told the immigration officer who had been standing outside.
Next the Detectives interviewed Johnny Walsh as they decided to let Reggie sweat while he waited. Johnny Walsh said nothing to the coppers, he just gazed down at the floor as if he was in another world, they had him in there for over forty minutes trying to get some response but Johnny never said one word.
Finally when they brought Reg in they were sick to see that he was as calm as anything, they were hoping he would be angry and get into some sort of argument with them in the hope that in his emotion he might let something slip.
"Reggie, sit down." Detective Jones said offering him a cigarette which Reggie Declined.
"Reggie we know you had something to do with the Hennessey's." Jones replied and then went into silent and staring mode.
"Is this a fucking wind up? We were in Spain!" Reggie replied.
Detective Jones smiled broadly then leant back in his chair put his hands behind his head and just looked at Reg sarcastically.
"You gonna nick us for that, you got fuck all on us Jones."
"We got your confessions Reg."
"Argh here we go! You gonna verbal us up now are ya, Detective Bill 'the verbal Jones. Taking us back to the Old Bailey with just a confession, don't make me fucking laugh Jones! You got fuck all on us, and you know it. We've got passport stamps, holiday snaps holding newspapers and the statements from about a hundred fucking people saying where we was, stop wasting our fucking time and piss off back to the yard!"

Detective Jones stood up violently pushing the table to one side, Reggie quick as flash jumped up as well.
"Go on fucking try it!" Reggie shouted as he put his hands up.
"I'll fucking ave ya Kray, might not be today but I'll fucking get ya and when I do your gonna spend the rest of ya stinking life rotting in a fucking cell." Jones shouted as Detective Crawley put an arm out of front of him worrying that a fight may start.
"Yeah… in your fucking dreams." Reggie said smiling.
The Twin's and Johnny Walsh were freed an hour later, they were escorted out of the building by four immigration officers which Reggie thought was way over the top specially as immigration had just completely wasted four hours of their time, then let them go with not even an apology.
When Violet Kray heard her boys come in through the front door she immediately knew it was them, she threw off a cover that she had been knitting for a neighbour and ran into the hallway.
Ronnie embraced his Mother warmly and so did Reg, she asked them if they were okay and commented how well they looked with their suntans.
Ronnie's Father walked out and shook their hands.
"The laws been round ere." he said.
"What for!" Ronnie replied.
"Little Firm of Irish fellows got done down the road, been in all the papers, everyone's had a tug."
"It's got nothing to do with us Dad, we've been in Spain." Reggie replied.
Charlie Kray Snr shrugged looking like he couldn't care less.
"Well just marking ya cards boys," he added before disappearing back into the kitchen.
"You look marvellous Mum, let's ave a cup of tea and were tell ya all about Spain, we got some great news for ya." Ronnie said.
"Right well sit ya self's down, ya Dads just lit the fire and I'll get ya something to drink, you hungry boys."
"Bacon sandwich mum!" Reggie replied.
Later that night the twins went down the Carpenters arms, Tony Lambrianou was already there with Trousers Johnny and Eddie Brenner, Dennis Smith was there with his cousin Tom and sitting in the corner playing cards was Slice'em Sid and Sammy Carpenter. The twins walked over and said hello to everyone before sitting down at their usual table, Tony brought them both over a Vodka and Tonic and then sat down besides Reg.
"How was Spain?" Tony asked Reg.
"Ar its beautiful Tone, wait till ya see the club we brought."
"You got a club?" Tony enthusiastically replied.
"Where's Chris?" Ronnie snapped suddenly interrupting Reggie and referring to Tony's brother.

"He's in Birmingham Ron."
"What's he doing up there!"
"Ronnie!" Tony said holding his hands up if defending himself. "He's gonna live up there, he's my brother and I love I'm but he wants to do his own thing Ron."
Ronnie's attention was suddenly distracted by a disturbance over at the bar, he got to his feet and saw that a man was holding a women by the wrist and shouting at her, Tony Lambrianou was standing in front of Ronnie and he got pushed clean out the way as Ronnie steamed over towards the argument, suddenly everyone on the Firm was rushing towards the man.
Ronnie grabbed him by the collar and pushed him away from the women who was now in tears.
"All right, alright!" the man shouted holding his hands up in a pleading fashion.
Eddie Brenner grabbed him by the arm and along with Dennis Smith and his cousin Tom they forcefully dragged him out the pub and into the alleyway besides it.
"Ronnie that fucking tarts no good, she's been giving me the run around now for two fucking weeks." he pleaded as he saw Ronnie walking over.
"So you decided to rough her up in front of my company did ya."
"Ronnie she's a slag, a fucking whore!" the man screamed.
Eddie Brenner chinned the guy hard knocking his head back against the brick wall "Shut ya fucking mouth!" Brenner then shouted at him.
Ronnie advanced like a wild animal, he grabbed the man's neck with his left hand while he slashed away at him with a knife in his right, it was over in seconds as the man dropped to the ground screaming trying to find what was left of his face on the wet pebbled ground.
Ronnie then turned violently towards his firm,
"Is this what I gotta fucking come home to!" he shouted, his eyes nearly coming out of his head with rage, "Cunts, acting like that in front of us."
Ronnie then pushed Brenner hard in the chest, Brenner backed off quickly as he knew how dangerous Ronnie could be when angered. Reggie jumped in front of everyone and told them quickly to go back in the pub.
"Ron, C'mon bruv, it's over now, we don't want to have rows with our own."
Ronnie was panting heavy as he bit his lip.
"What they all been doing Reg? This fucking asshole wouldn't have dreamed of doing this in front of us a year ago." Ronnie snapped as he slashed the man's back with a heavy blow.
"Ronnie!" Reggie shouted "That's enough!" he added as he bravely grabbed the knife off him.
"Our pub Reg! In our fucking pub!" Ronnie snapped as Reggie pulled him away and led him to the car. Tony was standing by the door still and as soon

as Reggie put Ron in the car he walked over to him. Reggie pulled out a couple of hundred pounds and stuffed it in Tony's pocket.
"I'm taking Ronnie home, sort that ponce out round there will ya, get him down the hospital and give I'm a few quid, tell him if he don't wanna get this again then keep his fucking mouth shut."
"Don't worry Reg I'll sort it out."
Reggie took his brother home and put him to bed he knew that Ronnie hadn't been taking no medication lately and while he was like this then anything was possible with him, Reggie gave Ronnie a couple of sleeping pills and a glass of milk and sat down on the bed next to him.
"Reggie I tell ya, they're all fucking plotting against us bruv I can feel it."
"Get some rest Ron your see things differently in the morning."
"We should do em all in, every fucking one of em, they think there fucking big time, then we'll fucking do em big time, then get ourselves a new Firm."
"Ronnie please, get some rest, we'll be alright I promise ya."
Reggie stayed holding Ronnie's head till he fell asleep then went quietly downstairs and picked up the phone,
"Dr Metcalf its Reggie Kray."
"Reggie how is you I have been meaning to call to congratulate you and Ronnie, I am very happy for you."
"Thanks doc but I need to see you about Ron."
"How is he?"
"Not good Doctor he had a bad turn tonight, he hasn't had no medication for a couple of weeks and I'm very worried about him."
"Where is he now?"
"I put him to sleep Doc."
"Ok where are you I will come straight away."
"At our Mums Doc."
"See you soon Reg."
Dr Metcalf was a long and trusted friend; he had looked after Ronnie now for a number of years, the twins always paid him well so no matter where he was or what time it was he was always available to them. The doctor arrived in thirty minutes and sat down with Reg in the lounge
"Tell me what happened Reg?"
"It's his temper again doc, he feels that everyone is against him."
"Paranoia!"
"Well yeah."
The doctor then reached into his bag and pulled out a few bottles of pills.
"Take two of these bottles Reg and make sure he takes four a day, I will give you something to sedate him as well, now it's very important he has rest for a couple of days, keep him away from work or anything that might annoy him."
"He's just wound up about a few things doc."

“Reggie.” the Doctor replied sincerely “Keep his mind of your work, we both know what he is capable of when he’s like this.” added Dr Metcalf as he got to his feet, Reggie also stood up shook the doctors hand and gave him a good drink then thanked him sincerely as he showed him the way out.
The next morning Tony Lambrianou and Eddie Brenner knocked at Vallance Road just after ten, Johnny Walsh answered the door as he had been there all last night looking after Ron and had just come downstairs to make himself a cup of tea and a piece of toast, Johnny ushered them in and asked them to be quiet.
“Be quiet! Ronnie’s asleep.” Johnny said motioning with his hand.
“How is he?” Tony asked quietly once Johnny had led them into living room and shut the door.
“He’s not good Tone, he’s gone right into one, Reggie called out the doctor last night and he put him on sleepers, told Reg that Ronnie needs a few days’ rest.”
“He went fucking crazy last night John, shivved someone up terrible, I thought he was gonna do me.” Eddie said.
“Yeah Reg told me about it, did ya get the geezer to the hospital?”
“Yeah should ave seen the fucking claret in the back of Tom’s motor, phroah, we gave him a few quid, he won’t say a fucking word.” Tony replied.
“Where’s Reg?” Eddie asked.
“He’s still a kip, ad a late night.”
“Johnny we need to see him mate, were gonna go down the Grave Maurice now, then we’ll be in the Carpenters about one let him know will ya, tell him it’s important.”
“Alright Tone no problem.”
Reggie walked into the Carpenters Arms at ten past one with Bill and George Hayes who had just got back from Spain, over in the corner he saw Tony and Eddie, Reg and Billy went over there while George went to the bar for some drinks.
“Alright Tone what’s up, did ya take care of that mug last night.”
“Reg done!, gave him the dosh and told him to keep his fucking mouth shut, turned out that the bird he was hassling was Jimmy Dazza’s little sister.”
“Jimmy down the car site.” Reggie said.
“Yeah we met him at the Maurice earlier, and straightened him out, he told us that the bird was terrified of him, the slag’s bashed her a few times, and anyway he told me to give you his word that his sister won’t say a word, they’re a good family Reg!”
“Good work Tony.” Reggie said as he reached up to get his drink Georgie had brought over.
“Is that what you came round for earlier?” he asked after taking a mouthful.

"Partly but when you left here last night, about an hour later, that copper Brooker turned up, he walked in and stood over the other side of the bar."
"Nah did he! What's he fucking want!" Reggie snapped surprised.
"I went over to him Reg; I let him stand for there for a minute then I went over."
"Who was he with?" Reggie interrupted.
"On his own, I pulled him about what the fucking hell was he doing here, the fat arrogant slag smiled at me, fucking smiled at me like we were long lost pals."
"Well what he say?" Reggie again interrupted.
"Asked where you and Ron were?"
"The fucking mug, what for?" Reggie snapped.
"Don't ask me Reg but he said it right flash."
"What'd ya tell him?"
"I told him you weren't here, and to thank his fucking stars that you weren't."
"What'd he say to that?" Reggie asked smiling
"He finished off his drink, wiped his mouth then said he will be back!"
Just as Tony finished Johnny Walsh came tearing into the pub he ran straight over to Reg sweating profusely.
"Reg! Ronnie's just left the house with Sammy and Slicem, he looked in a right fucking mood!"
"Where's he gone?"
"Don't know Reg, Slicem Sid and Sammy Carpenter knocked about twenty minutes ago, I told them Ronnie was kipping but Ronnie heard them and called em upstairs, next thing I know, the three of em are flying out the house, didn't even speak to me Reg, just pushed me out the way, should a seen the fucking look on his face."
"Bollocks!" Reggie snapped, "What the fuck are Sammy and Sid doing." he added.
Tony grabbed Reggie arm.
"They were both in ere last night Reg, they might a gone over to tell Ron about Brooker."
"Drive faster ya cunt!" Ronnie raged.
"Going as fast as I can Ron, there's a fucking hold up." Sammy Carpenter replied as he drove, while Ronnie sat angrily in the back of the Mercedes and slicem Sid sat in the passenger seat.
"Just get me to Carters fucking pub!" Ronnie growled.
"Ron we don't wanna have a row with him in there mate, too many eyes."
"When we get there I want you Sid, to find out if he's in there, don't get seen, Brooker's an old bill and they got eyes in the back of their stinking heads."

Once they reached Ladbroke Grove, Ronnie made sure they parked the car about fifty yards from Tommy Carters pub, Sid got out and walked up the road then returned a few minutes later.
"He's in there, Ron."
"Right were gonna stay here till he moves, Sid I want you to go and stand near the pub, buy a coffee or something and stand by that bus stop over the road and don't take your eyes of the pub. If he comes out and walks, then follow him from a distance, see where he's going, if he comes out and gets in a car then come back ere and were all follow him in this alright."
"Yep got it Ron." Sid replied as he jumped out the car.
Ronnie and Sam sat in the car for nearly three hours until Sid returned to the pleasure of Sammy who was getting more and more nervous at Ronnie's agitated state.
"Right he came out the pub and walked round the corner Ron." Sid said excited and out of breath.
"Where the fuck he go!" Ronnie shouted as he looked out the window.
"It's all right Ron I followed him, he walked up the road a few hundred yards then went into a basement flat, I walked over and took a peek through the window, I can't swear it but I think it was his place."
"Was anyone there?"
"Couldn't see anyone Ron but judging by the fucking mess I don't think it was a place where any women or kids lived."
Ronnie pushed Sammy in the back and ordered him to start the car; the three men drove off as Sid instructed Sammy where to go. They parked round a corner out of sight of Brooker's basement flat and then quietly but quickly walked over to Brooker's front door. Ronnie whispered to Sid that they should barge the door open, Sammy walked up a couple of stairs and looked around to see if anyone was about. Once the coast was clear he nodded to Ronnie who along with Sid barged open the old wooden front door.
Brooker was in his small kitchen frying himself some sausages when the door crashed off its hinges, to his horror he saw Ronnie Kray storm his way into the hall which was in clear view from his kitchen. Within the blinking of an eye, Ronnie advanced towards him, Brooker in panic grabbed hold of a carving knife. But before he could do anything Ronnie had ran up the small hall grabbed hold of the frying pan that was frying Brooker's sausages and threw it all over his face. Brooker dropped to his knees in agony as the boiling fat burnt his eyes. Ronnie Kray and Slice'em Sid then dragged Brooker out of the kitchen and into his small living room and threw him onto the floor. The old bill was then given a barrage of kicks and punches and stamps around the head.
"So ya wanted to see me, well here I fucking am!" Ronnie shouted.
Brooker rolled himself up in a ball and screamed.

"Shut up you fucking pig." Ronnie shouted as he stamped on his face.
"STOP!,STOP!, PLEASE, STOP." mumbled Brooker through the boiling fat and blood that now covered his face.
Ronnie then suddenly did as he asked; he picked up a cushion and threw it at Brooker.
"Wipe yourself down." Ronnie calmly said before turning to Sammy and telling him to go and fetch some water. Ronnie then picked Brooker up and placed him in an old ripped armchair, Sammy returned with the water and began wiping the coppers face.
"Don't kill me, don't kill me Ron."
"I ain't gonna kill ya, not unless ya tell me what I wanna fucking know." Ronnie replied
"Why were you down the Carpenters last night?" Ronnie then added.
Brooker coughed and grimaced before he replied.
"I came down to have a drink with ya, see if there was any work we could do together." he mumbled.
Ronnie cracked Brooker straight in the face with a hard right punch, which knocked Brooker's head into the back of the armchair, and then he slumped forward on the verge of unconsciousness, Ronnie picked up his head and pushed it back.
"Don't fucking lie to me!" he shouted before he reached into his suit and pulled out a hammer to which he pushed into Brooker's face. "That was the only fucking chance I'm gonna give ya, next time you lie, I'm gonna smashed this hammer right across your fucking jaw, now why was you in the Carpenters last night."
"Alright, we was gonna squeeze ya, put some pressure on you."
"Who's we!" Ronnie raged.
"Me! The old bill, get some money from ya and turn a blind eye."
Ronnie then grabbed his face.
"What was ya gonna put me on Scotland Yard's fucking weekly donation list, now what I tell ya about fucking lying, who was we?" Ronnie snapped as he slapped Brooker hard again and again until Brooker cried out.
"Alright, alright it was Tommy Carter's idea, he told me to go over to see you and threaten you with the law, I told him it wasn't a good idea but he made me do it."
"What else he want?"
"He wants to take you out, he's spoke about nothing else since that day you done him in the pub, he wants to skint ya, then put ya away somewhere, he wanted me to get close to ya, find out some things and then if he couldn't find a way to kill ya he would have enough shit on ya to ave ya nicked,"
Ronnie's face screwed up with rage as he began to punch Brooker.
"Fucking take me out!, kill me ya fucking slags."

"Ronnie Ronnie!" Brooker screamed.
"Don't kill me Ronnie!" he added trying to shield his face from the blows.
"Ronnie I can help you, I know everything about Carter's operation, don't kill me I can help you, I'll tell ya everything about him, we can do him together."
Ronnie then stopped punching and got to his feet.
"So you gonna help me now are ya."
"If ya want, I don't wanna die."
"So your help me kill Carter!" Ronnie calmly replied.
"If that's what you want." Brooker pleaded.
"Then give Carter this message for me!"
Ronnie then raised the hammer in his right hand and with every ounce of strength he brought it crashing down onto the top of Brooker,s head. It made a sickening noise as the top part of the hammer crashed through Brooker's skull and embedded into his brain and caused Brooker's head to tilt with the momentum of the blow. Ronnie had to twist the hammer to release it from his head as Sammy and Sid turned away in horror.
"Won't be fucking nicking no one now!" Ronnie calmly smiled.
Reggie Kray and Tony Lambrianou had been searching all day for Ronnie, Reggie had got everyone on the Firm out looking for him, it was now eight in the evening and Reggie was becoming very worried. Tony pulled the car up outside the Grave Maurice pub in Whitechapel.
"We'll give it another try Reg!" Tony sighed in a tired tone as they had already been in there three times already. Reggie jumped out and ran into the pub, he looked around and saw that Ronnie was not there then just as he was about to leave the landlord called out.
"Reggie, got a message for ya son, I was told to tell ya Ronnie's down the Carpenters and waiting for ya."
Ronnie Kray was on his sixth double vodka and tonic when Reggie and Tony stormed into the pub, he was sitting at his usual table with Sammy Carpenter and Slicem Sid, Eddie Brenner had just arrived and was busy at the bar trying to phone round for Reg to tell him that Ronnie was here. Reggie looked over and saw Ronnie sitting proud and menacing he turned to Tony and told him to phone Johnny Walsh and tell him to stay at home before he went over to his twin.
"Ronnie where ya been, I been looking everywhere for ya?"
"Had a bit of business Reg." Ronnie coolly replied.
Reggie gazed at Sammy and Sid who both looked as white as ghosts then he looked down onto the table to see at least two dozen empty glasses, he quickly wondered what kind of business Ronnie meant as they had all come back to the pub and began to drink themselves silly.
"Sid, Sam I'd like to talk to Ronnie alone."

When the two men left Reg moved closer to Ron and spotted blood splattered on his suit.
"Ronnie where ya been there's blood on ya suit?"
"That cozzer Brooker was down here last night came here looking for us."
"Yeah I know."
"Well he won't be coming here anymore." Ronnie whispered as he grabbed Reggie's arm.
"What'd ya mean?" Reggie asked although he had a good idea.
"I did him!" Ronnie replied with a huge smile.
"Fucking hell, fucking hell." Reggie sighed.
"C'mon Ron lets go, we gotta get you out of ere." Reggie added as he got to his feet and helped Ronnie up, once Reggie had put Ronnie into the car he called over Tony, and told him to go and get Johnny Walsh and Ronnie's medication, and bring him over to the house of the twins cousins Billy Smith who lived in Walthamstow, Tony knew the house well and told Reggie he would do it now.
"And tell Sammy Carpenter and that fucking idiot Slice'em Sid to wait here till I get back!" Reggie shouted.
Ronnie never said one word on the drive over to their cousins; he sat motionless just staring out the window as Reggie drove through the rain.
Billy Smith was related to the Kray's on their Fathers side of the family, Smith was a big man of Romany origin, in his youth he travelled up and down the country making a name for himself taking part in Bare Knuckle fights within the English and Irish Gypsy communities. When he gave up his fighting he went into business buying and selling caravans, another trick he had was to find an old plot of unused land near where the Government were building roads or motorways and place ten or twelve caravans on it, Smith would then bring over twenty to forty Irish travellers get them jobs on the building sites. Then charge them rent to stay in the caravans, this proved to be a good money spinner for Smith as he could always get the Irish to work for a cheaper price than the English. Work back in Ireland for these people was non-existent so he could always rely on getting the manpower. Smith would then charge them right over the odds to stay in his caravans, the Irish didn't mind as they were getting paid something rather than nothing, which was what they'd get back home. Every Saturday Smith would go to his sites for collection; he would take them three large barrels of beer along with bread and meats. He'd collect the rent then at a small profit charge them for the food and drink. The Irish travellers loved it , they would work all week get drunk in there caravans at night then send what was left of their pay back home to their families in Ireland.

Ronnie always liked Billy Smith he would say that his cousin was a modern day outlaw; never paid a tax in his whole life, never worked for anyone other than himself, and never turned away a friend.
Once Ronnie and Reggie reached Billy's house, Billy wasted no time in taking care of Ronnie, straight away as Ronnie walked in he noticed the blood on his clothes, he told his wife to go out round her sisters then ordered one of his eight sons to build a fire.
"Dada it's fuckin raining outside." pleaded his boy.
"Then build it in the fucking shed." Billy Smith replied.
One of Billy's other sons then fetched a bottle of scotch and brought down some of his Dads clothes for Ronnie to change into, Ronnie laughed as he saw the state of them, typical gypsy clobber, big fucking trousers and a big string vest and an old cardigan that stunk of tobacco.
"I ain't fucking going out dressed like this." Ronnie joked.
It wasn't long before Tony and Johnny Walsh arrived, Johnny walked straight over to Ron and gave him a couple of pills from his medication while Tony waited in the hallway where Reggie and Billy Smith came out to him.
"It's not good Reg, I spoke to Sid and Sammy, listen Ronnie topped Brooker."
"Yeah I know, were gonna have to get him away for a few days, but firstly I'm worried about if anyone saw him."
"I asked the same thing to Sammy, he said they done him in Brooker's flat."
"Did they have gloves on?"
"I doubt it Reg." Tony replied.
Reggie then turned to Billy.
"Billy have you got a couple of guys who can torch the place?"
"Not a problem Reg, I'll get a couple of the Irish fella's off the site, there'll do anything for a couple of extra bob."
"Good, can you go and get em and bring them down the red Lion in Stepney straight away Bill, we need to get a move on with this."
"I'll go now Reg." Billy replied as he reached for his coat then shouted out for one of his boys to come with him.
Reggie then walked over to Ronnie and Johnny Walsh and knelt down.
"Ronnie I gotta shoot off and take care of a couple of things, Johnny's gonna stay here, now wait here till I get back and I'll bring you back some clothes, I've gotta make sure we don't get nicked for this, now is there anything you can tell us."
"I can't see there being a problem Reg, no one saw us do it."
"I'm worried about prints Ron."
"Nah that's alright I didn't touch anything apart from a frying pan but I made sure wiped it down, but I can't vouch for Sam or Sid they were shaken up when we left."
"The fucking frying pan, what was you cooking breakfast." Reggie laughed.

“Right well you wait ere, I’m gonna get someone to torch the gaff.” Reggie added as he got up.
“REG!” Ronnie snapped as grabbed his arm.
“Keep an eye on Tommy Carter, that slags got ideas.”
Reggie winked at his brother before he left the room, once in the hall he pulled Tony over in a way to say let’s go and the two men walked outside and got into the car and disappeared into the night’s rain…..

Not Guilty Your Honour
Chapter Four
'The only good copper's, a dead un!'

Tommy Carter sat in his pub The Carters arms in Ladbroke Grove West London, like a Prince among men, Tommy was the eldest brother of four who all their life's had lived and robbed among the rough streets of Notting Hill and Ladbroke Grove. Tommy had spent over ten years of his life in prison and had been arrested over thirty times on various spiv charges.
Everything about Tommy Carter went against Ronnie Kray's morals, Carter pushed dope and pills from his pub to the blacks who would flock to the area at night, he ponced off the backs of women and ran numerous brothels, he had been a shoplifter, a pickpocket and he thought nothing about grassing someone up to get rid of his competition. The Carters until recently, were thought of as nothing, less than nothing, just petty spivs polluting their own manor with their sick and twisted ways. They never ventured in to the West End or showed any ambition to do so, they were just local hard men, Ronnie

Kray couldn't give a fuck about Notting Hill or Ladbroke Grove so until they teamed up with the crooked old bill Brooker no one cared less about them. Tommy was beginning to get anxious as he gazed up at the clock on the wall.
"What time do ya make it." he asked his brother who was sitting next to him as he thought that the clock on the wall could be wrong.
"Quarter past eleven."
"Where the fucking hells Dave?" Tommy gasped referring to Brooker by his first name.
"Why what's the matter Tom?"
"He was meant to be here at ten, we gotta go on the rounds, phone his house up will ya, see if he's there."
Over the other side of town in the East End, Reggie was in the Red Lion in Stepney, Tony Lambrianou had fetched Sammy Carpenter and Slice'em Sid and along with Billy Smith, they were sitting in a corner deep in conversation. Sid was telling Reggie everything that had happened earlier in the evening at Brookers flat.
"Fucking hell, there could be a thousand fucking bits of evidence in that drum." Reggie snapped as he looked at Sid with disgust.
"I thought you had more fucking brains than this Sammy, you should know better."
"Reg, we didn't know what Ronnie was gonna do, it all happened so fast mate, one minute were there giving him a slap then the next fucking thing I know is Ronnie's decorating the fucking walls with his head."
"Well ya gonna have to go back and torch the gaff." Reggie replied.
"Reg it could crawling with the fucking law." Sammy pleaded.
"That don't matter, you pair of cunts get back there and finish the job or we'll all end up fucking nicked."
"Ah fucking hell Reg." Sid sighed only to be pushed hard by Reg.
"Fucking hell you say, you take my brother into a fucking row and then piss off leaving him in a position to get lifed off, you wanna watch ya fucking mouth Sid, and your fucking step, we still gotta have a chat about this once you put things right, so right at this moment, you wanna be worrying about pleasing me and not the fucking law."
"Sorry Reg, I'm just a bit shaken up still."
"Yeah well stop pouring that fucking booze down ya throat and get ya head together."
"Sorry, sorry." Sid pleaded.
Reggie then turned to Sammy.
"Right can you remember Brooker's flat?"
"Yeah course Reg".
"Right then, Billy's got a couple of fella's outside in his car, I want you and Sid to drive them over there, show them the gaff and there do the rest alright."

"Yeah" replied Sammy.
"Then what ya fucking waiting for." Reggie snapped.
"When it's done come back ere!" he added.
Tommy Carter was now getting worried about his policeman friend, Brooker was now over an hour and a half late and Tommy knew that that just wasn't like him at all, one thing you could always rely on Brooker for was his punctuality, it came from being a copper for all them years, where being on time was part and parcel of his job.
"Something's not right Jackie, Dave should ave been here by now."
"He mighta got called back to the nick on something." Jackie replied.
"He would have called."
"I'll ask June." Jackie answered as he called out to the barmaid and asked her if Brooker had called at all that night.
"No, he ain't called here Jackie; he was in ere earlier then said he was going home for something to eat."
"That's it Jack I want you to go round and see if he's at home."
"Tommy it's pissing out."
"Take the fucking car." Tommy replied.
Sammy Carpenter parked the car across the road opposite Brooker's flat, Slice'em Sid sat in the passenger seat and the two Irish gypsy's sat in the back with a huge five gallon can full of petrol that was choking everyone with the fumes. Sammy wiped the condensation off the inside of the window.
"Looks sweet Sid, can't see anything about."
"C'mon lets fucking do this." Sid replied as he and the two gypsy's got out the car and into the rain.
"See ya in a minute Tom." Jackie Carter said as he pulled on his rain Mac.
"If he ain't there, leave a note for him to call me urgently." Tommy replied as Jackie left the pub.
Slice'em Sid and the two Irish boys slowly and carefully pushed open Brooker's front door, Sid had left it resting against the frame earlier as Ronnie had knocked it clean off its hinges. Sid placed the door on its side in the hall and told the Irish boys to give it a good dowsing with petrol, when Sid walked into the living room he wretched as he smelt the blood which was now covering half the floor as it had leaked from Brooker's fallen body.
"Firkin hell!" one of the gypsy's said as he saw the mess.
"C'mon get that petrol over everything and leave some for the kitchen."
Sid then walked into the kitchen and pulled out the gas main at the back of the cooker, the Irish boys followed and poured the rest of the petrol in there, once the can was empty Sid told them to leave the can and get out. Outside Sid told them to wait one minute then throw the matches in the front door and run down the road about a hundred yards where he would be waiting in the car for them.

Just as Sid got to the top of the stairs he saw a car pull up, Sid hid amongst some bushes as he saw Jackie Carter get out and begin to walk towards the flat.
“What the fucking hells going on here?” Jackie Carter shouted as got to the top of the stairs and saw the two gypsies.
“Oi!, who are you!” he shouted at them.
Slice’em Sid jumped from the bushes and picked up a large rock and smashed it onto the back of Jackie Carter who in turn then fell down the steps and knocked himself out, Sid followed him down frantically and ordered the two gypsy’s to help him pick Carter up and throw him in the hall so that he could burn with the flat.
The biggest of the gypsy’s put a hand on Sid.
“We’re not Firkin doing this.”
“What!” Sid answered surprised.
“Were not firkin murderers.” the gypsy added as he pulled Sid’s hands off of Carter.
“What are you fucking mad, he’s just fucking seen us.” Sid Screamed.
“He’s seen fuck all, now I’m telling ya right fucking now were not were not killing him, C’mon Jones pick the man up.” the gypsy replied as he and Jonesy carried Carter up into the street and laid him in the gutter sort of hidden by a car.
“Listen your making a big fucking mistake pal.” Sid said as the two paddies came back down the stairs.
“I don’t give a fuck, I don’t answer to you, Billy told me to torch this fucking place and that’s what were gonna do, but he didn’t say nothing about killing people, now out my fucking way ya blood thirsty bastard I’m throwing these fucking matches.”
With that the gypsy pushed his pal and Sid up the stairs then followed them up, Sid walked away with his pal as he threw the matchbox into the porch.
Next thing there was a massive explosion that knocked all three men off their feet and into the road, Sammy Carpenter spun the car round quickly as the three men jumped in.
“What the fucken hell happened there!” Sammy Carpenter screamed as drove up the road “I thought you was gonna wait till I turned the car round and who was that fucking fella you whacked?” he added.
“Jackie Carter.”
“What! What ya do with him?”
“We threw him in the road.”
“Did he see ya?”
“Nah he saw no one, didn’t see a thing Sam.” Sid replied quietly.

Four big Burly policemen guarded the door to Jackie Carter's Hospital room; he had been unconscious for three days since the fire and the murder of Policeman Dave Brooker.
The Metropolitan Police force had really been putting the pressure on most West London's known faces but after many arrests they had come up with little or no leads.
Jackie Carter however was a mystery to them; he was discovered in the road outside Brooker's burning house with a fractured skull.
Detective Chief Inspector Richard LaSalle was convinced that Carter in some way or another had been involved in the killing; everything was resting on Carter gaining consciousness so that he could be questioned or even charged with the killing of Brooker.
Mavis Carter, Jackie's Mother had sat by her son's bed since he was brought in, her three other sons had disappeared since the death and apart from a couple of hours each day where she went home to wash she had barely left his side.
The Police had questioned her a few times as to what her son was doing there and also the where a bouts of her other children but she said she was just their Mother and she had no idea or interest in what her sons did.
Inspector LaSalle was standing outside Carter's room; he had just spoken to the doctor in charge and now turned to his colleague Detective Len Vasallo with an angered look on his face
"Still no change Len, the doctor just keeps saying he's lucky to be alive."
"Fuck it!" Vasallo sighed, "Just came from the yard guv, the top boys ave ordered a result on this, the fucking press are having a field day on this one." he added quietly.
LaSalle nodded at his colleague's remark with a look that he already knew.
"Don't worry about that Len; we'll nail some bastard for this!"
Detective LaSalle was a legendary and feared figure of London's underworld, he had arrested and convicted many of the well-known villains, he was known as the verbal king, as his trade mark was to verbal someone up or to put it simply, he made up false statements from the people he arrested and lied with the skill of a Shakespearian actor once he took to the box in a court.
LaSalle knew full well why he was chosen for this case, It had been front page news for the last two days and the public and the houses of parliament were hungry for an arrest, he was the man to get one and he was trusted well enough by the top men at Scotland Yard who couldn't really care less if LaSalle got the actual man who murdered Brooker, it was more of a case of arrest and convict the right man who could satisfy the press and parliament.
It was politics and the police were under pressure, the orders were sent down the ranks; nick anybody we don't care who just as long it is someone who we can convict.

Over the other side of town Reggie Kray sat in Pillano's café in the Bethnal Green Road reading the morning paper while sharing a pot of tea with Tony Lambrianou and Georgie Hayes.
"Fucking papers, still going on about this slag Brooker." Reggie snapped as he threw down the paper.
"On everything Reg! We were listening to some Cunt on the radio this morning, fucking going on about how crime in London was spiralling out of control." Tony replied.
"I can see us all getting nicked for this." Reggie sighed shaking his head.
"We're in the clear Reg!" Georgie said, "They got their idea's but fuck all else." he added.
"It's their fucking idea's that I'm worried about George, they Know mate! No two ways about it they fucking know! Since we been out, there's been the Hennessey's murders and now this Cunt Brooker, it don't take fucking Sherlock Holmes to fucking work out what's going on here does it!"
"Fuck em Reg!" Tony said loudly.
Reggie pointed a finger at Tony and looked at George in a manner that was jest fully mocking at Tony's bravado, which in turn had all three men break into smiles, Reggie then picked up his paper and began to playfully smack Tony with "ya gonna say that to the fucking hangman are ya." Reggie added laughing.
Suddenly Reggie stopped as he saw Eddie Brenner storm through the cafes front door, Brenner marched over to the table and threw down his paper onto the table
"Reggie! This is fucking bollocks mate!" He cried.
"Oi!, oi! Calm ya fucking self-down." Reggie angrily answered as he reached out his arm and pulled over a nearby chair.
"Now sit down and tell me what's on ya fucking mind, and nice and calmly remember where we are, alright."
"Reggie I don't know what the fucks going on here, I got the fucking law all over me, Dennis has been nicked because of all this shit, I got the fucking old bill down the car site now, going over every poxy car, this is chaos mate."
"Hold up, what'd ya mean Dennis has been nicked?"
"He's down fucking Limehouse now! The filth come over the car site this morning looking for shooters, all to do with this fucking Hennessey turnout."
"So what's Dennis nicked for?" Tony interrupted.
"They spun the yard and found all the fucking snide fivers he had!" Eddie shouted.
"All right just keep ya fucking voice down!" Reggie added trying to calm Eddie.
Eddie leaned closer to Reg as he calmed himself.

“Reg, everyone’s got the fucking needle over this mate, the laws spinning everyone, none of us can fucking move mate.”
“Alright just calm down Ed, we know we got trouble but just keep it tight amongst ourselves and we will get through this, first thing we gotta get a brief down to see Dennis.”
“It’s done Reg, I got hold of Manny Freedman earlier, and he’s sending someone down there.” Eddie interrupted.
“Ya told his family?”
“Yeah, yeah I’ve took care of it all Reg.”
“How many fivers did they find?”
“Bout ten grand’s worth Reg.”
“Alright let’s see what Manny can do then we’ll get something sorted out for him.”
“Yeah but we got bigga fucking problems Reg, everyone fucking knows that Ronnie topped Brooker and everyone’s going fucking mad about it, Jimmy Ryan calls me last night going fucking berserk, he wants a meet with ya today four o’clock over Clerkenwell Reg.”
“Well what’s the matter with him?” Reggie asked.
“He’s had a tug Reg, over all these fucking killings, he’s trying to get his brothers back into the country quietly and now he’s got the law all over him”
Reggie leaned back in his chair and sighed loudly. “ah for fucks sake!”
“Reggie you gotta have a talk with Ronnie mate, this has gotta stop, its causing fucking bedlam mate, and I can do without having the Ryan’s on my case!”
“Don’t worry about them there not gonna have row with you, you’re with us.” Tony said.
“Don’t talk so fucking stupid Tone; the Ryan’s don’t give a fuck about me.” Eddie snapped back before turning to Reg.
“Reggie, we don’t need that mate, if we have a row with them then that’s fucking war, and we got enough on our plate as it is.”
“Nah Tony’s right there mate, don’t worry about Jimmy Ryan, his family and mine go back to our school days, I’ll go over and see him at four and see what he’s got to say, I’m more concerned over him getting pestered over the things we’ve done rather than having a row with him.”
“Well just marking ya card Reg, he was well pissed off last night mate.” Eddie replied as he held up his hand.
Reggie nodded as he poured himself another cup of tea and then offered one to Eddie.
“Oh yeah he asked me to ask ya if you would see him on yer own, without Ronnie.” Eddie added.
“Yeah that’s alright, Ronnie’s not about anyway.”
“Is he alright Reg?” Eddie asked.

“Yeah he’s down the coast with Johnny staying at my Mum’s bungalow in Worthing; get him away for a few days while all this fucking heats on us.”
“A few days!” Eddie sighed sarcastically “I don’t think this heats going away mate!” He added.
Ronnie had just finished a huge breakfast that Johnny Walsh had cooked him, he was sitting in a big armchair dressed in a fine pair of slacks and a plush smoking jacket and he just lit up a cigarette as Johnny brought him over a cup of tea. The TV was on and Ronnie was looking at the news it had just finished a report on the Brooker murder explaining how the police had been clamping down on all the major underworld figures in the hope that if they created enough pressure upon London’s underworld then someone somewhere would crack.
Ronnie smiled from ear to ear as the programme finished.
“I got every fucking copper in London, running about like headless chickens.” he gloated to Johnny who sat down opposite him.
“There’s a lot of heat on the manor Ron, spoke to Reg last night on the phone while you was sleeping, he said everything is okay and he told me to tell ya he spoke to Charlie in Spain and that everything was going real good out there.”
“Think I might go home tomorrow John.” Ronnie replied totally ignoring what Johnny had just said.
“Reggie asked me to tell ya Ron, that it would be best if we stayed here till everything calms down.”
“We’re missing all the fucking fun John.” Ronnie snapped.
“What fun Ronnie? Everyone’s got the law all over them, they’re nicking everyone on this one, we should stay away mate. You’re feeling much better now, we don’t want to go back home and get pulled in do we?”
“They got fuck all on us, I feel useless sitting here doing nothing, just wanna go back and have a few games with the bastards.”
Tony Lambrianou parked the car just off the Clerkenwell Road; Reggie told him to stay with it as he got out and made his way across the busy road heading for the side entrance to Jimmy Ryan’s offices. Reggie rapped on the door and was greeted swiftly by one of the Ryan’s Associates Frankie Lester.
“Reggie.” Frankie warmly greeted him as he held out his hand and motioned for him to enter.
“How are you Frank?” Reggie replied smiling.
“Not too bad Reg, Jimmy’s upstairs you know where to go don’t ya.”
“Yeah nice one Frank see ya in a minute.” Reggie answered as he walked up the stairs and then into Jimmy’s office.
“Reggie! Hallo mate you better sit down.” Jimmy Ryan warmly said as he first saw Reg.
“Alright Jim.” replied Reggie as they shook hands and Reggie sat down.
“Right where do we start Reg? This shits got way out of hand mate.”

“Well what’s it gotta fucking do with you lot?” Reggie snapped back sharply but not over threatening.
“What’s it gotta do with us Reg, I’ve had the fucking law all over me, south of the rivers going fucking crazy, Fred’s had a spin, did ya know that Reg?”
“No I didn’t.”
“Well he ain’t too pleased mate, none of us are, the Hennessey’s was one thing but this business with the copper is giving everyone fucking grief.”
“How was we meant to know all this would happen.”
“Reg what’d ya thinks gonna happen when a copper gets topped, the laws on everyone’s fucking cases, Joey Pine’s been nicked, Charlie from south of the river had all his slot machine arcades shut down, Harry boy the Jew and Moysher from Dean street have had all there spielers shut down, no one can fucking breathe Reg and everyone’s blaming you and Ron!”
“What’s Joey been nicked for?” Reggie asked.
“He’s been pulled in over Brooker!, Jackie Carter came out of his coma, Jimmy Lago from Bayswater phoned me he told me Carter woke up and pointed the finger at Joey. The old bill got Joey out of his pub about an hour ago; he’s being questioned over this fucking copper and a couple of tools they found in his motor.”
“Ah its gotta be Bollocks Jimmy! Joey wouldn’t have tools in his fucking motor.”
“That’s what I’m trying to fucking say Reg! That bastard LaSalle’s nicked him and I
guantee that slag put the shooters in his car.”
“This is out of fucking hand Jim.”
“Reggie!, get hold of Ronnie and get yourselves right out the fucking way, I’m telling ya mate ya both gonna get nicked on this one, get away and get the best fucking alibi’s you can buy.”
“What about you Jim, you gonna be alright?”
“Don’t fucking worry about me, they already gave me a visit but I was water tight, I was at a charity dinner show at the Savoy that night.”
“Well that’s one bit of good fucking news!”
“Reggie get away mate, this is bad news on a World War two stage, get out of here till things calm down,”
“How’s ya brothers anyway Jim?” Reggie asked.
Jimmy Ryan sighed loudly at Reggie’s question.
“They were coming back this week but there’s no fucking way now! When they get back here, they’re still wanted for questioning so they’re gonna have to go in, but with all this shit happening, they’d have to be off there fucking minds to walk into a nick now, the old bill are looking to score brownie points, looking for examples, show the public there doing there fucking jobs.”

"It's a right mess Jim, me and Ron will get out the way, were meant to be going to Spain next week anyway, were see if we can sort a few things out before we go."
"Reggie just get away mate, I'll take care of things here, right now you and Ron are in every fuckers wrong book, and everyone's got the needle."
"What'd ya mean Jim in everyone's wrong book, if anyone's got something to say let em fucking say it! And if they wanna have a row then they can ave it!" Reggie interrupted angrily.
"That ain't the point Reg, the point is if the law don't nick ya then someone's gonna say something that'll piss Ronnie off, with all this business going on mate you can hardly start having more rows can ya, let's take Dave and Billy Williams out of Hoxton for example, they've been planning a nice job over the airport, bout hundred grand they were looking at, Old bill hit em this morning laying on the pressure, fucking jobs off, six months they'd been plotting up on it, now you're hardly in their best fucking books are ya."
"Jimmy I couldn't give a fuck about Dave and Billy Williams, or Charlie from south or any other cunt, where were they when we was banged up, now you fucking tell em and any other ponce if they wanna ave a pop then were fucking oblige em."
"So ya wanna cause war? With every fucking one"
"I don't wanna cause anything but we certainly won't fucking walk away from it."
"C'mon Reggie! You can see what's happened here mate."
"Jimmy I hear what ya saying and I appreciate it, but let me just make one thing fucking clear, me and my brother run our affairs our way and if anyone doesn't like it, then let em come and tell us, we don't take orders from no one, if we gotta ave a row with some slag and put him away then that's what we'll do be yesterday, today or tomorrow."
"Reggie that's not what I'm saying!"
"Jimmy we got a lot of respect for you and ya brothers, go back a long way, but that's what it sounds like to me, I come up here to see ya and you start saying he's got the needle this one's got the needle, he's had his work stopped, he can't do this, this one can't do that, well fuck em Jim, I couldn't care less, fuck the lot of em!"
Paddington Green just on the Edgware Road was London's highest security Police station,
Joey Pine and his brother Ted were both sitting in different cells waiting for a solicitor to arrive, Joey was going crazy, he had already chinned the sergeant who had asked him to strip then six big coppers came into his cell and forcefully removed his clothes and gave him a good hiding as a bonus, he was left standing in a cold dark cell in just his underpants when the sergeant opened up the hatch on his cell door

“You fucking calmed down now ave ya?”
The sergeant asked sarcastically.
“Go-on fuck off.” Pine replied without even looking at him,
Joey Pine then heard another voice calling out his name he turned round sharpish as he recognized it to be the Voice of Detective Chief Inspector Richard LaSalle whose eyes he could see gazing happily through the hatch.
“You dirty Bastard” Pine mouthed as he walked over to him.
“All’s fair in love and war Joey.” replied LaSalle being patronizing.
“You fit me up ya slag.”
“We don’t want you today Joe, but we’ll fucking ave ya if you don’t give us what we want.” LaSalle said quietly after looking quickly over his shoulder.
“You won’t make this stick, I got fucking witnesses, I was in the pub all night.”
“No!, a long and violent feud with the Carters, Two guns in your car, a piece of rag stinking of petrol and I’d like to bet the clothes we took off you today come back from the lab with petrol on them.”
“You fucking slag!” Joey shouted as he spat at LaSalle through the hatch and kicked at the door.
“It’s not you we want, its Kray! Stick him up or you’re gonna spend the rest of ya life inside!”
“Fuck YOU! LaSalle.”
Reggie Kray left Jimmy Ryan’s office feeling like the world was closing in on him, he had only been home for a few weeks and already it looked like the old bill had a holding charge hanging over him but the fact that he or anyone else close to him had not already been visited concerned him,
“Looks like were gone get pulled in Tony.” Reggie said just as Tony started the car up
“Is that what Jimmy thinks?”
“Yeah he says there’s a lot of talking going on about us doing Brooker, have you heard anything Tone.”
“Ain’t heard nothing about Brooker but a lot of people know about the hiding we gave Tommy Carter at his pub, he told everyone he had a row with ya.”
“Yeah I know that but it still don’t put us right in the frame for Brooker does it.”
“The night Brooker come over the Carpenters asking where you was, wasn’t his first stop Reg, he’d been in about six or seven pubs beforehand mate, a few people knew him and it don’t take a lot of imagination when the next day he’s found dead.”
“Then why haven’t the fucking law nicked us for it?”
“Well what they got on ya?” Tony replied loudly.
“I don’t Know, but something ain’t fucking right Tone, if they ain’t paid us a visit then there’s only two reasons for it, one were under obbo and there just

waiting for us to fuck up, or two there gathering a ton of fucking evidence against us so that when they do pounce there'll be no way out for us, either way it ain't fucking good."
"I don't think they got anything on us Reg, they'd have nicked us if they did."
"I don't know Tone, they can't just nick us again mate, not after the last time, if they nick us again and we walk out from it there be crucified, they know they've got a have a case airtight before they pull us in again."
"So what we gonna do?"
"I'm not sure mate, I need to speak to Ron but one things certain were out of fucking work, you gone a have to tell everyone to back off of everything, till we get all this mess sorted out, I want everyone round us clean as a whistle do ya understand?"
Later that evening Reggie Kray was sitting in his front room at Vallance Road with Tony Lambrianou, Slice'em Sid, Sammy Carpenter, and Georgie Hayes, they were all waiting for Eddie Brenner who had just arrived.
"Alright Eddie what's happening, what's the news on Dennis?" Reggie asked as Tony gave Eddie a half filled bottle scotch and a clean glass.
"No Bail Reg, the old bills really opposing it, pressure tactics mate."
"Is that what Manny says?" Reggie asked referring to Manny Freedman the solicitor.
"Manny says if he's found guilty he's looking at a couple of years, he's got no chance of bail at the moment, not with all the heat on, maybe in a month's time we can get him bailed."
"How's his family for money?"
"Don't know Reg."
Reggie then reached into his pocket and pulled out a wad of cash to which he handed over to Eddie without counting it.
"Give this to his wife tonight, count it I don't know what's there, a few hundred quid I think, should help her out for a little while and tell her if there's anything that she needs then just ask for it and try to tell her not to worry Ed, tell her were gonna do everything we can to get him out but even if he does go down for it, tell her were look after her with her bills or anything else she needs alright."
Eddie Brenner put the money into his pocket then sat down and looked at Reg.
"Right now you all know we got some problems at the moment, there's not much we can do about it apart from sit tight and be careful. All of London knows about the row we had with Tommy Carter, so it looks like me and Ron could get a tug over this coppers death. But what I want from all of you here is to keep things very close to your chest, we're all gonna have to lie low for a little while until we find out exactly what the fucking laws game is."
"When you say lay low Reg, do ya mean on our toes or just stop everything?" Sammy Carpenter asked.

“It’s up to you, if you wanna fuck off somewhere for a while then go but I don’t want no reasons for the old bill to pull us in, everything’s got to stop, no card games, no rows, no jobs, I want everyone clean till this is over alright.”
“What about the pension’s list?” Tony asked.
“That will carry on the same, I’ll leave that in your hands Tone, in fact step it up, I want you to put the prices up, put an extra tenner on em weekly ok.,”
“I should think that with all this fucking agro going on Reg it’s probably the ideal time to put the money up, most people out there are scared fucking shitless at the moment.” Eddie added.
“Yeah good point Ed, tell em all the moneys gone up Tone, just a tenner more a week that way there all get the message we’ve still got control, and don’t forget the nipping list either, I don’t want them getting any idea’s we’re worried.”
“Don’t worry Reg, it’s done!” Tony Replied.
“Now has anyone heard anything about Joey Pine?”
“In a lot of trouble Reg, they got him over Paddington Green nick and it looks like they’re gonna charge him mate.”
“For Brooker?” Reggie asked.
“Manny didn’t know too much Reg, but he thinks it might be conspiring to commit murder or maybe even the murder, LaSalle’s nicked him and the words out, it’s a get up!” Eddie replied.
“Get hold of Bert Smith Sammy, his he still stationed at Wandsworth.”
“Last time I heard, he was Reg, haven’t spoken to him in over a year, but I heard a rumour he was promoted to the Flying squad.”
“That’s interesting Sam, get hold of him and see if he can find anything out for us from the inside, he had a nice few fucking paydays off us.”
“Do it tomorrow Reg.”
Reggie then stood up and knocked back the rest of his glass of scotch then nodded to Tony as he reached for his Jacket.
“All right lads, Tony and me are driving down the coast to see Ron, get on with everything quietly and I’ll see ya all in the Carpenters tomorrow night at seven.”
Manny Freedman the old Jewish Solicitor sat impatiently in the visitor’s room at Paddington green police station, waiting to see his client Joey Pine; he was getting extremely frustrated as Detective LaSalle had kept him waiting for over one and a half hours. Freedman once again asked at the desk why he was being refused to see Pine but was told he would have to wait for the officer who was in charge of the case to answer any questions.
“Well where is he?” Freedman demanded.
“He’s a busy man!” answered the desk officer rudely.
“Well so am I!” Cried Freedman

"Look if you don't like then come back later, I've had orders not to let anyone see Pine and that means you as well, if you don't like that then tell Detective LaSalle ok."
"I bloody well will, this is outrageous!"
"Please yourself! Now if ya don't mind, I got work to do."
Manny Freedman waited a further thirty minutes until finally Detective's Richard LaSalle and Len Vasallo decided to make an appearance.
"Can't say I'm surprised to see you Mr Freedman." LaSalle said smiling.
"What is the meaning of this Detective? I have been waiting here for two hours! I demand that I see my client now."
"Can't do that Manny." LaSalle replied completely UN perturbed.
"What do you mean cant, it is my clients right to have legal representation, if I am refused I shall go before a magistrate first thing tomorrow morning and demand a court order to see him, upon which you will be dragged into court where you will have to give good reason as to why I was refused."
"You can do what you bloody well like Freedman, but no one gets to see Pine tonight, not until were finished with him."
"Is he being charged?"
"Can't comment on that."
"What are the grounds that you are holding him on?"
"I can't comment on that either."
"So I am correct to presume that Joey Pine is here at all!"
"Can't comment on that."
"So you're not going to tell me if Joe Pine's here, if he has been charged, or what he's being questioned about, in a nutshell you're not going to tell me sod all!"
Detective LaSalle laughed out loud which angered Manny Freedman.
"I'll see you in court Detective LaSalle!" Freedman added before he stormed out the building.
"Well that's gonna piss the magistrate off Rich."
"Don't worry about that, I need some more time with him, if he's gonna give us Kray then we've only got tonight to get it out of him, I want him shitting himself, don't need that fucking Jew going in with him telling him everything will be alight."
"What d'ya wanna do Rich?"
"I want one more go at him see if he'll crack, if not were beat it out the fucker."
"Could be dodgy Rich if we go down that route."
"Don't worry about it Len, I'll take full responsibility, we got a free hand on this one, I've been told to whatever is necessary to get a conviction!"
When Reggie arrived at his mother's bungalow in Worthing he could not believe how well his brother Ronnie looked, the medication he was taking had

completely calmed him down and sea air had seemed to put a complexion of health on his face. The two brothers embraced warmly as they met.
Ronnie poured his brother a huge glass of very expensive port he had been drinking and the two men began to drink. Tony and Johnny walked into another room as the twins wanted to talk alone.
"How ya feeling Ron?"
"Feeling great Reg, I really like it down here, bit boring though, miss all the action back home."
"Miss all the action! Ronnie this Coppers caused a lot of trouble mate."
"Everyone is talking about us Reg!" Replied Ronnie almost proudly.
"Too many people fucking talking about us Ron ain't good for business."
"It will be you wait and see."
"Yeah, well I think we could get nicked on this one Ronnie."
"Nah it won't happen Reg they got nothing on us, they need evidence to pull us in again or some slag to go QE against us, I'm not worried about the law, I'm more concerned about all the other firms about, been a lot on TV about how the laws clamping down on everyone, must be a lot of pissed off fella's out there."
"Yeah your right there Ron, had a meet with Jimmy Ryan he's not too happy."
"Don't worry about Jim!" Ronnie interrupted.
"Nah he's sweet but Joey Pine's been nicked, looks like they're gonna put the Brooker murder on him."
"How can they do that? What the fuck they got on him."
"Jackie Carter told the law all about the feud his family has been having with the Pine's, LaSalle went over to Joey's pub and found two shooters in his car."
"LaSalle! Stitch up LaSalle…the dirty fucking dog."
"Yeah he's head of the case Ron."
"What the fucks LaSalle doing on this case, I'd like to put money that he stuck the guns in Joe's car."
"Course he did Ron, Joey ain't that fucking stupid to have tools in his motor."
"LaSalle's not interested in Joe, I know the way the fucker works he's nicked him hoping he'll give him us, that's his game divide and conquer, are there any witness's Reg?"
"Not what I know of Ron, Manny's gone in to see Joe tonight, should find out some more tomorrow."
"Never known LaSalle to nick someone without a witness Reg, not his style, I've heard a lot of fucking stories about him and he always relies on grasses."
"Like I said Ron, don't really know too much at the moment."
"Where gonna have to get Joey out of this Reg."
"We could be in it ourselves Ron"

"Nah, won't happen Reg, LaSalle's shown his hand and he'll be trying everything in the book to get Joey to roll over on us."
"Well that won't happen."
"Fucking right it won't, Joe's as staunch as they come, never do it! Never in a million years would he turn slag."
"I still think we should lie low for a while Ron."
"No we can't do that Reg , we got to be back on the manor, LaSalle's blown it, we got nothing to worry about, all we have to do is get Joe out of this."
"How the fuck we gonna do that Ron?"
"Don't know but it's gotta be done, there's no fucking way I'm gone let that cunt LaSalle stick this on Joe!"
Joey Pine lay bleeding in a pool of his own blood on the cold concrete floor, only his strength from being an ex-professional boxer was keeping him conscious, he could feel that his ribs were broke and the knuckles on both his hands were swollen and bruised, he spat out a large mouthful of blood as he tried in vain to pull himself up.
"Slag's! Fucking slag's!" he half shouted at the closed metal cell door.
He could feel himself still shaking, as the adrenalin still pumped through his body from the beating he had just taken from LaSalle and five big policemen; he suddenly began to smile as he thought of the frustrated look on LaSalle's face.
"Give me Kray, give me Kray!" LaSalle repeatedly shouted as the blows crashed down on him.
"Bollocks!" Joey had replied again and again with every punch and kick that landed.
Joey laughed out loud which hurt his ribs.
"Come on I'm still fucking here!" He shouted out to the empty cell.
He was embraced with pride, pride that after such a terrible beating his spirit still remained unbeaten, then he smiled again at how LaSalle must be feeling, he had lost, he was the loser, he walked into the cell six handed there was never any doubt who would come off worse physically, but he left the cell beaten, Joey was left on the floor punched and kicked almost to his death but it was LaSalle who walked out defeated.
What he wanted Joey would never give him.
The next six weeks past very slowly, the atmosphere in London was still very tense especially in the East end. Joey Pine had been charged with conspiring to commit murder and the possession of two firearms, Ronnie and Reggie Kray had just returned from Spain where they had taken all the family with them for the grand opening night of their nightclub, Frank Sinatra didn't make an appearance but Ronnie's contacts in America sent over one of New York's top Jazz bands, anyone who was important on the Spanish celebrity and sporting circuit was there , Ronnie had flown over a lot of his old show biz

pals from London where he had let them all stay at the villa , it was a huge success and the party lasted for two days, it didn't seem to stop it was in the club till dawn then back to the Kray's villa which Ronnie had called the 'Old Bailey' for drinks , grab a few hours' sleep , wake up, start drinking again, then back to the club.

Everyone in the East End knew about the party as Ron flew over a local reporter from one of the Daily papers and got him to take pictures of everything. Page two in the daily Mirror had a huge picture of Ronnie standing next to a member of the Spanish royal family at the party, with the words 'Kray's Empire' written above it. And down the page was another picture of Ronnie, Reggie and Charlie standing beside the gates of their huge villa next to a plaque on the wall with the name Old Bailey written it. Ronnie quoted that he always enjoyed himself at the Bailey and had a lot of luck there so he wanted to name his new house it.

Business all seemed to get back to normal as the weeks went by, Ronnie spent most of his time socialising back in the West End, while Reggie took care of the business in the East End. The snooker hall that had been took off their hands by the Irish gang the Hennessey's was now back in the hands of George and Billy Hayes, and the card game in the back room was taking a hell of a lot of money for them. The pension list had grown as everyone wanted to be under the Kray's protection. Reggie had invested some money into a local boys boxing club which had got them a lot of good publicity and Ronnie had decided to back a local businessman who wanted to be a professional boxing promoter, his first show was at Shoreditch town hall, everyone knew that Ronnie was his partner and the hall was full to the rafters, it was a great evening with some cracking fights.

Ronnie would spend most of his time in the up market establishments of the West End, he nearly always began his evening at Quaglino's restaurant just off the Haymarket, it was a very high profile joint where its clientele were made up of celebrities, sportsman and politicians.

Ronnie loved Quaglino's as he felt it was a great place for opportunities, it was where the rich and famous hung out, people with money and standing, to Ronnie it was the Land of opportunity.

Ronnie hung around in the west end usually always with Johnny Walsh who's handsome and debonair ways charmed everyone they would meet. Another friend of his was a gentleman named David Polson Smyth who was the son of Lord William Polson Smyth, the ex-cabinet minister for the Labour party. Ronnie loved to be around David and David loved to be around Ronnie, it was exciting for this ex public schoolboy who was heir to the Polson-Smyth estate, to have a friend like Ronnie Kray, it made him the leader among his own little click of friends.

Ronnie Kray had his own table at Quaglino's, he was sitting on with Johnny Walsh and Tony Lambrianou when David Polson-Smyth walked over, Smyth had two scantily clad women draped over each arm both looking worse for wear.
"Look what I found swaggering around Soho earlier Ron, this is Sheryl and this Delilah, and Sheryl's been asking to meet you all evening."
Ronnie smiled and motioned for Johnny and Tony to stand up and politely greet the girls.
"So you're Ronnie Kray?" Sheryl purred as she threw her arms all over him, only for David Polson-Smyth to pull her away and sit her next to Johnny Walsh "Now be a darling and wait your turn, Johnny could you please get these vixens a drink while I pull Ronnie away for a moment." he said to Johnny Walsh who in turn winked cheekily as if to say my pleasure.
Ronnie walked over to a quiet table with David and sat down.
"Is there something the matter David?"
"Not with me Ron, my life's just one big fucking party, but a friend of my Fathers has a need of your services."
"Yeah go on what's he want?"
"It's his son actually, got himself in bother with drugs and gambling, nice chap but a fucking magnet for trouble, what are you drinking there Ron, I need a drink."
"For fucks sake David what's the coup?"
"His Father's name is Lord Watkins a very influential gentleman if you get my drift, he was in the shadow cabinet just before the war, very important man Ronnie, he has more money than fucking Rockefeller, owns half of Devon or something like that, but it's his son, his eldest son and heir to all his worldly goods who's in trouble."
"What kind a trouble?" Ronnie asked.
"Got himself involved with a gang of ruffians in Soho, Maltese I think, they have been giving him drugs to which he's now hopelessly hooked, and cheating him rotten at cards. The poor lads always in debt with them, old man Watkins paid for his son's debt but this happened four times with each time the debt increasing substantially. Now his son has just surfaced in intensive care, overdosed on heroin and the Maltese gang are asking old man Watkins to pay his debt, the bastards have even threatened his wife whose seventy two years old and a complete lady."
"Why doesn't he just call the law on em?" Ronnie asked.
"I asked the same question Ronnie but old man Watkins is dying of cancer, he'll be lucky to last out the year, he is worried sick that when he's gone his son will fall back into the hands of this gang and everything that he has worked his life for, could be blackmailed or extorted from him, he is seeking a more permanent solution to his problem."

“I bet he fucking he is, how can I trust this fella?”
“He says money is no object, just name your price and he added that he would give you anything you need to assure you that your deal would not be discovered.”
“Nah tell him to see someone else David, were nobodies fucking errand boys.”
“He envisaged you saying that Ron, so he asked me to plead on behalf of him, he told me he would love to see you over dinner and if by the end of dinner you refuse his request, then that would be the end of it.”
“So what do you think David, should I see him?”
“I wouldn’t have brought this to you if I thought otherwise, and like I said he is an extremely influential man, he would be a great string to add to your bow.”
Two days later Johnny Walsh was driving Ronnie Kray and David Polson-Smyth through the country roads of Devon, David was giving Johnny the directions and he told him to drive down a slip road, half way down Ronnie saw a sign that pointed to Freinheim Palace,
“They got Palaces down ere too David.” Ronnie smiled.
“Frienheim Palace is Lord Watkins home Ron.” David replied.
Johnny drove the car through a large set of gates that gave them their first view of Lord Watkins home, the home was magnificent it reminded Ronnie of Blenheim Palace in Warwickshire home of the Spencer’s which he visited once as a young boy when he was evacuated. They were met by the butler who introduced himself as James and led into the house and into a large lounge with a huge stone fireplace that you could walk into without bending over, after James asked them what refreshments they require he asked them to sit down and Lord Watkins would be with them shortly.
They didn’t have to wait very long before a very smart dressed gentleman pushed Lord Watkins into the room, Ronnie got to his feet as he saw the old Lord dressed in a shirt and tie with a blanket over his legs, he could see immediately by the look on the old man’s face that he hated being in a wheelchair, he looked very proud in his facial expression but his body had obviously began to let him down, Ronnie could almost sense that this man welcomed his death, he had lived a full and prosperous life and now his body had given way to old age and disease.
The old Lord gave Ronnie a slight smile as he struggled to hold out his hand, Ronnie shook his hand gently, which was something Ronnie never did almost as if he was shaking a women’s hand.
“Good afternoon Mr Kray, this is my youngest son Peter, I trust you had a nice journey.”
“Yes it was fine Mr Watkins.” Ronnie answered.

“Please call me Nelson; I hate the term Mr Watkins makes me feel like a bloody MP again.”
Ronnie smiled and nodded.
Peter then pushed his Father over to a table that was next to a large widow, he meticulously looked after his Father’s needs before leaving, he made sure his Father was pushed under the table just in the right position then fetched his Father a large ashtray then lit his cigar carefully for him. After a long puff and a large exhale Lord Watkins began.
“Let us not play games Mr Kray, I am a man who believes there is no need for trivializing between men of importance, I have a problem, a problem that is beyond my control, a problem I believe and hope you can solve.”
“Your son!” Ronnie added.
“Yes! And the bastards who are ruining his life.” replied Watkins before taking another large drag of his cigar and shifting his position to make himself more comfortable.
Ronnie noticed the old lords anger as his hands seem to tense towards a fist and he noticed a frustrated tone in his voice as the lord began to talk again.
“All my life I have adhered to the laws of this land and God, and now in the twilight of my life I find myself abandoned by all of which I upheld, I feel betrayed and naïve to have lived my life believing that as a citizen of the realm I have been protected.”
“There are people in this world that couldn’t care less about the law.” Ronnie interrupted.
Lord Watkins acknowledged Ronnie’s remark with a nod.
“How do I outfox the fox Mr Kray, I have tried to be cunning, I have tried to be forceful but I see no other way now, than to give my problem of the fox, to the mercy of the hounds.”
“What you want is peace of mind, you want this problem to go away and never come back again, that’s not the law of the land is it, you want justice by my law, by my hands but are you willing to pay the price, Pay my price?”
“Name whatever pri…”
Before he could finish Ronnie stopped him by waving his hand.
“Before you offer me any money Nelson I want to be assured and convinced that this problem of yours is worth my concern.”
Lord Watkins leaned back in his chair and seemed surprised at how Ronnie had answered him, it had never occurred to him that Ronnie Kray might turn him down, He suddenly found himself respecting Ronnie more than the image he had heard of, he was going to have to sell this problem, and the currency was more than money.
“Has Polson Smyth filled you in with the facts of this predicament?”
“Briefly, but not much.” Ronnie replied.

"It is a problem that my son, my eldest son by his own devises has created. But nevertheless as his Father and guardian, I am impelled out of love and duty to seek out the best help there is for him that money and favour can buy."
"Well he's your son." Ronnie answered.
"Whatever the price, I want these bastards out of his life, I want these bastards taken care of!" Replied the lord who suddenly filled with emotion.
"I'm not for sale Lord Watkins." Replied Ronnie thoughtfully and completely poker faced.
"I will give you anything Mr Kray."
"What you're asking me to do is a very serious request, How can you justify such revenge or even more so how can you assure me of your trust, you speak of giving me anything I want as if your money can buy anything, but I look around here and I see that money doesn't hold the same need to you as it does to most other people."
Ronnie then hesitated before continuing.
"Does a man who owns grape vines, offer his friend grapes for his favour who or would a more sincere man, offer him wine"?
Lord Watkins nodded in agreement at Ronnie's reply; the old Lord took a moment to compose himself as he knew that his emotions had blurred his clarity of thought and unwillingly insulted his guest.
"My apologies Mr Kray, you are wise to correct me, my feelings have clouded my reasoning."
I did not mean to offend you, or turn this meeting into a cattle market but this has happened to my son, and my whole being is full of vengeance for the men who have caused me such strife."
"That's understandable, just tell me what I need to know then maybe we will talk about how to rid you of this problem." added Ronnie.
"To your first question, the question of justification, does my son being beaten an inch of his life, forced into heroin addiction, extortion, my wife assaulted, she was slapped and spat upon, the countless threatening phone calls and letters, all the dread and worry, does this not justify my thirst for retribution Mr Kray!, as for your second question and the emphasis on trust, I am not a fool Mr Kray and neither are you, I will reserve myself to any assurance that are requested, whatever you want or need if it is in the boundaries of reason then I will do!"
Ronnie Kray leaned back in his chair as Lord Watkins finished what he was saying, Ronnie looked at him sternly as if studying him "I can see that he is desperate." Ronnie thought quietly to himself.
The two men relaxed into silence as Lord Watkins eagerly awaited Ronnie's reply; both men occasionally glanced across the table at each other until Ronnie lit up a cigarette and leaned forward.

“I wanna know everything there is to know about these Maltese?” Ronnie finally asked
For the next hour Lord Watkins gave Ronnie every detail of his sons relationship with the Maltese, Ronnie heard how it had been a complete set up from start to finish, the crooked card games, the introduction to drugs, the intimidation, everything Ronnie heard convinced him that this was a very clever shakedown, scrupulously construed by a gang who obviously knew what they were doing.
As soon as Lord Watkins finished talking he leaned across the table and reached out to Ronnie’s hand.
“Will you help me Ronnie, please; I must have peace before I leave this world?”
It had been one week since the meeting at Freinham Palace had taken place and Ronnie had hardly left his mother’s house in valance road, only a select few had been allowed to visit him, amongst the his brother Charlie who had been summoned back from Spain.
Tony Lambrianou had been one of the Firm who was told to stay away, this worried him along with a few other members so he arranged a meeting with Reggie down the Carpenters arms to find out what exactly was going on.
“Reggie what’s appening mate, we’re all in the dark, has Ronnie got the needle with us or something?” Tony asked.
“Nothing like that Tone, Ron’s got a lot on his plate at the moment, just sit tight and we will put you all in the picture when the times right.”
“Well what’s the matter with him; if he’s got troubles then we can help?” Slice’em Sid added.
“The best way you can all help is to just sit tight, and remember that no matter what any of you hear, we don’t want nothing done unless you speak to me or Reg first, that’s very important.” Charlie Kray replied.
“Look just don’t worry about anything, we got things we’re doing at the moment that’s best you’re not involved in, everything’s gonna be fine you just gotta trust us and sit tight.” Reggie added.
Tony Lambrianou patted Reggie on the arm.
“Well were here if ya need us Reg.”
Three days later Ronnie’s ex POW friend Jeff Samuels was sitting in the White lion pub in west London, the lion was about two hundred yards from slain policeman Dave Brooker’s burnt out house. Samuels had been drinking heavily for the last three hours. He finished his pint of stout before getting up to go back to the bar but in his drunken state he stumbled into a couple of fella’s which caused them to spill there drinks
“OI! Mind where ya fucking going, ya old Cunt!” one of them shouted.
Jeff Samuels gave a half smile before he smashed the pint glass he was carrying into the man’s face, suddenly the pub broke out in pandemonium,

Samuels still strong for his age continued to thrust what was left of the glass countless more times into the man's head and shoulders, then almost as if rehearsed Samuels stopped and adjusted his clothes and walked over to the terrified bar hostess and calmly ordered himself another drink, everyone in the pub either left or had got as far away from Samuels as possible, the beaten man was laying at his feet as he collected another pint from the bar girl then calmly walked back over to his table and sipped at his drink while he watched the man who he had just cut to pieces being nursed by a few regulars.
"Fucking animal!" a brave lady cried out at him as she felt horrified by the deep wounds on the man's face.
Samuels raised his glass and just smiled at her.
Before long four policemen walked into the bar with their truncheons in their hands and after Samuels was pointed out they walked over to him.
"C'mon mate your nicked." the biggest one said.
Samuels rose to his feet and raised his glass to his mouth "After I finish my fucking drink." he replied.
Jeff Samuels was taken to Notting Hill Police station where he was charged with grievous bodily harm; he was thrown in a cell and told he would appear before the magistrates in the morning. After only one hour in the cell Samuels rang the bell and asked to see the desk sergeant.
"yep whad ya want?"
"I got some very important information that I need to tell detective LaSalle." Jeff Samuels said.
"LaSalle! What does a fucking down an out like you want with him?"
"Just fucking get him."
The desk sergeant grimaced as he shut up the cell hatch.
"Sergeant! Sergeant!" Samuels screamed angrily.
The desk Sergeant turned angrily and forcefully opened the hatch.
"Look pal, it's been a long fucking day, now ya not gonna be causing me trouble all fucking night are ya?"
"I ain't fucking around, get LaSalle on the blower and tell him you got me here and tell him I wanna speak to him about Ronnie Kray!"

Not Guilty Your Honour
Chapter Five
'Another day at the Bailey'

Detectives LaSalle and Vasallo arrived at Notting Hill police station just after midnight; they were escorted down to the cells and introduced to the desk sergeant

"Hello Sir, I don't know if this is a waste of time sir but the prisoner was very insistent that he saw you regarding the Kray's."

"What's he charged with?" detective Vasallo asked him.

"GBH sir, cut and dry case sir, glassed someone in the lion in front of about twenty witnesses."

"Did you get any statements?"

The desk sergeant picked up a file from his desk "Yes Sir about a dozen, we are still waiting for the victim's statement as he is being operated on but we have a sworn statement from his brother who was standing next to him."

“Well its looks pretty tight.” Vasallo added commenting on the evidence against Samuels.
“He’s got no chance sir.” the sergeant added cheerfully “He’s going down for at least a couple of years Sir.” he added.
The desk Sergeant then escorted the two Detectives down to the cell that was housing Jeff Samuels; he unlocked the door and let the two men enter.
“That will be all sergeant.” LaSalle told him as he ushered him away.
Jeff Samuels stood up from his bed as he saw LaSalle.
“Been a long time Jeff.” LaSalle said as he held out his hand.
“Been ten years Sir.” Samuels replied as he shook it, while reminding LaSalle of the time that had passed since his arrest with Charlie Kray ten years previous for fraud.
“Now then what was all this crap about, you know you’re gonna get some porridge don’t ya?”
“I can’t do a prison sir.”
“Should a fucking thought about that, before you sliced that poor fella’s boat up.” Vasallo added.
“Yeah that’s not like you Jeff, you probably killed a lot of people in the war, but I always had you down as a shrewdy, that was a bit silly what you done tonight.”
“I been going off my fucking rocker sir, see yesterday I was told I had leukaemia, the Doctor says I’ve only got a year to live, can’t get my head around it so I’ve been on the piss nonstop, didn’t mean to hurt that fella but I just snapped.”
“Just snapped!” Vasallo sternly added “That poor fuckers got a nose where his ear hole used to be.”
“Just what the fuck am I supposed to do, that fucking Doctor tells me I got a year left so I went out on the piss wouldn’t you?”
“Yeah I would properly have a shant, but I wouldn’t have did what you did, least not in public, now that year you got left is gonna be spent behind a fucking door.” LaSalle added cruelly.
There was a slight pause before Samuels spoke again.
“That’s why I have asked for you sir.”
“You got something to tell us?” Vasallo replied.
“If it cuts me a deal yeah.”
Detective LaSalle sat down next to Samuels.
“We don’t make deals Jeff.”
“O cut out the bollocks will ya, if you get me off of this, I’ll give ya Ronnie Kray.”
LaSalle quickly gazed up at Vasallo.
“And just how are ya gonna do that Jeff?” LaSalle replied sarcastically.

Jeff Samuels walked over to the spy hole in his door and looked out to see if anyone was within earshot before continuing.
“Do ya know where I was on the night of Brooker’s Death?”
“Go’ on.” LaSalle said.
“Just what would My testimony be worth to say I bumped into Ronnie Kray and Joey Pine just fifty yards from Brooker’s flat, alf hour before the fire, what would that be worth to ya?”
“And you would say that in the box?” LaSalle asked now more interested in what Samuels was saying.
“If you give me protection, and sort it I don’t do any bird, I’ll mount the box.”
Chief inspector LaSalle gazed excitingly over to his fellow Detective Vasallo and gave him a slight grin followed by a flick of his head, which motioned him to leave the cell with him.
“Where ya going!” Samuels asked as he saw what LaSalle did.
“We’re be back in a minute Jeff.”
“Could it be enough, to nail him for it Rich.” asked Vasallo once they were outside the cell in the small hallway.
“It could be, we have a statement from Jackie Carter telling us about the row he had in their pub with Brooker, if Samuels gets up and gives evidence that he saw Kray at the scene of the crime minutes before, it could just be enough to convince a jury.”
“We haven’t got any solid evidence though.” Vasallo replied.
“Well that could change couldn’t it, it’s not so much what we haven’t got it’s what we have got, we got motive from Carter and now we got sworn testimony that Kray and Pine were at the scene of the crime, we will have to introduce this for Pine anyway, so I say we nick Kray and see what develops.”
“Could Samuels be lying?”
“Cause he could be, but for what, it certainly isn’t doing him any favours putting the finger on Ronnie Kray is it.” LaSalle snapped.
“If we go with this guv we got to keep him right out the way, Kray and Pinewill put everything they got into getting at him, were gonna have to nursemaid him twenty four hours a day, can we get the money for that.”
“They want a conviction, they’ll just have to find the fucking money won’t they!” answered LaSalle referring to the bigwigs at Scotland Yard.
“Looks like we could have deal Jeff!” Detective LaSalle said smiling as he entered back into Samuels’s cell.
“So this charge I’m on tonight…. will go away then.”
“Don’t worry about that Jeff, I will deal with that.” LaSalle replied as he glanced across to Vasallo and motioned him to leave the cell and take care of it.
“I want a statement now, I want it down on paper just how well you saw Kray and Pine that night, I want the times and what they were wearing and don’t

forget to mention the petrol can they were carrying and how they stunk of petrol."
Samuels looked up at LaSalle and smiled, the last comment about the petrol can and how they stunk of it was typical LaSalle, but Samuels couldn't care less if he added that into his statement, all that mattered to him was not going to prison.
"Oh yeah the petrol can." He commented smiling.
"Don't forget that will ya." LaSalle added sternly almost like a schoolteacher chastising his pupil.
"So how do I know you'll get me out the shit if I write this statement?"
"Don't fuck about with me Jeff, just write down what you saw and I'll make sure you don't do any bird, it's up to you, or I'll walk out the fucking door now!"
"Detective alright! I'll do what you want just get me out of ere."
With that Chief LaSalle left Samuel's cell and went out to find Detective Vasallo in a heated conversation with the desk sergeant.
"Sergeant!" LaSalle interrupted.
"Samuel's will be coming with us tonight, get whatever forms you need me to sign and do it quickly, we have a lot of work to do." LaSalle added to the sergeant who had been protesting with Detective Vasallo.
"But Sir with all due respect." the sergeant added as he rose to his feet and opening his hands.
"Samue'ls is charged with a very serious offence, we have him scheduled to appear in court in the morning, I can't just release him."
"Your releasing him to the custody of me Sergeant, now pick up the phone and make the relevant calls, I want him ready to leave in thirty minutes!"
Both Detectives then left the charging room for the staff canteen to get themselves a cup of tea.
"So what'd ya think Rich?" asked Vasallo as both men sat down in a corner after getting their drinks.
"I think it's enough to charge Kray on, it's not cut and dry but we've got Carter's statements about the row he had in the pub with him, and we now got a statement putting Kray and Pine at the scene of the crime smelling of petrol. We'll spin Kray's house and find a can of petrol and if we get one of his suits with traces of petrol on it then we have a good case against him."
"What about the charge on Samuels?"
Inspector LaSalle then laughed out loud.
"The silly bastard doesn't even know who he had a row with tonight."
Detective Vasallo smiled sheepishly as he didn't know either.
"Who'd he have a row with?" he asked coyly.
"Little Danny Reilly and his brother Eddie, Jimmy the cosh's younger brothers, I saw the charge sheet."

“Jimmy the Cosh!” Vasallo laughed.
“Fuck me Rich he was lucky then weren’t he?” he added.
“NO there Just a couple of boys, There not muscle Len, they’re nothing like their elder brother, but Jimmy would never allow them to make statements, but just to make sure we’ll pay the cosh a visit in the morning.”
With that both men stopped talking as they both sipped their drinks.
“How about Jackie Carter’s evidence Rich, Tommy Carter might lean on him to withdraw it, if he does that then it takes away the motive, our case could crumble like an house of cards.”
“That won’t happen and anyway Tommy Carter’s on his toes, he’s fucking scared shitless of us and the Kray firm, one way or another I’d be surprised if we see him again.”
“Yeah right about him being scared shitless he’s fuck all without Brooker.”
“He’s nothing Len! Ronnie Kray finished him the day he gave him a clump in the pub, funny thing is I bet Kray doesn’t even realise it.”
On the morning of Friday the 22nd of June at seven o’clock, Detectives Richard LaSalle and Len Vasallo along with twenty other officers raided the home of Ronnie Kray. It was a damp and dark morning as they positioned themselves by the front door of Valance Road. Two officers stood waiting with sledgehammers in hand but before they were given the nod by Chief inspector LaSalle to crash the door in Johnny Walsh suddenly opened it from the inside and invited them in.
Once inside LaSalle found it strange to find Ronnie Kray awake, dressed and clean shaven all ready as if he had been expecting him, sitting next to Ronnie was his brother Charlie, his mother Violet, Father Charlie snr and his solicitor Manny Freedman, there was no sign of Reggie.
LaSalle couldn’t believe the sight he was seeing, someone had obviously tipped Ronnie off that he would be visited today why else would his solicitor Manny Freedman be sitting there; he gave Freedman a very dirty look before he walked over to Ronnie and cautioned him
“Ronnie Kray I am arresting you for the murder of Police officer David Brooker, You have the right to remain silent, and anything you do say will be taken down in evidence.”
“Give it a rest will ya I know the drill.” Ronnie Kray suddenly said as he interrupted LaSalle and got to his feet. Ronnie then turned to his Mother and gave her a large hug as Manny Freedman turned to Detective LaSalle.
“Don’t worry Mum it’s all in hand, they got nothing on me.” Ronnie softly said.
“What station will you be taking my client to Detective.” Manny asked LaSalle.
“Paddington Green!” replied LaSalle resentfully.

Manny Freedman suddenly grabbed hold of Ronnie Kray's arm and turned to face LaSalle.
"I want it made perfectly clear to everyone here that I am advising my client to remain silent at this time, if any verbal statements Detective suddenly arise at any further date, then they will be ardently scrutinised, do I make myself clear?"
LaSalle snarled angrily at Freedman's statement, it was solely directed at him and his underworld nickname as verbals.
"Get out the way Freedman or you'll be nicked for obstructing police business."
The atmosphere was suddenly twisting to one of anger and Ronnie sensing this and not wanting any kind of trouble in front of his Mother decided to hurry things along as he walked towards the door.
He was forcefully pushed into a police car, which caused his brother Charlie to cry out
"Oi easy does it!" he shouted at the offending officer.
Charlie Kray jnr then turned his attention to three other police officers that were walking out from his Mothers with a large amount of Ronnie's clothing,
"Ere some of them are mine! what'd ya doing taking all his clothes?" Charlie asked only to be greeted by silence as the men placed the clothes into one of the police cars.
LaSalle climbed into the front seat of the car that was carrying Ronnie and Manny Freedman rushed over to the window.
"I wish to travel with my client." Manny demanded to LaSalle.
"Take the fucking bus!" LaSalle replied angrily as he slammed the door closed and ordered the driver to speed off.
Charlie Kray snr and Charlie jnr along with Manny Freedman stood motionless as the police cars sped off down the road with their sirens blazing; the three men remained silent until the cars were out of sight when Manny Freedman turned to young Charlie.
"I hope he knows what his doing!"
The cells in Paddington Green police station were just as Ronnie remembered them only a little more dirtier and a lot smellier, he was kept locked up in only his underwear for over three hours till someone finally came to speak to him.
"You're briefs upstairs, they'll be coming to get ya for questioning in a minute." said a duty policeman through the metal doors hatch.
"I ain't going fucking nowhere unless ya get me some strides." Ronnie snarled back.
Ronnie waited by the door for about ten minutes until LaSalle and Vasallo along with three uniformed officers opened his door.
LaSalle threw Ronnie a pair of old white overalls to put on; they were the kind that you saw painters and decorators wearing.

“Put these on Ronnie.” he said cheerfully.
Ronnie pulled on the overalls and followed the Police down the corridor and up a flight of stairs till they came to a room with a sign on it that read interview room no1, once inside Ronnie greeted his Solicitor Manny Freedman who was already in there with a notebook laid out on the table in front of him, Ronnie sat down next to him where many very quickly whispered to him to make no comment.
Detectives LaSalle and Vasallo sat opposite them with another uniformed officer ready to make a note of the interview. LaSalle asked if the uniformed officer and Manny Freedman were ready, both nodded they were so he began his interview.
“Are you Ronald Kray of 178 Vallance Road, Bethnal Green?” asked LaSalle.
“If I wasn’t then that would make you aright idiot wouldn’t it.” Ronnie answered as he felt the icy cold stare coming from his solicitor.
“I want you to cast your mind back to the 14th of April, can you tell me where you were on that evening between the hours of ten till twelve?”
Ronnie gazed up at the ceiling and creased up his face as if thinking.
“The 14th of April did you say?”
“You know full well what day I mean.” LaSalle sternly replied.
“I object to that!” Manny Freedman suddenly blurted.
“Object to what!” LaSalle answered.
“I object to you insinuating that that date has a meaningful purpose for my client, at this stage in the investigations I see no reason why the 14th of April should have any more significance than any other date you could pull from the air.” Freedman replied.
“Ok the date that police officer David Brooker was brutally murdered to which Mr Kray you are charged with others for conspiracy to murder, now can you or maybe your solicitor tell me where you were on that day between the hours of ten and twelve.”
“Yeah, yeah I can remember now.”
“Ronnie you’re not obliged to answer that question.” Manny Freedman frantically interrupted Ronnie for fear he was going to.
“Will you leave your client alone to answer the questions Mr Freedman?” LaSalle cried out angered by the solicitor’s interference.
“Detective LaSalle I was merely stating my Clients right to silence.”
“Mr Freedman if you continue in your outbursts then I will eject you from the room, this is a very serious matter.”
“It’s alright Manny, I got a few things I can tell em.” Ronnie softly interrupted.
Freedman once again gave Ronnie an icy look as if begging him to keep silent but Ronnie just winked at him and grinned before he turned his attention to LaSalle.

"See I do remember where I was on that night, I was at Buckingham Palace having tea and cakes with her Majesty, she was drinking Earl grey and I was eating scones with clotted cream, Prince Charles kept burping, really loud but he did apologise and told us it was all that gin he'd been swigging down."
"Mr Kray I will ask you one more time, where was you between ten and twelve on the evening of the 14th of April." LaSalle asked very sternly and angered by Ronnie's last comment and even more agitated by the look on Manny Freedman's face as he tried to hide his smiles.
"I told you I was with er Majesty at the Palace give her a call, she'll tell ya and ask her about that leather coat I sold her."
LaSalle bit his lip hard and turned his head to the side, as Ronnie lit up a cigarette he could see that LaSalle just wanted to throw the table up in the air in frustration, there was an unerring silence for a while as the Detective composed himself before getting back to his next question.
"Have you ever met Police officer David Brooker?" LaSalle asked.
"Yeah I met him." Ronnie replied but suddenly stopped as he saw his solicitor rolling his fingers on the table in a tapping noise which once again angered the already agitated LaSalle
"I met him at Winston Churchill's funeral."
"What!" LaSalle cried.
"Yeah it was Churchill's funeral, I remember him as we were both pall bearers, he had a nice pair of shoes on, I remembered them cos when you've got a coffin on your shoulders you can't help but look at the ground."
"Winston Churchill!" LaSalle replied as if puzzled as he was not sure if Ronnie was taking the piss again or if there was in fact another man by that name that both Kray and Brooker knew.
"Which Winston Churchill are you talking about?" He asked coyly.
"Winston Churchill the fella who used smoke those big cigars and tell us all to fight them on the beaches, you know him." Ronnie replied.
"Are you taking the piss Kray?" LaSalle coldly answered.
Ronnie just sat staring at him poker faced.
"No sir I wouldn't do that to a policeman would I."
LaSalle sighed out loud and reached into his pocket and pulled out a packet of fags.
"Are you gonna fuck around all day Ronnie?" he asked as he put a cigarette to his mouth.
"You're asking me questions, I'm answering them, write em down in ya fucking book."
"Did you kill Brooker?" LaSalle suddenly asked.
"Don't be so fucking stupid!" Ronnie replied.
"Did You Kill Brooker!!" LaSalle repeated loudly as he banged his fist hard on the table

"No comment." Ronnie calmly replied.
Detective Vasallo reached out and gave Richard LaSalle a reassuring pat on the arm before he took it upon himself to ask the next question.
"Did you ever in any way have or have reason to argument with David Brooker?"
"Only once." Ronnie calmly replied which resulted in everyone taking more notice.
"Go on Ronnie." Len Vasallo sincerely tried to say.
Ronnie sighed out loud before answering; he ran his fingers through his hair and wiped his face as if wiping sweat.
"It was a long time ago when LaSalle's wife came to me complaining that Brooker farted all the time they were in bed together."
Richard LaSalle violently jumped to his feet he snatched his packet of cigarettes from the table and pushed his way past his fellow detective.
"That's enough of this fucking bollocks, this interview is over, charge the fucker and sling him back in the cells."
Ronnie Kray got to his feet and snarled back at him.
"What's the matter?... Ya fucking stitch up merchant, fuck ya and fuck ya questions."
Manny Freedman quickly grabbed a hold of Ronnie's hand and tried calming him down
"Leave it Ron, just let it go, we'll have our day, keep it cool son, keep it cool."
Ronnie Kray was charged for conspiracy to commit murder along with Joey Pine, he was remanded in custody with no bail; Manny Freedman didn't even try for bail, as he knew it would be a complete waste of time. Three days after he was arrested Ronnie was taken to Brixton prison in South London, within Brixton prison, was a prison within a prison, a secure unit where only Britain's most dangerous prisoners were kept. This was to be Ronnie Kray's new home until he and Joey Pine were to stand trial for murder.
As Ronnie was walked on the wing he was immediately given a warm welcome by one of the great armed robbers Tommy Woodley, Ronnie knew Tommy well from past and was pleased to see him looking so well.
"Hello Ronnie we heard you were coming, we're all sick you're here but we got a nice cell for ya."
"Hello Tommy, that's very nice of you, thanks very much." Ronnie added as he smiled at his old friend and shook his hand.
"Lot of old faces in here Ron." Tommy said as he helped Ronnie with his bag and began to lead the way to Ronnie's cell.
"Yeah that's nice Tommy, where's Joey Pine?"
Tommy Woodley suddenly stopped in his tracks and turned to Ronnie.
"He's down the block Ron, he ain't doing his bird too well mate, you're gonna have to have a chat with him."

“What am I going to say to him?” Ronnie replied not sure as to just exactly what Tommy was getting at.
“If he’s got a row with the screws or someone Tom then I’ll make one with him, I’m not gonna fucking just stand there and let him have alone.”
“I ain’t saying nothing like that Ronnie, but he’s having rows for fucking nothing, all the time, it ain’t too bad for us in ere, the screws leave us pretty much alone.”
Ronnie suddenly changed his attitude.
“Tommy Listen we go back a long way mate, but if you’ve greeted me today in the hope that I’m gonna be some kind of calming influence on this wing then believe me it’s not gonna fucking happen, I couldn’t give a fuck about whether the screws leave us alone or not, if they get in my face then I’m gonna break their fucking jaws.”
Frith Street in the heart of London’s Soho was well regarded, as an Italian quarter. Years ago the famous villains like Darby Sabini the Italian Godfather, Georgie Sewell, the Cortesi clan and the infamous Jack Spot could always be found sitting outside its many cafeterias.
The area was still full of the café’s and coffee shops but its colourful past had now been replaced by seedier kind a villain, prostitution had and always will be a big part of any city but it had become rife in Soho. The Maltese had pushed their way into Frith Street from Dean Street where they had many basement-drinking clubs. With them they brought prostitution right out into the open, The Italian Pizzeria restaurant on Frith Street was once famous for its classy clientele, had now become infamous for its trade in sex. And very much the strong hold for the Maltese gangs that now roamed its streets.
Reggie and Charlie Kray sat calmly by the window waiting for the men they were supposed to meet to turn up, they could not help feel a little out of place as most of the crowd they were sharing the place with were dressed a lot more casual, the music was blaring loud music which made Reggie feel agitated and he could not believe how some of the women who were obviously whores were acting, they were dancing and shouting, one of them even exposed her bosoms to two young Maltese men who were jeering her on.
Charlie pointed this out to Reg who had already seen it but looked away slightly embarrassed.
“You seeing this Reg?” Charlie smiled.
Reggie just ignored his brother’s question as he turned his head to look out of the window which in all honesty wasn’t much better than what was going on inside.
“Used to be a nice fucking area this didn’t it Charlie, somewhere you could bring a girl to and have something to eat.”
“I wouldn’t want to bring my girl up ere Reg; I’d get a right hander just for walking her down this road.” Charlie replied playfully.

"Where the fucking hells this Messina?" Reggie suddenly snapped as he looked at his watch and noticed that the man he was meeting Carmine Messina the self-pronounced king of the Maltese gangs was fifteen minutes late.
"He's probably got held up Reg, it happens mate." Charlie replied trying to calm his brother down as he had seen the signs of Reggie's impatience plenty of times before.
"Got held up! I'll fucking hold im up, I don't know why Ronnie wants us to meet with these mugs anyway."
"Reg just calm down mate, you know how important this is, Ron's depending on us to do this."
"Yeah alright, just gives me the needle when fuckers are late."
Fifteen more minutes and with Reggie now seething Carmine along with four associates strolled into the restaurant, Carmine Messina was greeted like a king as he walked in, straight away the music was turned down lower, everyone in there seemed to stiffen their composures and the waiters immediately stopped whatever they had been doing to quickly prepare Messina's usual cup of black coffee. One of Messina's associates removed his three quarter length coat that had hung loosely over his shoulders, which revealed a very expensive looking silk suit. Messina quickly looked at himself in the mirror and ran a hand through his greased back black hair before one of the waiters pointed out Reggie and Charlie to him.
Messina looked around with a slight urgency that Reggie noticed and calmed him a little.
"Reggie, Charlie my apologies for my lateness but I had a small problem with one of my establishments but anyway I am here."
Charlie got up and shook his hand while Reggie remained seated, Messina then turned to the waiters and very angrily shouted out to them something in Maltese, straight away a little waiter ran over to the table and asked if any more drinks were needed.
"Reggie we are all sorry to hear about your brother, it saddens my heart when a friend is taken away, and I give my sincerest blessing that he will beat this problem that hangs over your Familia,"
"He's gonna be ok." Charlie replied.
"So you are confident he will overcome this problem, that's good." Carmine replied.
"Carmine where not here to speak about Ronnie, there's another problem we need to talk about."
"Hey Reggie straight to the point, I like this."
"Look we got a problem which we wanna know if it's your problem, out of respect for you, Ronnie has asked me to talk to you first."
"Go on I am listening."

“There’s a group of Maltese fellas who have shook down one of our friends, he’s been conned and forced onto junk, and they’ve had a lot of money out of him.”
“The Aristocrats son.” Messina replied.
“You know about it?” Reggie asked.
“I know what has happened, this man owed them money at cards and when he did not pay, he was punished, what would the world be if men reneged on their debts, I cannot blame these men for the actions, I know them well, they are good boys who come from good stock, I know there family’s.”
Reggie gave a quick glance at his brother before grabbing Messina’s hand tightly.
“Look don’t give me none of that bollocks, I ain’t here to ask you fucking permission, these ponces are finished, one way or another they’re fucking history, all we’re here to discuss is when, and how it’s gonna happen.”
“Carmine listen it doesn’t matter to us whether we do it or you do it, but we’re here to help you not lose face amongst your own people.” Charlie added.
“What you ask of me is difficult!” Messina whispered.
“I can’t see what’s difficult about it, we’re gonna do em, make no fucking bones about it, but it ain’t gonna look too good on you if we come down here with a Firm and take care of four of your men, is it? So the best solution is for you to do it, like Charlie says we don’t care just as long as it gets done.”
Messina sat back in his chair; he waved his hand once again through his black hair before replying in little more than a whisper.
“You come to my place and ask me to perform murder, even though I have no interest in these boys’ deaths, and ask me to slay the sons, of men I call friends. Tell me why from your own mouth why these boys’ deaths should mean more to me than… as you say, losing face.”
“It’s a matter of business Carmine, as a matter of our business we have to do this, these boys have attacked someone who is under our protection, you understand this I know, and also one day you might need our friendship, one day one of these sons from the friends you call them, might feel that your position is weak. They are into drugs and out of control anything could happen, they may plot against you, plan for your death… but if they know of your connection with us then this assassination becomes more difficult. This is a business we are in, if a member of our Firm embarrassed us, then he would have to go! Or we risk losing everything that we have gained, there’s also one other thing you should consider, if your reply is a refusal and we come in here to do this task, and there is a fuck up or something happens that shouldn’t then we will look at this meeting with questions.”
“Do you speak for Ronnie?”
“I speak for everyone!” Reggie replied.
Carmine Messina picked up his espresso coffee and downed it in one.

"I can see that my back is against a wall, if I perform this duty that you demand then for the sake of business would seek to attain a levy."
"What kind of levy would that be?" Charlie asked.
"To begin with £5000. For the families of the men who will be killed, this will help them in the grieving and I would request that all their funerals be paid for, by yourselves or the aristocrat that you protect, once you have respected this wish then I would seek to nurture this friendship or alliance between our families that you speak of, if you are men of business as you stated… then you can see this is a small price to pay for my ethics and favour."
Reggie hesitated in his reply as he thought about what Messina just said, it sounded fair but it was not Reggie's way to be hasty in replying.
"I can't see there being a problem in that, but what I will say is it's got to be done right with no mistakes, all four have got to go and we want it public, I wanna read about their deaths in the papers."
Messina nodded his head silently then reached out his hand.
"Then we have deal Mr Kray." he added softly as Reggie shook hands.
After one week inside Brixton Prison Ronnie had already got back into the swing of prison life, he bumped into two old acquaintances from Mile End, Sammy Walker and Paul Largo, Ronnie knew both of them from the outside well, where they at one time used to do the odd jobs for him, now inside Ronnie had turned both of them into errand boys where it seemed their sole existence was to serve Ronnie Kray.
"Sammy! Go down stairs and get the PO will ya, tell him I need to see him up here."
Ronnie ordered him from his cell on the second floor.
A few minutes later officer Green knocked on the door of Ronnie's cell.
"Kray you wanted to see me?" he asked.
"You've got my Co-defendant banged up in solitary, how much longer is he down there for?"
"You'll have to speak to one of the Guvnors about that Kray."
"Well I'm fucking talking to you about it."
"I don't have the answers you want."
Ronnie then stood up and walked over to the door, officer Green backed away slightly as he felt the menace in Ronnie's composure.
"Then I suggest you go and get one of the Guvnors, we got a fucking case to prepare and only three weeks to do it, I don't wanna cause trouble in here but your fucking up our chances of acquittal so believe it when I say, if you don't get him out of there in 48hrs then this fucking wings going up in smoke."
Officer Green backed away from Ronnie as Sammy Walker and Paul Largo arrived and stood menacingly beside him.
"Now you don't wanna be talking like that Kray, we don't want any bother either, but we won't be ordered about, and I suggest you keep those remarks

to yourself, it's not too hard a task to have everyone on this wing disbanded to other prisons."
"Just go and get the Guvnor, errand boy, and don't fucking threaten me, I'm not a little boy, do yourself a big fucking favour and stay off this landing till you get someone to see me."
Green felt the anger at Ronnie's remark, any other time he would put him on report for this threat but he felt strangely unnerved by Ronnie's stance and with Walker and Largo blocking his escape, this was not the time to agitate Ronnie Kray who in this mood was capable of anything.
Green nodded at Ronnie before he slipped past his henchmen. Five minutes later a shout came out for bang up which meant everyone should return to their own cells.
Ronnie quickly leant over his landing and shouted out to a few of the fella's below; Tommy Woodley was with Christian Armour an Irishman, who was on remand for murder,
"Tommy listen mate we're not being banged up, you with us!" Ronnie shouted.
Tommy and Christian ran up the stairs and joined Ronnie who was now with Largo and Walker and Sonny Sacomo an Italian who was also on remand for murder.
"What's the matter then Ron?" Tommy asked.
"I wanna see the Guvnor about Joey, there taking fucking liberties with him keeping him down the choky,"
"Alright were with ya Ron,"
The six men stayed outside Ronnie's cell and shouted out to the screws to get the Governor, after about five minutes there were over twenty screws standing on the floor below, the senior screw asked Ronnie to end the dispute and return to their cells adding that they would all be in trouble for what they were doing, Ronnie told him to fuck off and go and get someone in charge who could make decisions.
Tommy Woodley was the first one to see the Governor arrive on the wing; he turned and pointed him out to Ronnie.
"It's Groves! He's alright Ron." Tommy shouted.
Edward Groves was Governor No3 in Brixton prison; he was one of the youngest senior prison officials in the system and was known to be fair, he had a nickname which was well known as BB which was short for big bad Eddie Groves a name he was given whilst single handed he once detained notorious prisoner Mad Frankie Fraser who was trying to get onto the roof of Parkhurst prison.
Groves walked up the stairs and headed straight for Ronnie, he was dressed unconventionally for a governor with slacks on and an open shirt with no tie and he carried himself a mug of coffee.

“What’s happening here Ronnie?” he very casually asked.
Ronnie looked him up and down with surprise, firstly that he called Ronnie by his first name and secondly with his relaxed and casual style.”
“Who the fuck are you?” Ronnie replied.
“My name is Edward Groves, I am governor No3.”
“Well where’s fucking governor No1?” Ronnie snapped.
Groves took a sip of his coffee before very casually replying.
“Can we talk Ronnie, none of us want this to get out of hand.” he said as he held out his hand in the direction of Ronnie’s cell, offering to go in and sit down.
Ronnie asked Tommy Woodley to go in the cell with him and Groves.
“Now then what are we doing here?” Groves asked once the three men were sitting down.
“We want Joey Pine out of the punishment block now!, Tommy told me he was sentenced to twenty eight days and that was over forty fucking days ago, you’re taking liberties with him groves, we got a case to prepare and all the fucking time you got him down there you’re playing with his fucking mind, we want him out now, on this wing so he can get his head together and start preparing for his trial.”
Governor Groves lifted his hand up to gently interrupt.
“Ronnie I think you have your facts wrong, Yes Pine was given 28 days but while he was down in solitary he has assaulted two of my officers and he is now on a dirty protest, since he has been here his behaviour has been diabolical, I have been warned by members of staff on this wing that if he was allowed to return he would assault more officers.”
“That’s bollocks Groves I know Joey well, he ain’t the kind to start something without a good reason.” Tommy Woodley said.
“I was told he was given a lot of warnings whilst he was on this wing, but nevertheless he refused to toe the line, none of us want trouble here Ronnie, this is a special unit which houses the country’s most violent prisoners, it is a boiling pot, every one of the officers on this wing has been chosen for their common sense and their past records, where they have shown reserve instead of anger, Joey Pine was trouble whilst on this wing, we all have a duty to perform and my duty was to look after my men,”
“Well then we got a real problem don’t we,” Ronnie said “By morning time the word of what we’re doing here would have spread to whole prison, tomorrow morning’s vans taking people to court will all be empty, by lunchtime you’ll have a full scale riot on your hands, Brixton prison will be on every newspaper and TV station across the country.”
“I could have you up on a charge for that Ronnie; you would be moved out of here by the morning.”
“It’s a stand-off then!” Tommy Woodley added.

“We won’t be threatened!” Groves replied.
“Let’s then reason.” Ronnie replied calmly, which surprised Groves.
“How! How do you suggest we do that Ronnie?”
“Look both of us here cant back down now, it’s gone too far but we can both give a little bit to calm the waters.”
“I have that authority.”
“Well let’s just say then that at this moment you have a situation that is under control but it could easily spiral way out of control within the blinking of an eye, you yourself could easily be held our hostage but we’re not that fucking stupid, in the long run that achieves us nothing, then you got Joey down in the solitary on a dirty protest, now that can’t be nice for your men down there can it, we want him back here with us but you say that can’t be done all the while he is breaking the rules, so why don’t you let me see him, let me speak to him see if I can get him to calm down, I’ll tell him if he comes off his dirty protest and behaves himself he can come back on the wing in a couple of days’ time, how does that sound.”
Groves thought carefully about Ronnie’s suggestion before answering.
“If I agree to this then can you convince your friends to return to their cells immediately?”
“Won’t be a problem, there only supporting me anyway, if I tell em it’s over then it’s over”
“If he comes off the protest and we have no more abuse at my staff then Pine will have to do one week from today then he’s back on the wing” Groves replied as he held out his hand to shake Ronnie’s purposely changing Ronnie’s request of a couple of days to one week so that Ronnie would not think him a pushover.
Ronnie shook Grove’s hand, as he knew the deal was fair, another governor would have just called in the “Mufty” or security prison staff to just flood the wing with manpower and truncheons and just bust who’s ever head they came across first.
Charlie Kray’s wife shouted out for her husband to wake, it was nine thirty in the morning; she had just put a nice cup of tea and the morning paper on his bedside cabinet,
“C’mon Charlie its gone nine.” She hollered as she left the room.
Charlie pulled himself up the pillows and wiped his eyes, he smiled as he looked out of the window and saw that the sun was shining, Charlie always loved the warm weather and since he had been staying out in Spain he had grown to like it even more, he was now the colour of bronze and had changed his wardrobe so that he wore more light coloured clothing, Reggie taunted Charlie about his white slacks and silk shirts and found it funny but Charlie paid no attention.

"There ain't too many fella's fucking walking about Marbella in wool three piece suits." he argued back.
Charlie yawned out loud as he reached for his cup of tea and paper, he blew the tea slightly then sipped at it as he opened up the paper on his lap with the other hand, what he saw on the front page nearly made him drop his tea, he placed it back on the cabinet as he picked up the paper with both hands to read its headlines.
"Four Men found Murdered in Soho."
Charlie opened up the front page to read the details and very quickly confirmed it was the Maltese men who he had asked Messina to take care of over a week ago.
"YES!" he shouted as he threw the paper at the wall and jumped out of bed.
When Charlie arrived at his mother's house in Vallance Road he found Reggie sitting on a deck chair in the small back garden enjoying some sun, Reggie was dressed in a pair of suit trousers with a white vest, he had positioned the record player by the window and had a classical opera record blaring out into the garden, as Charlie walked out he could see Reggie trying to mouth the words he was listening to in Italian.
"Can I turn this fucking thing down?" Charlie shouted.
Reggie jumped and smiled as he ran over to the window where he leant in and turned the music down low
"You heard?" he asked Charlie pleased.
"Yeah, is it them!" Charlie whispered.
"Fucking got a be in it Charlie."
Charlie then smiled and patted his brother on the arm before asking him if he wanted a cup of tea, Charlie made two cups then pulled himself up a deck chair.
"Has he been in touch?" Charlie asked referring to Messina.
"I haven't heard a thing since our meeting last week."
"Has anyone been arrested?" Charlie replied.
"Not what I know of."
"It'll make Ronnie's day!" Charlie laughed.
Reggie smiled broadly.
"Fucking hell Charlie can you see it now, Ronnie will be smiling from ear to ear humming Madame fucking butterfly all day long."
Charlie then leant over closer to Reg so to whisper.
"We're gonna have to go down the country now this is done."
"Yeah I've already called Johnny Walsh to drive us; he'll be here by twelve."
Just like Reggie said Ronnie was smiling from ear to ear, all morning long he had been shut away in his cell singing and in a really great mood, Joey Pine was now back on the wing and had been running around all morning, he banged on Ronnie's cell door before entering

“It’s true Ronnie he’s in reception now; he should be up here in a couple of hours.”
The man Joey Pine was talking about was Moshe Fleckman.
Moshe was a middle age Jewish man who all his life lived in Bethnal green, Ronnie had known him as a kid as Moshe was always around the pubs and snooker halls laying off bets, Ronnie liked Moshe who used to tell Ronnie he was a relation to the legendary east end hardman Wassle Newman, Ronnie didn’t believe Moshe but he still enjoyed hearing all his stories that went all the way back to the times of Jack the Ripper.
Moshe Fleckman was being held on the charge of murder, it was a big case that was headlined in all the papers, he was not known as a violent man but he just flipped , he was out with his young daughter of twelve when a drunken driver swerved off the road and killed her instantly, Moshe for four days was inconsolable, he buried himself in drink and on the fourth night he was so drunk he went round to the drunken drivers house and petrol bombed the front room, everyone in the house died. It was a terrible crime but because of what Moshe himself had gone through most people in the east end sympathised with him. When the police raided his house they found Moshe sobbing in his daughter’s empty bed and when they arrested him his mind was so gone with drink and grief he stabbed one of the policemen dead.
When Moshe arrived on the wing Ronnie couldn’t believe how old he looked, it looked as if he had aged twenty years, he was unshaven and dishevelled and his head was low as if he was sedated, Ronnie called out to him and Moshe acknowledged him back with a slight wave.
Two men on the wing mouthed an insult at Moshe as he walked past which caused Ronnie to fly over and throw the prisoner onto the floor, Ronnie jumped on the man’s chest and placed his knee on the man’s windpipe while his hands grabbed his face, Joey Pine and a few other cons stood over to block any view that the screws might have as Ronnie punched the guys face,
“You ever say anything to him again and I’ll smash ya to fucking pieces!” Ronnie told him.
The next day Ronnie and Joey Pine were sitting in Moshe’s cell, Ronnie was trying to tell Moshe to pull himself together and have a shave and a wash but Moshe was in another world.
“C’mon Moshe you got to pull yourself together mate.”
“But what Ronnie, my life is finished, I will never get out, they have told me this.”
“You never know Moshe, you could do.” Joey said.
“No I will die in here.”
“Ah don’t speak like that Moshe.” Ronnie added.
“Ronnie what I did was terrible, I deserve to die.”

"Yeah well so did that bastard who killed your daughter, now you got to think of the rest of your family, you got another daughter ain't ya."
"Judy, my lovely Judy."
"Well, be strong for her then." Ronnie added.
"How can I be strong Ronnie, how can I be a Father from in here?"
"Course you can Moshe, you can write to her, you can ask her to visit you."
"I don't want my family up here; I have caused them enough shame." Moshe said as he buried his hands in his head which made Ronnie sit down next to him and put a reassuring arm around his back as he gazed up over Moshe's head and looked at Joey.
"Maybe there is a way we can help you Moshe." Joey suddenly said as Moshe raised his head to look at him "maybe there is still a way you can be a Father and a husband and do some good, help us, and be a friend and we will help your family."
"Are you in trouble Ronnie?" Moshe asked him as he raised his head and spoke softly.
"Well we're not sightseeing in here mate are we." Ronnie gently and pleasantly said.
"You think I can help you?" Moshe asked quietly.
"You can do us a favour Moshe, if you do it we will return it." Ronnie said.
"We're make sure your family is taken care of Moshe, they won't go skint, I promise you." Joey Pine added.
"What can I do for you Ronnie, how can I help you?" Moshe asked as he lifted his head up.
"Will you do it?" Ronnie asked slightly stern.
Moshe looked into Ronnie's eyes and then glance at Pine he did not want to refuse but he felt scared at what Ronnie might ask him.
"I want to help you Ronnie but your scaring me, I want to help my family but what if I say yes to this favour then I don't want to do it, what will happen to me then Ron?"
Ronnie looked deeply and sincerely into Moshe's eyes and held the look for a few moments before answering him.
"Trust me old friend it's not nothing bad, I will not ask you to do anything that can cause you any pain, no one will get hurt by what I ask you to do, it will help me and Joe beat our case that's all, Summers here now if you help us we will get someone to drop a nice few quid off to your wife, we'll let her use our house down the coast let her take your daughter away for a bit of fun, get away from everything, it's a good thing for you to do Moshe trust me, it'll help us and help your wife."
Ok I'll do it Ronnie." Moshe replied after a short moment.
Ronnie gazed up at Joe and both men's eyes met as they both silently felt pleased.

"We want you to have a wash and clean yourself up first then we want you to ask to see a guvnor, when you're with him I want you to ask, or demand to see Chief inspector Richard LaSalle, tell the guvnor it's urgent and you need to see him concerning an ongoing crime."
"LaSalle he's the one who's nicked you Ronnie."
"That's him, when he comes to see ya I want you to tell him that he has arrested the wrong men for the Brooker murder, tell him you was in the area that night running with your bets and you saw Brooker having an argument with a couple of black fella's."
"I'll tell him Ron but he won't believe me." Moshe added.
"It doesn't matter Moshe, if he comes here which he will, it will be logged that he came to see ya, now officially your statement will be evidence but I know him, he won't declare it , he'll keep it to himself, now when our trial comes around we will introduce you as late evidence and once the jury and the judge hear what you got to say and that LaSalle came here to hear it but decided to keep it quiet, then it will help us to tell the jury this is a vendetta by the Police to convict us."
"It's a bit of a long shot Ronnie." Moshe added.
"So is everything but we have to try, and listen whether he believes it or not we will still owe ya mate."
"But he'll know were in here together wont he."
"Yeah but I know the way he fucking thinks, he's such a crooked bastard he won't declare it."
"Look Moshe if we just called up a witness who says he saw someone else do it no one will believe it, but when you stand in the box and say you told LaSalle this and he kept it silent then he'll have to answer why he didn't declare your conversation. Now that's the thing we want, we just want to put that little bit of doubt in the juries minds." Joey added.
On the day of the trial Vallance Road was alive with people, the press had arrived early hoping to get a quick word with someone from the Kray family. In the kitchen Violet Kray was making herself some sandwiches to take with her while her husband was sitting at the table talking Charlie and Reggie about the case, Johnny Walsh had fetched the jaguar and was waiting in the front room as he was going to drive them back once again to the old bailey. As the family left there house the press cried out different questions, Reggie said that his brother was innocent as climbed in the back seat and his mother replied to one of the reporters that she just wished the police would leave her boys alone. As the car sped off Reggie turned to see a tear in his mother's eye.
"What's the matter mum?"
"I just don't know Reg if I can go through all this again love." she cried.
"Don't worry Mum Ronnie will get off."

On the 28th of August 1969 Ronnie Kray appeared back at court No1 at the Old Bailey courts in central London, once again he was on a charge of murder.
He was taken in separate vans with Joey Pine from Brixton prison early in the morning, his solicitor Manny Freedman had just finished talking to Ronnie in the Old Bailey cells, he left Ronnie a packet of cigarettes and smiled as he walked out the cell.
"You got balls of an ox Kray!" were the last words he said before going upstairs to the court to prepare the case. The public gallery was filled with people from all walks of life; there were boxers, film stars, musicians, and a fair amount of Ronnie and Reggie's friends and family,
As Ronnie walked up the stairs into the court with Joey Pine he turned and gave his mother a smile and his brother Reggie a wink.
The atmosphere was electric as the press three rows deep penned there first viewing of Ronnie Kray.
Both men were read out the charges before both men pleaded not guilty, the prosecution then went about presenting their case, the court heard how Joey Pine had been having a long and violent feud with a family called the carters from west London, the victim police officer Dave Brooker was a friend of the Carters who had innocently been caught in the cross fire between these two warring families, the court was then told how Ronnie Kray on the behest of Pine had intervened and was involved in a heated exchange in carters pub with Brooker when Brooker tried to protect a barmaid who Ronnie had insulted.
The prosecution then added that Jackie and Tommy Carter were attacked by Ronnie Kray and his men upstairs, at this point Ronnie Kray's Queens council Jonathon Van-Hilary objected because it was unproven that this attack took place.
The prosecution next introduced the evidence of Jeffery Samuels who had made a statement claiming to have saw Kray and Pine on the night of the murder in vicinity of the crime carrying petrol cans and stinking of petrol.
The court heard next how on the arrest of the two men, items of clothing were taken, which forensics had found traces of petrol on, they also heard how guns were found in the boot of Joe Pine's car.
The QC for the prosecution was David Jansen, Jansen was regarded, as being one of the finest prosecutors around he was a thoroughly educated man who was ruthless in his presentation, he would not be hurried in the slightest and he dwelled on every point of the prosecution's case in order to explain very carefully to the less educated jury exactly what the evidence was.
He dragged this out for the whole day finishing only fifteen minutes before four o'clock where the judge thought it best to adjourn till tomorrow morning where the defence could reply and the prosecution would call its first witness Jackie Carter.

Ronnie Kray sat poker faced all day long in fact he looked bored by it all while Pine looked agitated and annoyed. As the two men walked down the stairs Ronnie once again turned and waved to his Family, Reggie raised his fist up to his chest in determination as if telling Ron to be strong.
Day two of the trial began with Ronnie Kray's barrister telling the jury how weak the prosecution's case against his client was, he claimed he would produce witness's that would contradict every aspect of the police evidence, Van-Hilary decided to keep things short and sweet, he commented to Manny Freedman that he thought the prosecution had bored the jury and came across patronising so he would shorten his affairs and give them more credit for their intellectual abilities, Joey Pine's QC Steven Frale followed his lead and did also.
Jackie Carter was the first Prosecution witness, he walked into the box with the aid of a walking stick, he was sworn in and asked his name before the jury.
"Is your name Jackie Carter?" the prosecutor asked.
"Yes your honour."
"We can see that you are carrying an injury can you explain to the court how this injury occurred?"
"It was on the night Dave Brooker was killed."
"Where were you on that night?"
"First I was at our pub then I went around Dave Brooker's flat, when I got there I was attacked."
"Did you see who attacked you?"
"No sir I did not, it was from behind and very dark."
"Can you describe to the court what you saw when you arrived at Police officers Brooker's flat?"
"I saw that the door had been kicked off from its hinges, I went over to have a closer look and saw the outlines of two men standing by the door."
"What did you do then?"
"I shouted out and asked what they were doing."
"What happened next?"
"I don't really know sir, I was hit with something from behind, and the next memory I had was waking up in hospital sir."
The prosecutor then picked up his papers from his desk.
"I now want you to go back to before that ill-fated night and tell me off your correlation with Joey Pine."
"Sorry sir." Carter replied.
"What was your relationship with Pine?"
"Relationship, we ain't got no relationship sir, we hate each other, his family and mine have been arguing for years."
"Has this arguing between your families ever resulted in violence?"
"Yes sir it has quite a few times."

“Fights, petrol bombings?”
“Yes sir.”
Manny Freedman gave Ronnie Kray’s QC a Firm nudge as if asking him to object; Van Hilary turned around and whispered to Freedman.
“Don’t worry about I am going to give him enough rope to hang himself with.”
“But he’s talking about fire-bombing?” Freedman replied.
“Don’t worry about it Manny I’ll destroy him.”
“Can you expand to the court on this petrol bombing?” the prosecutor asked.
“Pine’s petrol bombed a few of our cars and a flat went up in flames once as well.”
“And you have reason to believe it was Pine who did this?”
“Yeah he did it all right!”
“So in your view are Joey Pine and Ronnie Kray capable of violence?”
“Very much so sir.”
“Ok, now I want you to tell the court about the fight you had with Ronnie Kray?”
Jackie Carter then explained everything down to even what Ronnie was wearing on the day when Ronnie and Reggie attacked him and his brother Tommy in there pub, this lasted for ages as Carter tried his hardest to paint the worst picture of Ronnie that was possible, finally after about ten minutes he decided to stop.
“You didn’t tell em what colour shoes I was wearing.” Ronnie Kray shouted out which resulted in the judge giving him a very stern warning.
“So in a nutshell Mr Carter we have heard you testify to the court that your family has been involved in a long running battle with the pine family and that the pine’s called in their friends the Kray’s to help them in their arguments with you.”
“Yes sir.”
“Could Dave Brooker have been mistaken as being involved with this feud?”
“He was a very good friend of ours.”
“I’m sure you have lots of friends but I doubt they all end up murdered.”
“He was closer to us than most sir.”
“So he could have been mistaken as let’s say a powerful ally by your side?”
“Yes sir he could have.”
“And in your mind you have no doubt that both Kray and Pine are capable of such violence such as murder?”
“No doubt about it your honour, Pine especially, he is an evil bastard”
“Objection!” Pine’s QC suddenly shouted
With that the prosecutor finished his cross examination and sat down, Jonathon Van-Hilary Ronnie Kray’s barrister then rose from his seat and with a flick of his robes to get them back on his shoulders he took to the floor.

"Good afternoon Mr Carter." Van-Hilary began.
"I want to ask you about your testimony where you stated you was attacked by Ronnie Kray, why didn't you report this to the police?"
Jackie Carter hesitated in replying as he felt everyone looking at him.
"Where I come from sir you just don't do that."
"What reporting a crime?"
"Yes sir, we take care of our own affairs."
"So what changed your mind today?"
Jackie Carter once again hesitated.
"What do you mean sir?"
"It's simple!" Van-Hilary snapped as he raised his voice "You have just told the court that you do not report crimes so why are you here today! What changed your mind?"
"Well nothing changed my mind, I was asked to."
"Ah you were asked to, by whom?"
"By Detective LaSalle your honour."
Jonathon Van-Hilary then walked over to his desk and picked up his notes before returning back over towards Carter.
"Have you ever been in trouble with the police Mr Carter?" He asked still looking in his papers
"Yeah a little bit." Jackie Carter smiled coyly.
"Do you find that funny?" Van-Hilary suddenly snapped now looking sternly at Carter.
"What!" Carter replied.
"I asked you if you had been in trouble with the police.... you replied yeah a little bit, with a smile on your face, is it a laughing matter, is the question I asked amusing, tell me?"
"I didn't mean it funny, but ain't everyone had a bit of bother with the law."
"No they have not!" Van-Hilary snapped back "Could you tell the court what trouble you've been in?"
"I was arrested a couple of times for theft and a few punch ups, nothing that serious."
Van-Hilary smiled with a look of disbelief at Carter, he then turned to face the jury.
"In my hand I have the police record of Mr Carter, he has been convicted a total number of fourteen times , let me read them off, theft, theft, theft, theft, theft, ABH, ABH, GBH ,theft, offensive weapon, LIVING OFF IMORAL EARNINGS!, what was that?"
"I just looked after a few people, that's all, they gave me money in return."
"You took money from prostitutes! That is what you did, wasn't it?"
"Yes it was but so what!" Carter shouted back at him.

"You're earning money today for representing a murderer! Who's worse?" Carter added to which the judge butted in and asked him to refrain from such outbursts again.
Once things calmed down Van-Hilary resumed.
"Theft, Theft, and then I see another crime you were convicted of the crime of perjury."
Carter just looked at him angrily.
"Could you explain to the court what that is?"
"I was convicted of telling a lie."
"No sir that's not the whole truth is it; you were convicted of telling a lie whilst under oath, such as you are under today."
"Yeah!" Carter replied.
"I beg your pardon?"
"I said yeah alright but it weren't the same as this."
The prosecutor then intervened,
"Objection your honour, the witness is not on trial." he said rising to his feet.
"Your honour I am just cross examining the soundness of this man's character, if he was convicted of dishonesty under oath, then I think it imperative that this jury hear about it."
Replied Van-Hilary.
"I will permit this line of questioning but I will caution you Mr Van-Hilary to tread very carefully and be reminiscent that this gentleman isn't on trial."
"Yes your honour, I have nearly completed this line of questions anyway."
Van –Hilary walked back over to his desk where he placed his papers on top.
"Earlier you said that Detective LaSalle asked you to testify today, could you give us more details as to how this arose?"
Jackie Carter once again hesitated; he looked lost for a reply as looked around the court, finally he seemed to shrug his shoulders and say, "I don't know really when it happened, it just did."
"When did you first meet Detective LaSalle?"
"At the hospital."
"After you were attacked yes."
"Yes sir."
"So you were attacked at the scene of police officer David Brooker's death, as a result of the attack you were taken to the nearest hospital unconscious, and when you awoke you were questioned by detective LaSalle yes?"
"Yes sir that is correct."
"Were you a suspect in the murder Mr Carter?"
"I don't know what you mean, you better ask LaSalle."
"You were found unconscious at the scene of a crime, you were questioned upon waking in hospital, surely you were questioned as to why or what you were doing there?"

“Yeah they asked me, so I told them I just went round.”
“At that precise time.”
“Yeah unlucky for me.”
“Or police Officer Brooker.”
“Mr Van-Hilary! Could we have less of those kind of adlibs.” the judge intervened.
“Sorry your honour.”
“So let me just sum up, you were found insentient at the scene of a crime, then taken to hospital where you were questioned, at some stage in these questions you was asked what you was doing there, but out of the blue you decided to tell detective LaSalle about a completely unrelated incident which involved yourself your brother and the two gentleman who stand accused today, Am I correct.”
“It didn’t just happen like that but that is true.” Carter replied.
“Well I’m sorry but I fail to see why an altercation between yourself and the accused had any bearing on what had just happened to Officer Brooker, the only connection between Kray, Pine and Officer Brooker is you, who were the initial suspect in Brooker’s death!”
“No it wasn’t like that; I told the police Ronnie Kray had an argument with Brooker a few weeks earlier.”
“Yes this so called argument where Ronnie Kray insulted a bar women, are there anyone to substantiate this except you.”
“What do you mean?”
“Are there any other witnesses who could testify that this argument took place?”
“It took place the whole pub saw it.”
“But no one has stepped forward to confirm this.”
“Well I can’t help that can I.”
“What about the barmaid, why is she not here today?”
“She left the pub shortly after; we don’t know where she is.”
“How convenient.”
Jackie Carter just shrugged his shoulders in anger.
“I put it to you Mr Carter that this argument is a figment of your imagination and that it never took place at all.”
“So you’re saying I lied!” Carter snapped angrily.
“I am saying you told the court about an argument where no one else except you have come forward to testify it took place, all we have is your word and in all honesty your word is questionable sir.”
“Well the court can please itself if it believes me or not cant it.”
“I think you’ve made that problem very easy for us sir!”
“Please yourself.” Carter replied nonchalant.

Van-Hilary nodded slightly at the judge to motion that he had finished with his questioning; on his way back to his desk he smiled gently to Ronnie Kray.
The clerk of the court then arranged for Carter to be helped from the box before calling for the prosecutions next witness Jeffrey Samuels.
As Samuels walked into court there was a few hisses and comments aimed at him from the public gallery, the judge immediately ordered them to refrain from any further outbursts or he would clear the gallery.
Jeffrey Samuels was sworn.
"Your name is Jeffery Samuels?" The Prosecutor asked.
"Yes your Honour."
"Before we hear your testimony I would like the court to hear a few things about your past, is it true you fought in the Second World War?"
"Yes sir."
"And it is also true that you were shot down in enemy territory and held as a prisoner of war?"
"For Two years sir."
"Did you receive any medals for your service?"
"I was decorated four times sir."
"For valour and service for your country yes."
"Yes sir."
"And am I correct to tell the court that you were indeed one of first men to escape from the infamous Colditz?"
"Yes Sir." Samuels replied slightly embarrassed "It was a classified mission sir so we was not permitted to speak about it until after the war." he added.
"Outstanding!" the prosecutor remarked.
"Have you ever been convicted of a crime Mr Samuels?"
"No sir I have not!"
"So you appear today with a completely unsoiled character"
"Yes sir I do!"
"Right then let's begin with the statement you made to Detective LaSalle, where was you on the night of Police Officer Dave Brooker's murder?"
"I was drinking in the unicorn pub."
"That would be the unicorn public house on the corners of Trafford road and mulberry road yes, more or less fifty yards from Brooker's flat?"
"Yes sir that is correct."
"What time did you arrive and what time did you leave?"
"I arrived at just after six thirty and left around eleven sir"
"Did you bump into anybody as you left the pub Mr Samuels" the prosecutor asked as he was reading from Samuel's statement where he said he bumped into Ronnie Kray and Joey wheeler on his way out.
Samuels hesitated in giving his reply.
"No sir I didn't see anyone, I left the pub and caught the train home."

The prosecutor suddenly fingered through his notes, he felt unsure of himself and he asked the judge for a slight pause as he conferred with he's colleagues, the judge soon became fed up with David Jansen's delay and called out to him.
"Mr Jansen, the court is waiting."
"My Apologies Milord but I seem to be reciting from the wrong papers, won't be a moment."
"Mr Jansen!" The judge cried out again.
"Yes Milord I am coming!" the prosecutor replied as he called out from the heated conversation that was going on between his colleagues and Detective LaSalle who had now joined in.
"My apologies Mr Samuels but it seemed we had our paths crossed, I will start from the beginning and read from your statement you made to detective LaSalle."
On the evening of the 14th of April 1969 between the hours of six thirty and eleven o'clock you were drinking in the unicorn public house on the corner of Mulberry road is that correct?"
"Yes sir it is." replied Samuels.
"Good!, now in the next paragraph you say you left the premises at eleven o'clock and turned left into Mulberry road, is that correct?"
"Yes sir it is."
"You then walked approximately ten yards when you bumped into the accused Ronnie Kray and Joseph Pine, is this correct?"
"No sir it is not." Samuels replied.
David Jansen turned abruptly to his own bench and looked confused at his colleagues; Detective LaSalle was now sitting amongst them and made a gesture with his hands to indicate that he didn't know what was going on.
"Mr Samuels I have a sworn statement here where you stated you left the premises at eleven o'clock, you then walked ten yards down Mulberry Road and bumped into Ronald Kray And Joseph Pine who were both carrying petrol cans, are these your words?"
"It might say that in that statement but I'm telling you now that's not what happened."
"But this is a sworn avadavat!"
"It doesn't matter what it is I'm telling you the truth right now."
"Are you saying that this statement I am holding here is not your words?"
"It's not the truth!"
"But it's signed by you!"
"It's not the truth, LaSalle forced me to say what's in there, it's all lies, the lot of it."
The prosecutor David Jansen slapped the statement he was holding against his leg and sighed out aloud. The judge then leaned across to address Samuels.

"Mr Samuels may I remind you, you are under oath and if you continue with this line of replies then It is my duty to inform you that you could be investigated for perjury."
"Thank you your honour but what evidence I give here today will be the truth." Samuels replied.
Up in the public gallery Reggie Kray was beaming from ear to ear, he turned and made a fist of defiance to his brother.
"I will give you one last opportunity Mr Samuels; did you bump into Mr Kray and Mr Pine on the night of Brooker's murder?"
"No sir I did not!"
"No further questions Milord!" the prosecutor bitterly added.
Jonathon Van- Hilary, Ronnie Kray's Barrister was quickly out of his chair; he raced over to face Samuels
"Mr Samuels you said Detective LaSalle asked you to make this statement, did he care if it was an accurate account of what occurred that evening?"
"Objection your honour!" The Prosecutor cried.
"Disallowed, I want to hear why."
"He didn't care sir, in fact he encouraged me to reiterate about the petrol can, all he wants is to convict Kray and he couldn't care less if he's guilty or not!"
"So there was no petrol can."
"How could there have been sir I never met them that night."
"So the statement you made to the police is in fact full of falsehoods?"
"It's a lie from start to finish."
"One other thing Mr Samuels, since the arrest of Mr Ronald Kray where have you been?"
"I've been in police protection sir."
"So you have not been in any situation where you could have met any of the accused men's friends or family?"
"No sir, all I have seen is Policemen!"
Jonathon Van-Hilary then turned towards the judge.
"Milord in view of this testimony I would like to call an adjournment where I might address you in your chambers."
"I thought you might, I want to see all councils in fifteen minutes." the said then turned to the clerk "Now might be a good time to take the jury down for a short coffee break." he added.
Inside the judge's chambers the atmosphere was very heated indeed, the council for Ronnie Kray were arguing rigorously with the prosecution.
"Milord I must request that you order an acquittal here today, the case for the prosecution has completely fallen apart."
"Your honour I object strongly to the defences claim."
"Well I do not." the judge replied.

“Milord I would point out at this moment that without this key piece of evidence and the total unreliability of the prosecutions first witness I feel it would be very dangerous to push for a conviction on the grounds of what little evidence is left.”
“Yes!” the Judge replied as he flicked through the prosecution papers.
“Your honour the prosecution still has to produce the forensics of this case and whether the defence like it or not we have clothing belonging from each of the accused that has traces of petrol on them, we have further testimony to introduce, we also have the word of Inspector LaSalle.”
“And not forgetting the guns your honour.” An assistant prosecutor added.
Jonathon Van-Hilary sat down opposite the judge.
“Your honour without the testimony of Jeffrey Samuels, the prosecution having nothing except circumstantial evidence to link my client to the crime.”
“I agree with the defence you are on very shaky ground Mr Jansen, but I am going to carry on but I warn you that the court will not tolerate any more prosecution witness’s like we have seen, do you understand?”
Van- Hilary left the judge’s chambers feeling deeply annoyed, he returned to find Manny Freedman by the bench waiting patiently for him.
“It’s carrying on!” Van-Hilary declared.
“What, with what, they have no case!”
“Don’t worry too much Manny we are still way ahead and we haven’t even begun our case yet.”
“I’m going to go and see Ronnie.”
“Tell him not to worry, its early days yet!”
For the next two days the prosecution kind of waffled on with the rest of their case. The jury were given the testimony of two forensic experts, one of which took over two hours to explain the chemical breakdown of the petrol that was found on the suit belonging to Ronald Kray.
There was also evidence heard from a police colleague stationed at the same station as the murdered officer Brooker who alleged Brooker told him he was having trouble with the Kray’s and Pine. The defence argued that it was un-collaborated testimony and that its content be questionable. Detective LaSalle was also questioned where he gave his usual academy award performance, the defence declined to question him.
On day five of the trial the defence had their turn at presenting its case, Ronnie Kray walked up into the court with a spring in his step, he sat down next to Joey Pine and watched his council and the prosecution at loggerheads with the judge.
The defence were asking for some late evidence to be included whilst the prosecution were objecting.
“I can’t see how you would need much preparation for cross examination on this, it’s pretty plain if I may say so.”

"Milord this evidence has to be included; it has already been a sham as to why the prosecution did not allow the defence to see this."
"We were unaware of it." The prosecution replied.
"No I will allow it!" the judge replied.
The councils returned to their seats all except Ronnie Kray's QC whom the judge had asked to stay.
"You knew about this evidence yesterday didn't you?" the judge told him suspiciously
"Milord I was aware of something but I was not sure if it was evidence until I had the proper time to study it"
"Yesterday when LaSalle was in the box, I found it strange you declined to question him, now I see why, be very careful Mr Van-Hilary I will not stand by for any more of these stunts, I'm on to you!"
"Yes Milord!"
Moshe Fleckman took the box at 11.30 on the fifth day of the trial; he was the defence's first witness.
"Mr Fleckman could you please tell the court of the conversation you had with detective LaSalle in Brixton prison, start at the beginning."
"I asked to see Detective LaSalle because I had some information that I thought might be important, Detective LaSalle came to the prison where I told him I was in the area on the night off the killing, I told him I saw two black fella's having a very heated argument about quarter past eleven."
"How did you know it was Brooker that the two black men were arguing with?"
"Are you sure! I would know that bastard in my sleep, for donkeys years he's been taking money off me for turning a blind eye when I was laying my bets."
"Laying your bets Mr Fleckman."
"That was what I did sir, I took bets off of people for the horse racing."
"In public bars?"
"Mostly yes but I would go to snooker halls, card games, just about anywhere I had a very good name."
"Yes quite! Back to Detective LaSalle what did he say when you told him this?"
"Nothing sir, I just went a funny shade of pale and told me to keep it to myself."
"Why haven't you, kept it to yourself!"
"Because I don't want to see innocent men being weighed off for something they never did."
"Was the contents of this conversation written down?"
"LaSalle wrote it in his notebook sir."
"Thank you, Mr Fleckman"
The prosecutor then had his turn

"Did anyone else hear this story of yours Mr Fleckman?"
"Yes sir there was a prison guard in the room but Detective LaSalle asked him to leave halfway through what I was telling him."
David Jansen ended his questions and Jonathon Van-Hilary asked to judge for permission to recall Detective LaSalle back to the witness box.
"Detective LaSalle can you tell the court why Mr Fleckman's evidence was not made available to the defence?"
LaSalle for once looked rattled as he wiped the sweat from his forehead.
"I didn't think it important enough." he finally murmured.
"Didn't think it important enough doesn't the law state that all evidence relating to a case must be made available to the defence?"
"I am aware of the law sir but what Fleckman told me had nothing to do with this."
"He told you he saw two black men arguing with Brooker just moments before his death."
"That's a lie sir, he said nothing of the sort, he wanted to see me about a matter to do with his own heinous case."
"So he never spoke to you about Brooker?"
"No sir he did not."
"Ah so he is here today for nothing more than just a day out."
"I don't know why he's here; maybe Kray put him up to it!"
Van-Hilary then stepped back and waited a moment before changing the tone of his voice to a more softer tone.
"Detective, is it common practice for an officer to be required to make notes whilst on an interview?"
"In some cases it is."
"Was this one of those cases?"
"No sir it was not."
"Mr Fleckman has told the court that you made notes in your notebook, is this true?"
"No sir it is also a lie."
"Can we take a look at your notebook?"
"No sir you cannot."
"Why?"
"I have information in there which includes very confidential material; I would feel invaded if I just let anyone look at it."
"Hmm!" Van-Hilary replied with a look of suspicion before turning to the judge.
"Milord may I suggest that the notebook is then shown to you and you alone, and then you could make judgement as to who is telling the truth here."
The judge thought silently for a moment before turning to LaSalle.
"I would only look at the dates referring to this trial officer."

"Yes your honour."
The prosecutor walked over to LaSalle at LaSalle's behest and after a minute or so of whispering he turned to the judge.
"My apologies Milord but it seems that Detective LaSalle has lost the notebook you require."
"Milord!" Ronnie Kray's QC declared, "This is a complete sham!"
"I suggest it is Detective LaSalle who should be on trial here today, we have failure to produce evidence, perjured witnesses, witnesses who revoke their statements, your honour I beg of you this case is a farce."
"That's enough Mr Van-Hilary that is for me to decide, and I will not tolerate any more outbursts like that!" the judge shouted.
Van-Hilary turned back to LaSalle.
"So this notebook you deny any notes were made in is now lost?"
"Yes sir." LaSalle ungraciously replied.
"How convenient!" replied Van-Hilary ironically.
Detective LaSalle was dismissed from the witness box and defence called their next witness.
Lulu Taylor was then sworn in and questioned.
"You are telling the court that police officer Brooker used to take money from you and other girls like you and in return he would protect you?"
"I don't know about protection love but he wouldn't nick us."
"He would turn a blind eye as to speak?"
"Yeah he would let us work on his patch."
"You're a prostitute?"
"I prefer to say I'm a working girl."
Three other girls in the profession of Lulu Taylor were called and all of them gave the same replies. The judge became somewhat tired when another girl by the name of Sunset Down was called so he called out to the defence.
"Mr van-Hilary, are we going to hear the evidence from another prostitute?"
"Yes milord, I have three more witnesses in that genre."
"Is that necessary Mr Van-Hilary, I think we get the point, my god the waiting room outside must look like the Moulin Rouge!" the judge added which caused everyone in the court to burst into laughter.
The next morning Ronnie Kray was held below in the cells, it was now ten forty five and he had yet to be called up into the dock, Ronnie offered Joey Pine a cigarette as he asked him a question.
"What the fucks going on up there Joe?"
"Fuck knows Ron, probably that cunt LaSalle up to something mate."
Ronnie lit up Joe's cigarette and then his own just before the cell door opened and he saw Manny Freedman enter.
"What's going on Manny?" Ronnie asked.

"It's good news Ronnie." Replied Freedman in a whisper as he walked shiftily over to the two men.
"The judge has asked to see the prosecution in his chambers."
"He's in with the fuckers!" Ronnie loudly interrupted only to have Manny plead for quiet with his appearance and a gentle wave of the hand.
"It doesn't matter Ronnie, your defence lawyer says that the judge is getting extremely uneasy about the case against you."
"They gonna drop it!" Joey asked.
"I don't think they will drop the guns charges Joe but we have a good possibility on Brooker, just think how can the judge address the jury in his summing up, now that Samuels has withdrawn his testimony there is nothing but the word of a convicted perjurer to connect you with Brooker, think of it Ronnie they have nothing, all they have is a so called petrol can and a suit that has petrol on it, there is no way they can convict you on that, plus we still have more witnesses to come!"
The two co-defendants were kept waiting in the cells for a further forty five minutes, Ronnie entered the dock first and quickly looked over at his Solicitor Manny Freedman who gently grimaced and slightly shook his head as he walked over.
"He's going to continue Ronnie." he whispered.
"It's a fucking joke Manny!" Ronnie replied quietly.
"Please Ronnie don't despair now, everything is going fine."
The Judge apologised to the court before allowing the defence to call their next witness,
Harold Decosta.
"Is your name Harold Decosta?" asked Ronnie's QC Mr Van-Hilary.
"Yes sir that is my name."
"What is your trade sir"?
"I am a tailor!" Replied the frail Decosta with his Greek accent sounding more Louder as he added pride in his answer.
"Is that your full time trade and do you have any shop or trade premises?"
"I have been a tailor all my life sir, my Father was a tailor who came over from Greece during the war."
"And you have a shop in Whitechapel yes?"
"Yes I do, it is called Decosta's."
"Do you see anyone in this court today who you would call a client of yours?"
Harold Decosta pointed gingerly at Ronnie Kray.
"I see Mr Ronald Kray."
"He is a client of yours?"
"Yes sir he is a fine gentleman."
"Have you made clothes for Mr Kray?"
"Yes sir many times."

Van-Hilary then walked away from the witness box and spoke briefly to one of the court clerks who then moments later produced a dark blue herringbone suit that was marked with an exhibit number; Van Hilary showed the suit to Mr Decosta and asked him to identify it
"Did you make this fine suit Mr Decosta?"
"Yes sir for Mr Kray."
"When did you make this suit for him?"
"I made this in June of this year."
"June of this year, not June of last year?"
"No sir absolutely not."
"So by looking at this suit could Mr Kray have been wearing this same suit on the night of April the 14th?"
Harold Decosta grinned sheepishly as if embarrassed.
"I do not understand sir, is this some kind of trick question." he asked coyly.
"Mr Decosta, could Ronnie Kray have worn this suit on the 14th of April of this year?"
"I said before that this suit was not made then, I made this in June!" Decosta replied still sounding very uncomfortable as he tried not to offend.
Mr Van-Hilary then turned to the jury and held up the suit.
"This is the very same suit the prosecution have insinuated Ronnie Kray wore on the night of Brooker's death!"
"Your Honour!" the prosecution shouted. "Defence is giving a speech!" he added.
"Mr Van-Hilary you will have plenty of chance to adlib when you sum up." the Judge sternly spoke.
Van-Hilary smiled and nodded at the judge before turning his attention back to Decosta
"So there is no way this suit Mr Decosta, this same very suit that the police state had traces of petrol on it could have been worn by Mr Kray or anyone else on the 14th of April 1969?"
Decosta grinned again and shrugged his shoulders before answering.
"It was just a roll of material at that time sir."
"Thank you Mr Decosta, I have no further questions."
The prosecutor rose slowly to his feet and walked even slower over to Decosta.
"Good afternoon Mr Decosta, are Mr Kray's only Tailor?"
"I don't know sir; I would like to think so!"
"Do you think Mr Kray has only your clothes in his wardrobe?"
"How would I know sir what clothes Mr Kray has in his wardrobe."
"Ok let's put it another way, would you say you have made every suit that Mr Kray owns?"
"I don't know!"

“Well could he have other suits from other tailors?”
“I don’t know sir.” Decosta replied.
“So would you at least admit that there is a very good chance that Mr Kray owns items of clothing that have not come from you?”
Suddenly the judge butted in.
“Mr Jansen, where are you going with this?, you have asked the witness the same question three times now and I fail to see how he can answer you any plainer than he has already.”
“Milord I am merely trying to find out if Mr Kray has any clothing that has not been made by Mr Decosta.”
“I understand that but Mr Decosta has answered you three times that he doesn’t know, now what is your point Mr Jansen?”
“The point is milord that I want Mr Decosta to admit that Mr Kray has items of clothing that were not made by him.”
The judge sighed loudly.
“How can the witness give you an honest answer as to what Mr Kray’s wardrobe consists of?”
“It’s the possibility Milord!”
“Carry on, but I warn you I will not tolerate this line of questioning much further.” The Judge huffed.
“Mr Decosta is it possible that Mr Kray has items of clothing in his wardrobe that was not made by you!”
Harold Decosta smiled broadly and raised his hands up.
“I don’t know sir.” he answered in a frustrated tone.
The prosecutor nodded his head and briefly walked back to his papers, he knew that he could not ask the same question again so he purposely took his time reading through his papers as he gathered his thoughts, he knew that the judge was getting extremely frustrated with him but he wanted to try to divert the juries attention away from the damaging evidence against the prosecution that the jury had just heard.
“Mr Jansen the witness is waiting!” the judge finally reminded him.
“My apologies Milord, I won’t be a moment.”
“Mr Decosta, the defence barrister for Mr Ronald Kray has just shown you a suit, did you make it?”
“Yes sir.”
“Are you sure, it’s one of yours, could Mr Kray have two suits of this colour and material?”
“It’s my cut sir; I know instantly that I made this suit and when I did it.”
“And we have only your word for it that this suit was made in June as you earlier stated?”
“Not really sir.”

“Not really sir, how not really, I put it to you that this suit was made before April the 14th!”
Decosta shook his head.
“No, no, sir that’s impossible.”
“Well I suggest it was!”
“Then why sir would it have my name and the month of June written in its pocket sir.”
The prosecutor frowned at Decosta’s remark before turning swiftly back to the bench where he stared at Inspector LaSalle who in turn just shrugged his shoulders.
Prosecutor Jansen then asked the clerk to examine the suit jacket, and after a frantic few minutes of looking they found no tag, the garment was then presented to Harold Decosta at the Judge’s suggestion who very quickly showed them a very cleverly concealed tag with his name and date written very clearly upon it.
The garment was then shown to the jury and then to the judge where he took his time examining the complexity of how the tag had been concealed, once the judge satisfied himself he handed the jacket back to the clerk and immediately gave the prosecution bench and in particular Inspector LaSalle a very stern look indeed.
David Jansen the prosecutor for the crown looked speechless, he frantically racked his educated brain for a quick and witty response gazing up sceptically at Inspector LaSalle but he could find nothing, this was a shattering blow for the crown who were claiming that this suit this petrol stained suit had been worn by Ronnie Kray on the night of the murder but here now was undisputable evidence that this suit had not even been made until six weeks after the death of Brooker,
Prosecutor Jansen looked up unhappily at the Judge and mouthed in dismal tones.
“No further questions Milord.”
“That would be a wise choice.” the judge sighed quietly to himself as he peeked over his spectacles at Jansen.
Judge Charles Grantham in his last year as a high court judge decided that due to the time being close to four o’clock it would be best to adjourn the court until the morning, once the jury had dispersed he asked the prosecution and Ronald Kray’s queens council to approach the bench.
“Mr Jansen one of the reason’s that I have adjourned early today is that I want you to seriously take stock of the crowns prosecution. I am not a fool Mr Jansen, there is a very sinister tone beginning to emerge in this case, frankly I am not convinced either way of Mr Kray or Mr Pine’s innocence in this matter but I am beginning to be appalled at how the Police have gathered their

evidence, I will be revising tonight and take everything into consideration and by morning I may order the jury to return a not guilty verdict."
"Milord I agree totally that this case has thrown up a few peculiarities but I must ask you to look at the bigger picture sir."
"Mr Jansen this is a court room of Her Majesty's law!, we are not here to second guess the bigger picture as you quote it, but to assess the evidence of the case presented before us, and the evidence of the crowns case is disintegrating before our eyes."
"Milord with all due respect I feel you are being harsh."
Judge Grantham lowered his head to look over the top of his spectacles.
"I suggest you reserve that judgment for tomorrow morning."
Across the road from the Old Bailey was a pub called the quill and barrister, Charlie and Reggie Kray sat quietly in a corner discussing the day's events whilst they waited for Manny Freedman to come from the cells of the bailey after seeing their brother Ron.
Charlie was getting a bit worried as today Manny was taking a bit longer than usual.
"Fucking hell Reg, what's fucking keeping him?"
"I don't know mate, but I think it was a good day today, did ya see that fucker LaSalle's face when old man Decosta told him about the clothes tag."
"Ah fucking hell Reg, I wish I had a camera, he looked pig sick!"
"Yeah the slag! There tie him up by the balls when this case is done."
"I can't see how they can convict em now Reg can you."
"On what Charlie! They got fuck all now, Ronnie l be home in a few days."
Just as Reggie finished he saw Manny Freedman enter, Tony Lambrianou who was standing by the bar with a couple of friends pointed out where Reggie was and told Manny he would bring him over a drink.
"Hello Manny how's Ron?"
"He's in good spirits Reg" Manny replied as he sat down next to him.
"Any messages Manny?" Charlie added.
"No Ronnie is fine Charles, I took him down a couple of packets of players and he was happy."
"That's Good Manny, so how did it go today?"
"It went great Reg, your saw with your own eyes the state the prosecution got themselves in."
Yeah but what's was all that at the end when the judge called everyone over."
Manny smiled broadly as he reached out and grabbed Reggie's arm friendly.
"The judge is feeling very pressured to drop the case."
"What an acquittal!" Charlie barged in excited.
"Calm down." Manny pleaded.
"It's not as straight forward as that boys, but the crowns case is very weak, every time a witness has stepped in the box it has weakened them, but what he

is getting worried about is all the grounds to appeal that have cropped up, he knows full well that if everything here goes wrong for Ronnie and Joe and they get a guilty plea then there's grounds everywhere for a retrial."
"Why don't they just throw it out now?" Charlie snapped.
"The game isn't played like that, look we have destroyed the prosecution's case, their first witness Jackie Carter, he was shattered in the box, it was a master stroke how you found out he was once found guilty of perjury. His testimony now is almost inadmissible, he is a proven liar and the judge will have to instruct the jury not to rely on his evidence, Jeff Samuels turned into a nightmare for the crown, without him the crown has nothing to link Ronnie and Joe to the scene of the crime, all they had then was a suit that it has now been proven was not even made when Brooker died, we have beat them on every point but the judge will exhaust every avenue before he throws this case out."
"So he will throw it out Manny?" Charlie asked.
"No!" Manny sternly replied. "In my opinion he will not, in all due respect your surname is too high profile for him to do that, he is not a fool and he knows if he did that at this stage then it is almost as if he is accusing the police force of corruption and with you guys that's news at six."
"That's a fucking liberty Manny, so were being persecuted for who we are!" Reggie snapped.
Manny threw up both his hands and sunk his neck into his shoulders in typical Yiddish fashion and replied, "What's new!"
The next morning began in the usual fashion; Ronnie was led into the dock first followed by Joey Pine where they both looked up into the public gallery to see who was there. The Kray family were sat in their usual seats accompanied by many of their friends and showbiz personalities.
The court was told to all rise as the judge walked in and sat down, Ronnie Kray's Qc rose to his feet as the clerk of the court called out for the next witness.
"I call the honourable Lord Nelson Watkins MBE."
His youngest son Peter wheeled Lord Watkins into the court in his wheelchair; Mr Van-Hilary asked the judge if Lord Watkins could give his evidence from his wheelchair, as he was too poorly to mount the witness box.
"He most certainly can." the judge replied as he smiled and nodded warmly at the ex-shadow cabinet minister.
"Good morning Lord Watkins, thank you for coming to court today in your condition."
"Don't worry about me laddey, I'm fine I've seen better days but there's still plenty of fight in me yet son!"
Jonathon Van-Hilary smiled warmly at the old lord before beginning his questions.

"Lord Watkins could you tell the court where you were, on the fateful night of April the 14th of this year?"
"Yes I was at my home Freinham having a business dinner."
"Could you explain to the court Lord Watkins who was present at this business dinner?"
"It was I, my youngest son Peter, Mr Ronald Kray and Mr Joseph Pine."
"That's fine Lord Watkins could you now tell the court the duration of this meeting,"
"Mr Kray and Mr Pine arrived at my home late afternoon, we ate dinner at around eight o'clock then discussed business over a bottle of port, the evening ended at 11.30, my guests were shown to their guest bedrooms, they stayed the night we spoke briefly again over breakfast then they left at around 10.30 in the morning."
"And this night they stayed was definitely the 14th of April?"
"Yes!"
"Could I be so bold Lord Watkins as to enquire what your business was with the defendants that evening?"
"I will give you a reply to that question but my reply shall be vague as my ventures in business are not under scrutiny here, I first met Mr Ronald Kray a number of years ago at his Knightsbridge Casino Esmarelda's Barn, he was introduced to me by a mutual friend as a good business man in the area, More recently I have been informed that I have a terminal illness, the doctors have given me less than a year to make my peace, My son Peter has voiced a wish to remain by my side and act as my nurse, to do this he will have to give up his time that he spends in London on business, this was the reason Mr Kray and Mr Pine were dining with us that evening."
Van Hilary smiled at Lord Watkins statement before he replied sheepishly.
"Indeed your reply was vague sir; I would like to ask you one further question if I may?"
"I'm Waiting!" growled the Lord sternly.
"Can there be no mistake that the evening you dined with Mr Kray and Mr Pine was in fact the evening of the 14th of April this year?"
"Absolutely none! The 14th of April was Napoleon's birthday!"
"Napoleon as in Bonaparte?" Van-Hilary cautiously replied.
Lord Watkins smiled as if frustrated.
"No not in the Bonaparte, Napoleon was my horse; he was the first horse I owned."
"Agh your horse!" Van-Hilary quipped.
"YES 14th of April, never forget it; he was the finest damn horse I ever had!"
Van-Hilary smiled coyly and turned his head to the judge.
"On that note Milord, I have no further questions." he said warmly.

Prosecutor Jansen rose slowly from his chair, and deliberately took his time walking towards Lord Watkins.
"Good morning Lord Watkins, I like the rest of the court would like to give gratitude for your attendance here, it couldn't have been easy for you in your condition."
"Never mind my condition son, I have a duty to the crown, if I was lying on my deathbed in the final hours of life I would not malinger my charge to justice!"
David Jansen QC chief prosecutor for the Crown purposely hesitated as he decided what his next move should, here before him was a very well respected Lord, a man of considerable substance who's aristocratic bloodline reached back into the echelon of British society. A monument of British peerage whose reputation was unequivocal, a man who had rose from his sickbed to be here today to give evidence for the defence. Never in all of his years of giving service to the Bar had Jansen found himself in such a delicate situation.
After a short pause which seemed to last an age the prosecutor began his cross examination,
"lord Watkins what we have here is a very important dilemma, the crown claim that the two defendants were elsewhere on the 14th of April, I would like to ask you again for the clarity of the court, could there have been any mistake in your statement as to the correctness of the date the 14th of April this year?"
"Once again! Mr Kray and Mr Pine were dining at my home on the 14th of April this year, there is no mistake in that date, the times, or who were present on that evening," replied Lord Watkins very sternly but calmly,
"The crown says otherwise Sir" replied Jansen abruptly which raised the eyebrow of the judge,
"Did you hear me Sir, the crown state otherwise?" added Jansen after his first remark failed to get a reaction from the pokerfaced silent lord.
"You have heard my testimony!" The lord finally replied.
"Yes but your evidence has contradiction with the evidence of the Police, something here is amiss!"
Lord Watkins suddenly stiffened his posture; he pushed himself back into his chair using his arms against the witness box and raised his voice significantly.
"If you are insinuating something is amiss with my attestation then stop covering behind your hesitancy son and get it off your chest!"
Prosecutor Jansen gave a wry smile before answering.
"My insinuation is that someone is lying, and please sir refrain from calling me son, like yourself I have also given a life's service to the crown, my title is Sir or Mr Jansen, this is a gentleman's court where protocol and tradition claim weight over all manner of subtleties."

"My Lord!" Van-Hilary snapped to the judge as he suddenly rose from his chair in objection to the prosecutor's outburst.
"My lord this is a court of her majesties realm, I am a queens council barrister is it too much to ask that the proper courtesy's be followed." added Jansen.
Van-Hilary still standing, raised his hands in desperation.
"Can we not get back to the matter at hand?"
The judge looking quite agitated leaned over towards Lord Watkins.
"Could you please use the appropriate pleasantries Sir?"
Watkins smiled condescendingly at the judge and prosecutor but the previous outburst hardly made a dent in him.
Jansen after a brief pause where he shifted his silks once again began questioning the lord
"May I ask of your relationship with Mr Kray?"
"There is no relationship."
"But you say he was dining at your house, is it a usual occurrence to invite strangers into your home?"
"Mr Kray was an associate of my sons, he was well recommended as a businessman and he came to my home discuss a business matter, because of my illness it is much easier for me to conduct my business from home."
"May I ask what this business matter was?"
"No you may not!"
"My Lord may I remind you that you are under oath!"
"I am fully aware of the oath I took, but that does not entitle you to the question me on my business."
"I am fully entitled to ask questions regarding the defendants; they are on trial here for murder."
"That maybe so but I nor my business concerns are on trial here, the nature of this business is not a matter that can be shared in an open court, however even if it were I would decline to answer your question regardless."
"Once again sir, what was the nature of your business meeting that you claim was held on the 14th of April?"
"And once again I will tell you it is none of your business!" replied the Lord adamantly.
Prosecutor Jansen turned and pleaded to the judge.
"May I have your instruction to the witness to answer the question my lord?"
Before the judge could reply Van-Hilary jumped from his seat.
"My lord could I ask the prosecution as to what the relevance to this question would be?"
"The relevance here is to determine the truth" Jansen added
"Is it the crowns view that this meeting on the 14th of April did indeed take place?" said the judge only to bring a speedy response from the prosecutor.

"My lord I am midway through my cross examination, the crowns perception will be given in my summing up."
"I totally object to this line of questioning my lord, the witness's business concerns are not on trial here, I fail to see how the nature of what was discussed at this meeting has any bearing on this trial, many matters in business are confidential."
"I agree Mr Van-Hilary, I to fail to see the relevance of what was said at this meeting, the matter here is to explore the truthfulness and the accuracy that this meeting took place and on what date it took place." replied the judge to Jansen's obvious displeasure.
The prosecutor once again ruffled through his papers with his back to the witness, an awkward silence fell over the court that forced the judge to intervene.
"Mr Jansen have you finished your cross examination?"
"No my lord!" Jansen said turning around.
"Then the floor is yours sir!" The judge added.
"Lord Watkins, I have asked you on the accuracy of the date that this meeting took place and I have been refrained from asking you any further questions on the substance of this meeting so I would like to ask you a query regarding a question of character?"
"Are you aware of Mr Kray's reputation?" Jansen added.
"My lord this is outrageous!" Van-Hilary suddenly shouted.
"Have you or any of your family been threatened or approached by anyone regarding this trial?" Jansen added quickly.
"MR JANSEN!" the judge shouted.
"My lord what kind of questioning is this!" cried Van-Hilary.
"Mr Jansen you will cease immediately from this line of questioning."
"I am sorry my lord but I do not believe that this meeting between the defendants and Lord Watkins ever took place!"
Van-Hilary banged his hands down onto the table.
"I cannot believe what I am hearing here, my Lord you must instruct the jury."
The judge held up both his hands as if to hush silence from both QC's, council was then called over to the judge and in no uncertain terms they were told to act in a more responsible and applicable way. Mr Jansen was told to finish his cross examination but to tread very, very carefully as to what he was saying, if he was accusing that this meeting never took place then he was insinuating that Lord Watkins had with unknown persons conspired to pervert the course of justice and that he was in fact perjuring himself here today.
"One more time Lord Watkins, are you sure that this meeting took place on the evening of the 14th of April this year?"
"As from my previous replies I am certain!"

“What’s keeping Manny?” Charlie Kray jnr asked his bother Reg and Father as the three men sat opposite the Old bailey in the quill and barrister pub.
“It’s nearly seven o’clock.” he added looking at his wristwatch.
“He ain’t forgotten us has he Reg?” old Charlie added.
“Nah don’t be silly Dad he’ll be ere.” replied Reggie as he sipped again on his gin and tonic and Tony Lambrianou walked over with a fresh round of drinks.
“Do you want me to go over the court Reg, see where he is?” Tony asked just catching the last part of the conversation.
“Give it five minutes Tone, if he ain’t here then go and see what’s taking him.”
“Tony nodded as he lit up a cigarette.”
“He’s here now Reg!” Tony suddenly shouted as he saw the solicitor crossing the street.
“Alright Manny, we were getting worried.”
“Don’t worry about that Reg, I got some good news.” replied Manny Freedman as he took off his coat and sat down.
“Get me a coke will you Tony.” he asked before lighting up a cigarette from a packet of players that had been resting on the table.
“Well! What the fuck was all that about today Manny, I thought old man Watkins was gonna kick right off at one point?” asked Charlie jnr.
“Unbelievable wasn’t it, Van-Hilary couldn’t believe it, Jansen almost accused Watkins of conspiracy, if that makes the papers tomorrow then the judge will go mad.”
“What’s the good news then Manny?” Reggie suddenly interrupted.
“Right I do not want you to get your hopes up, but I think there is a very good chance that the case will be thrown out in the morning, the crowns case has totally fallen apart, that is why I am so bloody late, the judge called Jansen and Van-Hilary into his chambers, it seems that the judge is concerned at the prosecution’s evidence or should I say lack of evidence now that we have discredited most of their case.”
“Well what they got left Manny, everything they have said we have answered! Old Charlie added.
“Not just answered it Charlie, we’ve destroyed it, just look at their case now, Jackie Carter, the jury now know that he has been convicted of perjury, the judge will have to remind them of this, his testimony is utterly unreliable and cannot be relied on. Jeffery Samuel’s evidence now totally denied, LaSalle’s failure to reveal vital evidence to the defence mainly Fleckman’s statement saying he saw Brooker arguing with two black guys. We have also proved that Brooker was involved in criminal activities, taking money from prostitutes. We have proved that the suit, the suit they said was splattered with petrol had not even been made when the murder took place, and now we have Lord Watkins statement saying that Ronnie and Joe were two hundred miles away

on the night of the 14th, they have nothing left! For a judge to sum this lot up would be almost an acquittal anyway."
Later that evening Vallance Road was a house in cheerful anticipation, Violet Kray and her husband had already gone to bed when the clock struck ten o'clock. Downstairs in the living room now sat Reggie and Charlie sharing a bottle of wine.
"Manny seemed very confident tonight Charlie." Reggie sighed.
"Well its looks like it's all come together Reg, it's how we planned it."
"If Ron gets out tomorrow I think I may ask him if he wants to come out to Spain, make a nice break for him after all this."
"Be a nice break for all of us mate." Charlie replied.
"Have you spoken to Mario Chas, how are things going out there?"
"The clubs going well Reg, he called yesterday to ask how Ronnie was."
"What'd ya tell him?"
"I told him things are alright." replied Charlie opening his hands open in front of him.
"That's good, make sure we keep things sweet out there mate, and keep on top of it every day, that Mario's too much of a fucking playboy for my liking."
"He's all right Reg."
"They all are till they fuck things up!" replied Reg angrily.
"Don't let yourself worry about it Reg, I'm on top of it OK!"
"Besides that we got other, more important things to worry about." Charlie added.
"What the trial?" Reggie said.
"Nah other things."
"What fucking other things!" Reg snapped.
Charlie hesitated before replying, his face gave away the fact that it was a delicate topic
"Well what other things!" snapped Reggie?
"Well I'm worried about Ron, if things go well tomorrow then how long will it be till were in another trial."
"What ya trying to say Chas?"
"You know full fucking well what I'm saying Reg, Ronnie's not well! What he did here was way over the fucking top."
"He's fucking sitting in a cell tonight Chas, I don't like what I'm hearing here."
"It's a fucking miracle we're not all in there with him." Snapped Charlie.
"Ah leave it out Charlie!" sighed Reggie.
"No Reg while we're talking about, let's bring it out in the open, this Brooker situation has nearly destroyed us!"
"Ronnie did what he had to do, it's over with."
Charlie suddenly sighed out loud at his brothers care free attitude about this.

"Reggie there's a fucking dead copper, a copper, not a thief or a villain but a fucking copper, do you think the Yard are going to forget this?"
"What ya talking about Brooker was fucking dirty, he was bent as a nine Bob note Chas."
"He was still a fucking copper Reg!"
"FUCK HIM!" Reggie snapped back.
"Reg do ya know they closed the game down last night at the snooker hall, while you been locking yourself up in here and at the Bailey, the laws been leaning on everyone, we aren't getting no money Reg."
"Hold-up when did the game get closed and by who."
"The fucking law closed it Reg, three fucking CID went in there last night and fleeced the fucking gaff, took everyone's money, Billy Hayes got chinned by one of em, they told him until they nail someone for Brooker everyone's out of business."
"Fucking liberty!" Reggie replied.
"Why they doing this now, I thought things had got back to normal."
"I don't know Reg, maybe cos things aren't going to well for them with the trial, but the laws making themselves right fucking busy."
"And while we're talking, Tony got fucked off the other day by the William's, he walked into a pub over Islington, Dave Williams and about six fellows were in there."
"What'd ya mean he got fucked off, what happened there?"
"They never said anything, but Tony said there was an atmosphere, so he left."
"So what's the fucking matter with them?"
"It's over the pull they had when Brooker got it."
"They wanna mind their own fucking business Chas, I'll go down there tomorrow and see what they got to say for themselves, and anyway whys all this going on and no one's fucking telling me about it!"
"That's exactly why no-one's told you Reg, we don't need rows at the moment."
"Don't need any fucking rows Charlie!" Reggie snapped as he jumped from his chair.
"Everyone's out there trying to have a pop and we're turning a fucking blind eye!, what are we retired or something. I'll tell ya right now Charlie tomorrow night regardless what happens at the Bailey I'm going out on the rounds, and if any fucker so much as blinks in the wrong direction I'm gonna rip their fucking head off!" he added angrily.
"Reg calm down, it's not as bad as all that."
"Yeah well we're fucking see wont we!"
The next morning began with ominous undertones, when Johnny Walsh parked Reggie's Daimler outside their mothers house in Vallance Road the

rain was pouring down, Johnny ran from the car over to the front door which despite being 6.45 am was already half open in expectation of his arrival, the sound of thunder crashed above as he closed the door behind him.
"Is that you John?"
"Yeah it's me Mrs Kray" Johnny replied as walked down the hall and into the kitchen where Violet Kray was busy making sandwiches.
"I've just made some tea Johnny, do you mind pouring yourself a cup love."
"No problem Mrs Kray." replied John as he sat down.
"Terrible morning Mrs Kray, it's been raining all night, you'd think it was the middle of winter not the middle of summer."
"I know John I been up most the night, Reggie didn't go to sleep till the early hours."
"Where's he now is everything ok?"
"He's having a wash, I found him with three empty bottles of wine sprawled out on the sofa half five this morning, front room looked like a bomb had hit it." she replied jokingly.
"Three bottles of wine, oh don't Mrs Kray, I know what kind of mood he'll be in today then." Johnny said smiling.
"He was like a bear with a sore head when I woke him up."
"Who was like a bear with a sore head?" Charlie Kray snr suddenly said as he entered the room overhearing the last sentence of the conversation.
"Alright John!" he added tapping Johnny on the shoulder.
"Make us a cup of tea will ya love."
"There's a fresh pot I just made on the side."
"Well pour me a cup will ya I'm doing my tie up."
"Pour it yourself, can't you see I'm busy." Violet snapped abruptly back.
"Fucking good init Johnny, first thing in the morning can't even get my wife to give me a cup of tea."
"I'll get it for ya Mr Kray." Johnny replied before fetching it over for him.
Charlie Kray lit up a cigarette and sipped on his hot tea, Johnny Walsh noticed the look that Charlie was giving his wife as he dragged on his fag, it was an angry look that Johnny had seen countless times on the face of Ronnie just before Ronnie was about to have an argument, it was a trait that ran in all the males of the Kray family. It began with an intense stare; followed by silence, anyone unlucky enough to be around the Kray's while they was in this state of concentration could feel the uneasiness about the atmosphere. Charlie's eyebrows hardened and his face grimaced as the look he was giving his wife turned to a glare.
"Why you trying to embarrass me in front of guest Vi?"
"Oh please Charlie Kray, don't start your silliness with me today, I've been up half the night, just leave me alone will you, all I'm doing is making sandwiches for today."

“What and can’t pour me a cup of tea.”
“Charlie please I have more important things on my mind.”
“Fucking women!” Charlie mouthed quietly in the direction of Johnny before taking another drag on his fag.
“I’ll be in car Mrs Kray.” Johnny said as he got up suddenly but politely excusing himself.
“Don’t go outside love, its okay don’t let old moaner scare you off Johnny.”
“No its okay Mrs Kray.”
“No don’t be silly Johnny it’s pouring out, wait in the front room if you like, it’s nice and cosy in there, you can put the telly on if you like.”
“Alright Mrs Kray.” Johnny replied as he left the room.
Johnny Walsh flicked on the telly and threw himself down in front of it, after a brief look over his shoulder he said quietly to himself.
“Jesus doesn’t anyone in this family ever stop fucking arguing.”
Outside the Old Bailey courts Tony Lambrianou and a few of the Firm rushed over to the car as Johnny Walsh pulled the Daimler up onto the kerb, the rain was still pouring down yet it never deterred the usual press from running over and start snapping away with their cameras.
Reggie jumped out first and pushed two of the photographers out of the way so he could open the back door to let his Mum out.
After a brief struggle with an umbrella violet Kray helped by her husband pulled herself from the car, accompanied by her husband and two sons Tony Lambrianou and a few of the Firm they were ushered quickly into the main doors of the old bailey courthouse.
The first face Reggie noticed when inside was that of detective Richard LaSalle, he was standing by a conference room with seven other senior Scotland Yard detectives
“LaSalle!” Reggie nudged his brother Charlie.
“Don’t look too fucking pleased.” Tony Lambrianou commented on as he noticed as well.
LaSalle dragging on a large cigar was standing with his back against the wall, he was an old fashioned copper, nothing like the young up and coming fancy boys that were rising up fast through the ranks. LaSalle was a tough man, he stood over six foot tall and his rugged appearance made him look like one of the Irish Dockers that used to work down in the East End, just off Watney street.
He sneered hatefully across the room at Reg, Reggie noticing the look that LaSalle was giving him suddenly opened up his arms as if inviting LaSalle to come over.
“YEAH! YOU GOT SOMETHING YOU WANNA SAY!” Reggie shouted challengingly.

LaSalle's face just sneered more at Reggie,s remark while his Police comrades acted like peacocks sticking their chests out as if rising to the challenge that Reg had just thrown out to them.
"WHAT YOU SILENT NOW, LETS HAVE SOME OF YA VERBALS C'MON!" Reggie added as he started, only for Lambrianou to stop him to walk over towards the police.
"Reggie, leave it, we can't win here mate." Tony said.
Hearing all the commotion Manny Freedman who had been standing in a corner came rushing over to Reggie.
"Reggie! Reggie!" Manny cried jumping in between Tony and Reg.
"Reggie come over here." he added sincerely as he pulled Reggie's arm.
Reg turned with the solicitor and noticed the look on the old Jewish man's face.
"You've done it ain't ya, we've won in we?" Reg sighed as he was being led away.
"Come over here Reg, come on, we've beat them, come on don't get involved with them"
"What they gonna throw the case out." Reggie sighed in anticipation as he suddenly just stopped as the next moment nothing else in the world mattered apart from what the solicitors next few words were going to be.
"The judge is going to order the jury to return an acquittal."
Reggie's face broke into a smile from ear to ear as he grabbed Manny's cheeks with both his hands and planted a big kiss on his forehead.
"YES!" he shouted.
"Mum! Mum we done it! Their throwing the case out Ronnie's coming home!"
"Oh thank god!" Violet mouthed as she grabbed a hold of her son and sobbed, Tony and Charlie jnr did also and grabbed hold of Reg.
After a short moment where everyone congratulated each other Reggie broke free and locked eyes with detective LaSalle who while all the celebrating had been going was standing by silently seething at what he was looking at.
"Fuck ya!" Reggie mouthed mockingly at him.
"I'll have ya, one day I'll fucking have ya!" LaSalle replied quietly.

Not Guilty Your Honour
Chapter six
'Business & Bullets'

Two weeks passed since Ronnie Kray and Joey Pine walked out of the Old Bailey courts as free men. The national press had had a field day with the verdict; Ronnie's face had been plastered across every front page of the national papers. The daily express had a full page picture of Ronnie with the caption *'The Colonel'* as the headline and underneath it had the words *'Above the Law'*. Ronnie absolutely loved it; he must have brought over a hundred copies and ordered everyone to put them up in all the pubs, Clubs, restaurants and cafes that the Firm frequented. He even had one of the Firm put one up on a placard outside the New Scotland Yard headquarters. The trial had been a dreadful embarrassment for the Law. For the last two weeks not a day had passed when a national paper didn't write something about the trial. Even the Commissioner of the Metropolitan Police force was interviewed where he vowed to put an end to all gang related crimes. Politicians made statements suggesting that Britain like the USA should introduce a racketeering offence, RICO as it's called to clamp down on the London gangs. Ronnie however loved all this attention; he woke everyday eager to read what was being said about him in the papers. Reg on the other hand was quietly seething at all of the attention.

"Another fucking article Ron!" Reg mouthed with disdain as he walked into Ronnie's bedroom.

"What's it say?" Ronnie replied picking up the paper from where Reg had thrown it on the bed.

"Just another fucking MP throwing in his two penith again."

Ronnie quickly read the article and obviously found it exciting.

"Don't know why you're smiling bruv, we're getting more publicity than the poxy Beatles." Reg added as he unbuttoned his waist coat and sat himself down in a chair.

"What's all this?" Reggie suddenly asked as he noticed that the room was full of new suits hanging all around the walls.

"Decosta brought them round this morning Reg."

"What you going fucking mad Ron, how many's here?" added Reggie as he counted at least ten new suits.

"Didn't pay for them, well not directly anyway."

"What he give em to ya, well where's mine?"

"I gave him a grand last week Reg, you know as a sign of my appreciation for speaking for us at the trial."

"You shouldn't have done that Ron, he's had plenty of business from us, and anyway where did you get a grand from, you was blagging me for a few quid last week."

"Well I ain't gave it to him yet Reg, do you remember the bookie, Davies who owed us a few quid?"

"Yeah twelve hundred quid."

"Well I told him that if he pays up early I'll make it a round grand, told him to give it to Decosta, don't mind do ya Reg?"

"Fucking hell, that's marvellous Ron, so you get a dozen new suits I lose six hundred quid and get fuck all."

"Well take a couple Reg, there fit you."

"What wear your suits?"

"There nice suits Reg look at the cut." Ronnie added as he pulled on a jacket.

"One of us walking down the road looking like Al Capone is enough Ron."

Ronnie laughed loudly at his brother's joke.

"What's the matter with my suits, I thought you liked the cut off them." Ronnie added.
Reggie chuckled.
"Like the cut of your suits, you walk down the road like fucking James Cagney; you look like you just fell out of one of those old black and white gangster films."
"NAH." Ronnie smiled as being compared to Cagney gave him a thrill.
"Yeah seriously Ron, looking at you walking down the road you'd think it was 1920's Chicago, someone should tell ya mate, we're nearly in the seventies now, fashions changing."
Ronnie smiled again at Reggie's remark and looked himself up and down in the mirror admiring the suit.
"Fuck fashion!" he joked.
"I think I look smashing." he added proudly.
To be a passenger in a car when Reggie Kray was behind the steering wheel was an experience that you did not want to be repeated. Ronnie and Johnny Walsh sat in the back while Tony Lambrianou sat nervously in the front next to Reg.
"JESUS! REG." Tony screamed as Reggie mounted the pavement while doing a right turn.
"FASTER!" Ronnie shouted out from the back jokingly as he crashed into Johnny.
"Leave off Ron!" Tony pleaded.
Reggie now laughing at Tony's reaction decided to wind him up even more, he pushed the accelerator down making the Daimler drop down a gear and race up the road.
"REG!" Tony shouted as he extended his legs and pushed himself back in his seat. The next turning Reg once again hit the kerb, the car seemed to buckle.
"You've done the wheel Reg." Ronnie laughed.
Reggie kicked the accelerator down again, the car's V8 engine roared as it raced away.
"THAT'S IT! STOP THE FUCKING CAR!" Tony screamed.
Ronnie in the back was now in hysterics; he leapt forward and playfully grabbed Tony around the shoulders "You'll never make it alive!" Ronnie shouted.
Outside Quaglino's restaurant there was the usual crowd gathered waiting to see if they could get admittance, the crowd all turned to see the Daimler racing up the road towards them. Ronnie screamed with joy as the car slammed to a halt crashing two of its wheels on the kerb outside the restaurant making most of the crowd jump out of the way. Tony Lambrianou jumped from the car in a flash followed by Johnny Walsh, and the laughing Ronnie. Reggie as if totally oblivious to the spectacle just got out of the car calm as you like straightening

his tie then threw the car keys casually at one of the restaurants doorman in a manner that said *'now park the fucking car.'*
The four men walked into the building without a second glance to the other doorman who in turn acknowledged them and opened the doors for them.
Once inside Johnny led Ron and Reg over to their usual table where they found Eddie Brenner, Billy and George Hayes, Slice'em Sid and Sammy Carpenter already sitting down. Johnny Walsh pulled out a chair for Ronnie and let him sit down, Reg sat down next to him as Eddie Brenner poured them both a glass of Scotch.
Tony Lambrianou playfully squeezed Brenner's arm as he sat down next to him
"Give me that bottle" he sighed.
"Reg been driving again?" Brenner joked which made everyone laugh. Tony in turn didn't wait for a glass he just took a large swig straight from the bottle.
"I tell ya, if we ever fight the Nazi's again we should threaten them with Reg." he added as he took another swig.
"How long you been here?" Ronnie grimaced to the Firm as the whiskey burned his throat.
"Not long Ron." George replied.
"Is that music fella here yet?" added Reg.
"He's over the bar."
"Shall I go get him Ron?" Johnny Walsh added from his chair slightly behind Ronnie.
"Yeah go and get him John."
Don Harding, Jewish, mid-thirties was commonly known as the enforcer amongst the music industry, he was a tough guy in person and a tough guy to negotiate with, yet all the acts under his management had lucrative recording contracts. One of the stories about Don was how he dangled a Record label executive out of a fifth floor window and told him he would let go unless the exec signed one of his acts to his label. Don was a very successful businessman; his company had made fortunes in the music world. Ronnie Kray since hearing that Don Harding had wished a meeting with him had done his homework on Don. It surprised Ronnie a little bit as too why this successful music mogul was now reaching out to him. Whatever the reason was Ronnie was going to be at his most charming as this was an industry that he very much wanted to be a part off.
Don Harding sat down at the table as the rest of the Firm excused themselves leaving only Ronnie and Reg remaining,
"Hello Don, I'm Ron and this is Reg, we've heard a lot about you," Ronnie said,
"Likewise Ron," Don smiled as he shook the man's hand,
"Do you want a drink?" Reggie asked.

“I’ll have whatever you’re having.” replied Don trying not be a burden.
As Reggie poured the drink Ronnie as usual wasted no time in getting down to business.
“What can we do for you then Don?”
Don took a large gulp of whiskey before he answered.
“I got this problem, an ex-partner of mine, the piece of shit is really costing me a few quid, I’ve tried everything to get this fuck out of my life but he’s like the plague he just won’t go away.”
“You say he’s costing you a few quid, well how many?” Reg added.
“A lot of money Reg.” Replied Don.
“Tell us more Don, it sounds to me like we can solve this problem for you very easily but I want to hear what we are getting ourselves involved here.” Ronnie asked.
“Right ‘I’ll start at the beginning, me and this fuck were partners on this band, the bands red hot at the moment. They’ve just had a number two over here, and the American’s are crying out for them over there. Everything was going along just fine before this fucking idiot got in their ears. See with me when I manage a rock act I only give them enough money to get them by, sure I get them all the clothes, the cars, the birds, but I won’t spoil the fuckers. We’re talking mostly about young working class kids here, if say the record labels gave me two hundred grand to sign them then I would be a fucking fool to give it to the act.
Within a fucking month most of them would be shooting up so much junk, they’d be fucking useless, the game is to treat them well but don’t spoil them, keep them hungry and ambitious for success.
“Yeah that makes sense.” Ronnie interrupted.
“This works well for me Ron, it’s a proven and successful method, but like I say this guy who brought the band to me and was my partner started telling them all about how much money I was getting, everything, this fucking idiot told them the lot, things came to a head and the band started asking me questions. To cut a long story short this ex-partner of mine has pulled the band away from me and is telling them to just go with him. There young kids and they don’t know what to do, but all these arguments are damaging them, their hot NOW. They need to be out there doing the business but this idiot has them sitting around doing fuck all. If they hang about doing nothing any longer then there gonna lose their chance.
“And this band is that important to you Don, you know what you’re asking us to do here?”
“Number one it’s the fucking principle, I pull this guy into the industry and he treats me like a fucking jerk-off and secondly this band are worth fortunes. At the moment I have a two hundred grand deal sitting on my table from the Americans, it’s been sitting there for a fucking week doing nothing cos I can’t

get a hold of these fucking guys. And not to mention my reputation, if I let this fuck get away with this then I'll have every fucker having big ideas. So sure Ron, I know what's needed here and it's very important to get it done."
"Two hundred grand's a lot of money, how much of that are you willing to split to get this thing done?" Reggie interrupted.
"A quarter was a figure I had in mind Reg."
"Fifty-fifty sounds better Don." Reggie replied.
"A hundred grand Reg! I could get the British army for that Reg." Harding pleaded
Ronnie suddenly waived his hand in a motion to stop what was being discussed.
"Hold on a minute Reg." he firmly said.
"I've heard a lot of stories about you Don, and let's just say that from what I have heard you don't seem the kind of man that would tolerate this kind of behaviour, what's different with this situation."
Don raised his glass up to Ron before answering.
"Your right Ron, under normal circumstances I would have got this guy in a room with no witnesses and laid down the law to him but this time I let my emotions get the better of me, when I heard what he had been saying to the band I just couldn't believe the set of balls on this guy, I flew down the studios and slapped him around, the law got called and dragged me out of the studio."
"They didn't nick ya?" Reggie added.
"Nah they know of me Reg, it was just a fucking silly assault thing, I just got a slapped wrist and told not to be so fucking daft."
"If the Laws involved Don, then it makes things difficult mate."
"Yes for me Ron, but let's say he should get run over while I'm in America, well what can the law have on me for that?"
Ronnie took a large sip of his Whiskey before leaning closer to Don.
"The moneys a nice offer Don but this fucking slag could be smoking in hell by tomorrow if we could work out a better deal."
"Ron fifty grand's a lot of money."
"NO I'm not talking about the money Don, look we'll do this for ya, for nothing! But you got a new partner."
Don Harding leaned away from Ronnie and sighed loudly but not in a threatening way
"Ron I don't need a partner, in all due respect I'm not about to give away half of all my companies over just one of my acts."
"NO! NO! NO! You misunderstand me Don." Ronnie interrupted by placing his hand on his arm "No, we'll only be your partners on this band, fifty-fifty between you and us on everything that this band doe, now and in the future.

Now that sounds like a fair deal to me Don, after all mate you haven't come here today mate to walk away without an arrangement have you?"
Don Harding hesitated for a moment as he lit up a cigar, once the cigar was lit he held out his hand.
"Fifty-fifty!" he said as he shook Ron then Reg's hand.
"Just do a good job Ron."
"Don't worry about that Don; let's have a toast to our new partnership."
When Don Harding left the rest of the Firm returned to the table.
"Ronnie looks happy." Tony nudged Reggie.
"Ronnie's the new manager of a rock band!" Reggie loudly said.
"Well done Ron." Eddie Brenner added.
"A fucking rock band!" Slice'em Sid laughed " You'll have to change your style Ron, start wearing them flares and flowery shirts, maybe even grow ya barnet long." he added jokingly.
"FUCK OFF....!" Ronnie added smiling as noticed out of the corner of his eye David Polson-Smyth the flamboyant aristocrat walking over to the table.
"My sincerest greetings gentlemen." David uttered as he shook Ronnie's hand.
"Grab a chair David." Ronnie added only for him to notice the slight grimace on his brother Reg's face.
"Fucking ponce." Reggie uttered into Tony Lambrianou's ear obviously aiming his remark at the aristocrat.
"So is it onto the Astor Tonight Ron?" David blurted out.
"Maybe David, ain't made our minds up yet mate." replied Ronnie.
"Cabaret should be good tonight; I've heard on the secret that they have a big surprise for tonight."
"Not fucking LULU again is it?" Eddie Brenner said.
"OH Christ I hope not" Polson-Smyth replied laughing.
Suddenly the atmosphere was interrupted by the sound of loud laughter coming from a table over the far side of the room; Tony Lambrianou was the first to recognise one of the men seated in a group of ten.
"Is that Billy Williams?" he asked angrily to Eddie Brenner.
"Yeah, Billy and his brother Dave." Brenner replied.
"That's fucking nice, why didn't ya tell me they were here?"
"I don't know Tone, what's the fucking big deal?"
"What they doing here anyway?" Reggie suddenly added.
"Same thing as us mate, having something to eat and drink." Brenner replied.
"But why here? They fucking know this is our place." added Reggie.
"Fuck knows Reg." Brenner replied now getting pissed off.
The conversation was suddenly interrupted by Ronnie and David Polson-Smyth both getting to their feet.
"Reg you alright?" Ronnie asked looking over at the William's.

"Yeah everything's good Ron."
"You look like you're getting wound up by that lot over there." added Ronnie.
"Nah fuck them! I'm alright, where ya going anyway?"
"That actor Roger Moore, the Saint has just walked in, me and David are going over to the bar to have a drink with him, coming?"
"Alright Ron, be over in a minute."
Ronnie downed what was left of his glass of scotch, grabbed a packet of players that were on the table, put them in his pocket and then tapping Reggie on the arm walked off with David in the direction of the bar. Reggie watched his brother walk off before turning back towards Tony.
"You ain't said nothing to Ron about that time you felt funny over in Williams's manor have you Tone?"
"Nah! You told me not to tell him, we gonna go over there and give em a pull?" Tony replied sternly and nodding over in the direction of the Williams table.
Reggie sighed loudly as he dragged on his fag.
"It won't be a fucking pull with Ron here will it?"
"So Ron knows fuck all about all the things they been saying about us?"
"Don't be fucking stupid Tone, would he be standing by the bar if he knew."
Tony gave a small laugh before he replied "No he'd over there throwing the fucking table up in the air, this whole fucking place would be off."
"They're out celebrating Reg." Sammy carpenter suddenly added.
"What!" Reggie snapped.
"They had a right touch yesterday Reg, it was them who done the wages snatch down in Bow, heard they walked away with seventy grand."
"Well what we gonna do Reg, we gonna go over and say something to em?" Tony asked.
Reggie once again took a large drag on his cigarette as he looked around the restaurant.
"I don't know, there's about two hundred fucking witnesses in here, can't just go over there and have a fucking row can we?"
"They'll be tooled up Reg." Eddie Brenner added.
"What shooters?" replied Reg.
"Million percent mate; they've always got a tool on em."
"You carrying Eddie?"
"Yeah I got a 38 on me Reg." Eddie whispered back.
"Well what we doing Reg?" Tony again asked.
"Dunno let me think, don't wanna turn this place into the fucking OK Corral." Reggie said as again he dragged hard on his fag. "Right listen; keep your eye on em Tony, when one of them goes into the karzee let me know."
"Done!" Tony replied abruptly.
"Eddie you me and Tony will follow him in alright."

“We gonna clump him?”
“That depends on him don’t it, but I’m gonna give him a right fucking pull.”
Reggie and the Firm waited for about twenty minutes before Dave Williams, the younger brother and another one of his gang got up to go to the toilet. Reggie, Tony and Eddie jumped from their chairs and followed the two men in; Reg opened the door and saw the two men standing up at the urinals with their backs towards him. As Dave Williams looked over his shoulder to see who was there, Reg ran across and struck him with a left hook, Williams’s head banged against the wall forcing his nose to bleed as Reggie hit him again with a hook to the ribs. Eddie Brenner grabbed the other man and threw him hard onto the floor
“I’ve heard you got a fucking problem with us!” Reggie shouted as he pushed Dave Williams’s head into the wall.
“Williams quick as a flash elbowed Reggie’s arm and broke away from him.
“Yeah that’s fucking right! Jump me from behind; what ya wanna fucking do something about it then?”
“I’m not behind you now cunt!” Reg snapped back at him.
Just as the two men began to square up to each other for a fight, the toilet door swung open and Billy Williams followed by the rest of his gang pushed their way in, once Billy saw what was going on he pulled out a gun from his waistband.
“Leave my fucking brother alone!” he snarled as he pointed the gun at reg.
Eddie Brenner meanwhile had reached for his own gun and pointed it at Billy Williams.
“PUT THE FUCKING TOOL AWAY!” he shouted at Williams.
Reg turned to Brenner.
“Point it at his head.” he shouted as he pointed at Billy’s brother Dave.
“GET THAT FUCKING GUN AWAY FROM MY BROTHER, I FUCKING SWEAR Reg I’L TAKE YA FUCKING HEAD OFF!” shouted Billy Williams after seeing Brenner point the gun at his brother.
As Billy Williams finished shouting the toilet door suddenly slammed open, where George and Billy Hayes, Slice’em Sid and Sammy Carpenter ran into the room, the four men then uneasily pushed themselves past the Williams gang and walked over to reg.
“Now were even.” Reggie said confidently.
“What you waiting for Williams! C’mon, you been saying things about us, and what you’re gonna do when you see one of us, well theirs a Kray in front of you now cunt!” added Reggie now seething with anger.
Billy Williams looked around, you could sense him thinking about the situation, everyone looked edgy, the atmosphere was on a knife edge, one wrong move and this was going to explode into bloodbath.
“So what now Reg, who’s gonna make the next move!”

“It is how it is.” Reggie replied.
“Then I’ll make the move, I’ll stand down, let my brother over here and we’re walk away, lets save this for another time.”
“What’s wrong with right now, you’re a big fucking man, got a big pair of fucking balls, big fucking mouth, c’mon lets fucking do it now!”
“NO Reg another day, we’re walking out, Dave come over here!” replied Billy as he lowered his gun.
Reggie nodded to Eddie Brenner to relax as Dave Williams walked over to his brother.
“Any fucking day you want Williams.” Reggie snarled.
“Watch ya back.” Williams smiled as he walked out towards the door backwards.
“Don’t worry about my fucking back.” growled Reggie.
Dave Williams wiped the blood from his noose and spat violently on the floor as he left with his brother.
“Out now, Ronnie’s outside on his own.” Reg snapped as the door shut.
The Williams gang walked back over to their table and gathered their belongings, as Reg and the rest of the Firm walked over to the bar and surrounded Ron.
Reg never once took his eyes off the Williams’s as they shuffled their way past the busy bar and walked out of the restaurant.
“Has something just gone on?” Ron suddenly asked Reg as he noticed the sudden change in atmosphere. Reg just looked away still looking at the door where the Williams’s had just left.
“WHATS JUST FUCKING HAPPENED!” Ronnie demanded as he violently grabbed and tugged Eddie Brenner’s arm.
“We just nearly had off with the Williams’s Ron.” Eddie replied.
“WHAT!”
“Yeah nearly went right fucking off, shooters and everything.”
“WHAT YOU FUCKING TALKING ABOUT SHOOTERS, WHERE ARE THEY NOW?”
“They just left Ron.” Tony added.
Ron pushed Eddie Brenner right out the way, so violently that Eddie fell against the bar knocking a few guests over as well.
“RON LEAVE IT!” Reg shouted as he tried to stop his brother, Ron however was having none of it he pulled his arm away and flew off towards the door, Reg and Johnny Walsh gave chase behind him.
“Get out the fucking way!” Ronnie shouted at two doormen as he pushed everyone to one side and marched into the night’s air.
Billy Williams sat in the passenger seat of the car driven by his brother Dave, as the car drove past the entrance to Quaglino’s he looked out the window. He

saw standing on the top of the stairs Ronnie Kray looking back at him; he noticed the hate in the face of Ron.
Billy smiled as the car drove past.
"It's begun now Dave." he sighed to his brother.
Ronnie Kray carried the foul mood he was in onto the Astor club that evening, he had been seething all night at the front that the Williams's had showed earlier. Johnny Walsh had managed to quietly phone up Charlie Kray from Quaglino's and explain to him about what had happened , he told Charlie that Ron was in a terrible mood and that Reg had been drinking very heavily, and that Ronnie wanted everyone to go onto the Astor. Charlie told Johnny that he would meet them down the Astor later and that Johnny should try to keep the twins out of any more situations.
The Astor club just off Berkley Square in London's Mayfair was a very high class joint; every major London Firm frequented it. The Astor was also on the Kray's weekly pensions list although it was shared with the Ryan family from North London and Joey Pine. The arrangement between the Kray's, Pine and the Ryan's worked well as the combined weight of the families stopped any other Firm from approaching the club for protection.
"Johnny just make sure you keep everyone away from the twins, especially Ron OK, I'll be down before midnight." Charlie had said anxiously as he put the phone down worried that his brothers in this mood were an odds on bet to hurt someone.
As they walked up to the door Johnny could see that the Astor club was packed to the rafters, standing outside Johnny saw Tommy and Alex Jones out of Walthamstow, the Jones brothers were both members of the Firm but as Ronnie would call them they were Firm heavies. Both fierce fighting men who stayed close to Ronnie, and Ronnie alone. Johnny quickly realised that Ron must have called them from the restaurant to check out the club if any of the Williams's Firm was here. Johnny felt a little relieved as he knew that for Ronnie to do this then at least he was thinking straight through his angered mood. But nevertheless he knew that both the Jones brothers would be holding guns on them.
"Alright Ron, there not here mate, the Maltese are here though, and little Jock and mad Ronnie's in there as well." whispered Tommy Jones as Ron and Reg walked in the entrance.
Johnny Walsh heard the conversation between Ron and Tommy and was pleased that none of the Williams's Firm were here, he knew full well that if they was then there would be a bloodbath, but the mention of little Jock and mad Ronnie made him silently curse. Mad Ronnie a pest at the best of times and was the last person that Johnny would want around him now. If anyone could wind Ronnie up, it was him! He was a real dangerous fucker with strong ties to a major South London Firm. Ron and Reg couldn't stand him but he

was tolerated because of the Firm that he was with. But Johnny Walsh knew that tonight Ron or Reg would not be tolerating anyone.
Ron, Reg, Eddie Brenner, Tony Lambrianou, Sammy Carpenter, Slice'em Sid, George and Billy Hayes and now Tommy and Alex Jones were politely escorted down to their usual table. Johnny Walsh stood slightly back looking around to see if he could spot any potential problems.
As the Firm sat down numerous people shouted over their greetings towards the twins, Johnny out of the corner of his eye spotted standing at the bar mad Ronnie Fromer and little Jock. Mad Ron all six feet four of him had his shirt unbuttoned half way down his chest and was holding a bottle of champagne in one hand, he was jumping around and messing about and obviously making a nuisance of himself to anyone who was unfortunately enough to be near him. Johnny thought it best that he would walk over to mad Ronnie as Ron and Reg were ordering there drinks.
"Hey Johnny Walsh!" mad Ronnie cried as he saw Johnny.
"Johnny Walsh from the Elephant, South London boy!" he added drunkenly as the arm that was not carrying champagne and gave him a hug.
"Hello Ronnie enjoying yourself mate?"
"Fucking right! That's what life's all about mate, getting pissed around all these cunts!"
"Alright Ronnie, but don't cause any agro in here will ya." Johnny replied reminding him silently that this place was under the Kray's protection.
"WHAT! You cheeky little fucker, I ain't gonna cause no grief." Mad Ronnie said squeezing Johnny's face.
"Anyway where's the Colonel?" he added loudly.
Johnny Walsh motioned with his hand for Ronnie to keep his voice down.
"Him and Reg are over there Ron, but do yourself a favour and leave them alone will ya, Ronnie's not in the best of moods and their just having a quiet drink."
"Ronnie's in a mood, what's the matter did he forget to take his fucking funny pills, fuck it!, I'll cheer him up, we're swap asylum stories." he added arrogantly as he began to walk towards the table.
"Ronnie I told ya, leave them alone!" Johnny said now more assertive as he pulled the man's arm. Mad Ronnie Fromer suddenly stopped dead in his tracks and violently moved his arm away from Johnny Walsh's clinch.
"What do you fucking mean, your telling me, don't get fucking saucy with me John!" he shouted in a threatening way as he waved his finger in the face of Walsh.
"For fucks sake don't start Ron." Walsh mouthed back at him.
"Don't fucking start, you wanna mind ya fucking manners Walsh, just cos you hang out with that lot don't fucking impress me, I remember you, you little runt when you was a fresh arsed boy running round the gyms in Bermondsey,

you wanna have a fucking second think before you get fucking brave with me."
"It's not like that Ron; I just don't want any incidents."
"Yeah, well ya fucking causing one now ain't ya! Who'd ya think you fucking are? You're nothing but their fucking errand boy anyway, ay! What the fuck you done, where the fuck you been, I got respect for them but your just a little cunt. A little mug errand boy tying up his masters shoe laces or wiping his fucking arse….. I don't wanna cause a scene in here but I'm fucking telling you, if you don't fuck off away from me now I'm gonna smash this bottle right over ya fucking head!"
Any other night Johnny Walsh would have had no other option other to punch Ronnie Fromer right on the chin for what he had just said. But with the mood that the twins were in tonight he knew that if him and Ronnie Fromer started fighting then the first person to run over would be Ronnie Kray and he would pull a trigger no matter who was about.
Johnny put up his hands defensively.
"You're right Ronnie, I was a bit out of order mate, I tell ya what, you and Jock go over to the corner bar and have a drink on me, I'll tell the twins you're here and I'm sure when they've finished there meet there come over and say hello."
Mad Ronnie Fromer didn't get his nickname for being a tolerant person, he listened to what Johnny Walsh had just said to him and remained silent, his mad eyes bore a hole into Johnny's face with an evil stare.
"Can't be fairer than that Ron." added Johnny.
Little Jock who had been silent during the argument tugged gently on mad Ronnie's arm
"That's alright Ron, come on were go over to the corner bar mate."
Johnny Walsh smiled at both men.
"I'll see ya both in a minute." he added with a wink.
Mad Ronnie stood still for a moment as Walsh walked away.
"Flash little cunt!" he said to Jock.
"Leave it out Ron, we don't want any agro with the twins mate." little Jock replied
"FUCK EM!, words out there on the fucking slide anyway"
Johnny walked over to the table and caught the eye of Tony Lambrianou who in turn got up and stood next to him
"What's up john?"
"We got a fucking problem tone, I just nearly had a row with Fromer, he's over there pissed as a fart shouting out where's the fucking colonel, we gotta get him out of here tone before winds the twins up mate"
"Fuck me john, of all the fucking nights to have that fucking loon performing"

"Tone if he comes over to this table performing, the mood these two are in, well anything could happen"
"Fromer will kick right off john, the mans a fucking psychopath"
"Tony what are the options mate, Ronnie and Reg are sitting just begging for someone to come over and wind them up, Jones has already slipped Ronnie a piece, he's got it in his fucking pocket, I'm telling ya tone if Fromer walks over here drunk and starts calling Ronnie the colonel and cheer up and all that bollocks then Ronnie will shoot him straight in the head, we'll all be back at the bailey before we have time for a fucking shit"
Tony lit up a fag and took a very large drag
"Ah this is gonna be fucking murder" he sighed frustrated as he knew full what a fucking hand full Fromer was going to be.
"Where's Fromer now john"
"I got him over at the corner bar standing next to the fire exit"
"That's good thinking john, at least we ain't got too far to get him out, right me you Eddie, Billy and George will do it alright"
"we're be plenty mate, little Jock wont perform" John added
"Maybe we should tell Reg what we're doing here john"
"Nah don't be fucking mad tone, Reg can hardly stand up mate"
"Yeah but theirs consequences here mate, his Firm ain't gonna be too happy about this"
"FUCK THEM TONE!, let the twins sort it out when everyone's sober, anyway his Firm know what a fucking pest he can be when he's pissed"
"This is your decision then john; I don't want the twins on my case over this"
"It's down to me tone!"
"That's good enough for me, let's do it!"
Tony Lambrianou walked over to Eddie Brenner and whispered in his ear
"We got a problem ED, get Billy and George away from the table without the twins noticing will ya."
Eddie motioned with a nod of his head to Billy and George Hayes and the three men stood up.
"Oi where you going?" Ronnie snapped as he noticed them all getting up
"Going over to the bar Ron, get a proper fucking drink, only be over there mate and we won't be long alright."
"Well don't fucking disappear alright."
"See ya in a minute."
Tony pulled the three men away.
"Right Ronnie Formers over there making a right nuisance of himself, we got a get him out of here now."
Eddie Brenner laughed at what he heard.
"Just like that Tone" he said sarcastically.

“How do ya wanna do this mate, he’s gonna make a right fucking scene.” Billy Hayes asked.
“The direct approach sounds best to me, were just walk over pick him up and sling him out the fire exit.”
“And what we gonna do once he’s in the fucking fire exit?”
“We’ll tell him to fuck off.” Tony replied.
“Tone you know as well as me mate were gonna have to give him a fucking hiding, he ain’t going nowhere quietly.”
“If he’s gotta have an hiding then that’s what we’re fucking give him, now c’mon lets fucking do this, I wanna get back to my fucking drink.”
Moments later Tony, Johnny, Billy, George and Eddie walked over to Fromer and little Jock, mad Ronnie noticed the body language on the men walking towards him and immediately put up his guard. Tony noticing Fromer stiffening greeted him with a smile and held out his hand.
“Hello Ronnie.” Tony smiled.
Fromer hesitantly reached out to shake Tony’s hand. As soon as their hands touched Eddie Brenner and Billy Hayes flung their arms around him, seconds later mad Ronnie Fromer and little Jock were in the fire exit hall.
“Get ya fucking hands off me.” Ronnie shouted as he broke free.
“We don’t want no agro in here tonight Ron.” Eddie Brenner shouted using all of six feet five eighteen stone body to sound authoritative.
“Yeah well ya fucking got it.” Fromer shouted back as he pulled of his jacket.
“NOW FUCKING TURN IT IN!” Eddie added.
Mad Ronnie didn’t even wait for Eddie to finish speaking, he threw a wild right hander towards Eddie, Eddie dodged slightly but the punch still grazed his forehead. The next thing all chaos broke loose, Eddie retaliated along with Billy, Tony, George and Johnny and all five men began steaming into mad Ron. The scuffle seemed to go on and on as the five members of the Firm punched and pushed Fromer towards the street but Fromer was fighting like his life depended on it. Tony Lambrianou got a bloody nose and Johnny Walsh ended up with a kick in the bollocks, the fight only ended when once out the street someone shouted out that the old bill were coming. Mad Ronnie broke, his face was in a right mess but there was still fight in him,
“You just signed ya fucking death warrants you cunts,” he snarled wiping away the blood from his face.
“Just fucking go home.” Tony shouted.
“I’m gonna kill the fucking lot of ya” Fromer added before little Jock pulled him away
Once Tony and the boys were back inside the fire exit Johnny Walsh leaned up against the wall.
“My fucking nuts are killing me.”
Tony laughed.

"I saw that kick, fuck me he put some boot in it, I'm fucking glad it hit your balls and not mine!" Tony said trying not to laugh.
"Ah fuck off Tone, their killing!"
"Jesus! Have we just thought a fucking gorilla, the fucking nutcase was strong as an ox." Brenner said.
"Told ya he was a psychopath."
"I hit him with a punch in the guts that would have dropped a horse, he just fucking growled, he went cunt as I hit him." Billy Hayes laughed.
"C'mon lets go and have a fucking drink." Tony said "Johnny tell them upstairs on the door just what's happened will ya, don't want that fucker coming back in alright." he added.
The five men tidied themselves up and went back inside the club and sat down. Surprisingly they found Ron and Reg now looking very much more sober and deep in conversation with the Jones brothers.
"I'm telling ya Ron, just tell me when and I'll put the fucking William's in the grave." Johnny Walsh heard Tommy Jones say as he sat down next to Ron.
"I just don't get it, why would the Williams Firm want to have a row with us?" Ronnie added calmly.
"Because they're flash cunts Ron!" Reggie replied.
"Reg someone's definitely behind this mate, there's no fucking way they would start this unless they had another Firm backing them."
"Like who?" Reg snapped.
"I don't know." Ronnie replied throwing his hands open.
"They're very tight with the Ryan's Ron, out a their manor." added Sammy Carpenter
"Nah it can't see it being them."
"You never know mate."
"The Ryan's, we go back fucking years with them, why would they want us out the way?" Ronnie said.
Reggie lit up a fag and waved at Ronnie.
"Sammy might not be too far wrong about the Ryan's Ron, they were fucking livid over Brooker, tell ya what, if it is them, then there's gonna be one hell of a fucking war."
"Well we will soon find out Reg, whoever's with the Williams will have to stand up once we make a move on the slag's."
Charlie Kray was driving frantically over London Bridge, the E-type Jaguar he was driving was roaring as he kicked down the accelerator.
"Fucking traffic lights!" he shouted as a red light forced him to stop.
Mad Ronnie Fromer reached under the driver's seat of his Ford Corsair and pulled out an old semi-automatic pistol, he cocked it to put a bullet in the chamber and then wiped the blood away from a large gash above his eye.

“Ronnie for fucks sake let’s just go home tonight.” little Jock pleaded sitting next to him.
“What just fucking drive away from this.” Ronnie snapped back angrily.
“Look at me, look at my face, I’m gonna make those cunts pay, pass me that bottle of scotch in the dash.” he added.
“Listen Ron, we can’t just declare war, we better speak to Terry first mate.” Jock said implying that they speak to Terry Anderson, the leader of the south London Firm who they both worked for.
“They fucking declared war! Not me, I’m gonna sit here till that cunt Walsh comes out and then put one in his fucking head!”
“Tony I want you to get all the Firm over at Vallance Road tomorrow evening, get them all there by six, we need to decide how were gonna sort this business out with the Williams.” Ronnie said authoritatively.
“Yeah it will be done Ron.” replied Tony in his own stern way.
Charlie Kray parked his car just off Berkley Square, he never liked anyone parking it for him and always parked in the same row of parking spaces about fifty yards from the entrance to the Astor. He slammed the door and put the keys in his pocket and then trotted up towards the club. Twenty yards from the club he noticed two men sitting in a car, Charlie slowed his pace so he could get a look at who was in it, his first thought was that it might be the Williams so he tried his best to be quiet, when he got near he realised that he recognised the man who was sitting in the car. Mad Ronnie Fromer was sitting with his arm out the window smoking on a cigarette.
“Hello Ronnie!” Charlie said smiling as he put his hand on formers arm.
“What the fuck happened to you?” Charlie added seeing all the blood on Fromer’s face. Fromer pulled his arm away where Charlie saw the gun on his lap.
“What the fuck you got that for!” Charlie asked.
The customers waiting to get into the Astor suddenly jumped to the floor as the sound of three gunshots echoed down the street. Bert Hemming, the head doorman saw a car screech off just along from where it sounded like the shots came from, Bert walked down the stairs and saw a man staggering against the railings and holding his stomach, he ran to give the man aid,
“Charlie!” he sighed in horror as he saw that the man with a stomach full of bullets was Charlie Kray.
Ronnie Kray had just finished ordering a fresh round of drinks when his and everyone else attention was drawn towards a commotion coming from the stairs that led to the Astor clubs entrance. Ronnie nodded at Eddie Brenner to go and see what all the fuss was about and Eddie followed by Tony and Billy Hayes got up from the table to go and investigate.
The three men only got half way across the floor when they were met by one of the doorman. Ronnie stood up when he noticed Tony talking to him, then

Eddie and Tony ran up the stairs while Eddie Brenner turned and ran back towards the table.
"RON ITS CHARLIE HE'S BEEN SHOT!" Eddie shouted.
In an instance everyone at the table jumped up and ran towards the door pushing anyone who was in their way out of the way.
Outside Tony Lambrianou had ran over to Charlie who despite drifting in and out of consciousness had managed to crawl nearly all the way to the clubs door.
"Charlie it's me Tony! You're gonna be fine mate, come on stay with us!"
Ronnie and Reg ran down the street both horrified when they saw the bloody mess that their elder brother was in.
"CHARLIE!, CHARLIE!, its RON" Ronnie shouted as he rubbed his brothers face, Charlie for a moment regained consciousness as he reached out and grabbed his brothers hand.
"You're gonna be alright, were gonna get you to the hospital, don't worry." Ronnie cried.
Ronnie tried to wipe the blood away from his brothers face "WHO FUCKING DID THIS?" Ronnie suddenly screamed as his concern suddenly turned to rage.
Reggie nearby stood at his brothers feet looking like he was in shock, he had both hands on his head motionless and it was only when Billy Hayes bumped accidentally into him did he move.
"WHERE'S THE FUCKING AMBULANCE!" Billy Hayes shouted at the doorman.
Reg turned suddenly and in a calm voice shouted out to Johnny Walsh.
"Johnny, get the car mate."
"Where's the nearest hospital?" he added to Hayes standing next to him.
"Charring Cross, I think Reg, Fulham Palace Road."
"Fuck it we're taking him ourselves." Reggie added.
"Reg look at all the claret mate, maybe we shouldn't move him." said Sammy carpenter standing nearby.
"If we wait for the fucking ambulance he'll be dead, he needs treatment now."
Ronnie tried to cup his brothers head as Charlie began coughing up blood, Ronnie frantically wiped the blood away but then let out a gut wrenching scream as his brother went limp, Ronnie got to his feet and wiped his face, Charlie's blood smeared across it, "HE'S DEAD REG!" "HE'S FUCKING DEAD!" Ronnie screamed.
Within a second Ronnie pulled out the gun that was still in his waistband, everyone jumped as he started firing it at all the parked cars.
"WHERE ARE THEY!" he screamed as he fired at a nearby shop window.
"FUCKING WILLIAMS'S, CARTERS, BROOKER, CORNELL!" "I'LL FUCKING KILL ALL OF YA!" he screamed hysterically.

Reg ran over to his brother and tried unsuccessfully to calm him, Ronnie was now so upset he was way out of control, Reg called Eddie Brenner to help, Eddie and the Jones brothers ran over and tried to control Ronnie, along with Reg all four men struggled to restrain him.
As this was happening Johnny Walsh skidded the car up beside them, Tony and Sammy Carpenter picked up Charlie and placed him on the back seat.
"Get him to the hospital." Reggie shouted out to Tony, within seconds Tony and Sammy had jumped in the car and Johnny Walsh had sped off up the road.
Reggie wrestled the gun out of his twin brother's hand and gave it to Tommy Jones.
"Get these fucking tools out of here." he told Tommy.
Reg turned back to his brother Ron and saw that Eddie Brenner along with Billy Hayes was really struggling to restrain him. Reggie grabbed Ron face and told him to calm down.
"RONNIE!,RONNIE!, CALM DOWN!"
Ronnie was now in a such a state of rage that he never even heard his brothers screams, not coherent to what or who was around him Ronnie head-butted his brother hard in the face. Reggie staggered back reaching up to a large gash that immediately opened up, Reggie gathered his thoughts and in one deliberate move he punched Ronnie square on the chin, the punch had the desired effect as Ronnie's body went limp in the arms Brenner and Billy Hayes.
Reggie turned to the road as he heard a car pulling up, he quickly saw that it was George Hayes behind the wheel, Brenner and Billy carried the knocked out Ronnie and put him in the back of the car followed by themselves, Reggie jumped in the front seat and called over Slice'em Sid who had been standing nearby.
"Sid, get your own car and meet us at the hospital mate but get hold of the Jones's first, tell them I want them there."
"Reg!" Sammy replied as he grabbed his arm.
"The fucking press have photos of everything mate."
"Well fucking get em!" Reg snapped.
"They've legged it mate."
"FUCK IT! Look I can't be thinking about that now just make sure you and the Jones's get to the hospital, get Trousers there too alright."
"Don't worry it's done."
Johnny Walsh screeched the car to a halt outside the accident and emergency unit at Charing Cross hospital, moments later two Doctors and three nurses came running out to the car, one of the doctors jumped into the back of the car and immediately began to examine Charlie.
"I got a faint pulse." he shouted back to his colleague.
"He's been shot!" Johnny Walsh shouted.

“This man needs theatre now!” the Doctor added as he began lifting him out, Tony and Johnny quickly reached over to help and along with the two Doctors they urgently rushed Charlie inside the hospital. Once inside Charlie was put onto a trolley and within seconds was whisked away through two large doors on his way to the operating theatre.
One of the nurses remained with Tony, Johnny and Sammy; she asked them if they would like to use a bathroom as the three men especially Tony and Sammy were absolutely drenched with Charlie’s blood.
“Is he gonna be alright?” Tony asked the nurse.
“He is very poorly.” she replied gently.
“Can we go with him?” replied Tony.
“I’m sorry but he’s gone straight into theatre the Doctor will give you some news as soon as we know” said the nurse trying her best to sound sympathetic, as she finished talking another nurse, one who helped Charlie outside came walking over with a clipboard in her hand.
“I’m going to have to take some details from you sir.” she asked Tony Lambrianou.
“What’s the patient’s full name?” she added.
“Bob Taylor.” Tony replied hesitantly.
The first nurse smiled at Tony’s reply.
“Even I know that that was Charlie Kray.” she said.
“Look love it’s not my place to give you answers darling.” replied Tony coyly.
“Look love your friends in their fighting for his life, if we are to have any chance of saving him then we need as much information as possible.” the second nurse added.
“Alright.” Tony sighed.
“What time did the shooting take place?”
“About twenty minutes ago.”
“So within the hour.”
“Yeah.” Tony said.
“Do you know what kind of a gun he was shot with?”
Tony tilted his head.
“Now that’s a question I can’t answer.” he replied sarcastically.
Ten minutes later the car carrying Reg and Ron ground to a halt outside the accident and emergency unit, Tony, Johnny and Sammy were standing outside the entrance having a cigarette as the car pulled up. Tony ran over and opened Reggie’s door.
“Fuck me Reg what’s happened to you two?” he asked Reg as he noticed the large cut on his brow and Ronnie unconscious in the back.
“How is he?” Reggie snapped back “Is he alive?” he added as he walked towards the entrance.

"Barely mate, they've taken him straight into the operating theatre."
Reggie forcefully pushed open the hospital doors and walked over to the reception desk.
"My names Reg Kray, you have my brother in here and I would like to see a Doctor about him."
"If you could bear with me for a moment sir I will fetch someone to speak with you."
Moments later a senior looking nurse walked over and pulled Reg over to the side.
"Mr Kray your brother is in a very critical condition, his blood loss has been substantial, however we have stemmed the loss of blood and at present we have him in a stable condition."
"Can we see him?" Reg asked.
"Not at present, he needs to be moved into surgery immediately."
"Is he going to be alright?"
"I'm sorry but I can't answer that, all I can tell you is that until the surgeons find out the extent of damage that the bullets have caused we will just have to wait and prey that all will be well, but on a positive side he is stable at the moment, he is very, very poorly but his condition is not deteriorating, there is a very good chance that surgery will be a success."
"Thanks love." Reggie sighed as if the nurses slight optimism was exactly what he wanted to hear "If it's okay then were just hang about round here until we find out how he'll be." added Reg.
"That's no problem, although I would suggest that you let a nurse take a look at that cut on your head." answered the nurse pointing to Reggie's wound.
Reg felt a deep feeling of fear for Charlie as he walked out into the nights air and made his way over to Tony Lambrianou, Johnny, Sammy, Billy and George Hayes and Eddie Brenner, who were all standing by the parked car that Ronnie still unconscious was in the back off.
"Gis a fag Tone." Reg asked.
"You alright Reg?" replied Tony as he handed re a packet of cigarettes.
"How's Ron?" Reg asked ignoring Tony's question and gazing into the car.
"Out like a light mate." Tony replied with a smile.
Reg took a long drag on his cigarette and blew out a large channel of smoke that drifted up into the night's sky.
"Listen Johnny, I want you to take one of the motors and go and pick Mum and Dad up." "George I want you to go and get Charlie's wife alright."
"Alright mate, shall I go now." Johnny replied.
"Yeah get going now John."
"Ave you let everyone know Reg?" Eddie asked.
"Nah, not yet, after this fag I'll give them all a call." added Reg with a sigh in his voice.

“Are the Jones’s ere yet?” Reg Asked.
“Not yet mate.” Eddie answered.
“Right well as soon as they get here, let me know straight away, I want those fucking Williams’s taken out tonight.”
“Williams’s.” Tony hesitantly added as he slyly looked across at Brenner in a tone that made Reg curious, Reg looked at Tony and frowned at the worried look on his friends face.
“WHAT!” Reg snapped.
“What I say something wrong, what’s the matter with ya?” he added.
“WHAT!” Reggie impatiently demanded at Tony’s silence.
“Reg it weren’t the William’s who shot Charlie mate.” Tony said swallowing hard.
Reg looked hard at his friend and then at Brenner who was purposely looking down at his feet.
“Well who the fucking hell was it?” Reg Growled.
Tony hesitated in replying as he looked over to Eddie Brenner as if asking for some support.
“What ya fucking keep looking at him for, TONY WHO THE FUCKING HELL DID THIS?”
“It was Ronnie Fromer.” Tony finally uttered.
“mad Ronnie Fromer, why the fuck would he shoot Charlie?” snapped Reg his voice deepening by the second into a angered growl, Tony and the rest of the men all noticed Reg tense, it was like a wild animal cornered, his face began to flush and his hands moulded themselves into fists, each man had witnessed this volatile state countless times before, both Reg and Ron in this angered state were highly unpredictable.
“Fromer! He’ll be dead by morning, but why’d he jump into bed with the William’s.”
“Reg!” Johnny calmly said as he walked over and affectionately reached out at Reggie’s arm in a calming gesture.
“It’s got fuck all to do with the William’s mate, last night after the row in Quaglino’s I phoned Charlie to tell him what had happened, Ron was in a terrible rage see and I thought it best to let Charlie know that we was going on to the Astor Reg, Charlie told me to try and keep you and Ron out of any more situations and told me he was on his way. I told Eddie and Tony about the conversation I had with Charlie and we all agreed to keep our wits about us and make sure that we kept everyone out of harm’s way, when we got to the Astor and I saw that Fromer was in there Reg I couldn’t fucking believe it, of all the fucking people we could bump into last night it had to be him. The biggest fucking nuisance going, I went over to see him as I didn’t want him coming over to you and Ron, I knew Ron was holding a tool and in the mood he was in and the fucking drunken state Fromer was in I thought it would be

certainty to go off, like I said I spoke to Fromer but he was out of his fucking box Reg, all he kept saying was *where's the Colonel, where's that fuck*, shouting out about funny pills and asylum stories, I told him to calm down and he fucking fronted me, so we slung the cunt out."
A strange silence fell between the men as Johnny finished explaining, as Reg looked coldly at John, Tony and Eddie.
"So all this is down to you three?" Reg aggressively mouthed.
"I wouldn't put it like that Reg." replied Tony gob-smacked at Reg's reply.
"What other fucking way would you put it?"
"We made a decision Reg, Ron's was sitting at the table dying to get in a fight with a tool down his pants, Fromer's acting like a cunt, what would you do mate, we just didn't wanna see ya get into any aggravation." added Eddie.
"Aggravation, what'd ya fucking call this!" snapped Reg.
"Reg were sorry mate, Charlie's like a fucking brother to us as well." said Tony.
"So you saw him being shot then." Reg asked.
"Fuck off Reg, do ya think we would just stand there watching if we did." replied Tony sternly.
"Charlie told us on the way to the hospital Reg, until then we never had a clue it was Fromer." Johnny added.
Reg shook his head and sighed, he felt angry but he knew that his friends had acted in the correct way, slinging Fromer out was the right thing to do, Reg nodded slightly to show his friends that he was not angry at them.
"Tony I want all the Firm down here tonight, get on the phones and squeeze every fucker we have to find out where Fromer is, someone somewhere will know where he is, he's our first priority, I want that mug strung up within forty eight hours, get someone to give Terry Anderson a pull as well, let's hope he was acting on his own but if he wants to hide behind the Anderson's then they can fucking have it as well."
Four hours after Charles Kray jr was shot, Charring Cross hospital was like a magnet of activity, the Police had turned out in force along with countless members of the national newspapers and two TV news crews. The accident and emergency department looked like a war zone with all the different gentlemen roaming around.
The operation was a success and three bullets were safely removed from Charles abdomen, he was wheeled into a private room where his Mother violet, Father Charlie, and his wife were anxiously waiting. Violet upon seeing her son wheeled into the room jumped up and ran to his side, she affectionately caressed his face as she bent to kiss his cheek.
"Charlie." she cried through a face of tears.

“It’s all right love he’s sleeping.” her husband quietly comforted her as he ushered her gently away to a nearby chair. Just as violet Kray sat down Reg and Tony Lambrianou quietly walked into the dimly lit room.
“REG!” violet sighed as she grabbed her son in her arms.
“It’s alright Mum, the nurse says he’s gonna be alright.” Reg whispered back.
“I don’t care what it takes Reg; I want the bastard who did this taken care off.”
“ssh don’t worry Mum, just try to relax.”
“NO REG! That’s my son there, we take care of our own, do you understand this, we take care of our own.”
“Mum please don’t worry yourself.” Reggie pleaded as his Father put a comforting arm around his wife.
“C’mon love, sit down.” Charles Kray snr implored her.
“Where’s my Ron!” violet suddenly realised.
“Ron’s alright mum, he’s down the coast, we can’t have him here.”
“That’s his brother lying there.”
“Yeah I know Mum and theirs half of Scotland Yard’s coppers standing down the corridor.”
“Sod the law.” violet snapped.
“Mum look.” Reg said seriously so that it grabbed his mum’s attention.
“Listen I don’t want you to worry but me and Ron can’t be here now, there’s too much activity going on at the moment we need to sit down quietly away from all this and get things sorted out, I’ll not be far and I’ll be in touch, try not to worry about nothing Mum everything will be fine, Rosie’s boys, Fred, Jim and Docky are outside now they’ll look after you see, anything you need they’ll take care off.” Reg added calmly.
“Don’t worry about us son, you go and do what you got to do, and mind ya backs.” Reg’s Father Charlie said as he embraced his boy.
“I’ll be in touch dad, mums don’t worry about nothing, I love you” Reg replied as he wiped a tear from his eye and left the room with Tony.
Once outside Reg wiped his face and breathed in deep he took two steps before noticing the cumbersome silhouettes of six burly men standing at the far end of the dimly lit corridor.
“Here they fucking are.” he mouthed quietly to Tony.
“Reg Kray we’d like a word.” said the first cop as Reg approached.
“Fuck off!” Reg snapped nonchalantly back.
“Didn’t you hear him, we want a word.” another cop said as he stood in front of Reg blocking his path.
“Didn’t you hear me, I said fuck off!”
“Now look son don’t be fucking stupid, you know the drill, if that’s how you want then we can do this down the station.” said the first cop.
“I couldn’t give a monkeys where we do it, my answers still the fucking same.”

"Look we got reports that you and Ron were fighting at the scene of the crime." another cop piped in.
"With who?" Reg asked.
"With each other?" the cop replied.
Reg smiled mockingly.
"So some mug told you that me and Ron were fighting each other, is Ron nicking me?"
"Let's fucking nick him!" another cop aggressively said.
"For what, fighting with my brother, get out my fucking way, my solicitors standing out there, let's call him over or better still let's call over some of them paper men, we can tell them how the Laws harassing the Kray family again."
As Reg finished talking the flash cop the one who suggested nicking him looked as if he had run out of patience, he forcefully reached out and grabbed Reg's arm as if trying to restrain him, Reg twisted away with equal force and took a couple of steps back. The senior cop quickly moved in between the two men.
"Leave it Del we're wait." he said calmly to his police colleague.
"We're be watching you like a fucking hawk Kray." he mouthed angrily turning back to Reg.
"What's fucking new?" Reg replied as he and Tony walked off.
Johnny Walsh had just finished cooking Ron a nice big fry up, he placed it on a tray and took it into the living room of violet Kray's bungalow in Worthing, east Sussex. Ron had just woken up and had just finished the day's first cigarette as Johnny entered the room.
"Get this down ya Ron, it'll do ya some good." Johnny said as he put the tray on Ron's lap.
"What time is it John?" Ron asked.
"Just gone ten."
"Has Reggie phoned up?"
"He called at about seven Ron, Charlie's going to be alright, and Reg said he would be down before midday."
"Put the telly on will ya John." Ron asked as he took his first bite of bacon Johnny Walsh walked over and turned the on switch on the TV then sat down on a chair next to Ron as the two men waited for the TV to warm up."
"What a fucking night ay Ron." Johnny sighed as he reached for a fag.
"Yeah those Astor nights are killer's John" Ron quipped sarcastically which made John stiffen at the joviality that Ronnie could show at last night's events.
Both men's attention were then drawn to the TV as it flickered into life, Ron tried to kick the aerial with his foot as the picture was jumping.
"Fucking TV's, cost a fucking fortune and never fucking work." Ron shouted.

"It's alright Ron I'll do it."
"That's it John!" Ron said as Johnny's wiggling the aerial about produced a picture.
"It's the news Ron." Johnny added as he sat back in his chair. Ron took another bite on his bacon and then suddenly stopped chewing as a caption flashed across the screen saying.
"GANG WARFARE IN LONDON."
Good morning my names Trevor Atkinson.
Charles Kray elder brother to the Kray twins Ronald and Reginald was sensationally gunned down on a London roadside in the late hours of last night. The shooting took place outside a notorious haunt of London's gangland fraternity. We go over to our crime correspondent Alistair Stevens for a full report.
The shooting took place at approximately midnight last night where Charles Kray the elder brother to Ron and Reg Kray had parked his car and was walking along Berkley square on his way to the Astor club, a local haunt of celebrities and villains. Reports from eyewitnesses state that three shots were heard and Charles Kray was seen to collapse outside the entrance to the club. His brothers Ron and Reg shortly after ran from within the club and an ensuing gun battle then took place. Damage was sustained to various cars parked nearby and shop windows in the vicinity were shattered by gunfire. so far the police have made no arrests but the police are looking to interview Ronald Kray who shortly after the incident disappeared into the night. I spoke to a senior detective earlier today and he is extremely worried that further violence may result from this incident, he added that they were in the process of conducting their investigations and urged the public to not approach anyone whom they suspect of being involved in last night's shooting, anyone with any information should contact Scotland yard and he stressed that any contact will be dealt in the strictest confidence.
But once again gangland violence has reared its ugly head in the capital, an eyewitness said to me earlier that the scene last night was like something out of 1920's Chicago, bullets were firing in all directions and it was a miracle that no other wounding's or fatalities took place.
Alistair Stevens for the BBC in Mayfair London.
The TV coverage switched back over to the studio where the original newsreader was now sitting down with senior gentlemen opposite a desk.
"We welcome retired Detective Richard Wilson to the studio, Detective Wilson this is very serious."
"Indeed! Shootouts on the streets of London, thank god are not a common occurrence, like your reporter stated earlier it seems only by the grace of god that we are not here discussing a mass of fatalities."

"As an ex Scotland Yard detective could you give us any insight into what will be going on in the minds of the detectives at Scotland Yard this morning."
"Vaguely, I wouldn't want to comment on any points of process but rest assured they will be investigating this incident in a very thorough and professional manner."
"Can we expect a major clampdown on London's Gangs?"
"That's not for me to say, but we can pretty much guarantee that they will be using all of their resources to arrest the assailants in last night's shooting, as for a clampdown well that's possibly a question for parliament."
"Parliament you say?"
"There is a growing frustration within the force that the courts are too lenient on gang related crime, in the USA they have a racketeering charge, the RICO act that gives the courts the power to incarcerate these villains for extremely long periods of time."
Ronnie suddenly shouted out at Johnny.
"Turn the fucking thing off John; I've heard all this bollocks before mate."
Johnny jumped up and did as Ron asked.
"At least we now know for certain that the laws looking for ya Ron."
"Don't look so fucking happy about it John." replied Ron jokingly at Johns comment.
"Nah fuck off, I didn't mean it like that." added Johnny as both men smiled.
"I thought I might be going paranoid." Ron said poking fun at himself and his schizophrenic illness. Both men broke into a nervous laugh until abruptly they were interrupted by the sound of a car pulling onto the bungalow drive. Ron jumped up and grabbed a pistol that was on top of a cabinet and then ran to the window.
"It's alright John, its Reg." he calmly replied as he peeked through the side of the curtains.
Johnny opened the front door and let in Reg, Tony Lambrianou and Eddie Brenner.
"Fuck me Reg, you three look fucking terrible." Johnny sighed as he saw the three men enter.
"Don't Johnny, been up all fucking night, where's Ron?"
"Inside Reg, come on I make you all a cup of tea."
As Ron saw his brother enter the room he walked over to greet him, both men hugged shortly.
"You alright Ron?" Reggie asked as he broke free.
"Couldn't be better Reg, you know how I love mums bungalow, it's the sea air see, it livens me up." replied Ron as if he never had a care in the world.
Tony glanced across at Eddie Brenner who in turn returned the look, both had an expression of surprise and even disbelief, even Reg stiffened at the sight of Ron in such a fine and care free mood.

“Have you seen this?” Reg said as he passed Ron a rolled up newspaper. Ron grabbed the paper from his twin and sat down eagerly unrolling it, he knew it was something about him and he couldn’t hide the sinister smile that broke out on his face.
It was today’s daily express and on the front page was a full page picture of Ron with gun in hand and Tony , Reg and Eddie all trying to restrain him, it was a night picture so certain features were hard to make out but Ron’s face in the picture grimaced in rage was clear as a bell. Written across the bottom of the picture in great big letters was the word *‘PHSYCOPATH!’*
“They’re calling me crazy Reg!” Ron giggled.
“You look mad as a hatter in that fucking picture!” Reg replied sternly and clearly not as impressed with the paper as his twin was. Ron threw the paper over to Johnny.
“Read it out John.”
“Gang boss Ronnie Kray photographed here last night just after a gun fight in the streets of Mayfair which had innocent bystanders terrified, Ronnie brother Charlie was shot in the stomach during the gun battle and is in a life and death fight in hospital”
“That’s you nicked Ron!” Reg interrupted sternly.
“For what!” replied Ron.
Reg shook his head slightly in disbelief before he answered his brother.
“Ronnie, you’re on the fucking front page, holding a fucking gun mate, their hardly gonna give you the Nobel peace prize.”
“You never know Reg.” Ron joked.
Reg looked at his brother in amazement.
“Are you alright Ron, I’ve just had the night from fucking hell but I come here and your joking around, look bacon and eggs the fires on, cups of tea, right cosy, have I missed something mate, have we just won the fucking pools or something?”
“What you on about?”
“I just can’t get it through my head why you’re so fucking happy.”
“Oh bollocks! You’re just fucking jealous that it’s me in the paper holding a gun.”
If Reggie’s first look at his brother was amazement then the look he gave him now was one of sheer astonishment, he looked at Tony and Eddie who were both trying desperately not to burst into laughter and just sighed.
Johnny Walsh with perfect timing then butted in.
“How many sugars in ya tea Reg?” Johnny smiled.
“Two.” Reg shouted before sitting down opposite Ron.
John nodded and got on with the drinks, during the night he had already told Ron that it was Ronnie Fromer who had shot his brother but I didn’t matter to

Ron who had pulled the trigger, he just wanted revenge and who it was against was just not important to him.
Reg lit up a cigarette before beginning.
“We been banging on doors all fucking night Ron, look at us ain’t had a chance to get washed, changed or anything, had about half hours kip on the way down, that’s all, no one is saying a fucking word about Fromer, he’s just disappeared.”
“What about the cunt that was with him?” Ron said with menace in his voice.
“We kicked little Jock’s door in at six this morning, but he knows fuck all Ron.”
“How can he know nothing, he was with Fromer, he must know where he dropped him off.”
“I know he was with him Ron but he had nothing really to do with what happened to Charlie.”
“Your wrong Reg, he knew Fromer was going to do someone with a gun, he must have known Fromer was tooled up, and anyway he sat in the car and then fucking drove him off.”
“Little Jock’s not a hard man Ron, Fromer put him in a spot.”
“What’s he saying Fromer scared him?” replied Ron.
“Yeah like that Ron, he said Fromer was going crazy, he pulled out a gun from under the car seat and told Jock what to do, Jock says that he tried to calm the mug down but Fromer was having none of it.”
“So that’s what Jock told you happened?”
“Yeah.” Reg said.
“And you believe him?” Ron asked with a hint of sarcasm.
“Yeah I do believe him Ron.”
“Just like that!” Ron added now with even deeper tones of sarcasm.
“NO! It weren’t just like that Ron, it was after Eddie stuck a gun in his ear and I’d gave him a few digs.”
“A few digs, I’d have broken his fucking neck, he should have got out the car and came into the Astor and told us what Fromer was doing.”
“Why should he Ron, he’s not on our firm!” replied Reg in a frustrated voice.
“Well it don’t matter now anyway, that little scotch cunts gotta go!” Ronnie said banging the table with his fist.
“I left him needing over a hundred fucking stitches in his face, broke his fucking legs and kicked the cunt from one room to another.” Reg replied angrily.
Ronnie smiled broadly.
“That’s all I wanted to know Reg, innocent or not that fucker was with the cunt who shot our brother, we need to be seen to be sending out a message.”
“Ron he got the fucking message!” Reg snapped.
“Good.” Ron said nodding his approval and then taking a sip of his tea.

“Right then Fromer! Someone somewhere knows where he is.” Ron said as he put down his cup of tea on the table.
“My bet Ron is he’s holed up somewhere with the Anderson’s.” Tony added.
“Well let’s get hold of Terry Anderson then.” Ron replied.
“What if the Andersons are hiding him Ron, what’s our move then mate?” Eddie Brenner asked.
“Then we give Anderson a pull, tell him we want Fromer.”
“And if he refuses to give him to us?” asked Tony.
“Then he fucking gets it as well.” snapped Ron with a determined voice.
“The Anderson’s are a big Firm Ron, their no mugs mate.” Eddie added.
“What does that mean Eddie, what do we only fight mugs, if he makes himself busy over this then we’ll have to give it to him.”
“We need to think carefully about this Ron, we’ve still got the Williams to deal with, could be risky taking on two large Firms at the same time mate.” Reg said.
“Fuck the lot of em Reg!, this won’t be the first time we’ve had wars, the Williams can be dealt with anytime but this Fromer bollocks has to be done now, they shot our brother and that’s as personal as it gets.”
“I hear what ya saying Ron and I agree hundred percent but I feel we should tread carefully about all this, it’s a lot of problems, Williams, Fromer, Anderson’s and the old bill and maybe even the Ryan’s if they were something to do with what happened with the Williams’s.” Reg added seriously.
“Look Reg first thing first and that’s Fromer, number one its personal, he shot our brother and number two the whole fucking worlds watching us and waiting to see what were gonna do, for the survival of everything that we are we have to show strength, we have to show every fucker out there just what our grip of control is.”
“So it’s agreed, Fromer’s a dead man.” Tony added coldly.
“As fucking dead as Winston Churchill!” added Ron.

Not Guilty Your Honour
Chapter seven
'On The Hunt'

THE ANDERSONS

Terry Anderson was the eldest of eleven children, he had three sisters and seven brothers, Terry was born in Glasgow in 1935 in one of the most squalid sectors of the city. His Father Terry snr worked as a Docker in the day and as an enforcer for a major Glasgow gang at night. Most night's Terry snr would mind back street gambling dens where his job was to make sure no harm came to the staff. Glasgow in them days was like the wild west of America the only difference was that the yanks used guns and the Scots used razors, knifes and coshes. It seemed a night never passed without Terry snr having to cosh someone or another but on one night in the course of doing his job Terry was jumped by six rival gang members where they cut him with razors to within an inch of his life. Terry had two choices, mend and seek revenge or to take

up on an offer by a cousin to move his family down to London. It took weeks for Terry's wounds to heal and like everything else in his life he thought very carefully about his options. The push though finally came in the form of his wife Maggie, sickened by years of violence and endless worrying just to get by, she told her husband that she had had enough of Glasgow, Terry and Maggie had seven children and she feared that if they remain in Scotland they would only be bringing up their children into poverty and violence. So on hot sunny summers day in 1947 the Anderson's moved to Battersea, South London.
Terry Anderson jnr was a monster of a man, at first glance you could be mistaken into thinking that he was fat but once up close you could see that he was as solid as an ox. He wasn't particularly muscular but just a big boned brute of a man. Over six feet two and seventeen stone with a thick mane of ginger hair, Terry Anderson just oozed menace and danger.
He was a hard drinker, hard gambler,, hard talking, hard bastard, most people who knew him were terrified of him, at best people kept their distance from him. He was a bully, a bully in every sense of the word, anyone who upset him including women came to harm, Terry was known for his temper and stories about the beatings he gave to women and men were legendary around the streets and pubs of south London.
With his gang of friends and seven brothers the Anderson's absolutely terrorised South West London. It was said that there wasn't a pub, club, or spiel in Battersea, Clapham, Balham, Vauxhall, Fulham and Tooting that wasn't in some shape or form paying protection to the Anderson's. They owned three scrap metal yards, four car sites, six snooker and billiard halls and countless illegal underground drinking and gambling clubs. Times were good for the Anderson's, they had money and they had plenty of it and they had a reputation that was fearsome.
Terry Anderson sat in the office of his Balham car site with his feet on the table wearing a three quarter length sheepskin coat that made him look like a big ginger bear, he was sipping on a bottle of Brown ale and joking with his brothers Doug, Ian and Jason, there was one other man laughing and joking in the office as well, mad Ronnie Fromer.
"So how'd he go again when ya shot him?" Terry said mockingly.
Fromer jumped up from his chair and began to play act for his boss.
"Ron, Ron, what you doing here, what, what, why you got that gun, BANG, BANG, BANG, arrhhhhhhh." Fromer joked as he grabbed his stomach and fell onto the floor in a mock and callous re-enactment of Charlie Kray's shooting.
"Fucking mug, screamed like a fucking women Terry."
"Shame it weren't Colonel Kray, the fucking schizoid or his poncy twin brother." Doug Anderson added.

“Be careful what you wish for Dougie.” Fromer answered jokingly with a wink.
Jason Anderson suddenly jumped up as he heard a car pulling into the show room outside the office. Ronnie Fromer like startled cat followed suit by quickly getting to his feet and pulling out a pistol from his waist band and cocking it.
“It’s Jackie and Glenn.” Jason said as he looked out the door.
Terry Anderson still sitting and not having budged an inch noticed Fromer’s actions with a look of contempt; his voice seemed to growl as he spoke.
“I hope that’s not the fucking tool from last night.” he said tilting his head slightly towards Fromer’s gun.
“Nah don’t be silly Tel, that went over Vauxhall Bridge on mi way home last night.”
Terry Anderson didn’t bother to reply, he just nodded his head authoritatively as if to say well done and it’s alright then.
Jackie Anderson the second eldest of the brothers was a real rough and ready man’s man, with a habit of talking and acting fast, unlike his brother who spoke with a broad South London accent, Jackie still spoke with a slight Scottish slur, he had the same stocky and full build as his older brother, only Jackie chose to shave the ginger hair from his head. Jackie Anderson’s main characteristic though was a terrible looking botched scar that ran from his forehead down to just under his chin. As the scar crossed his eyebrows it pulled the skin slightly making one of his eyes slant gently, it also left his top lip out of shape from the difficult stitch job that he was unfortunate to receive. It looked like a result of a knife wound or as if someone had ran a machete across his face but in fact it was caused by a car engine falling onto him one day while he was working underneath one. The scar mixed with Jackie’s build, bald head and the way that he carried himself all blended together to create a very foreboding looking man. Wherever Jackie went he would draw stares, he was like a subtle version of Frankenstein’s monster. Friends and family often joked that he was Jack the ripper reborn because of the very sinister and frightening presence he put forward.
“It’s nay fooking right Terry, wee Jocks in a right fooking state.” Jackie growled as he burst into the office like a blue arsed fly followed swiftly by the youngest of the Anderson brothers Glenn.
“Reggie fooking Kray and that foreign cunt Tony lambri …fookin what’s his name prick sliced the wee poor fella ta fooking pieces.” he angrily added.
“Fucking liberty taking cunts, Jock had fuck all to do with last night.” Fromer snapped.
“He was with ya weren’t he?” Terry replied calmly.
“Still don’t make it right!” added Fromer shaking his head.

“what’ll ya on a different fucking planet Ronnie, you two fucking shot Charlie Kray, if I was Reg I’d have done exactly the fucking same, No worse, if someone put a bullet in Jackie, Glenn or anyone else would have carved up every cunt who was in the house including his wife.” snapped Terry angrily.
“Yeah I suppose.” Fromer sighed quietly.
“And in case its slipped your mind Ronnie, you didn’t just shoot Charlie last night, you put a bullet in the whole fucking Firm, they have a reputation that walks before them and they gotta fucking live up to it.” added Terry.
“Sounds like you’re expecting a lot more agro from this.” Jason Anderson rather naively commented.
“I couldn’t give fuck!, I don’t care either way if they want a row with us then we’ll fucking have a row with them, I won’t turn away from no man, but all of ya bare in mind that Ronnie Kray is one dangerous fucker. They’ve been around the rackets for a lot of years now, they put themselves about all over the fucking place, and there an open invitation with a big fucking reputation to protect, and they been protecting it and protecting it well. Reg Kray and the others on the Firm are game lads, but Ronnie’s a different kettle of fish, like all mad men he’s unpredictable, if he gets it into his head that he’s gonna do ya then given the opportunity, he’ll fucking do it anywhere, he don’t give a fuck where he does it, or who he does it front. you never know what he’s gonna do, with him your just as much in danger standing in the reception of Scotland Yard as you are in a dark alley at two in the morning.”
The North East London area of Hoxton had a long and dark history, its origins in London dated back to the doomsday book when it was called Hogesdon. History records that in the seventeenth century vast numbers of French Protestants (Huguenot refugees) desperate to flee the tyranny of the French church flocked to the areas of Hoxton and Shoreditch. As a result of the Huguenot invasion many of the wealthy locals who made their money from milling and metalwork’s moved away from the area.
Over the next two centuries the population grew from massive influxes of Jewish, Irish, welsh and Scottish immigration and by the end of the nineteenth century the boroughs of Hoxton and Shoreditch had descended into tremendous poverty, The whole area was just one huge sprawling slum where crime and prostitution were the order of the day. As the twentieth century broke across the world with it came a great optimism for the future, Victorian Britain was leading the world in its science, medical and political fields yet in the slums of London the dawn of a new century just passed like another normal soul destroying day. Hoxton in particular saw the rise of a fearsome alleyway gang society. Now with the 1970’s just beginning Hoxton for the last seventy years had been responsible for producing a large percentage of London’s crime families. The Kray’s were born in Hoxton as were fierce

fighting families like the Ryan's, the Hodge's, the Sabinis, the Jeffrey's, the whites and the Williams brothers Dave and Billy.
Jill's café in Hoxton square was often the regarded as a meeting place for the areas criminal fraternity, on some days it was like a who's who of the London's underworld history. The café was owned by Jill Williams, sister to armed robbers Dave and Billy. Every day the brothers and members of their gang would go to Jill's café at twelve o'clock to begin the day with a good fry up.
"I can't fucking believe it! Same fucking night Dav,e as we had a pop at em." Billy said quietly referring to Charlie Kray's shooting to his elder brother over a cup of tea in their usual corner of the café.
"It's odds on their think we had something to do with it." added Billy in a threatening voice
"Ain't you heard?" replied Dave surprised.
"Heard what?"
"It was South of the river who did it, Fromer and the Anderson's shot Charlie."
"Mad Ronnie Fromer?"
"Yeah, fuck me bill, where you been, I've had my blower going at least a dozen times this morning."
"I've been in bed." Billy sighed as he rubbed his head "Ronnie fucking Fromer!" he added with a smile.
"Yeah!" Dave laughed as he took another sip of his hot cup of tea.
"The twins know its Fromer." Billy added.
"I should fucking think so!, little Jock by all accounts was with Fromer when he did it, the twins kicked his door in early this morning, nearly killed the fella, smashed him right up Bill, I've heard they been kicking in doors all over London."
"What about our problems with the twins Dave?"
"I ain't given it much fucking thought really, I got woke up seven this morning and got told about all this bollocks but Jimmy and John wanna see us later on so I guess it's something to do with the twins."
"Dave I ain't gonna go and sit down in front of John and Jimmy Ryan, and be told what to do!" Billy suddenly snapped.
"Hold up, whose fucking saying that you have."
"They got businesses with the twins Dave."
"So have we!" Dave snapped back referring to their own mutual business partnerships with the Ryan's.
"I'm just not being told what to fucking do!"
Dave raised his hand in a calming motion.
"Let's just see what they fucking gotta say alright!" he mouthed in a condescending way.

By four o'clock in the afternoon violet Kray's bungalow down on the south coast looked like a doss house. Reg, Tony and Eddie Brenner were all sprawled out in the living room sleeping on chairs and couches. Ronnie Kray, Johnny Walsh, Sammy carpenter, slicem Sid, George and Billy Hayes and the Jones brothers Tommy and Alex were all sitting cramped around a table in the kitchen.
"Fromer likes to drink in the Castle pub in Tooting, south of the river, Ron." said Sammy Carpenter who was originally from Tooting in South London and was now giving Ron his knowledge of the pub and club scene down there.
"Then that's our first stop Tonight!" replied Ron with visible glow in his complexion as if all this planning was making him happy. Everyone in the room could feel Ronnie's excitement, this was what made him tick, he was in his element here sitting at the head of a table giving out orders and planning assaults like a strategic Colonel instructing his captains.
"I want numbers tonight!" Ron growled as banged the table.
"Don't worry about that Ron, when we hit the streets tonight there be a good twenty of us." Billy Hayes replied.
"Make it thirty; I wanna send out a right fucking message to these South London mugs."
"You spoke to Joey?" asked George Hayes meaning Joey Pine, the twin's fiercely loyal and dangerous friend.
"Yeah Joe's with us one hundred percent." said Ron.
"Is he coming tonight?"
"Yeah Joe ain't gonna miss all the fucking fun is he."
Sitting and talking in the Argyle Square, Hoxton office of their wholesale clothing business were the Ryan brothers John, Jimmy, Frank and Albert, the topic of their conversation was as usual the Kray's, and the conversation had been and still was very heated.
"Jim I've Fucking had enough!" John Ryan usually the calm brother ranted as he banged his hand on the table.
"I know it's all the fucking time, every week there's something in the linens about the twins." added Albert the eldest brother.
"It's beyond a fucking joke now, honestly, time and time again they've been told to turn it in." said Frank Ryan.
"Yeah I know, were gonna have to have a meet with them and sort this out." John sighed.
"Personally I'd fuck em off John, we don't need them, let's have nothing more to do with em, I've already had Fritz on the blower today, he's going fucking mad about last night." added Frank angrily commenting on the owner of the Astor clubs reaction to the shooting last night.

“Nah, hold on let’s get it right, someone fucking shot them, they never shot the place up, what happened last night could have happened to any of us.” added John.
“John!” Frank snapped, “It’s all the fucking time, they’re always getting into rows, what about the old bill, they’re gonna be all over us again.” he added with a mix of desperation and angered frustration in his voice.
“Alright this is what we’re do, we will call a meeting and see if we can arrange a way that we can break away from each other.”
“Well how’s that gonna work John?” Albert asked. “Take the Astor for an example, the twins ain’t gonna just walk away from their half of the pension, then what about the business with the yanks, the Chemin games, even this wholesale business they got a share of.”
“I know Al, there’s a lot that needs sorting but one thing is certain and that is we can’t go on like this anymore, if we carry on like we are then it’s a fucking sure bet were gonna end up in the fucking nick.” John added sternly which caused Frank to get up from his chair and sigh loudly in frustration.
“Might be easier just to get rid of em.” he said quietly “Permanently!” he added.
John snapped his head quickly in the direction of his younger fiery brother; he silently gazed as he witnessed him light up a cigarette and then sit back down in his chair again. John mentally took note of the confidence that his brother had just showed, getting rid of the Kray’s was not as easy as it was said yet John saw how his brother meant every word of the statement he had just heard. Frank waited for his brother to reply but as an eerie silence fell across them he spoke on further.
“John, if you think you’re going to get Ronnie Kray in here and tell him to listen and to be a good boy then you’re as fucking mad as he is, now we know that he has just had a row with Dave and Billy, there be here in a minute, all I’m suggesting is maybe the problem between the twins and the Williams could be in fact the solution.”
John although not the eldest was commonly thought of as the leader of the Ryan’s, between the brothers there was never a boss or any orders between them but subconsciously they all recognised John as the authoritative figure. He listened intently to what Frank had said and for a moment he played with the idea but to John it seemed too harsh or too premature, John feared no man but he always felt that discussion should be used before force.
“I hear what you’re saying Frank but NOW’s not the time for that, we go back a long way with the twins, they bent over backwards to keep us out of their last trial and I will not use my friendship as a weapon against them.”
“We were abroad for months because of that trial.” Frank replied.
“But we weren’t in the nick Frank.” Jimmy Ryan added.
Frank sighed in defeat and slapped both his hand frustrated on his knees.

“What about Dave and Billy, there be here in a minute and it’s an odds on bet there be asking our blessing to go to war with the twins.” Frank added.
“Well they won’t fucking get it, I want peace between us Frank, we got business with both Firms and I don’t want our income to get in the middle of this.” replied John in a very adamant voice.
“Do you think Ronnie Kray will listen to peace John?” replied Frank dryly.
“He’ll fucking have to!” snapped John in a calm but serious tone.
The castle pub in Tooting, South West London was a drab and dreary looking building; situated on Tooting high street the pub had a fierce reputation for violent and drunken behaviour.
The Jaguar car drove by Johnny Walsh carrying Ronnie and Reg Kray, Tony Lambrianou and Joey Pine pulled into the pub car park. The rain from this cold and wet November evening made the castle pub look even more miserable.
“He’ll be a fucking madman if he’s got the balls to be in here tonight Ron.” Joey Pine reiterated talking about Ronnie Fromer.
“It’s his local Joe, some mug will be here.” Ron answered as the car ground to a halt, Ron looked out the window as he saw five other cars all carrying members of the Firm pull in besides him and park facing outwards to face the road in case they would have to escape quickly.
Sammy Carpenter who had been sent on ahead to scope the pub for any old bill saw the cars pull in and walked over in the nights rain, overcoat done up to the top, he walked towards the passenger window of the jag, leaning over to talk to Ron he gave his report.
“Fromer’s not here Ron, can’t see any old bill floating about either.” he said in a low voice which got absolutely no reaction from Ron at all.
“Is any of his Firm in there?” Joey Pine asked from the back seat.
“Not really Joe, only Dickie the dollar’s in there mate.”
“He’ll fucking do!” Ronnie suddenly snapped as he reached for the door handle.
“Hold on Ron!” Reg said quickly as he grabbed his brother’s arm.
“Who the fuck’s Dickie the dollar?” Reggie then asked Sammy.
“He’s a fence for the Anderson’s, bit of a face over these parts.”
“He’s with the Anderson’s?” Ron asked menacingly.
“Yeah but nothing heavy Ron, he just runs a few errands for them.”
“IS HE ON THEIR FIRM!” Ronnie suddenly growled.
“Yeah!” said a startled Sammy Carpenter. “Yeah he’s with em.” he added slightly pulling back.
Ron didn’t need to here anymore, like a flash he leapt from the car and stormed off in the direction of the pub, Reg, Tony and Joe hastily followed trying to keep up with him, the other members of the Firm who filled the other five cars quickly ran into the night and ran over to join them.

You could have heard a pin drop when Ron and Reg walked through the doors of the pub followed by twenty four members of the firm. All through the day the pubs topic of conversation had been about the shooting of Charlie Kray, there was still a newspaper resting on the bar with a picture of Ron Kray under the headline of psychopath. When Ron dressed in a finely tailored wool suit and matching overcoat walked in bold as brass, the whole pub seemed to stop; it was a mix of panic and fear.
The landlord of the pub was a big man, a welsh ex rugby player called Alwen Davies, he was very adept and capable of looking after himself and dealing with the usual Saturday night drunks but before his eyes now was a different matter, he felt and knew that he was totally out of his depth here, this was his pub or his domain but right now his fate, and the fate of his customers were out of his control.
Alwen Davies like everyone else in London had heard about the Kray's, he had also heard about the shooting of Charlie, everyone had, his publicans nose smelt that this was something to do with the shooting, the colour seemed to drain from his face as he quickly became worried. He knew from listening to all the drinkers tales and stories over the years that if anyone was foolish enough to cross the Kray's then it was odds on, that they would end up dead. Davies bit his lip hard and sort of said a silent prayer.
Ron, Reg, Tony Lambrianou and Joey Pine walked over to the bar, as the other members of the Firm walked menacingly around the pub looking threateningly at the regulars in what was a clear show of intimidation. No one in the pub met this confrontation; everyone just lowered their heads and backed away from any kind of eye contact.
"Four Gin and tonics." Tony Lambrianou barked to the landlord.
Alwen Davies tried to stop his hands shaking as he carefully poured the drinks, two drinks at a time he placed them on the bar in front of Ron, no money was offered nor asked for.
"Ronnie Fromer been in here today?" Ron asked quietly as he sipped his drink.
"No Ron he hasn't been in here." Davies replied.
"You expecting him in here tonight?"
"No I don't think so."
"Are you sure?" replied Ron a bit louder taking his eyes away from his drink and staring intensely at Davies.
The landlord as a result of Ronnie's cold stare immediately began to feel his cheeks blush, knowing it was Fromer who shot Charlie Kray and now he felt he was being scrutinised as if he was someway something to do with the shooting. But in truth Davies like every other landlord in the area loathed Ronnie Fromer, he was pest, a bully, a man who would walk into pubs and

throw his weight around, Davies never had a clue when Fromer would come and go to his premises.
“He just comes in now and again, I don’t know when.” he replied nervously.
“I heard he collects a pension here for the Anderson’s?” said Ron lowering his voice again.
“Please Ron, whatever your business is, it has nothing to do with me, I’m just a publican trying to make a living, I don’t want to get involved.”
“Well I’m involving you!” snapped Ron.
“Please Ron I have nothing to do with your business.”
“Looks like you have now.” replied Ron casually as he took another sip of his drink then lit up a cigarette.
“From now on, you pay us, FUCK FROMER!”
“Please Ron I don’t want any trouble with you lot.”
“Then do as ya fucking told, you now pay us, if I hear that Fromer gets any more money from here, then I’ll burn the fucking place with you in it down.”
Suddenly Ron’s attention was distracted by a commotion coming from one of the pubs exits; he turned to see that one of the regulars in the pub had tried to leave only to be unfortunate to walk into the way of Eddie Brenner.
“Where you going, go back and sit down!” Brenner growled.
“I want to leave.”
“Listen do as ya fucking told or you’ll be leaving this life!” Brenner replied as he turned and pushed the man back to his chair.
“That’s Dickie the dollar.” Sammy Carpenter whispered after he swiftly walked over to Ron.
“Take him over there.” Ron replied pointing to a table next to the gentlemen’s toilets.
Dickie the dollar was frog-marched towards the table when moments later Ron, Reg and Joey Pine along with Tony Lambrianou and a few other members of the Firm sat down around him.
Dickie the dollar was a man in his forties, balding and slightly fat; he was a fence, a man dealing in stolen property or tin pot villain as Reg called them. He was a man of little principles who often robbed or ripped off ‘straight goers’ people who made an honest living. He was also known as a ‘knocker’ someone who blatantly ripped people off. Dickie got his nickname dollar over twenty years ago when he robbed a bank and mistakenly took only the money bags containing American dollars, subsequently he was arrested for the robbery and the press reporting on the trial mockingly called him the ‘Dollar-man’.
He was not what some would call a particular hard man but he was handy in using a tool, he was a bully whose trait was to glass someone while making them look away. Terry Anderson in his cheap South London way liked having

people like Dickie the dollar around him, most people loathed him, but Terry found him amusing and frequently gave him trivial little collection jobs.
“So you work for Terry Anderson?” Ron asked as he sat down opposite him across the table.
“Look Ron, what’s all this about? If it’s about what happened to ya brother Charlie, then that had fuck all to do with me.”
“You been talking about my brother?” replied Reg.
Dickie shrugged his shoulders.
“Look lads why you asking me all this, I haven’t done a thing to you lot.”
“Where’s that cunt Fromer!” Ron abruptly and angrily said.
Dickie the dollar nervously turned his head away from Reg and looked at Ron, one quick glance told him that Ron was getting wound up.
“I don’t know where he is, honest I don’t.” pleaded Dickie.
“Don’t give us any of that bollocks, where’s he staying?” said Reg butting in.
“Please believe me; I don’t have a clue where he is.”
“But you’re on their firm.”
“What Firm?”
“Your starting to really fucking wind me up!” Ron mouthed.
“The fucking Anderson Firm you ponce!” said Tony Lambrianou as he threw a beer towel at Dickie.
“What’d ya want from me?” Dickie sighed and made a face of ignorance.
“I want Fromer!” growled Ron as grabbed Dickie’s hand across the table and squeezed it firmly.
“I told you I don’t honestly know where he is.”
“Honestly!, you’re as fucking honest as Scotland yard.” snapped Reg.
“One last fucking time, where is he?” asked Ron menacingly still squeezing Dickie’s hand.
“Ron if I knew whe…..”
Ron Kray didn’t wait for him to finish, pulling him across the table by the hand he was squeezing he smacked Dickie with his other hand solidly on the jaw, Dickie reeled back in his chair dazed as blood began to spill from his mouth.
“Pick him up!” demanded Ron as he got to his feet.
Tony and Eddie Brenner picked Dickie up under the arms and followed Ron, Reg, and Joey Pine into the gent’s toilets. Once inside Ron wasted no time on going to town on Dickie, as Tony and Eddie held him Ron punched him again in the face and then twice in the stomach making Dickie spew up the pint of beer he had just drank.
“I fucking mean it, this is ya last chance.” growled Ron now squeezing Dickie’s face.

“We ain’t fucking around.” Reg shouted as he slapped him hard on the temple.
Dickie still groggy from the punches gasped for air, Ron silently waited for a reply, Reg slapped him again.
“Well!” he shouted forcefully.
Dickie just coughed and spat blood from his bleeding lip, some blood dripped onto Ron’s hand as again Dickie coughed from the blood that was going down his throat, he again gasped for air as he tried to get his words out.
Ron suddenly and for no apparent reason through impatience decided enough was enough, he let go of Dickie’s face and reached inside his overcoat pocket, as Dickie saw Ron pull out a 38 revolver his legs went limp, Tony and Eddie firmed their grip as Ron pushed the gun into Dickie’s nose forcing it to bend.
“Fuck this mug.” said Ron through gritted teeth as he cocked the gun.
Joey Pine standing nearby suddenly leapt forward and pulled Ron’s arm away.
“NO RON! Not like this.” he said with a potent voice.
Ron turned violently towards Joe, his eyes were narrowed and his face was tense, through rage and bravado he was on that vulnerable edge of forgetting reason and going out of control.
“Ron theirs fifty fucking witnesses out there.” added Joe determined.
“No one, will grass.” replied Ron.
“RON!” yelled Joe as he shook Ron’s arm trying to shake some sense into him.
“This ain’t the right way.” Joe added
“Ron, Joe’s right.” Reg suddenly said as he stepped closer.
Ron turned and looked at his brother, Reg was now holding Ron’s other arm, he quickly glimpsed back at Joe before relaxing his posture and a slight wry smile broke on his face.
“Yeah alright.” he sighed as Reg and Joe let go of his arms.
Stepping a pace away from Dickie Ron carefully released the hammer on his pistol and then pulled out a bullet from the gun.
“Open ya mouth.” Ron calmly said as he turned back at Dickie.
Dickie the dollar at this stage would have opened his arse if Ronnie asked he was so terrified, Ron pushed the bullet into Dickie’s mouth and grabbed his cheeks.
“Chew ya mug.”
“CHEW!” he shouted pushing his head back against the wall. Dickie closed his eyes and began to chew, Tony Lambrianou still holding his arms winced as he heard a tooth break in his bleeding mouth.
Ronnie smiled as he heard the sound of Dickie breaking his tooth
“Keep chewing!” he laughed grabbing his face again and pulling his cheeks as if helping him to chew.
“You know Dickie, I came here tonight with the intention to blow someone’s fucking head off, but as its getting near Christmas I’m gonna give you a pass,

how bout that, season of goodwill and all that festive stuff, so when we leave ya I want you to tell everyone what a great fella Ron Kray is."
Ron then smashed a right hand punch hard into Dickie's face breaking the man's jaw and sending him flying into the urinals. As Ron and the others walked out, Tony tapped Eddie on the arm to listen to Ron, Eddie looked in front and saw Ron humming the tune of 'O come all ye faithful' Eddie shook his head in amazement and smiled.
"No one would fucking believe this Tone, two minutes ago we had to stop him shooting someone in the head now look, he's singing fucking Christmas carols."
"And our birds wonder why were always pissed?" replied Tony quietly which brought a smile to both men's faces.
As the Firm walked out of the pub towards the cars everyone including Reg noticed the excited mood that Ron was in, Ron rubbed his hands together and walked with a new found spring in his step quickly over to the car.
"Someone's gonna get hurt tonight." Tony said quietly to Joey Pine. Joe in turn hung back as he waited for Ron to climb into the car before pulling Reg to one side.
"What the fuck was all that about Reg!" Joe angrily said.
"What?....what's the matter?" Reg replied a bit annoyed at the way Joe had tugged his arm and pulled him to one side.
"That Bollocks back there! The fucking shooter Reg."
"What'd ya expect Joe."
"I didn't expect Ron to start pulling shooters out in front of a hundred fucking people."
"He didn't use it, don't worry about it Joe."
"Listen Reg, I'm here as a pal but I'm not here for fucking surprises like that." said Joe pointing angrily towards the pub.
"Joe I don't know what you want me to say, you know what were here doing tonight."
"Course I fucking know, but there's a right way and a wrong way, that bollocks in there was definitely the fucking wrong way."
"We need to make a show, need to let every fucker know were here and we mean business."
"Reg, what's the fucking matter with you, you know what we did in there was nuts, making a show is one thing but pulling out shooters in packed pubs is fucking suicide, the only fucking show were gonna do like that is show everyone the quickest way to get nicked."
"Joe it'll be alright mate."
"It fucking wont Reg, if you don't pull Ronnie up, he's gonna use that fucking gun tonight and you know it."

“We gotta be tooled up, what ya would expect us to go looking with just our fists.”
Joe shook his head in frustration as a short tense moment of silence fell between them.
“Don’t take this the wrong way Reg, I owe you two a fucking lot especially Ron, but I’m not going to repay ya by acting like this mate, this fucking bollocks ain’t me, I don’t work like this.”
“Joe! Charlie’s in hospital with a belly full of bullets.”
Joe stopped Reg in mid-sentence.
“I know what they fucking did to Charlie but going into packed pubs pulling out shooters ain’t my scene Reg, if were gonna do some serious work then let’s talk quietly about it, let’s do it fucking proper without all the eyes.”
“Look don’t worry Joe.”
“No Reg I’m going, I’m not doing no more of this tonight, if you and Ron wanna talk to me on your own tomorrow then give me a call.”
“So your just gonna fucking walk away tonight.”
“That’s fucking right and if you had and sense you’d do the fucking same.”
“C’mon Joe.”
“No Reg, this is fucking crazy, call me tomorrow.” Joe said finally before walking off and pulling one of his pals Terry Millit out from one of the cars.
Reg shrugged and then got back into the car where Ron was.
“Joe’s going.” he said to his brother.
“Don’t blame him Reg.” Ron calmly replied.
“WHAT!” replied Reg shocked at his brother’s calm manner.
“Not his scene Reg, you know Joe he likes to do things his way.” Ronnie said.
“Joe’s with us Reg, he’s always with us, he’s as fucking staunch as they come but if he don’t wanna be with us tonight then I can understand that.” he added.
Reg sighed loudly and waved his hand in a frustrated gesture then just leaned back in the seat.
“Drive the car Johnny, c’mon let’s get fucking out of here.” Ron then demanded before starting to hum Christmas carols again. Reg tapped Tony’s arm and grinned at his brother.
The rain kept pouring and the next few hours seemed to waltz past as minutes, as the Firm visited half a dozen more South London pubs. Ron in this fearless mood was unstoppable, he pushed and punched his way about the pubs shouting his message loud and clear ‘we want Fromer and his paymasters the Anderson’s’. This was a declaration of war; once again East London and South London were going to lock heads. One way or another Ron was going to get mad Ronnie Fromer and if it meant going into a full pitched gang war with another major London crime family then so be it. The Kray’s had made their name fighting other villains so to Ron this was just another day of business.

As midnight approached the convoy of six cars led by Ron's Jaguar pulled over by a tea stall on Battersea Bridge. Eddie Brenner and Tony Lambrianou stepped out of the car and stretched their legs as Johnny Walsh went over to the tea stall to get Ronnie a warm drink. Eddie stretched out his arms as he watched the firms other five cars parking up behind.
"Alright Sam." Eddie sighed as Sammy Carpenter came running in the rain from a car behind only to pass him and jump into the drives seat of Ron's jag.
"What now Ron, what'd ya wanna do?" Sammy asked in his usual fast way.
"Fromer's got to be somewhere; some fuck must know where he is."
"He's had it on his toes Ron, we won't find him tonight." Reg added.
"He's around somewhere Reg; he's too much of a lippy bastard to be hiding."
"Are ya staying here for a bit Ron?" Sammy asked.
"Why?"
"Let me find a phone box Ron, it's a long shot but I asked a couple of card players from over this way to keep their eyes open."
"Be quick then Sam, you know the laws looking for Ron."
"Be five minutes Reg, there's a call box just down the road."
In a dimly lit room of a Lavender Hill pub barely two miles away from where Ron and Reg sat, there were six burly men sitting together deep in conversation, Ronnie Fromer, Terry, Jackie and Alan Anderson, Bob Ferris and Shamus O'Callaghan. They sat on a corner table sharing a bottle of malt whiskey keeping their voices down so as not to disturb the illegal card game that was being played just yards away.
Giles and Bill Anderson then entered the room and walked quickly over.
"They're all over the fucking manor Tel." Giles quietly but firmly said.
"We gotta meet this fucking head on Tel." Jackie declared angrily.
"I say let's get tooled up and go over their fucking manor." Fromer mouthed in his usual aggressive way.
"They're already in our fucking manor!" Terry replied.
"Then let's go and fucking do em!" replied Fromer aggressively and loudly enough to disturb the men playing cards.
"Keep ya fucking voice down will ya." Terry snapped. "Just fucking calm down, you've caused enough fucking agro already." he added.
"What we gonna do then Terry, Ronnie's got a point we can nay just fooking sit here all night." Jackie said.
Terry Anderson poured himself a very large whiskey and downed it in one.
"Right lets go and do some rounds then, you lot tooled up?"
"Nay fooking bother there Tel, am a tooled to ya fooking eyeballs." replied Jackie getting to his feet.
"Not you Ron, you're staying here." Terry then added as he saw Ronnie Fromer get up.
"What!" protested Ron.

"You fucking stay!" demanded Terry again.
"It's my fucking row." Ronnie pleaded.
"Not tonight it's not, I want you here, Bob and Alan are staying here with you too, no one knows about this place so your be out of harm's way, or better still if you're here then you won't be getting up to any more fucking mischief."
"Ah for fucks sake." Fromer sighed sitting down clearly showing his disappointment.
"Where the fucking hell is Sammy?" Ron Kray impatiently said as he threw the empty cup of tea he was drinking out the window.
"Can't stay here for long Ron, your right on offer here."
"Let's give him another couple of minutes Reg, and then were have to go."
"Hold up Ron I see him now." Eddie Brenner said standing beside the window.
Sammy Carpenter ran up to the car and jumped into the back seat besides Reg.
"RESULT!" he said happily. "He's in a pub over in Lavender Hill, upstairs they got a card game going on, he's up there with three of the Anderson's."
"Is this reliable Sammy?" Reg asked as his mind thought about the possibility of a trap.
"It's hundred percent Reg, one of the fellas gambling hates Fromer, I've known him since I was a kid we were both in Approved school together."
"Let's fucking go!" Ron snapped.
"Hold on Ron." Reg replied as he turned back to Sammy.
"Do you know the pub?"
"Yeah I know it well."
"Right I don't want us pulling up right outside Sam, we're follow you, so take us near the pub, somewhere quiet where we can park up, I don't want to mark their card that were outside alright."
"Don't worry Reg, the pubs next to an old abandoned bus garage, we can park in there."
"Right let's fucking go!"
"How'd ya wanna do this Ron?" Reg asked as the car pulled away.
"Don't know yet Reg, let's have a look at the pub and then we'll decide."
Moments later the car Sammy carpenter was in led Ronnie jag and four other cars into the gates of the abandoned bus garage, the garage was perfect, it was dark and completely out of sight from the pub hidden by its large surrounding walls.
Ron and Reg got out of the car and looked through a large crack in a wall and looked over the road at the pub, the street was completely empty and there was only the rain that was making any noise. Ron turned and spoke to his Firm who were all now out of the cars and standing huddled around nearby.
"That's the pub then Sammy?" Ron quietly asked.

“That’s it Ron, see that room on the first floor, that’s where they play the cards.”
Ronnie turned around again and looked through the crack.
“Listen” he said turning back, “Me and Reg are gonna walk round the pub and check it out, I want you lot to stay here but keep ya fucking eyes open, if any cars pull up I don’t want it to be just me and Reg having a row alright.”
“Don’t worry Ron we got your back.” Tony replied.
Both Ron and Reg almost at the same time pulled up the collars on their overcoats as if trying to hide their faces, Ron then took a cap off of one of his pals and put it on his head as the two men walked away.
“Can’t see many cars parked.” Ron whispered to his brother.
“I can see seven.” replied Reg.
“There’s no one downstairs.” Ron said as they quietly walked past the first door.
Reg stopped slightly as looked at the door.
“It’s reinforced Ron.”
“We’d have to drive a fucking car to open that Reg.”
The brothers then walked around to the next door and both saw that it was exactly the same, big old Victorian solid wood doors.
Moments later the twins were back behind the garage wall with the rest of the firm.
“What we gonna do Ron?” Tony Lambrianou asked.
Ronnie asked him for a fag and then put his head into his coat to light it so as not to make a glow with the match.
“We can’t kick the doors in, they’re fucking solid.” Reg said.
“Why not just knock!” Eddie Brenner asked.
“If we do that then we might as well just smash our way in through the windows.” Reg snapped back.
“Nah they’re bound to have some sort of secret knock or a hidden bell, if there up there playing cards then there not going to just open the fucking door at this time of night.” Billy Hayes replied giving his knowledge as host of these kind of card games.
“What about making out were old bill?” Slice’em Sid asked.
“Won’t work Sid, there think it’s someone trying to knock of the game?”
“Let’s just wait em out, they gotta leave sometime”
As this conversation was going on Ron had walked away by himself and was quietly smoking his fag, deep in thought he gazed intently towards the pub, he could hear the Firm talking behind him but he wasn’t listening. Once he finished the cigarette he walked back over.
“Tony, Eddie, Billy and George I want you standing over by the first door, now there’s a small ledge so I want you all to push up against the wall, it’s important that they can’t see you from any of the windows alright. Me, Reg,

Tommy and Alex will be by the other door, now Sid I want you to act drunk outside, start singing and falling over, make a right fucking racket but keep an eye out to see if anyone looks out from any of those windows above, when someone looks out I want you to start pissing up one of those cars. Its odds on they belong to someone in there, with a bit of luck someone will come down to clear you off, when they open those doors, we're in."
"You heard him sing Ron." Tony joked.
"Shut up, be fucking serious." Ronnie barked back as he walked over to Sid.
"Open ya jacket, pull ya shirt out." he said pulling and tugging at Sid.
"C'mon you gotta look a right fucking mess, like ya out of ya fucking head." Ron said as he messed up Sid's hair.
Moments later Sid was outside the pub staggering around "HE AINT HEAVY HE'S MY BROTHER" he sang loudly trying hard to sound drunk. Tony and Eddie had to cover their mouths to stop themselves from laughing
"HE AINT HEAVY HE'S MY BROTHER!" Sid sang over and over again trying to sing the hollies track that was currently No 3. In the music charts.
"What the fucking hells all that outside!" Ronnie Fromer said as he poured himself a drink. Bob Ferris and Alan Anderson got up and pulled back the curtain.
"Some fucking drunk!" Alan shouted back.
"OI! FUCK OFF!" Alan shouted as he knocked on the window.
Sid looked up and staggered against a car, "Bollocks!" he mouthed back as he then began to piss up one of the cars.
"Cheeky cunt just said bollocks." Alan Anderson laughed.
"WHAT!" Fromer said as walked over.
"THAT CUNTS PISSING UP MY CAR!" Fromer then angrily snapped and then banged hard on the window "OI! DO YOU WANNA A CLUMP!" he shouted.
"I'll go and get rid of the cunt." said Bob Ferris as he walked away.
"Yeah fuck him off quick Bob, we don't want the old bill round here." Alan added.
"Yeah and hit the cunt on the chin for pissing on my car will ya."
"Don't worry I'll kick him up the bollocks." Ferris yelled back as he left the room.
Ron tensed and grabbed Reg's arm as the hall light came on behind the door he was standing outside of "Get ready Reg." he whispered. Bob Ferris unbolted the door and opened it, Ron like lightening leapt out and pushed the door open, together with Reg they quickly covered Bob's mouth and threw him to the ground, Ron pulled out a gun and pushed it into his eye.
"Keep ya fucking mouth shut!" he growled quietly.
"Who's upstairs?"

“Fromer’s up there with Alan Anderson, a couple of dealers and six gamblers.” Bob Ferris replied terrified. Seconds later there were ten members of the Firm inside the door. Ferris was held down as Ron, Reg, Tony, Eddie, Billy and George Hayes and Tommy and Alex Jones shooters in their hands quietly crept up the stairs. When they reached the top, Ron motioned silently with his hand to stop, he then placed his ear at the door and listened for a moment what was being said in the room. Turning to his brother he held up three fingers “On the count of three.” he mouthed silently.
“1,…2…3” he then said.
Ron then hit the door with his shoulder smashing it from its hinges, they burst into the room. Fromer and Anderson jumped up in shock as the eight armed men poured inside. Ron seeing Fromer walked straight over and violently pistol whipped him across the face sending him crashing to the floor. Tommy and Alex Jones quickly rounded up the gamblers and the dealers and took them out of the room; Tommy locked them in the kitchen before returning to see Ron who was now kicking the living daylights out of Fromer on the floor.
“You fucking cunt!” Ronnie screamed with spit flying from his mouth in rage. “CUNT!” he shouted as he stamped on Fromer’s face breaking his nose. The beating went on and on until Alan Anderson begged Ron to stop.
“Please that’s enough, you’re killing him!”
Ronnie grabbed Anderson by the throat.
“He doesn’t deserve to die.” Alan added.
“Deserves got fuck all to do with it.” Ron said wincing in anger just before taking out a knife and slashing Anderson right across the face. Fromer was now a bleeding and battered mess but he still managed to get himself to his feet.
“Put the gun down and let’s fucking ave it Kray.” he barely managed to say. Ron turned ominously towards him, he gave the gun to Reg and then with knife in hand walked determinedly towards Fromer, Fromer barely managed to raise a fist as Ronnie sank the knife full to the hilt into his throat, Fromer screamed in a gargled voice as he grabbed Ron’s hand that was holding the knife. Ronnie stabbed Fromer so hard that the momentum forced both men to fall over, Ron landed on top of Fromer and then pulled out the knife and stuck it repeatedly back into his neck another five times. Blood shot everywhere as Fromer’s life left his body. Ron smacked the bloody face of Fromer before giving him one last stab in the heart.
“CUNT!” he mouthed as he spat in his dead face. Reg then walked over and helped up his brother, once Ron was up Reg bent down and pulled the knife out from Fromer’s heart, then suddenly Reg stuck it into Fromer’s face just below the eye.
“That’s it Reg, show that fucker that we’re a family.” Ronnie said.

Ron slowly turned and walked over to Alan Anderson who was standing by the wall holding his face almost in a state of shock at witnessing the severity of violence that he had just seen.
"Tell your brothers that I'm satisfied, I got what I came down here for." Ron said grabbing him by the throat, Alan nodded silently back, the sight of Ronnie looking at him with his face and hands smothered in Fromer's blood chilled his soul, never in all his life had Alan seen such a cold and intense man. It was all in the eyes, Ronnie would squint his eyes as if looking at something in the distance but when Ron looked deeply into someone's face this way, it somehow showed an inner strength that was difficult to comprehend.
As Ron was warning Alan Anderson, Reg began smashing the tops off of vodka and whisky bottles and pouring the contents about the room, on the curtains, carpets and sofa's,
"C'MON!" he urged Tony and Eddie to do likewise.
Billy Hayes then returned to the room after finding a tin of paraffin.
"Here ya go Reg." he said handing over the tin.
Reg splashed the paraffin over most of the floor as Tony Lambrianou threw a few found sheets and blankets and pillows in a heap.
"Ere Reg, give it here." Tony said grabbing the can of paraffin and then pouring it onto the pile.
Reg then turned to the Jones brothers and told them to get Ron back to the car. Ronnie in turn took off his blood saturated overcoat and suit jacket and threw them on the pile of blankets and sheets.
"Make sure these fucking burn!" he demanded at Tony.
Tony poured out the rest of the paraffin onto them as Ron disappeared out the room. Reg then told the Hayes brothers to put Alan Anderson and Bob Ferris into the kitchen with the rest of the gamblers and dealers, lock the door and fetch the key back to him.
"Tony you stay with me, the rest of you get back to the cars and fuck off, George bring one of the motors down the road and wait for me and Tony alright."
"By the bus garage Reg." George Hayes asked.
"Yeah just where we pulled in, but make sure the others get going now."
"Alright Reg."
Reg then sent Tony over by the window.
"Tell me when you see the cars going." Reg said.
Reg carried on saturating the room with booze until Tony called out.
"They're gone, everyone but George."
"Good give us a match Tony." replied Reg.
Tony walked over and gave Reg a box.

“What about them.” he said as he nodded in the direction of the kitchen and the trapped men.
“Let em fucking roast” Reg replied calmly.
“Reg.” Tony said sheepishly grabbing hold of Reggie’s arm.
“Half of those in there are innocent Reg.”
“They can tell the old bill can’t they.”
Tony sighed loudly; his whole body reaction showed that this didn’t agree with him
“I don’t know Reg.”
“What!” Reggie snapped back smiling.
“Don’t taste right mate, Ron wanted Alan Anderson to pass on the message”
“I thought you were tough.” Reg replied.
Tony couldn’t answer Reg; he felt a lump rise in his throat.
“Let’s fucking do it.” he hesitantly and very unconvincingly replied.
Reg fumbled with the matches, he threw one over at the curtains and they immediately burst into flames, Reg repeated this until all of the far side of the room was ablaze, Reg then pulled Tony back to the doorway and threw a match onto the pile of blankets, sheets and Ron’s blood soaked clothes, the pile burst into flames. The room was now filling with smoke and the heat was beginning to feel too hot, Tony pulled his collar up to his mouth to avoid breathing in the smoke.
“REG THAT’S IT MATE, LETS GO.” he shouted with panic in his voice, Reg pulled up his collar and then pushed Tony out the room, Tony went to run down the stairs but Reg called him back. Tony stopped and saw Reg standing by the kitchen door fumbling for a key in his pocket.
“You bastard.” Tony sighed relieved but slightly angry at Reg winding him up.
“Come on I can’t find the fucking key.” Reg shouted
Moment’s later Tony and Reg shoulder crashed the door. Reg burst into the room to tell the men in side that they could leave but he discovered that the men had already escaped through a broken window.
“Fuck me there gone.” Reg shouted through the noise of the fire.
“Are you sure.” Tony shouted back.
Reg gave the place a quick look over.
“Yeah they’ve legged it.”
“Let’s go!” Tony shouted pulling Reg with him onto the stairs.
Both men ran down the steep wooden stairs and ran into the freshness of the night, George Hayes saw them running and he pulled the car out into the street, both men climbed into the back as George kicked down the accelerator. The car was gone in a few seconds, the threat and the revenge of Fromer was also gone.

“I was just about to come in there looking for ya.” George said driving the car and commenting on how ablaze the pub was and how long Reg and Tony were inside.
“Fucking hell George, I’ll tell ya mate another couple of minutes and we would have been roast dinner” sighed Tony as he wiped the sweat from his face.
“Was you pulling my leg back there Reg?” Tony then asked lowering his voice and turning towards him.
“I felt sorry for ya mate, I saw you standing on the stairs and I knew you’re a bit of the religious type, so thought about your conscience.”
“So you was gonna let them burn?”
“I don’t know Tone; it seemed a good idea at the time.”
Tony shook his head slightly at the callousness of Reg but decided it was best not to say no more about it.
Reg looked out of the window and the words he just said ‘Seemed like a good idea.’ went over and over in his head, he lowered his head as if he felt ashamed, truth is at first he was just playing with Tony but he knew that for a moment back there, a hearts beat moment he did play with the idea of letting them burn, he felt himself feeling nauseous at the thought of killing a dozen people, he wondered what he was becoming but then he snapped out of it as he thought of his brothers
“Where’s Ron?” Reg asked George.
“Said for us to meet him at the Carpenters.” replied George meaning the Carpenters Arms pub in Bethnal Green.
“Alright get us there quick.”

Not Guilty Your Honour
Chapter Eight
'Another day in London'

Ron Kray always kept a spare set of clothes in one of the bedrooms upstairs in the Carpenter's Arms; it was like a little home from home for him as he stayed there many a time. Only Ron had the key for the bedroom as inside it you would think you was in a posh West End hotel, Ron had decorated the room in plush fabric wallpaper, the kind that you found in the west End Theatres, dominating the middle of the room was a huge four poster king-size bed with matching wardrobes and cabinets, he had Italian silk sheets on the bed and an Italian marble fire surround on the chimney breast. As the rest of the Firm were ordering their drinks Ron was busy lighting the coal fire, he took off every stitch of his clothes and threw them on the floor next to the fire. He waited for the fire to flame up by having a cigarette on his bed and picking up the phone. He dialled the number of his Mum's house in Vallance road. The phone rang a few times before it answered.
"Mum." Ron asked.
"Is that you Ron?" his Dad Charlie asked.
"Where's mum?"
"Down the hospital, you alright son?"
"Yeah I'm fine, how's Charlie?"

“He’s alright, he’s on the mend.”
“Alright dad, tell Mum I called, tell her I love her.”
“Is everything alright son?”
“Yeah don’t worry.”
Ronnie took another drag on his cigarette as put down the phone, the fire was now blazing so put his shoes on it one at a time, he then ripped up his shirt and trousers and placed them piece by piece onto the burning coals.
Reg walked into the pub through the back door just as Ron was walking down into the bar from his room upstairs, Reg noticed that Ron had showered and changed his clothes
“Is there anything up there for me to put on?” he asked Ron.
“Help yourself.” replied Ron reaching into his pocket and throwing Reg the key.
“Look at the fucking state of ya.” Ron added looking at Reg’s soot ridden face.
Reg just looked Ron up and down as if to silently say, well you look all speck and span.
“And make sure you burn all your clobber, there’s a fire going upstairs, sling ya gear on that, and don’t forget ya shoes.” added Ron.
“Our shoes!” Tony Lambrianou questioned.
“We’ve all done it!” shouted Eddie Brenner as he held up his socks and pointed at the large coal fire in the bar which now had eight pairs of smouldering shoes on it.
“I’ve just paid fucking forty quid for them, there Italian!” Tony snapped loudly.
“Burn the fucking things! Anyone who went upstairs in that room will have blood on his shoes.” Ron shouted back pointing seriously at Tony’s shoes.
“Are you serious Ron?” Tony pleaded “I’ll give em a good scrub.” he added.
“Burn the fucking shoes now!” replied Ron as grabbed Tony’s leg as if he was going to take them off him himself.
“Alright Ron alright.” Tony said as he raised his leg and slipped off the shoes.
“Fucking shame, beautiful fucking Italian shoes, it’s alright for him, he’s got clothes upstairs, I gotta go out in this weather now with no fucking shoes, not to mention what I’m gonna tell my wife when I get home in bare feet.” said Tony quietly to Reg as he walked across to the fire place.
“What’s that you said?” Ronnie shouted hearing Tony mumbling.
“Nothing Ron!, just joking that my feet are gonna get wet in the fucking rain.”
Ron squinted his eyes.
“Ah poor little Tony, look big fucking villain worried about getting his fucking little feet wet!, just burn the poxy things and stop acting the mug.” shouted Ron in a tone that always puzzled people even ones who were very close to him whether he was joking about or being serious.

Ron sat down next to Johnny Walsh and Johnny immediately got up and returned shortly with a large gin and tonic for him.
"You alright Ron?" Johnny affectionately asked.
"What about a drink for us." George Hayes joked.
"Get em ya fucking self!" Johnny replied.
Ronnie then called over the Jones brother's Tommy and Alex and told them to sit down at the table.
"Cheers." Ronnie said holding up his glass to Eddie Brenner, George and Billy Hayes, Slice'em Sid, Sammy Carpenter, Johnny, and the Jones brothers Tommy and Alex.
"To a good job well done." he added smiling broadly.
"Well done lads, help ya self's to the drink." added Ronnie standing up and raising his glass to the other members of his Firm scattered around the pub.
"Cheers Ron." some of them shouted back.
Johnny Walsh pulled out a packet of players from his pocket and lit a cigarette for Ron, Ron took a large drag and gulped at his drink, he then patted Eddie and Tommy whom were closest to him to come closer.
"One more job tonight, alright, I hear that the Williams's have got a café over in Hoxton square, lets burn the fucking place down tonight."
"Half of us ain't got any fucking shoes Ron." Eddie joked.
"One of them lot will do it, get ya cousins to do it Sid." Ronnie replied turning to Sid and pointing at his two cousins Jeff and Simon.
"There only boys Ron."
"What difference does that make?"
"Well if we want it done prop…"
Ronnie interrupted him.
"You underestimate people Sid, call em over."
The two lads just in their twenties at Ronnie's behest walked over and sat down next to him
"Do you know Hoxton square?" Ronnie asked warmly.
"Yes Mr Kray, we were brought up just round the corner."
"Good, now come closer lads, I need you to do me a favour, do ya think you can do it for me?"
"Yeah course whatever you want."
"That's good!, I knew you were good boys, now there's a café in Hoxton square, it belongs to someone I don't like so I need it burned down tonight, do you think you two can do this for the Firm."
The eldest of the two Simon, nodded his head.
"No problem, if that's what you want Mr Kray then it's done."
"Terrific, talk to Sammy he'll get someone to take you there, now do a good job wont ya, I want it burned to the ground."

“It will be done Mr Kray; if that café ain’t a pile of ashes by the morning then you can burn me instead.”
“I like your attitude son, make sure you come and see me, when you’ve done this.” replied Ron smiling.
Reg Kray threw a clean white shirt to Tony as both men finished burning their clothes on the fire in Ronnie’s bedroom.
“Ere Reg, this shirt has got RK on the pocket, Ron won’t mind will he.” asked Tony as he put it on and commenting on the embroidered initials.
“It’s either wear that shirt and these strides or go downstairs with your knackers hanging out.” replied Reg as threw Tony a pair of trousers.
Tony threw on the trousers and tucked in his shirt then turned and admired himself in Ron full length mirror.
“That fucker Decosta don’t cut my trousers like these.” said Tony commenting on the sharp cut of Ron’s trousers.
“That’s Ron, Tone, he likes his suits cut sharp, like a fucking 1920,s gangster, listen I’m going to see Decosta tomorrow, he’s doing me a lovely whistle, flared and wide lapels like all the stars are wearing.” Reg replied as sat on the bed doing up his shoe laces.
“Why don’t you come wit…” he added only to stop in mid-sentence.
“What’s the matter?” Tony asked noticing Reg pause.
Reg sighed before answering.
“Almost fucking forgot what we’d been doing over the last twenty four hours, was gonna say why don’t you come with me to Decostas but that’s not going to happen now is it.”
“Do’ ya think things are gonna turn nasty Reg?” Tony asked.
“I don’t think we’re gonna be having much fun for a bit are we, first things first we gotta get Ron out of the way Tone, the laws still looking for him and fuck knows what’s gonna happen when they find Fromer.”
“You worried about them nicking us?”
“Maybe, maybe not, but we better get a few alibis all the same.”
After a slight moment of silence Tony sat down on the bed next to reg.
“We really put our balls on the chopping block tonight Reg.” he said with an air of frustration.
“Don’t I fucking know it.” Reg replied in the same voice.
“Half of fucking South London knew we were looking for Fromer last night and there were a lot of people saw us in that room Reg.”
“Fuck it, it’s done now mate.”
“I’ll tell ya, Joey was fucking right to piss off like he did.” said Tony.
“For Joey Reg it was the right thing to do, but me and Ron never had a choice mate.”
“Charlie.” Tony added.

"He's our brother, when its family Tone you can't just sit on it, wait for a good time, you have to react, you gotta just fucking do it, and whether you get nicked for it doesn't come in to it."
"Bollocks to it all Reg!" Tony suddenly said with a more defiant voice "We've had the poxy law looking at us for years, so what's the fucking difference mate."
Reg's posture relaxed a bit as a result of his friend's carefree manner, he smiled and lit himself and Tony a cigarette.
"You know something Tony." he said pausing for a moment as he placed a hand of friendship on Tony's shoulder.
"It's at times like this that me and Ron are the luckiest blokes in the whole pissing world, tell ya mate all the fucking tea in china couldn't buy the friends that we got."
Tony nodded and smiled at what Reg had said and he placed his hand reassuringly on top of Reg's hand still on his shoulder.
"I'm always here for you mate, thick or thin, we're the fucking Firm ain't we!, like them musketeers, all for and one for all." he said in a loud and stern voice which made Reg grin.
"Came a long way ain't we Tony, brought up in a poxy tin box terraced house in a corner of London nobody gives a fuck about, deserters corner they called our street. Growing up on the wrong side of the blitz, fucking V2's and poxy doodlebugs bombing us every night! But look at us now Tone, look at us, clubs, pubs, suits, birds, FELLA'S, money, we got the whole fucking world at our feet,"
Tony got to his feet smiling abruptly as he stretched for an ashtray.
"Typical!" he snapped,
"What?" Reg Asked,
"Only a Kray could possibly say something like that at a time like this."
"What, what I say?"
"Got the world at our feet!, we got the law after us, god knows how many Firms have the needle with us and say we got the world at our feet, right about now Reg all I want at my fucking feet is bloody good pair of shoes." added Tony laughing.
"C'mon lets go and have a bleeding drink." Reg said jumping up and laughing.
By the time Reg and Tony reached the bar downstairs Ron was already on his third large gin and tonic, Sammy Carpenter had left with his cousins for the William's café in Hoxton and Eddie Brenner and the Jones and Hayes brothers were already half way to getting pissed.
Upon seeing Reg Johnny Walsh who was sitting next to Ron immediately gave up his chair for him.

“Looks good on you that.” Ron greeted his brother commenting on one of his suits on him.
“I don’t know about that Ron; look at the fucking shoulder pads.”
“What fucking shoulder pads!” snapped Ron.
“These fucking things, it’s like I got two bloody great boxing gloves stuck on my shoulders.”
“Oh piss off; you ain’t got a clue about suits.”
“Times are changing Ron, you gotta be in with the fashion now mate.” Eddie Brenner laughed.
“I couldn’t care less about what all these pricks are wearing.”
“What about growing your hair Ron?” Brenner added joking.
“Yeah!” Ronnie replied.
“Like all these filthy hippie bastards, tell Reg he might grow his hair long.” added Ronnie.
“Might just do that Ron, Decosta’s doing me this right nice pinstripe number, flared bottoms and flared lapels, I see the same whistle on John Lennon last week down at James’s gaff.” Reg said.
“John Lennon, how can you look like John Lennon, he’s from Liverpool.”
“What difference does that fucking make?”
“They walk different from us.”
“You mean talk different.” Brenner added.
“No I said they walk differently, they like playing football in Liverpool so it makes their legs bandy, it’s a fact.”
Reg shook his head at his brother and gave him a look as if he was stark raving bonkers, however Reg was used to Ron’s weird little ironies so he just sighed and winked at Tony and Eddie.
“Anyway like I said Lennon walked in the club with two Chinese birds on his arm wearing this black pinstripe suit with a white trilby hat.”
“Ah I bet he looked a fucking picture.” Ron interrupted sarcastically.
“The suit looked fantastic Ron, you should have seen it.”
“I would have chinned the flash bastard.” Ron calmly replied witch got everyone laughing.
“So how bout it Ron, we gonna see you in flares soon or better still what about one of those hippie beards they all got?” Brenner said joking.
Ron smiled excitingly.
“Not in a million years would you get me looking like a fucking Beatle, can you imagine what Mum would say Reg, if I grew a beard.”
“I think a beard would suit you Ron.” Reg replied.
“Piss off!” Ron snapped.
“Why not, you could have one of those pointed ones.”
Ronnie laughed then held up his hand to get everyone’s attention.

“listen seriously, you should never have a beard, and I’ll tell ya why, if you got a beard and you get into a fight then it’s no good, they can grab it and pull you down and then hit you over the fucking head with something, so I’m telling everyone now I don’t want none of our Firm growing beards alright,” Ronnie banged the table as he finished, suddenly the jovial mood in the room cooled, Ron was in one of his unpredictable moments, somewhere in between having a good time and being annoyed, everyone knew that with Ron you had to tread very carefully when throwing playful banter around, he could change viscously at the drop of a hat. Only Reg could push Ron at this stage and get away with it,
“Alright Ron, no beards.” Reg said trying hard to not laugh “Do ya hear this lads no one on the Firm is ever allowed a beard!” he shouted across the room.
“You taking the piss?” Ron calmly and suddenly said turning his head.
“Nah just agreeing with what you said.” replied Reg still in a playful mood.
“It fucking sounds like you’re taking the piss.”
“Ron I ain’t taking the piss.”
“You sure?”
“Yeah I’m sure.”
“Well you don’t want to take the piss Reg.”
“I ain’t taking the fucking piss.”
“Alright that’s good then.”
“Yeah good.”
At this point Tony whispered to Brenner.
“Here we fucking go again.”
Reg leaned back in his chair and lit himself a cigarette; he threw the match onto the table as if he had the hump.
“Thinking about it Ron, Dodger Mullins had a beard and he could have a right fucking row.”
“Dodger never had a beard!” snapped Ron.
“He bloody did.”
“He fucking never Reg, it was stubble.”
“Fucking stubble! It was half way down his fucking chest.”
“No it weren’t!”
“Yes it was!”
“Anyway it was different with Dodger” Ron snapped getting angrier.
“What’d ya mean different?”
“He was a tasty bastard!” Ron snapped.
“But he had a beard Ron.” Reg replied.
Ron turned his body towards his brother.
“What do ya keep going on about beards for Reg., you say you ain’t taking the piss but it bloody well sounds like you are to me, what do ya wanna make me look a fucking mug for?”

“Ron I’m only saying.”
“Yeah you’re saying too fucking much!”
“Bollocks!” snapped Reg.
“Bollocks to you.” replied Ron only louder.
Sammy Carpenter pulled up his car just on the corner of Argyle Street and Hoxton Square; he had been moaning all the way there,
“Do this, do that!, it’s getting on my fucking nerves this is, there all getting pissed where am I, out in the fucking rain that’s where. Right now the cafes round the corner, just get the fucking thing done so we can fuck off out of it!” he snapped angrily to his cousin Simon and Jeff.
“Ain’t you coming with us?”
“Am I bollocks, you got the paraffin, I’ve already done too fucking much tonight, you two wanna be big men so go and fucking do it.”
“Alright Sam, you’ll be here.” replied Simon.
“Yeah where else am I gonna fucking be!”
Simon and Jeff tried to hide in the shadows as they quietly walked towards the William’s café, the entrance to the café had a slight porch were both boys huddled together and looked around to see if anyone was about. The rain was still pouring down and the wind was blowing strongly it was perfect getting up to no good weather. Simon reached into his overcoat and pulled out a crow bar, moments later the lock on the café door was cracked open. Simon pushed the door open and told his cousin to wait in the porch and keep an eye out. Once inside Simon opened the five gallon can of paraffin and began splashing it over everything, he saturated everywhere, the chairs, tables, walls and the kitchen. Then shutting the door Simon and his cousin walked across the road and waited in an opposite doorway. Sammy had told them that they should wait a short while after they poured the paraffin so that the fumes could spread and cause maximum damage. After a quick cigarette Simon looked around to see if anyone was about and then walked purposely towards the café. He pushed the door slightly open with his foot and then stood back about five yards, he then took out a box of matches , struck one and put the lighted match back into the box which ignited the rest. Simon threw the burning box through the crack in the door and into the shop.
The shop exploded like someone had thrown in a hand grenade, the display windows blew out throwing Simon and thousands of pieces of glass across the street, Jeff ran over and helped pick up his bleeding cousin and then the two of them ran back towards Sammy and the waiting car.
“FUCK ME! It sounded like a bomb went off!” Sammy shouted as they jumped in
Once in the car Jeff took a good look at his cousin Simon who was bleeding from hundreds of tiny scratches caused by the flying glass.

“You’re supposed to stand outside when you light the match.” Sammy joked looking at poor Simon’s face.
“Just went up like a fucking bomb Sammy.” sighed Simon.
“It might have been cos I kicked the cooker off the gas main.” he added.
Sammy gave a slight giggle as he kicked down the cars accelerator causing the car to wheel spin up the wet road.
“Let’s fuck off before the whole fucking street goes up.” he added in excitement.
In the light of the morning what was once Gills café was now a large smouldering pile of ash and charred brickwork. Through the window of their wholesale clothing business John, Jimmy and Frank Ryan could see the smoke and the fire engines up the road. They could see that it was the café that had gone up in smoke and John had sent his brother Albert to investigate. When Albert returned he burst into the office shaking his head.
“Firebombed! Someone lit the bloody place up.” he said.
“ARSON!” Jimmy replied.
“Yep, the fireman said it stinks of paraffin, god knows how he can tell that in that mess but that’s what he said to the law.” added Albert as he sat down.
John and Jimmy walked away from the window and joined there Brother Albert sitting by the desk. Frank remained by the window.
“Have you spoken to Dave or Bill?” Frank said meaning the Williams brothers
“Briefly Frank but their down there talking to the old bill.”
“What they saying to the old bill?” John snapped in an alarmed tone.
“Nothing John, it’s just fucking routine, ya know with it being an arson job.”
“Well they should be speaking to their sister Gill.” replied john.
“She’s in bits John, totally distraught.”
“This is the twins fucking handy work.” Frank suddenly said which had the effect of making his brother John turn quickly towards him.
“OI! We don’t know that!” he said holding up a finger towards him “If that’s your opinion then keep it to ya fucking self!” he added strongly.
Franks facial and body expression changed to a quiet air of defence.
“John I’m only saying it here in front of us, but I’ll tell ya this, Dave and Billy will blame the twins, bit of a coincidence this happening just one night after they had a bit of grief with them.”
“Let them come to their own fucking conclusions, this situation is volatile enough, it don’t need us fucking provoking things.”
“John, Frank was only saying.” Jimmy chipped in defending his brother only for John to cut him short.
“Only saying things gets people locked up, gets people killed jimmy, now we stay neutral in this situation, I don’t want any siding from us with this okay, especially you frank, I know your pally with Dave and Billy but were staying

out of it, I don't want things getting any more out of control than they already fucking are"
Suddenly the brother's attention turned towards a loud banging on the office door, "come in!" John shouted out.
Teddy Royston an old east end villain who now worked doing little odd jobs for the Ryan's came running in.
"Boys put the wireless on." he shouted urgently, John nodded in the direction of the wireless set to teddy who in turn ran over and switched it on so that the boys could catch the back end of a news bulletin he had been listening too downstairs.
'Fromer was said to have connections with a major south London crime family, his charred body was found in the ashes of a south London pub after firemen had to battle with the fire for three hours, the police have already stated that arson is suspected, they have put out a plea for any witnesses to come forward and they state that any information will be treated in confidence. Surprisingly at this early stage the police have also admitted that they feel this is part of an on-going feud between London's crime families and they are confident that arrests will be made imminently'
Teddy Royston left the room as the news bulletin finished, once he was outside Frank Ryan sighed loudly.
"There's no fucking doubt whose handy work that was!" he said.
"My blower never stopped ringing last night, they must have visited a dozen pubs looking for Fromer." added Jimmy.
John gritted his teeth in a frustrated anger.
"What was it fucking vengeance night last night! Stark raving fucking mad, the pair of em." he growled.
The atmosphere in the Anderson's car showroom in Balham South London was a mixture of tension, anger and caution. Terry Anderson sat prominently behind his large mahogany desk with his brothers Jackie, Dougie, Glenn, Mo, bill, and Giles scattered around the office. Alan Anderson the brother who was with Fromer last night was the only Anderson brother missing.
Bob Ferris sat nursing his bruised face as Terry and the brothers were giving him a real hard time regarding what happened last night.
"I cannae fooking undestand ya Bob, wha was ye fooking thinkin about taking wee Alan tae the hospital." growled Jackie angrily.
Bob winced as he touched his swollen eye; he was also having difficulty breathing as a result of the beating that he took last night.
"He was in a bad way Jackie, we just couldn't stop the bleeding." he struggled to say.
"Fucking bad way Bob, how'd ya think he's fucking feeling now banged up in a poxy cell?" Dougie Anderson said.

“How the fuck was I to know that those Pratt’s down the hospital would call the old bill.”
Terry gave a slight laugh as if amazed.
“You turn up in the middle of the night covered in blood, what the fucking hell did you think they’d do.” Mo Anderson added.
“Look I’m sorry lads, it wasn’t just my idea to go to the hospital, Alan was in a lot of pain, he was panicking and was blacking out through the blood loss, I thought he was gonna top it right in fucking front of me, what would you have said then, how would I be if I would have just let him bleed to death.”
Terry still shook his head in frustration.
“Alan wasn’t in a state to think straight Bob; you should have tried to give one of us a call.”
“Thinking straight Terry, look at me mate, I hardly walked out of there thinking straight, to tell ya the truth mate I don’t think I will ever think straight again after witnessing last night’s row.”
“What’d ya mean by that?” Terry asked.
“I mean having to stand there helpless while that fucking psychopath Kray butchered my pal.”
“Was it bad Bob?” Glenn Anderson asked.
“He fucking sliced him up like he was a piece of fucking meat, but what’s more fucking disturbing is the fucking excitement Kray was getting whilst doing it.”
The door of the office suddenly swung open which made every one jump and in walked Terry Anderson snr.
“The bastards are keeping him in.” were the first words from Terry snr mouth
.
“wha for?” Jackie asked.
“They say he’s a suspect in a possible murder.”
“How long are they holding him for” Glenn asked angrily
“How the fook should ar know, those bastarts law didnae let me speak wid him, I got a brief going there ta see if we canae sort this shite out.”
“I’ve already got Mitchell on it dad.” Terry jnr said.
“Where the fuck is he then! They were nae fooker there when I was there!” Terry snr growled.
Terry turned to his younger brother Glenn who was sitting by the phone.
“Call Mitchell’s office will ya Glenn, see if he’s found anything out”
Terry snr walked over to Bob Ferris and put a friendly hand on his shoulder.
“ya alright son?” he asked warmly.
“A bit sore Mr Anderson but I’m alright.” Bob replied.
“OK, now listen the laws looking out fa ya so do ya self a favour and be scarce for a few days, they havenae got ya name but the hospital have given a good description of ya.”

Bob Ferris nodded he appreciation for the advice.
"Do me a favour Bob, I wannae speak ta mi boys alone." Terry added asking for Bob to go outside. Bob nodded gently and struggled to his feet, Terry snr leant a hand pulling him to his feet and then Bob left the office.
"If ye need any money let Terry know." Terry Anderson snr said as he closed the door behind Bob and then turned back to his sons.
"Now listen boys, I want this feud to end, I got one of my boys sitting down the nick and I don't want any more."
"Are you asking us to walk away from this dad?" Mo asked surprised.
"I'm asking ya to use ya fooking heeds, that fucking Fromer was a loud mouthed gobshite, if it wasnae the Krays that killed him it wouldnae have been long before someone else did it, now I want youse all to take a step back from this and act fooking sensible."
"They fucking started this dad, now it's our time to teach them a fucking lesson." Mo Anderson snapped back.
"Shut ya fooking mouth and stop acting like a juvenile, open ya fooking ears will ye, do I have to spell this out to ya, DROP IT!, the fooking old bills got their eyes out everywhere, and I know about these Kray brothers, these bastarts didnae know how to take a backward step."
Terry Anderson jnr listened intently to his Father's words, being the eldest he still had memories of the poverty of where they came from in Glasgow, he remembered well the violent environment that his Father used to mix in and he could see through the words that his Father was saying, this was no back down. His Father never had a fearful bone in his body, this was his Father speaking through experience of his violent Glasgow background, he could smell trouble, he could feel that the police were ready to pounce, and now this was his way of telling his sons of his wisdom in violence.
"We're do as you say Father." Terry jnr suddenly and calmly said.
"We're step back and see what presents itself, and there will be no provocation from us, we're wait, but if, IF they come south of the river again with any intent then were gonna have to meet fire with fire." he added.
Ronnie Kray was still fast asleep as the clock struck midday, Reg and Tony pulled the car into a remote gypsy site hidden amongst the hills and undergrowth on the borders of Essex. There were a few gypsies scattered around who inconspicuously nodded hello as the car passed by. Tony drove to the far end of the site to a secluded corner where they stopped the car in front of an old tatty caravan. Johnny Walsh seeing them pull up opened the caravan door and walked out into the rain to greet them.
"Alright Reg, Ron's still sleeping?" he said as Reg and Tony got out.
"At this time in the day." moaned Reg.
"He couldn't sleep Reg, he was on a real buzz when we got him back here, I had to slip him two sleeping pills in his drink or he'd still be up now."

Tony, eager to get out of the rain hurried towards the doorway but stopped and stared, as he entered the door.
"Fuck me look at the state of this place." he groaned
Reg pushed him inside
"C'mon I'm getting wet!"
Johnny Walsh closed the door behind him and then walked over to the far end of the caravan and gave Ron a gentle push while he slept on a tatty old mattress.
"Ron, Ron, Ron its Reg mate, Ron."
Reg looked down at Ronnie sleeping.
"OI! Rumpelstiltskin, get up." he shouted jokingly.
Ron opened his eyes and sat up, after a great yawn he got up with the bed sheet wrapped around his shoulders and then walked in to greet Reg and Tony.
"Alright." he gasped half yawning with his hair all sticking up and walking past his brother and Tony with his head down.
"Welcome to the fucking world." replied Reg.
"Fuck off." Ron snapped sharply as he reached for a fag.
"What's happening? We heard anything yet." added Ron after lighting his cigarette.
"Been on the wireless about Fromer, they think it was murder." Reg replied as swept the dust of a chair before sitting down.
"Who thinks it was murder?"
"The Law."
"What's it got to do with them?" Ron replied still sleepy.
Reg just half smiled in amazement and ignored his brother.
"Put the kettle on John!" he shouted out to Johnny Walsh.
"Already doing it Reg, three teas." John shouted back.
Reg then reached for a cigarette and lit it before talking to Ron who was still having difficulty to stop himself yawning.
"We're not keeping you up are we Ron?" Reg asked sarcastically.
"Fuck off Reg, ain't you ever been tired before."
"Look I spoke with Manny today about you and this business outside the Astor, off the record as he said it he thinks its best that you stay right out the way for a bit."
"Is that what you and Manny think is it?"
"Yeah it sounds best."
"So you come all the way over to this damp muddy fucking pisshole in the middle of fucking nowhere, where I'm sleeping in a cold, leaking flea infested pit to tell me.... you think its best that I stay out of the way!"
"What's the matter with you?" Reg barked back.

“What the fuck do you think I’m doing in this pisshole! Simeys out there somewhere ask him, even his fucking greyhound dog won’t sleep in this karzy!”
Tony Lambrianou suddenly burst into laughter, he held up his hand as if to say sorry but still couldn’t stop laughing, the stink of the damp caravan and the sight of Ron sitting on an old torn sofa with a sheet wrapped round him and his hair pointing in all directions was too much to bear for him.
“I’m sorry Ron but you look a right picture sitting there.” he laughed.
“Yeah! Where’d you sleep last night” Ron snapped back.
“Over at Eddies, in front of a nice fire.”
“I slept over at the Carpenters in your room Ron.” added Reg.
“You bastards!” Ron sighed now himself laughing.
Johnny Walsh brought the teas over and after each man took a sip there mood subdued to more urgent matters.
“What about the Anderson’s Reg, have we heard anything from them?” asked Ron.
“Nothing yet Ron but we got people out on the streets keeping their eyes and ears open.”
“Good.” replied Ron as he took another sip.
“Right now it’s a waiting game Ron, we just got to sit back and see what happens.”
“Alright but just make sure everyone’s on the guard, when can we get the Firm together Reg, theirs a few things I want to get moving on.”
“I thought we just said that it’s best that you stay out the way Ron.”
“Yeah but theirs staying out the way and theirs staying out the way Reg, like I said theirs still things that I wanna do before I go away.”
“Like what Ron, what needs doing?”
“We’ve got them on the run; let’s finish the fuckers off now.”
“NO Ron… I say we should wait and see what happens, and anyway where you going away to?”
“Morocco!”
“MOROCCO!” Reg replied.
“Yeah I’ve been meaning to go there for ages, I’m gonna go out there and see Billy Hill.”
The Ryan’s office in Hoxton had two entrances, downstairs there was a large double shop front open to the public selling pieces of cloth at wholesale prices to tailors and seamstresses and at the rear of the property there was the ‘tradesman entrance’ a highly fortified door leading to the office upstairs from the car park. Teddy Royston opened the back door after hearing the buzzer go and he welcomed in Dave and Billy Williams.
“Hello boys there upstairs, you know the way lads.”

Both Williams's brothers just nodded at the old villain before silently walking up the stairs.
Frank Ryan opened the office door and greeted both brothers with a Firm handshake.
"What'd the old bill want?" John asked without greeting them as they sat down.
"Usual cobblers John, asked us if we knew anyone who would want to do this to the café."
"So what'd you say!" John replied in a strong voice.
"what'd ya think!, I told them the only person who had the hump with me was my three year old son because I never brought him a rocking horse for his last fucking birthday" snapped Dave back sternly with an angered tone at being asked the question.
"So it was arson then?" Frank asked.
"Course it fucking was, and we all know what pair of cunts were behind it." Billy snapped.
"You don't know that yet." John added.
"Come on John who the fuck else would it be." Billy added.
"By all accounts the twins were occupied elsewhere last night." said Jimmy Ryan.
"You mean Fromer." replied Dave.
"They've nicked Alan Anderson for it." he added looking at John.
"Anderson was his fucking mate." snapped Frank.
"Well he's banged up for it."
"Well it weren't fucking him." Frank added only for John to turn and give him a very severe look for his outburst.
Dave Williams noticed the look that John gave his brother and he turned his eyes away as if pretending that he never saw it.
"Anyway John, what's all this about mate, why'd ya call us up here?"
John purposely paused in giving his answer as he slowly poured himself a glass of scotch that was on his desk.
"We need to talk lads."
"What about?" Dave snapped even though he knew full well what was coming.
"I don't want bedlam in my manor." John replied sternly and loudly.
"Your manor John? We live here too mate."
John took a large sip of his drink and licked his lips and then banged the empty glass hard on the table.
"Let me say this loud and clear so you get this straight, if you two have any ideas about revenge then you forget them now, one more time, this fucking stupid row stops right now!"

Dave hesitated in replying as he saw the seriousness in johns face, both men held eye contact for a moment until Dave answered calmly and trying his best not to sound confrontational.
"John they've embarrassed us."
"That don't matter, this has got to end before it brings everyone down, now you boys are good grafters, you both got good heads on ya shoulders so leave it out, stay out of the mix, Ron Kray will burn his own candle."
"Is this what you want John."
"This is what I want Dave."
"Then for you and our friendship I'll do as you ask."
Detective chief inspector Richard LaSalle sat anxiously waiting in a small and quiet café in a back road just north of Walthamstow, he was already on his third cup of tea and on his eighth cigarette when the door opened and Slice'em Sid came hurriedly and nervously walking over.
"What fucking time do you call this? I've been waiting here forty five minutes." LaSalle groaned angrily.
"Sorry chief it's fucking lucky I'm here at all with all what's happening at the moment." Sid gasped as he sat down and looked nervously about to see who was about.
Eddie Brenner cursed his cars wiper blades as they left a smear on the window screen in the heavy rain.
"Fuck me Eddie I can't see a fucking thing!" Billy Hayes moaned.
"The fucking things have got grease on them." Eddie replied.
"Well pull over and let's give them a wipe, we're ave an accident if we carry on like this."
Eddie pulled over the car outside a busy Shoreditch high road pub where both men jumped out into the rain and began searching the boot for some sort of rag to clean the wipers.
"Here's one!" Billy Hayes said finding one.
Then out the corner of his eye something distracted Eddie, he tapped Billy Hayes on the arm and both men froze as they saw Billy Williams walking out the pub barely five yards away. The three men froze as they looked at each other. Eddie panicked first and reached into his coat and pulled out a semi-automatic pistol. Billy Williams dived back into the pub as Eddie Brenner fired off three shots at him, hitting the floor Billy Williams pulled out his own gun and within seconds Shoreditch high road was the scene of a full pitched gun fight. Bullets were flying in all directions until Eddie and Billy Hayes jumped back in to the car and wheel spinned off up the road.
"Who killed Fromer Sid, was it Ron or Reg?" Detective LaSalle questioned Sid sternly.
"Ron killed him chief, but Reg was there."
"Will you stand in the box and testify to that Sid?"

"Not at the moment chief, I can't."
"How much longer are we gonna dance to this tune Sid, we got two crazy bastards out there killing anyone they please, they need to be behind bars."
"You don't have to remind me of that chief, I'm with the fucking psychopaths every day, now nobody wants to get out of this crazy life more than me, but I have to do it right, I gotta make sure my family's safe before I jump."
"I could nick you right now for being an accessory."
"Listen are we talking seriously here or what, I've told you I'll say whatever you fucking want when the times right, but NOW's not the right time, leave me a bit longer chief, once I get my family out there yours!"
Johnny Ryan was absolutely livid when he heard the news about the shooting incident with Eddie Brenner and Billy Williams down Shoreditch high road; Frank had just finished a phone conversation with Dave Williams and gave his brother the news.
"Where are they now?"
"Down the yard John." Frank replied.
John jumped from his chair and made towards the door.
The Williams scrap metal yard was only a few hundred yards from the Ryan's office and Frank and Jimmy had to walk fast in order to keep up with their brother. Dave Williams seeing the Ryan's walk into the yard came out of the office to greet them.
"Where's your fucking brother!" John Ryan angrily said pushing Dave Williams out of the way.
"Hold on!" Dave pleaded.
John burst into the office and saw Billy Williams sitting on the desk talking on the phone, without a moment's pause John flew towards Billy and grabbed him by the throat; John forcefully pulled him off the desk and slammed him into the wall.
"What fucking part of keep ya hands in ya pockets didn't ya fucking understand?" John growled through gritted teeth as he banged Billy's head about like he was a rag doll.
"John, they shot first!" Billy mouthed in pain.
"LIAR!" John shouted as he threw Williams to the ground.
"John, its true mate, Billy just walked out the pub and Eddie Brenner and Billy Hayes were waiting for him, they just started shooting at him, if he hadn't fired back at him then he'd probably not be here now." Dave Williams cried.
Jimmy walked over and tried to calm John by gently putting an arm around him.
"It weren't his fault John."
"Just keep out the fucking way!" John mouthed angrily as pushed Dave Williams before walking out of the office.

“Get Reg Kray on the phone, this fucking cobblers ends now, I’ve had enough of it!” John shouted at his brother Jim.
Reg Kray sat in the back room of the carpenters arms with Tony Lambrianou and the Jones brothers as Eddie Brenner and Billy Hayes told him about the shooting.
“Did you hit him?” Reg asked.
“I don’t think so Reg.” Eddie replied.
“Are you fucking joking Reg, Eddie couldn’t hit a bus with a cannon.” Billy joked.
“I didn’t see you fucking shooting!” Eddie snapped back.
“Course you fucking never, I was hiding behind you.” Billy joked back.
Suddenly after a knock on the door Sammy Carpenter came in.
“Reg someone on the phone for you mate.”
“Tell I’m not here.”
“I think you’d wanna get this Reg.”
“Who is it?”
“Jimmy Ryan.”
“Ah, for fucks sake.” Reg sighed as he got to his feet.
“Jim its Reg.” Reg said picking up the phone in the pubs hall.
“Reg we need to talk mate.”
“What about?”
“What’d you fucking think.”
“Alright, I’ll see ya next week.” Reg replied.
“No, Reg lets do this today, can you and Ron come over the office?”
“Things are little hot over your part of town right now Jim.”
“No thanks to you fucking lot.”
“What’d ya mean by that Jim!”
“Listen Reg let’s not fucking do this over a phone.”
“I’ll get over sometime tomorrow Jim, can’t do today, Ron’s out the way.”
“What time?”
“Leave it with me and I’ll get back to ya in the morning.”
“Your give us a call Reg.”
“Yeah in the morning.”
The next morning the Anderson’s woke to the news that they were all dreading, Samuel Mitchell the family’s solicitor was first to break them the sorry news.
“It looks like they’re going to charge Alan for murder.”
“That’s fucking crazy!” Terry jnr snapped sitting next to his Father.
“How the fuck can they do that!” Terry snr added desperately.
“There saying that Alan stunk of paraffin when he went to the hospital, his clothes have been taken away for examination, if they return traces of the paraffin then Alan will be in a lot of trouble.”

“How can that prove he was guilty?” Terry added.
“It’s enough to charge him on, let’s look at it from the police’s view, a man is found dead in a fire and the fire chiefs have suggested arson which looks like it was started with paraffin, Alan turns up at a hospital three miles away with a deep wound and stinking of paraffin, to them it looks like Alan had a fight with Fromer and then started a fire to hide any evidence.”
“That’s not how it fucking happened.” Terry jnr said which made the solicitor sit up straight.
“Gentleman.” Mitchell said lowering his voice. “If Alan was in that place prior to the fire and he knows who lit the fire then off the record I suggest he testify against the persons who started it.”
“NO!” Terry snr sighed loudly. “That’s not our way!” he added strongly.
“Terry, it might be your son’s only way.”
“doesnae matter we don’t grass!” Terry snr stated.
“Has he made a statement?”
“According to the police he has admitted being there, that’s all I know.”
“Verbals, the fucking old bill have verballed him up!” Terry snr added.
“Can we get him bail Samuel?” Terry jnr asked.
“Absolutely no way, there is so much of this case waiting on the results of forensics; we’re just have to wait for the results.”
Reg and Tony sat talking to Johnny Walsh in the caravan as Ronnie washed and put on a fresh suit that his brother had delivered to him. They were there to pick Ron up and take him to a meeting that Reg and Jimmy Ryan had arranged for eight o’clock that evening. Jimmy Ryan had been hassling Reg all day to make the meeting earlier but Reg refused to drive Ron into the east end in daylight hours.
“C’mon Ron its quarter past seven.” Reg shouted.
“Alright! What’s the fucking rush, they’ll wait.” replied Ron as he did up his tie.
“I said we’d be there at eight!”
“Bollocks to em, we’re get there when we get there!” replied Ron as he walked out of the caravans bedroom.
“Pour me a drink will ya Johnny.” Ron asked Walsh as he walked by. John turned and quickly poured Ron a very large gin which Ron grabbed before sitting down next to Tony and reg.
“We can have you out the country tomorrow night Ron, Joey Pine knows a captain on a fishing trawler down in Kent, he’ll take you over to France, from there you have to make your own way.”
“A bloody smelly old fishing boat, can’t you get some documents so I can jump on an plane.”
“Don’t be fucking silly Ron.”
Ron laughed as he lit up a cigarette.

“Tomorrow might be a bit soon Reg.”
“We still got that business with Don Harding to take care of.” Ron added.
“Ron, Fuck Don Harding! We ain’t got time to worry about his business.”
“I gave my word.”
“Look Ron let’s get you away for a bit alright, that’s our first priority, leave Don Harding to me, I’ll deal with it when you’re gone.”
Ron sat quietly in the back seat of the Ford Zephyr as it drove through the depressing streets of the East end.
“How much did you give for this fucking heap?” asked Johnny Walsh sitting next to Tony Lambrianou who was driving.
“Three quid!” Tony snapped back proudly.
“He fucking robbed you!” Johnny joked back.
“Fuck off! You can’t even get a decent pair of shoes for three quid.” remarked Tony as he struggled with the cars gear lever causing it to make a loud grinding noise.
“I hope this fucking old thing makes it, I don’t feel like fucking walking.” added Johnny.
“Bollocks!” snapped Tony.
Ron found the conversation between his two friends in the front amusing as he laughed next to Reg.
“Where’s the Jag Reg?”
“It’s parked up Ron, it’s too hot to be driving about in that.”
As Tony pulled the car into the forecourt of the Ryan’s business, Ron looked up and saw that the light was on in the Ryan’s office, Ron next looked around the car park and counted the number of cars.
“There are a lot of cars in here Reg.”
“What’d ya thinking Ron?” asked Reg even though he knew what his brother’s thoughts were.
After a short pause where Ron looked around as if studying the situation he turned to Reg quietly.
“Let’s just keep our wits about u.” he said as he reached for the cars door handle.
“And that means you two as well!” he added sternly as he pushed Tony in the back.
“Don’t be having a fucking nap.” he added.
“Do you want me to come with ya Ron?” Tony replied.
“Nah just sit here and keep ya eyes open, anyone comes into this car park or near that door you beep the fucking horn.”
“Don’t worry about it Ron, I got ya backs.” Johnny Walsh replied.
Ron nodded and then with Reg they both got out the car, Ron gave the car park another look over before pushing the buzzer on the door. Moments later

the old villain Teddy Royston opened it and smiled broadly when he saw it was the twins
"Hello boys, how's my favourite couple of tearaways?"
"How ya doing Teddy?" Ron replied warmly and then reaching into his pocket and pulling out a crisp new five pound note and then pushing it into the old man's palm.
"Ah you don't have to do that Ron, you know the boys upstairs look after me."
"Please Teddy take the dosh, it's good to see ya again."
"Come in boys; let's get you out of the cold." Teddy said pulling Ron's arm.
"I still remember all the stories you used to tell us Teddy." replied Ron smiling reminding the old villain of the days of the blitz when violet Kray used to take her sons down the underground to escape the Nazi bombing raids and teddy along with other local villains would entertain everyone with their stories and songs.
"They were good day's boys."
"You was always on the run then Teddy, you're not on ya toes now are ya." Reg joked.
"Spent over half my life on mi toes lads, fuck all wrong with that." Teddy joked back before holding out his hands.
"I'm seventy nine now boys, still strong and the old minds still their but my old legs ain't what they used to be, these young bobbies wouldn't have much difficulty in catching me now, if it weren't for my legs I'd still be out there getting a few Bob don't fucking worry about that."
Ron and Reg smiled at the old boy, they loved and still admired the gameness of him, even though it was plain to see that old age had caught up with him they could still see the sparkle in his eye.
"You were the best dipper in the East End Teddy." Reg warmly said meaning pick pocket.
"What'd ya mean East End!, In London! I was the best all over, come on boys let's get you in, don't wanna keep the boys upstairs waiting now do we." Teddy replied as he gently pulled the boys in the direction of the stairs.
Reg walked first and as Ron passed Teddy the old boy gently pulled his sleeve.
"The Williams brothers are upstairs." he whispered leaning forward. Ron smiled and warmly patted his arm.
"Reg." Ron then whispered as he pulled his brother close half way up the stairs.
"The Williams are up here."
"Says who!"
"Teddy told me."
"What'd ya wanna do Ron?"

“Were going in!” Ron said sternly.
“It could be a trap” replied Reg
“Don’t worry about it, just keep your eyes open.” replied Ron pushing his way in front of reg.
As the twins reached the landing at the top of the stairs Ron gave his brother a reassuring look before reaching for the door. Ron never knocked he just turned the handle and walked in. inside the office were the four Ryan brothers john, jimmy, Frank and Albert along with two of the most staunch and toughest members of their gang, Danny Coyle and Charlie Roth. Sitting over by the desk were Dave and Billy Williams.
Ron’s eyes immediately focused on the two Williams brothers as he glared coldly at them
“Nice and fucking cosy in here.” Ron snapped calmly but with menace in his voice.
“It’s not what you think Ron.” John Ryan said quickly getting to his feet from behind his desk and walking over to greet the twins.
“So this was your fucking meeting Jim?” Reg cursed as he stepped besides Ron angered that the Ryan’s had not told them the Williams would be here.
“Let’s just sit down and have a drink Ron, c’mon let’s see if we can sort things out.” John said gently ushering Ron over towards the desk.
The twins sat down at one end of the table opposite the Williams as John sat down in the middle between them. On the desk were three large bottles of spirits and a consignment of glasses, John reached out and poured the four men a large scotch each as each man sat in silence, the atmosphere was mounting as the silence seemed to heighten the tension, the rest of the Ryan brothers pulled over there chairs and sat closer to the table, Ron getting more and more frustrated decided to break the silence.
“Let’s just get on with what you gotta say John, if I sit here any longer I’m gonna throw them two mugs out the fucking window!”
Dave Williams was just about to take a sip from his glass when Ronnie’s outburst caused him to sneer and bang his glass down hard on the table.
“You wanna say something?” Ron said angrily at him.
“What!” snapped back Williams.
“Don’t fucking sneer at me.” Ron replied with a chilling tone to his voice.
John Ryan rose to his feet.
“Ron please, let’s just hear what everyone’s go to say.”
“You can hear what I got to say right now!” Ron snapped back.
“FUCK EM! Fuck the pair of em!” he added.
“JOHN!” Dave Williams suddenly said in a kind of plea as he got to his feet.
“I’m not gonna sit here and listen to this.” he added angrily pointing at Ron.

“NO! well what ya gonna do?” Reg said, “You was fucking brave the other night with all ya Firm round ya, there’s two of us and two of you, why don’t you get brave now ya fucking mug.”
“I’m not scared of you!” Billy Williams snapped back getting to his feet with his brother, which in turn made Ron get to his feet only for John and Jimmy Ryan to get in between the four men.
“Ron let’s just calm down can we, just fucking hear what I got to say.” John said loudly.
“Who fucking asked you for help!” replied Ron.
“Ron please just give me five minutes will ya, for fucks sake just hear me out ok!” added John.
Reg grabbed Ron’s arm gently, Ron knew that Reg was asking him to calm down.
“Alright John, were listen to what ya wanna say.” Reg added strongly.
John waited for everyone to sit down before passing the bottle of scotch around, Ron noticed how John offered the bottle to the Williams first so he just ignored John when he offered him the scotch. Ron’s mind pondered on the reason as to why John had offered the first drink to the Williams, did his actions reveal his inner feelings, it was like asking your closest friend before others. Ron would always offer his brother a cigarette first, in a subtle way it was like showing his loyalty, did John’s action reveal where his loyalty lay thought Ron.
John offered Ron the drink again but like before Ron just ignored him.
“Ron.” John now asked holding the drink in front of him.
Finally Reg grabbed the bottle not because he was thirsty but because he could see what Ron was doing and all this delaying bollocks was driving him mad. John watched Reg top up his glass and Ron’s with the scotch before beginning to talk.
“Right I wanted to get everyone here today to see if we can sort this whole fucking mess out. One of the reasons why we can’t let this get out of control is the Laws all fucking over us at the moment. We’ll all end up nicked if we start having rows right now. So far nothing too serious has happened between the four of you, it’s just been a few harsh words and a couple of back handers, so there’s fuck all really standing in the way to sorting this shit out, before it goes any further. I’ve already spoken to Dave and Billy and they’re prepared to leave things where they are, we can all put this behind us tonight, we can move on, call a peace and get back to earning fucking money.”
As John finished he looked straight at Ron, the ball was in his court and the whole room waited for Ron to answer, Ron took his time as he looked back at John, then after lighting a cigarette he gave his reply.
“I remember a time John when you were with us no matter what!” Ron said calmly “Right or wrong we stood together.” he added.

"I'm still with ya Ron." interrupted John.
"Nah, you're now putting ya businesses first."
"What fucking businesses?"
"Your business with them two fucking idiots."
Both the Williams brothers sighed at being called idiots as Dave pushed his glass along the table, John's facial expression gave away his frustration with Ron.
"I'm trying to fucking sort this bollocks out, in a way that's best for all of us!"
"No deals!" interrupted Ron sternly.
"You haven't even heard what they gotta say?" replied John pointing to the Williams.
"I couldn't give a fuck what they say." replied Ron almost nonchalant.
"I think you owe to us, to hear them out!" Frank Ryan suddenly said making Ron turn to look at him.
"You do, do ya?"
"Yeah I DO!" answered Frank angrily.
""Frank! turn it in, stay out of this!" John Ryan angrily said as he pointed at him before turning back to the twins.
"Ron as a favour to me, at least hear what they got to say."
Reg grabbed Ron's hand in a way that said let him reply.
"We'll listen to what he's gotta say John, then we're make up our own minds."
John Ryan nodded gratefully and then turned to Dave Williams.
"Dave." he said giving him his key to begin.
Dave glimpsed briefly to his brother Billy who was sitting back in his chair with both arms flung over the back rest and balancing on the chairs back two legs, then Dave leaned onto the desk where he rested both elbows on the table. Ron noticed how both men sat, he could see that Dave Williams felt under pressure, he looked like he just wanted to get this over with as quickly as possible and get out, while his brother sat with a more casual arrogance. There was a flashiness about him as if he was sitting at the behest of his brother and the Ryan's but the way he sat, and the interest in his face looked like he couldn't give a damn if the twins listened or not.
Dave Williams cleared his throat.
"I don't think we ever liked each other, strange but that's probably the truth, we both come from the same part of town, run in the same circles, yet our paths have never really crossed. You got your interests and we got ours, we got our Firm and you've got yours. I'm here tonight only because John asked me, I'm here to see if we can nip this thing in the bud. If we carry on then someone's gonna get killed, either that or were all end up fucking nicked. Everyone in this room knows how to use a tool, anyone of us here can blow someone away, what happened at Quaglino's the other night nearly showed us

that, by some fucking miracle it didn't turn into a bloodbath. Now for the sake of common sense we're here to try and find a peace, try and find a way where we can all walk away from this, shake hands and get things back to normal."
"What about compensation!" Ron suddenly interrupted.
"What?" asked Dave Williams less than impressed by Ron's Outburst.
"No Ron, we just all walk away from this with a clean slate." John Ryan added.
"NO! Not without compensation."
"Ron, compensation for what mate, there's been no damage." John snapped in frustration.
"Compensation for spoiling my fucking night out."
"Ah for fucks sake." John Ryan angrily growled in disbelief.
"Compensation for having the fucking balls, to making themselves busy in the first place, they knew Quaglino's was our place and started the row."
"Ron now holds up."
"No John you fucking hold up, do you honestly fucking think that I'm just gonna sit here and listen to these two fucking idiots, do you think I'm just gonna sit here and let these mugs off? They start the fucking row then come knocking on your door and then all of a sudden everything's fucking rosy, bollocks to em!, If they want peace then it's gonna fucking cost them, they pay us compensation for the insult or they can have their peace whilst laying in the fucking grave."
"What about compensation for our sister's café!" Billy Williams said losing his temper.
"Fuck your sister!" Ron calmly said strongly back at him.
"Can't we just be civil ere!" John Ryan snapped.
Dave Williams held up his hand in the direction of John as if asking to be heard.
"Ron you've heard what we gotta say, like before we're willing to forget about all of this and walk away but we're no fucking mugs. They'll be no compensation, not now or never, we've said our piece now it's up to you, you've had our peace offering so take it how you fucking want."
Ron gazed down at his burning cigarette, he stared at its burning tip, 'just enough for one last drag' he thought. Ron put the cigarette up to his lips and sucked in hard lighting up all of his face from the glow. Then taking his time he firmly stubbed it out in the ashtray. Everyone in the room waited with baited breath for Ronnie's reply, the atmosphere was now at its most tense, there was a chill blowing in from the poorly fitted windows. Ron taking his time looked around the room, everything suddenly slowed as if in slow motion, Ron could hear his own heartbeat as he looked at Frank Ryan, Ryan's face was angry as he bit his bottom lip, and Albert Ryan was sitting back from it all in his usual laid back way. John Ryan with sweat on his brow growing

more and more frustrated with each passing second, the two Ryan heavies Danny Coyle and Charlie Roth both shitting themselves in case things turn ugly. Calmly Ron then turned his head in the direction of the Williams brothers, he looked at Billy first, Ron furrowed his brow as he saw how confrontational Billy Williams sat, he could see that the eyes of Billy Williams failed to hide his hate. Then he looked at Dave Williams, his face was contorted as he waited uneasily for Ron's reply, suddenly Ron broke into a wry smile as he knew full well what his reply was going to be. He looked once again at the Williams brothers and thought of how this meeting was giving them an importance, it was an importance that Ron felt they did not deserve, they were 'Blaggers' fucking robbers, as far as Ron was concerned the Williams shouldn't even be in the same room with him, let alone sit down in front of him saying what and what not they were going to do.
Calmly Ron slowly got to his feet.
"This is my peace offering." he said quietly.
Dave Williams looked up and then suddenly froze from fear as he saw Ron produce a handgun from his waistband. A second later Ron shot Dave Williams right between the eyes, the back of Williams's head exploded sending blood and brains splattering against the back wall. Ron moved closer and fired two further shots into the stomach of his brother Billy Williams who flew backwards from the blast onto the floor.
"Here's my fucking peace offering, what'd ya think?" Ron smirked before firing two more shots into Williams groin, Williams screamed as Ron knelt down beside him pushing the gun into his eye socket,
"Who the fuck do you think you are?" Ron added before pulling the trigger and blowing off the top of his head.
Ron turned and stood up, the smell from the gun and the open wounds of the Williams's was overwhelming, expecting a reaction from the others, Ron tensed his body in anticipation. He looked at the other men in the room. No reaction other than sheer horror or disbelief was shown by them. Ron wiped away some specks of blood that was on his face with his sleeve.
"Let's go." he said softly to Reg, who was looking at the two dead men speechless.
Placing the gun on John Ryan's desk Ronnie turned to him.
"Get rid of that." he said quietly as if he was a school kid admitting his guilt, John just stood there open eyed, his face looked in sheer panic and shock.
"C'mon Reg lets go." Ron repeated pulling his brother towards the door, then just before they left the room Ron turned with his head lowered and looked at John.
"Sorry John." he sighed almost in a whisper.
The twins reached halfway down the stairs when they were met by Tony and Johnny both with a gun in their hands running up after hearing the gunshot.

"RON!" Tony shouted pointing his gun.
"Let's get out of ere!" Reg said quickly.
"You alright?" asked Tony.
"Let's fucking go!" Reg called out again only this time tugging Tony's arm, Johnny Walsh was the better driver so he jumped into the driver's seat, Tony jumped in beside him but only after he made sure that the car reversed cleanly and was pointing in the right direction and the twins jumped in the back.
"Fuck me Ron, I almost shot ya." Tony sighed.
"What the fuck happened." he added as he looked at the strange and chilling look Reg had on his face.
"Let's just say the Williams's won't be too bothered about Christmas this year." Ron smirked with a sinister smile.

NOT GUILTY YOU'RE HONOUR

Chapter Nine

'Them & Us'

Dating back four hundred years Petticoat lane was London's oldest trading market, the origins of the market was believed to be created by the Huguenot refugee lace-makers and expanded by the Jewish refugees escaping Germany and Poland, over the years as the market grew it commonly became known as the best clothing market in the country.
Petticoat lane was sandwiched between Whitechapel and Shoreditch and ran along the notorious Middlesex Street. Notorious for its shady past Middlesex Street in Victorian and Dickensian London formed the boundary between the city and the English county of Middlesex. Criminals sought by the metropolitan police force would often seek refuge along the area so that they could make a hasty exit away from the city.
As the sixties drew to a close the lane was becoming a real celebrity haunt, music stalls selling all the newest records sprung up overnight, pop groups like the Rolling stones and the Beatles were an often sight shopping amongst

the clothes and record stores. London's King's road was regarded as being the fashion centre of the capital but the lane had a more Bohemian feel to it. Modern times were catching up with everywhere in London, but Petticoat blended modern and old in its own unique East End way.
The lane was a stark contrast, on one side of the road you would see Hippies listening to their music and smoking hemp and on the other side of the road as if oblivious to the new free love culture were the old east end villains, standing by the old traditional jellied eel stalls that usually always rested besides a pub the old boys mixed drank and ate till their hearts were content.
Every Sunday morning Violet Kray would try to visit the market, sometimes if she had money she would treat herself to a dress or cardigan but without fail she always visited Tubby's Ell stall to meet up with family and friends. Most of the older women from Bethnal Green and Whitechapel would gather there swapping gossip and tales of their husbands and sons, some would be returning from church while others would be returning from shopping to pick up a bowl of eels for their sleeping husbands at home.
As violet Kray neared Tubby's she was greeted by two senior gentleman who recognised her, the two men immediately gave up the wooden stall that they had been sitting on eating their cockles and drinking their sarsaparilla
"Morning Mrs Kray." one of them said tilting his cap.
"How's the family Mrs Kray?" the other one said.
"Here sit down here luvvy, tell us what you want at the stall and I'll ave someone fetch it over." said the first gentleman.
"No that's okay." protested Violet feeling a little awkward at the men's hospitality.
"Please Mrs Kray, it's our treat."
Violet smiled warmly looking a little embarrassed.
"Okay then, I'll have a half pint of cockles." she added coyly.
"It's on its way." replied the old gent with a wink.
As violet sat down she pulled her coat tighter to keep out the cold from around her neck and began adjusting her headscarf when out of the corner of her eye she saw two of her neighbours coming towards her.
"Vi!" said Val Roth who lived six doors along called out.
"Hello Vi." said the lady accompanying her Beth Campbell.
"Where's the old man?" Beth said sitting down.
"Phew, down the pub as usual, probably over Kings Cross with his gypsy mates."
"Aw girl you're in for a rough afternoon." Val joked.
"Sod him!, he'll waltz in early evening, moan a bit, swear a bit and then pass out on the couch." Vi joked back.
"Same as last week then girl." Beth said smiling before calling out to the two gentlemen who were still queuing to get violet her cockles.

"OI, we'll ave some of those cockles as well." she shouted cheekily.
"Alright love, three lots of cockles." the gent shouted back.
Violet turned away in embarrassment.
"I don't know where you get the front from." she said quietly in a sort of praising way to her friend Beth.
"That's old man Cossini, he was a right catch a few years ago Vi."
"Bert, Bert Cossini, he was married to Beryl." replied Violet.
"That's him, Bi Bop Bert we used to call him."
"Don't Beth, I didn't recognise him, it's a terrible shame what happened to Beryl."
"Who would have believed it Vi, walking across a bridge and hit by a bus." replied Beth sadly commenting on how Bert's wife was killed one morning while walking to work over Tower Bridge.
"Here, you remember her son, Frankie, he was in the army with your Charlie, he's got a really good job now, works in the print down Fleet Street."
"That's nice." said violet.
"Here Vi, talking of Charlie, how is he, is he still in hospital?" Val asked.
"Yeah but he's in Whitechapel now, won't be long and we're have him home."
"How's the twins Vi? Ain't seen much of them lately?" asked Val.
"Their fine, you know them two always up to something."
Two miles away in Bethnal Green Road, Reg sat in Pelicci's café eating a bacon and egg sandwiches with Tony Lambrianou, Eddie Brenner and George Hayes.
"You heard from Ron?" said Tony as he wiped his mouth.
"Johnny called this morning, he didn't say where he was but he said there alright."
"He's in France." Eddie added.
"I fucking know that." replied Tony.
"There was a couple of old bill nosing about last night." Reg said.
"Where?"
"Outside mums, I told them to fuck off." added Reg which made them all grin.
"They've charged Anderson for that slag Fromer." George Hayes suddenly said.
"When did you hear that?" asked Reg.
"This morning, Sammy called me."
"That's scandalous." sighed Reg.
"Takes the heat off of us though." added Tony.
Reg didn't reply, he knew what Tony had just said was true but it was not a satisfactory way to feel at ease, as Reg raised another sandwich to his mouth he was distracted by the sight of Billy Hayes barging his way into the café as if the blitz had returned.

“What’s the matter with you?” Reg asked as Billy pushed himself next to Tony.
“Got a problem Reg, little Lenny’s game got spun last night.”
“What the old bill?” interrupted George.
“NO the fucking Maltese!”
“Massina?” asked Reg in an angered way.
Billy just nodded in an over exaggerated wa.y
“You sure?”
“As sure as I’m fucking sitting here Reg.”
“I don’t fucking believe it, they know that games ours, what happened?” added Reg.
“Three fucking great lumps walked in, bold as fucking brass and grabbed hold of Lenny, gave him a few clumps and said there be back every week to collect a pension.”
“So what did Lenny fucking say, didn’t he say he was paying us?”
“He told em Reg.”
“What’d they say?”
Billy hesitated which made Reg even angrier.
“What’d they say?” Reg said now more loudly.
“Lots of things Reg.”
“Like fucking what?”
Billy looked anxiously at his brother first before answering.
“Like what” his brother asked with a mouth full of egg and bacon
“They said fuck the Kray’s, they’re finished, something about Charlie being an invalid and Ron was in hiding.”
“Anything else?” Reg growled.
“They said forget about Reg, he’s nothing without Ron.”
After a short pause as everyone looked hesitantly at Reg, after finishing off his tea Reg asked another question, surprisingly calm.
“And it was without a doubt the Messina’s?”
“They mentioned Carmine Reg.” Billy replied.
Reg thought silently for a moment as he lit himself a cigarette.
“I’ll show these flash bastards what I can do without Ron.”
Just as violet and her two friends finished eating there bowls of cockles she saw out the corner of her eye a friend of hers walking just past the ell stall, violet jumped up and called out.
Shirley Wilson the mother of Slice’em Sid who had lived down the Roman Road all of her life, turned her ageing weathered face in the direction of the call, as she saw Violet she stopped immediately and walked over.
“Hello Vi, Beth, Val.” she said slightly out of breath.
“Hello Shirley, how are you love?” replied Violet.

Shirley gave a slight smile but couldn't hide the fact that something was bothering her.
"VI, can I have a quick word love?" she asked quietly.
Getting to her feet violet reached out and held her arm.
"Of course Shirl." she said warmly.
Shirley smiled at Beth and Val before walking a few feet away with Violet.
"What's the matter Shirley is something wrong love?"
"It's Sid Vi, I'm at my wits end with him, I don't know what the boys have got him doing but he's not himself, its none of my business but some fella won't stop phoning him, he calls all through the night and never leaves his name, it's frightening me Vi, it's got so bad that I never want to answer the telephone anymore."
"Who is this fella?"
"I've asked him for a name, loads of times but he won't say, he's terribly rude, I've asked Sid about it but he just tells me to mind my own business."
"It sounds awful Shirl."
"If it's someone the boys know Vi, could you have a word with them and ask this man not to call anymore, last night he called at one in the morning."
"Don't worry about that Shirley, I'll have a talk to Reg and sort it out for you love."
"Thanks Violet." Shirley replied as she raised a hankie up to her face.
"O come here love you look in a right state." violet replied as she put her arm around Shirley who just burst into tears.
"Something's wrong Vi, I know it, Sid's worrying me to the grave, he's not himself, I'm sure he's in some kind of trouble, he's my life Vi, he's all I've got since his Dad died."
"Come on calm down love, I'll find out what's wrong, now don't you worry about it, it's probably nothing, you know what men are bloody like."
"Bloody nuisances! That's what they bloody are, you love em and all they bloody do is cause ya pain, since the day Sid was born I've done nothing but worry about him."
Violet smiled warmly.
"Bloody worries! I could write a dozen bloody books on worry with my lot."
Shirley suddenly pulled her head away from violets shoulder and rubbed her nose with her hankie.
"Oh I'm sorry Vi, how can I be so bloody selfish, you have enough on ya plate with Charlie in the hospital."
"Never you mind about that, look I'll have a chat with Reg and we're get this mystery man sorted out for you, ok!"
"Alright Vi."
"That's good, now come over here and have a chat with the gals."

As his colleague drove him through the dim and grey streets of Vauxhall in South London Detective Richard LaSalle sat motionless as he gazed blankly out of the passenger seat window. He was deep in thought reminiscing years ago when a fresh faced bobby on the beat he walked day and night along these dismal alleyways and streets. Nineteen years of age he was when he was stationed at Walworth road police station, It was then and still is today one of the toughest and most notorious areas in the whole of the country. LaSalle smirked as remembered his days chasing crooks around the Elephant and Castle and Lambeth Walk, in these streets the police were despised, it left its mark on the young LaSalle, this squalid little sector of the city had modelled him into the no nonsense villain hating copper that he was today.
“This fucking cesspit is where I broke my boots in.” he sighed as if disgusted to his colleague driving.
“In this piss-hole!” the driver replied turning up his nose.
“Yeah, in this piss-hole.” sighed LaSalle back to him quietly.
“See those arches.” LaSalle suddenly pointed.
“That’s where Taffy Williams got stabbed and killed, saw it with my own eyes.”
“I didn’t know you knew Taffy sir.” replied the driver remarking on the legendary detective Taffy Williams.
“The bastards opened him up like a can of fucking tomatoes.”
“It was the Daniel’s gang that killed him.” replied the driver.
“Little Del killed him, Del Daniel’s now he was a fucking evil bastard.”
“He was hung for the murder.” interrupted the driver.
“It was one of my first arrests, I took a cosh across the back of the head, Taffy got killed and I got twelve stitches, the day they strung that bastard up every copper in the country had a drink.”
“Jesus sir!, I didn’t know you was on that nicking, Taffy Davies and the Daniel’s gang was legend when I was at police college, it was part of our awareness program, you know never approach a dangerous suspect unless you had proper back-up.”
LaSalle sighed loudly at his colleague’s remark.
“There all fucking dangerous suspects in these manor’s, ya fucking college handbook don’t work down ere.”
“Get em out the game, and get them out quick!” the driver added.
“That’s right John.” LaSalle interrupted.
“This is a coppers education, forget all that bollocks at Hendon, ain’t worth a fucking light down here, it’s in these streets, these fucking piss-holes where a copper gets his stripes.”
The driver was nodding enthusiastically at LaSalle’s remark.

“I did my first station in Shoreditch sir, fresh out of college I thought I knew it all, fucking woke me up walking them streets, it terrified me what the real world was.”
“Shoreditch, tough first station, what’d ya learn?”
“I learnt that you look after number one first, there’s no right or wrong, justice or injustice, innocence or guilt, it’s just them and just us!”
LaSalle turned his head slowly at his driver and looked pleased at him before looking down at his watch.
“C’mon john, better put ya foot down mate, we gotta be there in five minutes.”
“No problem sir.”
Lavender Hill police station was one of the new police stations in London, positioned between Battersea and Clapham on the south banks of the river Thames it looked like a mini prison from the outside. Detective LaSalle’s car pulled up at the side gates where they were met by a security barrier, after showing his police card, where the policeman looked at it in great length finally the car was allowed to pass.
LaSalle left his driver in the car and walked over to the police entrance where he was met by another police officer who once again asked for his credentials
“Here ya go I’m here to see Detective Parsons,” moaned LaSalle as he pushed his identity card into the officer’s hand,
“He’s on the third floor,” replied the officer,
Detective Daniel Parsons was a young up and coming Detective with an ex-military background, he was known as a bit of a maverick amongst many of the old guard detectives, extremely stubborn and strong headed, he had a strong reputation for doing things his way.
Today’s meeting with LaSalle had annoyed Parsons, he was well aware of LaSalle’s legendary nickname ‘verbals’ and his way of policing. Parsons however was ‘straight’ as he called it, he hated crooks and villains as much as any detective but to him it was the law that mattered most, and if he couldn’t catch a suspect within the parameters of the Law then that was how it was.
Parsons had just finished a conversation on the phone when he heard LaSalle knock on his door.
“Detective, come in.” parsons warmly said.
“Daniel is it? Or is it Danny?” LaSalle replied smiling.
“Daniel will be fine sir.” parsons smiled back.
“Good you can call me Rich.” added LaSalle as he walked in the office and sat down.
“So then, what brings you down here, it’s not often that the top brass, dirties their boots in these districts.” Parsons said sitting down.
“I’m hardly an Eaton square copper sonny; my boots were dirtied on these streets before you were born.” LaSalle replied with anger in his voice.

"Firstly no insult was intended detective and secondly I ceased to be called sonny when I took up the queen's commission."
"Yeah your ex-army ain't ya?"
"Captain of the military police in the Royal fusiliers."
"You must have chased a lot of crooks in them days." answered LaSalle with sarcasm.
"My fair share."
"Year I bet."
"Look detective we can sit here shooting the breeze all day if you wish, but I would wager that your just as busy as I was before we were introduced, you haven't come down here just to trade insults, let's just get on with the reason shall we."
LaSalle smiled wryly, before lighting himself up a cigarette.
"You arrested Alan Anderson for the Fromer murder."
"Yes!"
"You've nicked the wrong man."
"Really." Parsons replied with sarcasm.
"Anderson was Fromer's pal, everyone knows that."
"And I suppose a pal has never killed his pal before, so if it wasn't Anderson then detective, who was it?"
"It was the Kray's"
Daniel Parsons closed his eyes and sighed at LaSalle's outburst, along with LaSalle's nickname the detectives obsession with the Kray's was also just as famous, after a short pause as the young detective composed himself he tried to sound rational.
"Detective, frankly speaking the ink has barely dried on the last case that you brought against the Kray's."
"I have it from a good and reliable source."
"Yes, I have evidence, solid bang to bloody rights evidence."
"I'm telling you Anderson never did it."
Parson once again sighed.
"So what are you asking?" he added with frustration in his voice.
"Drop the charge against Anderson, keep the investigation open, when the times right I'll give you all the evidence that you'll need to convict Kray."
"I can't do that."
"Why not? I'm telling you, you have the wrong man."
Parsons shook his head.
"I have a wounded man who was at the scene of the crime, his clothes are covered in paraffin and I have Fromer's blood on the arrested man's shoes, what more bloody evidence do we need, I can't just let this man go because you say so."
"He's the wrong man, everyone fucking knows it." LaSalle growled.

“When detective has that bothered you? What proof do you have.” replied Parsons raising his voice.
“I’ll have proof I told you.”
“We’re just going round in circles, unless you walk in here with a witness or concrete proof there’s nothing at this point I can do.”
“I can take this over your head if need be.”
“Then why don’t you!” replied Parsons with anger.
LaSalle leaned back in his chair.
“I wanna speak to Anderson.”
“Absolutely no way!”
“Then you talk to him, do this at least, tell him there’s proof that Ronnie Kray was in the room, make him a deal, see what way he goes.”
“I don’t make deals detective.”
“Everyone makes fucking deals, it’s how this thing works, you’re not that fucking pure are you.”
“Look I’ll interview Anderson, but they’ll be no deals.”
“If you mention that you know it was Kray who killed Fromer then he’ll turn.”
“They’ll be no deals.”
“Fuck me! Tell the fucking man that you know it’s not him! Tell him all he has to do is say who it was, and he’s in the clear, how fucking difficult is that.”
“I’ll interview him!”
“Well do it the fucking right way!”
Parsons rose to his feet and shifted towards the door.
“Thank you detective for your time.”
LaSalle rose slowly.
“If you fuck this up I’ll make sure you’ll never get another promotion even if you find fucking Lord Lucan.” snapped LaSalle as he walked out.
Narbonne on the south Mediterranean coast was the last big French town before reaching the Spanish border village of La Perthus. Ron Kray and Johnny Walsh sat happily in a Narbonne railway bar having just travelled five hundred miles from Paris on the superb French rail network.
“What times our train John?”
“It leaves in forty five minutes Ron.”
“I can’t wait to get down to Spain.” Ron sighed as he sipped on an espresso coffee.
“It won’t take long Ron, once we’re on the train we’ll have a couple of drinks then get our heads down by morning were be in Marbella.”
“It’s a fucking long way John.”
“Eight hundred miles, don’t worry about it Ron, I did what you asked and got us first class, we’re sleep like babies on the beds they got on this train.”
“No one gave you any funny looks when you brought the tickets.”

“I told you before, it was sweet, I made out I was Irish.”
“Fucking Irish!” Ron snapped.
“Yeah put on a real broad paddy accent.”
Ron laughed.
“Good thinking John, now they’ll have us down as two fucking paddie terrorists.”
“Don’t get paranoid Ron, they only wanna see ya for questioning mate, it’s not like we broke out of Wandsworth is it.”
“Well that’s reassuring John, I’m so pleased your so calm about it.” joked Ron.
“Fuck it! We’re be on a beach in twenty four hours.”
“Well come on drink that down, I wanna call Mario before we get on the train, let him know what time we get to the station tomorrow.” added Ron standing up and pointing to johns cup of coffee.
Johnny Walsh dialled the number and put in the adequate French coins before handing the phone over to Ron.
“Mario, its Ron, we get in at twelve tomorrow, midday alright.”
“Ronnie! Is that you?”
“Yeah!”
“I have been trying to call Reg; we have a problem at the club.”
“What kind of problem, what’s the matter?”
“It’s the Americans they want to buy us out.”
“Buy us out, what’d ya mean buy us out, we’re not for sale!”
“Ronnie! I cannot handle this, they are very heavy, I need someone here, I need help.”
“Well I’ll be there tomorrow, and I’ll see these fucking mugs.”
“I have a to see these bastards again today, Ron I am afraid.”
“Listen you cancel today’s meeting; tell them that the owner will talk to them tomorrow.”
“Ok Ron, okay I will do this.”
“Mario don’t go on that meeting without me alright.”
“Okay I understand.”
“Just pick us up at midday and I’ll deal with these mugs.”
“I see ya tomorrow.”
“Yeah twelve o’clock.” said Ron as he slammed the phone down which immediately alerted Walsh that something was wrong.
“What the fuck was that all about?”
“He says he’s got some problems with some yanks putting the arm on him trying to buy the club.”
“WHAT!”
“Yeah some flash bastards are putting it on him.”
“Who are they, do we know em?”

“Fuck knows John! But we’re find tomorrow who they are and they’ll fucking find out who we are.”
Frith street in the heart of London’s Soho on a Saturday night was a thriving concoction of bars, clubs, restaurants and cafeterias, During the nineteen twenties, thirties and forties and fifties Frith and its parallel Dean street had been predominantly under the wing of the Italians.
Old fashioned villains like the Sabbini’s and the Cortesi’s ruled this area with a rod of iron, they kept away all the petty villains and con men and made the area a respectable place to enjoy your days and evenings in. ‘somewhere one could dine his mother’ as old Darbi Sabbini would say. But as the old guards empire collapsed Frith street became a target for a more ruthless and unscrupulous breed of immigrant. For the last two decades the area had been overtaken by Maltese and French racketeers, and in their wake the area has fallen into prostitution and razor gangs. The once posh bars and clubs are just but a memory now; David wraith reporter for the Daily mail once wrote that this seedy part of London was the closest thing to Sodom and Gomorrah since the days of the Roman Empire. An overstatement of course but still it was an insight into the depravity that this once respectable area had fallen into. The once fiercely proud Italian proprietors who would polish there steps and boast of their freshly painted window and shop fronts of their cafeterias, bars and restaurants had been the first casualties, then the image suffered as the streets filled with vice Tsars from Europe and con men and spivs all eager to cash in on the easy life.
Little Lenny Goodman was part of a small Jewish minority that still traded in Immigrants alley as frith street was sometimes known. Lenny’s roots went back to the old days when his Father escaping the Nazi soldiers from Czechoslovakia settled in the area and opened a salt beef and bagel cafeteria and delicatessen, after only two years Lenny’s Father had saved enough money to buy the lease for the shop and the flats above. For a further decade the business boomed until the ever increasing rise in prostitution drove away all the customers. At the death of Lenny’s Father he inherited a business that was fast in decline, Lenny tried his best but the debts soon begun to mount, in the end he was forced to close and to find a new tenant, he rented out the shop to a French Algerian adult magazine trader who blacked out the windows and turned it into an shop to sell his pornographic items from. Lenny moved out his family from the flat above into a more predominately Jewish and calmer way of life in the London suburb of Stanford hill. The flat was rented to a Maltese businessman who traded the services of women in exchange for cash. The money from his two new tenants was good, slowly he began to get himself out of debt but Lenny was still troubled, he tried not to think about what his Father’s business had now become, but in reality Lenny had become a landlord to the vice world. Like it or not he was indirectly being paid from

the proceeds of prostitution. He tried desperately to justify it in his own mind telling himself that he was just renting out the flat and that it was none of his business what his tenant was doing. But his guilt or shame would not easily be forgotten, every Friday he would go to the synagogue and try to be a man of faith but the guilt the more he tried to forget chipped away at him even more. Then one day when the Maltese were late in a rent payment Lenny jumped in his car and drove over to the flat, Lenny walked up the stairs into his own home where he was met by a young lady, at first he thought it must be the Maltese businessman's teenage daughter but she propositioned him with her services. Sickened Lenny ran instantly from the flat and ran into the nearest bar where he asked to wash his hands and face, just being in the flat for a moment had made him feel filthy, he retched as he thought about what degradation was now going on in his once family home. Enough was enough Lenny whilst walking back to his car knew that for his own saneness if nothing else the Maltese were going to have to go but it would not be that easy, firstly he had a tenant's agreement and secondly the Maltese had built up a highly profitable business and would not give that up without a fight.
He looked for and found an old associate of his Father, Battles Rossi, Rossi was a very well respected villain son of Italian immigrants. After listening to battles Lenny agreed a deal, Rossi would evict the Maltese but would rent the flat out himself where he would turn it into a gambling house, during the daylight hours the flat would be used for runners taking bets on the horse racing and dogs while in the night it would be used for card games. The plan was successful and for many years until his death Rossi was the proprietor of one of the most prestigious and lucrative back room gambling establishments in the city. After the funeral of battles Rossi surprisingly to Lenny no one came forward to replace the Old Italian, forced into a position he didn't want to be in Lenny Goodman had to take on himself the day to day running of the spieler. The money side of things were good, very good but Lenny Goodman had one big problem, he was Lenny Goodman and he could supply the protection that the Italian once respected, he was on his own, a target and it was only a matter of time before a gang focused their attention on him. It was recommended that he talk to the Kray's, a meeting was arranged and Lenny gave Ron and Reg a piece of the action in exchange for their protection, it was how things worked with both parties happy with the arrangement.
It had just gone eleven o'clock in the evening as Sammy Carpenter pulled the car up at the beginning of Frith street where it joined old Compton street. Reg, Tony Lambrianou and the Jones brothers Tommy and Alex quickly jumped out and huddled together in a doorway.
All wearing overcoats they formed a circle as Reg gave them a final briefing. "Right if there in there, there's no fucking about, we're just steam straight in"

"I'm nearly certain they're in there Reg, Lenny called this afternoon and said they'd be here about now." Tony said.
"Good, you tooled up Tommy?"
"Got a 38 Reg." Replied Tommy in a low voice.
"Alright keep it in ya pants unless things go right on top and there's no other option."
Reg looked quickly around before patting both the Jones brothers on the arms "Right let's fucking go!" he said sternly.
The four of them then walked briskly to the entrance of the gambling joint where they were met by Stevie 'arms' McKenzie a black doorman who worked for Lenny, he got his nickname 'arms' because of the huge muscles he had built from years of weightlifting, Stevie stood well over six foot and was built like a tank but that was where the menace stopped, he was a front, a fraud, he could deal with the odd drunk because of the sheer size of him but he couldn't as Reg says 'ave a row'.
"Reg!" Stevie smiled as he opened the door.
"Alright arms, is Lenny up there?"
"He was in the bar Reg, shall I call him for you?"
"No that's alright mate, I'll find him myself."
"Ok Reg, can I take your coat?"
"Nah but you can do me a favour, shut this door and don't let anyone else in until I come back down alright."
"Stevie looked at Reg nervously, he was no way going to refuse him but he was scared of what Lenny would do if he closed the entrance."
"Don't worry about Lenny arms, I'll tell him I told you to do it."
"You don't want me to let anyone in Reg, what if its…."
"NO ONE! Don't matter who it is, no one else comes through that door."
"Okay Reg!"
Reg, the Jones brothers and Tony walked up to the first floor landing where the main bar was, the usual Saturday night regulars were there and it looked extremely busy. Reg walked in first and noticed a few old faces amongst the crowd. He saw Dave 'the tie', a good old Jewish gambler standing over at the far end of the bar and standing next to him was young Bert, the nephew of the infamous Bert Marsh, an old time heavy who was loyal to the Sabinni's back in the twenties and thirties. Looking round the room Reg also noticed four large olive skinned men standing by the window, the four men all seemed to meet Reg's eye as he gazed across at them.
Tony nudged Reg,
"That's gotta be them," he whispered nodding in the direction of the four men who Reg had just looked at.
Reg nodded back to Tony as he lit a cigarette, he could see by himself that the men were the Maltese gang, there actions gave them away, the way they stood

alone, and the way they looked out of place and the anxious look on their faces.
Turning to the bar Reg ordered four gin and tonics, the barmaid quickly poured the drinks and then refused to take payment for them, Reg insisted and put the cash on the bar, the barmaid left the cash and then disappeared quickly into an adjoining door before returning only with Lenny Goodman following her.
"Reg it's good to see you my friend." Lenny warmly greeted Reg.
"Is it?" replied Reg distantly.
"We never got last week's money." Reg added as he took a drag on his cigarette.
"I have it here for you Reg, and this weeks too."
"So you have two partners now then Len." added Reg remarking on the Maltese.
Lenny paused for a moment in replying, he felt himself becoming stressed as he wiped away some sweat on his brow.
"I was not sure if this was my problem Reg or whether it was yours."
Reg half smiled as he took a sip of his drink.
"It's my problem Len, but I can't understand why you never came to see me."
"I told Billy Hayes!"
"That's not what I said, why didn't you come over and see me in person, your silence makes me ask questions, I wonder to myself if you're still loyal or maybe you have something to hide."
Lenny shook his head from side to side disagreeing with what Reg had said.
"I am your friend Reg, we make good business together but in truth I was afraid to see you, I needed time to gather my thoughts."
"Gather your thoughts, after all the time we've been together you can't come to me when there's a problem, what am I meant to make out of all this Len, you pay someone else instead of us and then give us the silent treatment, anyone would think that you don't want to do business with us anymore."
"NO REG!, you and Ron will always be my partners, I was just afraid that you would be angry that I paid them, but I had no choice, I walk past these people every day, they hit me, threatened me, threatened my family, I had to pay them Reg."
"So there's no problem between us?"
"NO Reg I just want things back to normal, I want these bastards out of here."
Reg looked at how sincere Lenny looked so leaning forward he shook his hand.
"Is that them then over there?" Reg added nodding discreetly at the Maltese.
"Yes that's carmine's nephew."
"Good, what can you tell me about them?"

“I don’t know too much about them Reg, I’ve seen them around the area and I’ve heard that they are all dangerous men, the biggest one is the one who hit me.”
“Do ya know if there tooled up now?” Tony asked.
“Are men like these not always tooled up.” replied Len wisely.
A remark that made Reggie smile.
“Is there going to be trouble Reg?” asked Lenny now looking concerned.
“I would say so Lenny, no other option.” replied Reg.
“Not in here Reg, please not in here.”
“I can’t see there being anywhere else Len, not unless you wanna ask if they wouldn’t mind stepping outside.” Reg added somewhat tongue in cheek.
“It will be bad for business Reg.”
“Sorry Len, it’s gotta be now.”
“Please Reg.”
“No Lenny, they gotta go.”
As Reg spoke with Lenny, Tony Lambrianou winked at the Jones brothers telling them to get ready, Lenny Goodman then reached out and grabbed Reg’s arm.
“Please Reg; let me get some of the customers out of here.”
Frustrated by Lenny’s persistence Reg smirked and bit his lip.
“You got two minutes.” he said in a snarl before taking another sip of his drink, as soon as Lenny heard Reg he immediately ran off and began whispering to a few of his clients, telling them that he was closing this bar because it had been booked for a private card game the clients resentfully began to move to the bar upstairs.
As this was happening Tony Lambrianou made sure he kept his eyes on the Maltese, he could see that they were becoming anxious especially with what Lenny was doing so he studied them carefully, Tony saw that the Maltese could sense trouble, they’d be fools not to. Tommy Jones who was standing next to Tony was also keeping a keen eye on them, standing slightly in the back ground he kept his hand on his revolver that was in his pocket, if the Maltese had a gun on them then Tommy was going to make damn sure that he was going to get his bullets off first.
Reg took one final sip and finished his drink before putting the glass down on the bar, then turning his back on the Maltese he turned to face his friends.
“I’m gonna go over there on my own, it might drop there guard a bit, just make sure your ready as soon as it goes off alright.”
“Don’t worry Reg” Tommy Jones added reassuringly.
“Do ya want this.” Tony suddenly said as he moved closer to Reg and cunningly revealed a cosh that he had in his waistband.
“Nah you keep it tone, just make you smash that big cunt right over the head with it, I don’t wanna be rolling about on the floor with him.”

Reg then smiled and gave his pals a wink before turning away and taking off his overcoat, he then carefully folded it and placed it on the bar before walking towards the Maltese men who seeing Reg walking towards them all stiffened as they turned to face him.
"Alright lads." Reg said warmly as he neared them "Why don't we have a little talk." he added now only a few feet away.
"What about." said one of the men.
"About this." Reg said as he suddenly threw a devastating right hand punch which connected with a loud cracking noise on the largest man's jaw, the punch was perfect as it struck the man on the point of the jaw just as it met the ear, his jaw broke instantly as the power of the punch sent him flying back over a table. Reg then turned his attention on the nephew; a firm punch broke his nose as Reg then doubled him up with a powerful blow to the stomach. By now Tony had joined Reg and was attacking one of the other two men with his cosh, Tony hit the man once on the temple and he dropped heavily to the floor, the last Maltese man was being savagely beaten by the two Jones brothers who had forced him on the floor with wooden chairs and were now hitting and kicking him into oblivion.
Within moments the fight was over and the four Maltese men lay bleeding on the floor bleeding and battered.
"You paid these fucking idiots!" Reg shouted out as he turned to Lenny who was cowering behind the bar.
"Throw these fucking mugs in the street." Reg said turning back to his friends before picking up the nephew himself and throwing him onto his back on top of a table. Reg then tidied himself up as his top button had sprung open during the fight he then looked back at the nephew who was lying on the table barely awake, blood was pouring from his nose and mouth, Reg punched the man again knocking out five of his teeth and tearing his lip as the broken teeth ripped through his cheek. Reg hit him a further four times in the face causing it to tear, redden and swell, then grabbing him by the hair Reg shouted at him.
"Tell your fucking boss, to keep his fucking wog paws off our business."
Tony who had been doing as Reg asked and taking the other men down the stairs and into the street returned to find Reg shouting at the last man, Tony walked over and grabbed Reg.
"Reg, he's gone mate, look he's fucking out of it, it's no good telling him anything."
One more punch and Reg backed off, Tony sneered as he looked at the state of the nephews face while Reg had grabbed a place mat and was wiping the blood off of his knuckles, then as Reg pulled his overcoat on he thought of an idea.
"Pick him up." he said to Tony and the Jones brothers.
"What we doing with him?" Tony asked.

"Just bring the cunt downstairs."
The Italian pizzeria in the heart of Frith Street was always busy on a Saturday night, sat in their usual corner were the young Maltese men who worked with the Massina's. At the other end of the pizzeria near the front windows were the regular prostitutes, pimps and drug dealers carefully scanning the street outside for any potential customers? In the past the Italian pizzeria was once a high class restaurant but since the Italians moved out it had become a dregs dive, people openly sat in there smoking hemp. It was like a villains open office for all the insignificant immoral criminals. The pizzeria was also under the protection of the Massina's where the eldest brother carmine would often hold meetings in the back booth, open twenty four hours of the day this once respectable establishment was now a dark example of all what was bad in the area of Soho.
When Reg Kray burst through the doors of the pizzeria the whole place broke out into silence, everyone knew who was behind the restaurant so violence within the pizzeria doors was not a common sight. As Reg walked in he grabbed the first man he saw, a frail looking heroin addict pimp called Pascal, Reg grabbed him by his long hair and dragged him onto the floor.
"WHERES CARMINE MASSINA!" Reg then shouted as he began to throw a couple of tables in the air which forced a few people near him to jump out the way.
Recognising Reg the young Maltese men who had been sitting at the back of the bar all stood up and cautiously began to advance towards Reg.
"Easy, easy, he's not here." said one of them in soft tone trying to diffuse the situation.
Reg turned back towards the door where Tony and the Jones brothers walked in carrying Massina's nephew who was still barely conscious, Reg grabbed his hair and dragged him on to a table top and then turned back to face the men.
"Then give him this piece of fucking shit, and give him this message, tell him to keep his fucking nose out of our business!"
The Maltese men did not reply they could see the mess that their friend was in but more important they could see how angered and menacing Reg Kray looked, the man who spoke just nodded as if to show Reg that he understood.
Reg for a moment held a gaze at the Maltese men, he was waiting for a response, any response as Reg was ready for more fighting, or more to the point he wanted more fighting, finally he spat into the face of the Maltese nephew who was still on the table then very slowly he walked out the pizzeria.
"Job fucking done!" he mouthed angrily to Tony and the Jones brothers as he walked off into the nightlife in Frith Street.
Detective LaSalle walked angrily after parking his car in the car park at Tottenham swimming baths, he was still seething from his meeting with detective Parsons. Before the heated meeting he was hoping that detective

Parsons would play along with him and hold up the case against Anderson so that he would have more time to gather his evidence against the Kray's but Parson's refusal had given LaSalle a big dilemma. He felt confident that Slice'em Sid was going to at some stage give him what he needed. But if he wanted to stop the Fromer and Anderson case, he was going to have to force slice'em Sid to turn now. Or at the very least he would have to reveal Sid to his superiors, but LaSalle had grown up in the real world, he trusted no one, especially the crooked detectives at Scotland Yard. Half of them were on the take and he felt certain that if he revealed Sid as an informer then it was a certainty that some greedy detective looking to earn a quick pound would somehow get a message to the Kray's. For a detective this was always a problem, detectives would nurture their informers and gain a steady and reliable source of information from them whilst turning a blind eye to the informers crimes, sometimes detectives would pay the informers money, it was an ideal arrangement for a detective, he would be keeping up with his rota of arrests while the scum bag giving him information would continue to earn money with a near impunity to arrest. But once you revealed the informer and made him a witness at a trial then his cover was blown, that would be the end of the arrangement and the detective would have to start all over again and find another source.

Slice'em Sid sat anxiously on a wooden bench just behind the swimming baths in a small park area he was dressed in a large overcoat with a thick scarf pulled half way up his face and a large flat cap on his head, if it wasn't for the severe December weather he would look very suspicious.

"WHATS THE FUCKING MEANING OF THIS!" Sid snarled as he first saw LaSalle. "I can't keep having these fucking meetings, you're gonna get me fucking muellered you are!" he added as LaSalle reached him.

"Just shut ya fucking mouth and sit ya arse down!" LaSalle angrily replied as he pushed Sid back onto the bench.

"Who you fucking pushing?" Sid protested.

"Shut ya fucking mouth will ya, do ya know they've fucking charged Anderson."

"Course I do, everyone fucking knows."

"And that don't bother ya."

"That's down to your fucking lot, that's your end, not mine."

LaSalle sighed and wiped his head as he sat down next to Sid after a short pause of silence he leant over and spoke more quietly but still with an authoritative tone in his voice.

"I might have to bring you out into the open."

"No fucking way! I told you I can't do it now."

"There might not be a choice; we can't let Anderson go down for what Ronnie did."

"Then fucking do something about it, you're the copper."
"I can't! Their starting court proceedings soon, you gotta come forward, I gotta fucking introduce you."
"Look I fucking told you, there's no fucking way I'm doing this until I'm ready; bring me in at a later date as late evidence or something."
"I can't just bring you in half way through a fucking trial; they'll have my bollocks for withholding this."
"That's your fucking problem!"
"No its both of ours, I can't keep you a secret anymore, I'm giving you one week, after that I'm telling my seniors about you and I'm coming after you."
"I won't do it!"
"One week Sid, then you're out in the open."
The train pulled into Malaga train station at twelve ten, ten minutes late. Ron and Johnny got off the train and were happy to see that Mario was already there waiting for them, the three men greeted each other with a warm embrace before walking off towards Mario's car.
"Now what's all this about the yanks then Mario?" asked Ron as soon as they had got into the car and Mario had pulled the cars roof down as Ronnie liked.
"They won't leave us alone Ronnie, I've told time again that the clubs not for sale, but still they keep on asking, every night they come and every night I tell them the same thing, still they won't take no for an answer."
"What's so special about our fucking club, where'd these flash bastards come out from?"
"They just appeared, they say they love the area and our club is perfect for them, they have already brought two properties in the Puente Romano area, they have brought Valentino's old villa."
"What'd they mean perfect for them?"
"I don't know Ronnie, one night they just appear in the club, they spent a lot of money drinking champagne all night then one of them asked the waiter to see me, I went over to their table expecting there to be a problem with the bill but they said they wanted to buy the club, I tell them it's not for sale but his reply was 'everything and everyone is for sale'."
"What'd ya say to that?"
"Like before all I say is that the club is not for sale at any price, but still they ask me every day, I don't know what's going on Ronnie, last time we spoke they said that one way or another they always get what they want, it is scaring me Ronnie, I think that they are American Mafia."
"MAFIA what makes ya think that?"
"You know the way they act, the way they look and talk, plus they told me that they are representatives from a large New York organisation that are investing in the Costa del Sol, this is all too crazy for me Ronnie."

Ronnie smiled as he leaned his arm out of the window and looked up into the clear blue sky.
"Don't let it bother you no more Mario, I'll deal with these MAFIA."
"They'll be in the club tonight, they have told me to think of a price."
"Good, I'll give em a fucking price; just leave this to me alright."
"Ok Ronnie, where'd you want me to take you now?"
"Take me to the villa, I wanna get in some fresh clothes and make sure I got a clean suit for tonight."
Reg Kray sat round the fire at his mother's house feeling pleased with himself after last night's work, his mother had just brought him a cup of tea as he pulled the chair closer to the fire to warm his legs.
"I don't know what it is with you boys, what time did you get to sleep last night Reg?" said violet as she was making a comment on how'd Reg had slept in till three in the afternoon.
"Ah you know what it's like mum, half our business is in the night time, why, what's the matter, do ya want me to get a milk round or something,"
"No! I'm just saying you've missed half the day, it'll be dark in an hour,"
"Leave it out mum, don't worry about it."
"I'm not moaning Reg but why'd ya always come here after a late night, what's the matter with your own flat."
"I wanna be with you mum!" Reg joked "Anyway I got no one to make me breakfast in my place have I?"
"You wanna get yourself a nice girl Reg." violet replied and then winced as the words left her mouth.
"I tried that didn't I mum."
"I'm sorry Reg, I didn't mean that." replied violet sincerely as she knew that the suicide of Reg's wife Francis was still a very painful subject for her son.
"Don't worry about it mum, I know what you meant"
"Listen why don't ya get yourself washed and come and see ya brother with me?"
"How is Charlie Mum?"
"He misses you and Ronnie Reg."
"Ah I'll go and see him later." sighed Reg.
"That's what you always say."
"Nah I will, I'll definitely go and see him tonight."
"Anyway where's Dad, mum?" Reg suddenly asked and changing the subject.
"He's out on the Knocker."
"What's he doing that for I gave him a few quid last week."
"He's probably got a bird somewhere ain't he."
"Don't say that mum."
"He can do what he bloody likes for all I care, listen Reg I'm gonna go up the road now and see ya brother, is there anything you want before I go."

"Just a kiss Mum and tell me your look after ya self, crossing them roads."
Violet leaned forward and hugged Reg's head.
"I'll see ya later son." she said as she planted a big kiss on the top of his head.
When violet left the house Reg still feeling tired put his feet up on the sofa and decided to get another hours sleep in front of the fire but just as he closed his eyes the phone rang.
"Fucking hell, who the fucks this?" he said as strained to get himself up.
"HELLO!" he shouted in a grumpy tone as he picked the phone.
"Reg is that you, you alright." replied Tony Lambrianou after hearing Reg's crabby voice
"Yeah what'd ya want Tone?"
"I've had a call; they wanna have a meeting about last night Reg."
"Argh fucking hell Tone, look do me a favour, I feel fucked, come over in a couple of hours mate alright."
"I'll see ya then."
"Yeah I'll see ya."
As Mario pulled up to the gates of Ron's villa Ron was pleased to see that the resident house keeper Juan had kept his residence in a clean and pristine order, Juan was busy mowing the front lawn as he saw the car pull up, immediately he recognised Ron and came rushing over to open the large iron gates. Ron warmly greeted the old Spaniard with a friendly embrace as he got out of the car.
"Mr Kray it is so good to see you."
"And you Juan, how's the house?"
"It is how you left it senor."
"We had a problem with the boiler but I make it work again." Juan added proudly that there had been a problem but he was clever enough to have it fixed.
"Can I get you a drink senor?"
"Got any beers?"
"I think so."
"Then me and Johnny will have a beer each." Ron added with a smile.
Juan nodded and then marched off in the direction of the kitchen.
"I could get a proper service for you to take care of the house Ronnie." Mario said as Juan disappeared.
"Nah what's the matter with Juan?"
Mario shrugged at Ron's reply.
"He's a bit old Ronnie."
"He's fine, anyway I like him, I feel that we can trust him." replied Ron.
Mario just gave a slight smile at Ron's decision, he did not agree with it as he was from Spanish aristocratic background and house keepers and butlers were a way of life to him, he grew up in a Spanish mansion that was almost single

handily run by the staff of the residence, Ron's housekeeper Juan was an old Spanish vagabond who Ron and Charlie met one day when Juan was helping out selling ice cream on the beach. Ronnie took a liking to him and offered him a job, at the time Juan was homeless so Ron moved him into the house and made sure that Mario gave him a small wage every week. This kind of generosity Mario found hard to comprehend, maybe it was the difference between his and the Kray's background, his past was one of money and wealth while the Kray's were born into poverty and had had to fight for everything they had ever made. There seemed to be an affinity between Ronnie and Juan that Mario just couldn't understand.
Mark Ralindi and Tommy Spano arrived at the club at their usual time of 10.30pm, both men were dressed immaculately in $500 silk suits and hand stitched Italian leather loafers. Accompanying them were four associates or body guards all over six foot tall and built like tanks.
Mario's suspicion that the men were Mafia were correct as both Ralindi and Spano were both high ranking men in the notorious New York Genovese family, currently the most powerful crime family in America. The men had been sent to Spain by the bosses back home to test the waters or look for opportunities of expanding the mob's obsession with the casino business. Over the last decade the American mob had been expanding their casino expertise to all the four corners of the globe, drawn by the immense profits made from casino's it was now one of the mob's main investments.
The Genovese's involvement in international casino's begun in the fifties when boss Charlie 'Lucky' Luciano and Meyer Lansky with a Florida based gangster Santo Trafficante invested millions into a democratic Cuba, working hand in hand with the Cuban government the business was a gold mine. But in 1959 due to a government that was fast losing control to a ever increasing revolution the mobs luck finally ran out in Cuba. Luciano and Lansky held a last ditch attempt to rescue there Cuban involvement, they met face to face with a prominent revolutionary named Fidel Castro but at this meeting they were told that once Cuba becomes a communist state then their investments would become nationalised by the communist republic of Cuba.
Urgent talks were staged amongst the top Mafia dons to discuss their options, rumours say that at this meeting it was discussed the possibility of killing Castro but Lansky the principle investor made it clear that Cuba had fallen too far, it was now inevitable that it would become a communist state, the Italians persisted in their arguments to kill Castro but Lansky pointed out that all the murder would achieve is killing one communist to be replaced by another. With bitter rage the mob walked away, helplessly they saw there millions taken from them.
Lansky was quoted as saying 'when a people rise up against an oppressive government there is no force in the world that can resist, we was unlucky, if

had a been anyone apart from the communists then we would have cut a deal, but that's life'
The mob still had millions invested in Las Vegas but the spoils were shared on a more national basis, like mafia families from New York, Chicago, Cleveland, Milwaukee, Philadelphia, Ohio, and a few others all hand their hands in the Jewell of the desert. Unlike Cuba Las Vegas was under the control of the so called Mafia commission but the frequent power struggles amongst the nations crime families made it difficult to enact any kind of control regarding Vegas.
As a result of the increasing mob violence Las Vegas soon came under the scrutiny of the FBI and other government agencies. Soon prominent mob chiefs from around the country were being indicted to give evidence in front of senate hearings, the TV became involved and the whole thing became a circus. Meyer Lansky tried his best to control the Italians but before his eyes he could see that the mobs future in Las Vegas was fast becoming a distinct reality. Even the unions after a relationship that reached back nearly thirty years who helped launder money were trying to disassociate themselves from the mob,
Lansky growing tired of all the politics amongst the Italians tried to distance himself, working with a few childhood friends he knew trusted and respected, East coast guys and Angelo Bruno he advised them to invest internationally again, after Cuba this took some doing but the Genovese family had over the years generated millions of dollars from the advice of Lansky, hesitantly they put their money into London. Again times were good to begin with but the mobs nemesis the FBI once again caught up with them. In 1968 eight of the mobs top casino operators were barred from entering the UK. Dino Cellini a close associate of Lansky's who was in Cuba with him was amongst the eight along with the film star George Raft who was now a very much Mafia front man.
Once again the mob refused to let this setback stop them, after being kicked out of Britain they moved there operations to the Bahamas and parts of south America but Lansky had a dream about setting up in Europe, he believed that Europe was where the big money was. The Italian Mafia were not interested in the casino business so as far as Lansky was concerned Europe was like an open shop, ripe for the picking by someone who had the expertise.
Fat Tony Salerno the under-boss of the Genovese family and childhood friend of Lansky and Luciano had for a few years now heard that Spain could be a good place to invest. Reports had been coming back to him that the Spanish Franco government were relaxing its stance on international commerce, Franco had already named his successor as Prince Juan Carlos who himself had a much more open minded to his countries future, in his own words it was development rather than dictatorship that Spain needed.

Salerno thought Spain could be the next gold mine, it had the right location, weather and the catholic church was so set in its ways as its neighbour Italy, there were also no competition, there was no Spanish Mafia, Franco's harsh government had made sure of that, if Spain was to open up then Salerno wanted the mob in at the beginning.
"HEY! Look they gotta a fucking reserved sign on our table Tommy." mouthed Ralindi in his New York accent.
"What d fuck!" Tommy replied.
"Call over that fucking waiter." Mark said turning to one of his associates.
Moments later a very sheepish looking waiter came over.
"Senor." he said lowering his head slightly.
"Don't give me none of that senor bullshit, who d fuck put that sign on that table, we been sitting there all fucking week, this is fucking disrespectful, go get fucking Mario and don't go taking ya fucking time."
"Senor the table is reserved for senor Kray."
"Who the fuck is senor Kray? You fucking tell Mario we're sitting at that mother fucking table."
The waiter nodded back nervously.
"I will inform Senor Mario, can I get you a drink while you wait?" he added.
"Screw the fucking drink, just go get Mario!" Tommy barked.
Knowing that the Americans would be coming and not eager to see them without Ronnie by his side, Mario had been hiding away in the office all night.
As the waiter told him about the Americans anger with the table and their insistence to see them, his face filled with dread at the prospect of having to go downstairs. Resentfully Mario agreed and made his way down to them.
"Mark, Tommy!" Mario said as he held out his hand.
"Don't give me any of that handshake bullshit, Mario, what'd fuck goes here?, every fucking night we been drinking in this joint, spent a lot of fucking doe here, this is fucking disrespectful, maybe you don't know who we are? Let me fucking tell you, you don't wanna fucking find out who we are, do I make myself clear." snapped a very irate Mark Ralindi.
"Please." Mario pleaded "There was no disrespect intended, the table was reserved because the owner Ron Kray is arriving tonight." he added.
"The owner, I thought you were the owner." snapped Tommy Spano.
"He's my partner."
"Huh, ya fucking partner, good, we got business to talk about."
Feeling intimidated, Mario just apologised and gave in, he called over a waiter and told him to sit the Americans down at the table, in the back of Mario's mind he thought that this might anger Ronnie but he hoped that once explained Ronnie would understand.

“Make sure you bring your partner over, when he arrives.” Tommy said with arrogance in his voice.
“As soon as he arrives I will bring him over, I’m sure he will want to speak with you to.” replied Mario.
“Yeah you do that…. and make sure he thinks of a price.” Tommy added.
Still not dressed, Reg sat in his pyjamas with a blanket wrapped around his shoulders drifting in and out of sleep snugly in front of his mother’s fire, the night had now fallen onto the cold streets of London and Reg had not bothered to turn on the lights on, apart from the glow of the warm fire Reg was sitting in the dark. When Tony Lambrianou knocked on the front door he saw that the lights were off and wondered if anyone was in, he gave door another bang and was just about to walk off when Reg opened the door still wearing the blanket wrapped around his shoulders.
“Fuck me Reg, you alright, didn’t think anyone was in with all the lights off.”
“Yeah, come on, hurry up its fucking cold.” replied Reg.
“They reckon snows on its Reg.”
“Fuck off, its cold enough.” replied Reg as he led the way back to the fire.
“Shall I turn the light on Reg?” asked Tony as he walked in the living room.
“Nah leave it Tone, I gotta headache, must be coming down with the flu or something.” replied Reg as sat back down beside the fire.
“I won’t keep ya then Reg but I got a phone call from the Massina’s.” said Tony as he sat down.
“What’d they say?” snapped Reg.
Tony took in a deep breath before replying.
“Their angry about Carmine’s nephew Reg, but they say they understand, they reckon that they never knew that we had anything to do with the game.”
“Fucking liars!” snapped Reg.
“Course they are Reg, but it’s there way of trying to keep face mate, they’ve asked for a meeting, a meeting so as they can iron out any bad feelings between us.”
“What fucking bad feelings? I ain’t got any bad feelings, we got the game back.”
Tony shrugged.
“Their words were, ‘we need to sit down and discuss business so that things like this won’t repeat in the future’”
Reg picked himself up a cigarette and lit it as he thought about what Tony had just told him.
“What’d ya think there on a bout talk business, how did they sound Tone, tell me what do you feel in ya guts mate, do ya think they’re gonna make one with us.”
Reg took another drag as he finished talking, in his own mind Reg couldn’t really care less what the Massina’s wanted to do but more importantly he

wanted to know how Tony would react, Reg and Tony had been growing increasingly closer over the past couple of months and this was Reg's way of showing Tony that he now valued his opinion.
"Personally Reg I know they got the hump, they look at Frith street as their own bit of London, then right slap bang in the fucking middle of it there little Lenny's game, there manor and there not getting a penny from it."
"That's the way things are Tone, they don't own the fucking place."
"Yeah but reverse it Reg, let's say that there was a right good earner right in the middle of Roman road, what would we do if the Massina's were being paid to protect a gaff in our plot." asked Tony. "We wouldn't have it!" snapped Reg.
"There you go then."
After another drag Reg replied again.
"But it's not the same Tony, the West Ends always been open, you got different firms from all over the place working in the smoke, it's not like grafting on someone's doorstep is it."
"It is to them Reg, Frith street is their door step."
"So what you saying, make them a partner, fuck that Tony."
Tony shrugged.
"It might not be a bad idea, give em a small piece."
"Nah you're missing the big picture, we'd lose face Tone, if we let a Firm slip into us and then give em a piece, fuck me, we'd have every fucking one trying it on."
"So what's our stance then Reg?"
"We've shown them our stance, we protect ours."
"And if they wanna make one?"
"Then we'll fucking make a bigger one back!"
"A lot of people got the hump with us already Reg, do we need any more enemies?"
"It's the life we lead Tony, as long as we're all together then I couldn't give a fuck about any other fucker."
"So shall I tell Massina to fuck off?"
Reg thought for a slight second before answering.
"Just leave it for a bit Tone, let em sweat, if they call ya tell them you've spoke to me and that I'll think about after Christmas."
"Alright Reg, if that's what you want, I'll call them tonight."
"No, don't call them, let them call you."
"Alright." replied Tony as he got to his feet.
"Where ya going, sit down, ain't finished talking yet." Reg said.
Sitting back down Tony reached for a cigarette and lit it as he listened to Reg.
"Do ya remember Donnie Harding?"
"Yeah the music fella."

"Well we got a bit of business to take care of for him."
"Ronnie mentioned something about it, but with all that's been happening Reg I didn't know if we was going to do it."
"Ron gave his promise so we're have to do something but I don't want the fella topped, get the Jones brothers on it, and tell em theirs a monkey in it for em, now I want this slag fucking hurt, he's gotta be put in hospital for a nice few weeks Tony."
"Broken bones." Tony smirked.
"Yeah, smash his legs in, put him in fucking wheelchair I don't care but I don't want him killed alright."
"Don't worry Reg, it'll be done well."
"Nice one Tony,"
"Shall I call Harding and get all the details?"
"Yeah, you speak to Don and then tell the brothers what to do."
"Alright mate, I'll call him tomorrow."
"Good, right I'm gonna try and get back to sleep see if I can sleep out this poxy cold, come over about the same time tomorrow Tony, I won't be going out anywhere."
Deciding to wait outside the entrance for Ronnie to arrive Mario rubbed his hands together nervously as paced the doorway up and down. The Americans had unnerved him but now he was also worrying about how Ron would react when he found out about the Americans taking his table. He anxiously again asked the valet if he had seen Ronnie, again the valets reply was he hadn't. another twenty five minutes passed until Mario saw a car pull up carrying Johnny Walsh and Ron, Johnny jumped out of the driver's door and threw the car keys towards the valet who had just hurriedly opened the passenger door to let Ronnie out.
"Ronnie!" sighed Mario.
"Alright." replied Ron holding out his hand.
"What's the matter?" Ron added as he saw the stressed look in Mario's face.
"It's the Americans Ron, they are here, please Ronnie do not be cross with me but I had no choice but to give them your table, I…I tried to tell them that the table was reserved but they would."
Holding up a hand Ronnie suddenly interrupted his friend.
"Mario, calm down, look I'm here now don't worry I'll deal with it."
Mario sighed loudly and shook his head slightly.
"Thank you." he gasped.
"Come on let's go inside, let's get a drink then show me these mugs." Ron added leading the way.
Once Ron entered the club everyone made a point of greeting him, Ron made his way straight to the bar where Mario instructed the barmaid to get Ron and

Johnny a gin and tonic each, Ronnie eagerly took a sip then scanned the room eager to catch a glimpse of the yanks.
"Is that em." he nudged Mario.
"Yeah, the one with the blue shirt on is Mark Ralindi and the fat one with his back to us is Tommy Spano.
Ronnie took another sip then nudged Mario again.
"C'mon take over there." he said coldly and calmly.
Mark Ralindi seeing Mario coming towards him rose to his feet, Ralindi immediately noticed Ronnie walking besides him, he squinted as he looked Ron up and down and noticed how well Ron was dressed, he stiffened his posture as he noticed the cold fixed look upon Ronnie's face. Ralindi seemed to taste the presence of Ron, it wasn't a thought of fear that struck the American but more of a recognition of power, 'This guys no fucking club owner' Ralindi silently thought to himself. As Mario , Johnny and Ron got closer so did the feeling of Ron's presence, this was a guy coming over who had been told of the Americans intentions yet he showed no nerves at all, instead he looked like and walked like a wise guy himself.
"Gentlemen this Mr Ron Kray."
Mario said as he arrived at the Americans table.
"Hey Ron Kray! Mark Ralindi, and this ugly fucks Tommy Spano." replied Ralindi in his usual cocky manner.
"How'd ya do." said Ron quickly as he shook their hands.
Ron stood back as Mario pulled out a chair for him, once seated he turned rather abruptly towards mark Ralindi.
"So here I Am." he said as if challenging the yanks.
Ralindi ignored Ron's question as he busied himself lighting a large Cuban cigar, after what seemed an age he finally turned and faced Ron.
"You got a nice joint here!"
Ron gave a slight smile as now he ignored the American and then taking his time to take a cigarette out of his cigarette box to which Johnny Walsh immediately lit as soon as he placed it in his mouth, Ron took a large drag then blew the smoke away.
"Now what's all this about?" he asked Ralindi sternly in a no nonsense tone.
"We wanna buy the club."
"Why!"
"Hey, it's a fucking nice club."
"There's other nice clubs around here."
"Yep there is but we want this fucking club." Tommy Spano said challengingly.
"It ain't for sale!" replied Ron in a very final tone.
"Every fucking thing is for sale." Ralindi added.
"Well this ain't." mouthed Ronnie beginning to lose his patience.

"Yeah, I'd have a real good think about that if I was you." said Tommy.
"I've thought about it."
"Well think again." added Tommy.
"Why don't you fucking think again!" Ron snapped as turned and gave Tommy Spano a menacing glare which immediately had the effect of creating a nervous atmosphere.
"HEY!" Mark Ralindi suddenly shouted "Hey let's not get into a fucking beef about this, we're here to make you an offer, we like the club, we got business down here, so we're looking for our own place. All we wanna do is see if we can cut a deal, we've been gentlemen here, tried talking to that cocksucker Mario, but every fucking time we try to talk with him he just fucking freezes, now I can see your more of a sensible guy, now we're fucking talking dollars here. What's the matter with you fucking guys don't ya like talking about fucking money?" he added.
Ronnie nodded his head as he bit his lip then slowly took another drag on his cigarette before extinguishing it in the ash tray.
"Firstly that fella you're calling names, is my friend! And then you're telling me that your talking business… then stop playing fucking games, Mario's' my friend but I ain't no Mario, you wanna talk to me then fucking talk to me, you're wasting everyone's time with all this cobblers."
"What, what'd he say!" Tommy asked loudly only for Ralindi to wave a hand of authority before him.
"Where you from Ron, you're not from round here are you?"
"London!"
"Hey you're from London, you know how things work then, I may be wrong but looking at you I'd say you know who we are."
"Yeah I'v seen your kind about." replied Ron now sounding rather uninterested.
"If ya don't mind me asking, what'd ya do in London Ronnie?"
"I run things."
"You run things, what kind of things?"
"All kinds of things."
"Clubs?"
"We got our interests in a few of em."
"You ever heard of the Colony club in London Ronnie?"
After taking a sip of his drink Ronnie gave a sly smile as he now found the Americans question amusing, the Colony club was before his arrest for the murders of Cornell and Mcvitie a club where along with the Ryan's, he was getting a weekly pay cheque for protection. Backed by Mafia money the Colony club was where George Raft and Dino Cellini had worked on behalf of Meyer Lansky and mob boss Angelo Bruno.
"What's so funny, something he say amuse you?" Tommy Spano snapped.

“The Cellini’s, Dino and Eddie.” Ronnie said smiling.
“Yeah, Dino and Eddie, you know these guys Ronnie?” Ralindi replied now felling curious.
“Yeah I knew them well, and their Father, do you know them!” replied Ronnie.
“Know them! There like fucking brothers.”
Ronnie smiled again, suddenly he was getting the picture on these Americans and now the fact that they knew some of the fellas that Ronnie knew had the effect of easing the tension in the air.
“So who you with, A.B, Momo or fat Tony?” Ron asked quietly.
“How’d you know these guys?” Ralindi snapped now with suspicion.
Ronnie then got to his feet.
“We’re finished talking!” he said abruptly.
“Hey, what the fuck!” Tommy Spano said confused as he also rose to his feet.
“We’re just getting fucking started!” he added now looking bemused.
Ronnie went to walk away but then paused as he turned back to Ralindi.
“Reach out to any of them Colony fella’s, tell them you’re talking to Ron Kray, once you’ve spoken to someone then come back, maybe then we’ll talk.”
“You just fucking walking away?”
“There’s no point in talking now, not till were properly introduced, make a few calls and ask them who I am, then were sit down.”
sitting back down the Americans sat slightly aghast at Ron’s sudden exit, their initial reaction was one of anger but Ralindi and Spano knew that after Ronnie had said the names that he had just mentioned then their next action was a phone call back home, if Ronnie was indeed a friend of some of the guys he had said, then Ralindi and Spano would have to show that friendship the respect it demanded.
Ron had barely walked three steps before suddenly turning back round to face the Americans again.
“If you’re staying here for a drink then I’d think twice about being rude to Mario again, like I said before he’s my friend and secondly, if you fellas are serious about doing business down here then you should show him the respect he deserves, his uncles the Mayor of this town, and over here it’s the mayor who runs the fucking place.”
later that night Ron was feeling pleased with himself as he sat in the clubs office with Mario, Johnny Walsh had been keeping an eye on the Americans as Ron had asked him to do, for the third time now he burst back into the office to report that all was well and that the Americans were very much behaving themselves.
“I cannot believe it Ronnie” Mario laughed as if relieved. “Last week the yanks were bloody intolerable, they were grabbing hold of the bar girls and

shouting at the waiters, you are a miracle worker my friend." he added with a large smile.
"Storms not over yet Mario, I've just brought us some time, making them show their hand."
"So you think they are Mafia?"
"It looks like it, but don't worry Mario, I know their game, it's the same as they did in London a few years ago, Ralindi and Spano are like scouts, they're bully's, flash bastards sent over here to make a bit of a noise."
"Make a noise?" asked Mario confused.
"Yeah, bully's sent over here to case out the place, find the best sites and put it about a bit, see if they can intimidate a low price out of someone."
"So you think there will be trouble?"
"Nah not now, they know they can't fuck about with us, but there might be a bit of business with them."
"So are we going to sell the club?" asked Mario with a concerned look a upon his face.
"No way!" Replied Ronnie sternly.
"We're keeping the club, but we might be making a few changes if I'm right." Ron added.
"What Changes?"
Ronnie lit up a cigarette before answering
"If I'm right then they want this place as a casino."
"A casino! There are no casinos in Spain Ronnie."
"No casinos." asked Ron puzzled.
"No!" replied Mario "This is a catholic country Ron, the church would not allow it!" added Mario.
Ronnie furrowed his brow as if thinking.
"They must know something that we don't know then Mario, Cuba was a catholic country weren't it?" said Ron before reaching for his drink.
"Do me a favour Mario, speak to your Father and uncle, see if they can find out if anyone in the government has been spoken to, I can't see the yanks coming over here unless they had an invitation."
"I will speak to them in the morning Ron."
"I'll come with ya, there be back in tomorrow night, and the next time I speak to them I wanna know exactly what's going on."
"You really think that this is what they want Ronnie?"
"I'm positive Mario, and if I'm right then there's a fucking king's ransom to be earned here mate."

NOT GUILTY YOU'RE HONOUR
Chapter Ten
'Loyalties'

Christmas shoppers poured into Oxford Street, people stood packed deep on the buses that took them to the shops and overloaded Taxi's laboured on the sidewalk dropping off and picking up the frantic shoppers. Simon Allen the manager of rock group Blackjack stood quietly on the corner of Newport Street wondering on whether to hop on a bus for the short trip to Bayswater or call himself a cab. The nights air was freezing as he pulled up his collar and then followed by trusting his hands deep into his overcoat pockets, he seemed totally at ease with himself as he thought about his dilemma, it had now been a few weeks since he had had any contact with his ex-partner Donnie Harding, at the beginning of the arguments Allen was worried about the heated exchanges and threats of bodily harm but as the weeks passed and his contact with Harding disappeared he became more relaxed, with this care free attitude and the fact that he had just been smoking quantities of hashish all day in the

Westcliffe music studio's he stood totally unaware of the force that was coming to destroy him.
In his hashish haze he failed to react when he saw two hulking brutes walking menacingly towards him, the first man grabbed him forcefully by the arm and managed to almost lift him off the ground as the second man grabbed his other arm.
"Keep ya fucking mouth shut or I'll cut ya fucking throat." Tommy Jones snarled as he showed him a cut throat razor.
As the two men marched away from the busy Oxford street in the direction of a dark alley, Simon Allen his mind still stoned from hashish just couldn't comprehend what was happening to him, he thought of Donnie Harding but he just couldn't react, he couldn't put his thoughts together so strangely he just went along without a fight, hoping or wondering that he would not be hurt.
"You're the manager of Blackjack right?" Tommy growled at him.
"Yeah." sighed Allen.
"Then I suggest you find another business." said Alex Jones tightening his grip on his arm.
Within seconds of entering the dark alley Simon Allen was thrown head first into the brick wall, Alex Jones grabbed the hair at the back of his head and forcefully scraped his face down the brickwork tearing and cutting his skin, the pain was excruciating as Allen tried to scream out, Tommy Jones punched him in the stomach that winded him, Allen tried to scream out again but no sound came out, he was pulled back up where Alex Jones took out the cut throat razor and opened up his face, again and again he slashed at his bleeding face, every stroke opened up thick gashes from his forehead to his chin as the razor sharp utensil sliced him to the bone.
"You fucking forget Blackjack!" Tommy Jones mouthed over again and again.
Simon Allen collapsed in a heap, his face was in agony, he could feel the warm blood pouring onto the floor but couldn't say a word as the horror of what was happening became so stark reality he was sure that he was about to have a heart attack from the pure cold terror. For a moment he wondered if there was anything left of his face, he glimpsed at the ground and in the darkness he thought he could see his nose and lips upon the freezing ground. Suddenly he was slammed against the wall again, he was helpless, the strength from his body had totally gone. It seemed to take an age as sat helplessly on the ground watching Tommy Jones pull both of his legs out stretched and then raise his feet onto a step, motionless he then watched in terror as Tommy Jones jumped into the air and stamped down onto his ankles, he heard the bones crack and then a blanket of un-measurable pain swept over him
"Please." he managed to sigh through the blood and tears.

Tommy Jones began kicking and stamping on his legs and arms, even his hands were broken as one of the men stamped on them with their heels. Moments later in a heap of broken bones and ripped flesh he drifted out of consciousness, the message had been given and Simon Allen's betrayal of Donnie Harding would now haunt this man for the rest of his life.
Christmas time to the Eastenders especially the locals from Hoxton Square was a time when everybody would try to make the best of a bad situation. Being one of the poorest areas in London made no difference to the local churches and missions who stopped at nothing to make sure that everyone in the area had a chance to share in the festive spirits.
Every night as the early nights closed in the parishioners of the local Catholic Church huddled around a large Christmas tree they had erected in the square and served up hot soup and bread to those who needed it most. Frank Ryan and the Ryan brothers always gave a good donation at Christmas time to the church and every year Frank would always spend a couple of days helping out with the soup and bread.
It had just began to snow as the clock tower struck its chime at six o'clock, Frank decided enough as he and Charlie Roth who had been giving out blankets to the homeless for the past five hours walked into the Kings Arms pub just off the square. Tired and cold the only thing on his mind now was a large dram of scotch.
Franks brothers John, Jimmy and Albert were all standing at the bar besides a large log fire in festive spirits.
"Here he is!" John shouted out as he saw Frank walk in.
"Get me a shant, I'm fucking freezing!" Frank replied as he walked over.
"Two, large brandies!" Jimmy shouted out to the barmaid as John reached over and affectionately pulled Frank closer with an arm around his neck.
"Hoxton's very own Saint!" John said warmly with a slight slur to his words a result from drinking all afternoon.
Frank shrugged his brother off, not in a rude way but a way that silently said your drunk.
"Someone's gotta do it." he replied once he broke the hold.
"I dunno why ya bother, every fucking year you're out there, should just let the fucking church goers get on with it." replied John.
Reaching into his pocket Frank pulled out a packet of cigarettes and after lighting one he turned sullenly to his brother.
"Maybe you should think about giving something back John."
Sobering up John turned his head quickly.
"What!" he said in a slight confused and aggressive tone.
"You know what I mean." replied Frank.
"I gave them money didn't I?"
Frank grimaced.

“You can’t buy your way into heaven john.”
“Oh fuck off frank, don’t start all that that religious cobblers again.”
Frank shrugged as just in time before another Ryan family argument happened Jimmy eased the tensions by handing Frank his brandy.
“Mum would be fucking proud of him John, leave him alone!” Jimmy snapped as Frank walked off towards the fire to warm himself up with his drink as the men stood and watched.
“What is it with Frank, John, why’s he got this thing with the church?” Charlie Roth asked quietly as he walked over.
“When he was a kid Charlie, he was brought up by Father O’Brien, over at St., Matthew’s, it’s been with him ever since.”
“What’d ya mean brought up, weren’t he with you.”
“Most of the time yeah, but for a couple of years he lived at St. Matthew’s, it was when we all got banged up as kids for robbing the railway, Dad got two years, me, Jimmy and Al got 18 months and poor old Mum got 20 months for handling stolen goods.” replied John in a strangely proud tone of voice.
“I knew you was all in approve school but I didn’t know that was what happened John.” Charlie said.
“Dunno who was worse off, us in the fucking nick, or poor Frank living with that tyrant O’Brien.” shrugged Jimmy grinning.
Looking over at the fireplace John suddenly switched his attention towards his brother; John noticed an unusual quietness about Frank so grabbing his drink he walked over to his brother.
“What’s the matter frank, you look like you got things on ya mind bruv.” asked John affectionately knowing exactly what was on his brother’s mind.
Frank took a sip of his drink then leaned closer.
“They were my pal’s John, no matter how hard I try to occupy myself; I just can’t get the look in their eyes out of my head.”
John leaned forward and placed an arm around his brother.
“You gotta let it go Frank, you gotta forget about it bruv, if you carry on like this it’ll fucking tear ya apart, ……its over……finished!….just fucking move on, it’s hard but this is the life we lead.”
Grimacing Frank wiped away a small tear.
“The fucking life we lead!” he snapped back but still keeping his voice low “I fucking grew up with Billy, last week I had to fucking scoop up what was left of his brains and throw it in a cardboard box, I picked his fucking body up and his bollocks fell onto the floor from the hole in his trousers and you say forget it, move on,……this is the life we lead.” he added with a rage in his voice.
Tightening his grip John’s voice rose.
“Frank you’ve got to let it go.”
“I can’t!”
“It’ll eat you up.”

"Then fucking let it."
"I can't do that frank, you're my brother."
Frank rubbed his face as if trying not to get emotional; he breathed deep as he then took another sip of his brandy finishing off what was left in the glass.
"That's it Frank, come on let's have a drink, its Christmas remember."
"Fucking Christmas, I just saw Gill in the square, last week she had a café and two brothers, now what's she fucking got, she's in the square selling horse chestnuts over a fire trying to get a few Bob for fucking Christmas, I can't look her in the eye John, she knows I know who did it."
"Has she said anything?" John said suddenly alarmed.
"No what's she gonna say, she knows the fucking score, but I know she knows something, she's waiting for someone to tell her."
"Tell her nothing Frank alright."
"What am I gonna fucking tell her……that it was me who tied them both up and dumped them in the alley."
"Look don't worry about Gill, I'll give her a few quid alright."
"I've already done it john, I gave her a grand just now."
"You gave her a grand! What that grand I gave you yesterday."
"Yeah, I can't spend it can I? How can I? when I look out there and she's doing that, all the fucking grief she's got and yet she's out there grafting to get her Mum a few quid."
"Come here bruv." John warmly said as he hugged his brother affectionately.
"You gotta find a way to deal with this Frank." he whispered.
Frank stiffened in his brothers arms.
"I can't do that John, I want this feeling, I wanna feel exactly like this the next time I see Kray, I want this pain, this pain how I feel right fucking now, I don't wanna lose one little piece of it, that way I'll know exactly what I'm gonna do the next time I see that bastard!"
"Listen to me; I don't want you going near them boys, Ronnie's not right in the fucking head, you just fucking calm down, we're a family and what we do, we do together."
The weather this time of year was being extremely generous in the Spanish coastal resort, Marbella was renowned for its mild winter climate but to everyone's delight the Costa del Sol was basking in a glorious sunny spell blown in from across the sea from the Sahara desert. The sea in December was cold but that never stopped the busier than usual beaches as the temperature hit the mid-seventies.
"Let's go to the port." Ronnie asked Mario as he relaxed in the passenger seat of Mario's convertible E-type Jaguar.
"Yeah sure Ronnie, have you finished shopping."
"I've had enough of walking round shops let's get a nice drink Mario."

“Ok the port it is!” Mario snapped cheerfully back as Ronnie smiled and rested his head back on the seats headrest trying to enjoy the sun, with the countryside whisking by Ronnie’s mind began to wander, he gave himself a smile as he thought about the meeting with the yanks last night, the showdown had given him much pleasure purely for the fact that they were Mafia, to Ronnie dealing with the mob was like an accolade in the business of crime, it was a merit badge, a mark of just how far Ronnie had come from his humble roots of east London. Even as a boy he fantasised about the likes of al Capone and lucky Luciano, Genovese and Frank Costello, they were his role models in life especially Capone.
Mario looked over and saw Ronnie eyes shut face to the sun smiling like a Cheshire cat, it pleased him that Ron was in a good mood, Mario had seen Ron in action when annoyed and he hoped he would never have to be around him again when such rages engulfed him, Johnny Walsh had pulled Mario over to the side when he picked Ronnie up this morning and told him that if Ronnie should become agitated in anyway then he should get him back to the villa straight away, it was unusual for Walsh not to want to be by Ronnie’s side but the fact that when Mario had woke Ronnie at nine this morning with a bag containing three thousand pounds in cash, some of profits from the Kray’s share in the club, Johnny could see how delighted Ronnie was, and as Ronnie wanted to go shopping for clothes, Johnny knew exactly what his job would be today, carrying dozens of bloody shopping bags, sensibly and wisely as Mario’s boot was full to the brim with new clothes he decided to stay and rest at the villa.
Terry Anderson sat motionless staring out the window, Dougie had been trying to grab his attention but it was clear that there were other things on his mind.
“Terry!, Terry! Are you here mate?”
Dougie added as he waved a hand in front of his brother’s face.
“Sorry mate, just can’t get Alan off my mind, poor fucker banged up in those fucking cells.”
“unfuckingbelievable bruv, the Law must know it’s not him but I don’t think they give a fuck on this one Tel.”
“Everyone fucking knows it weren’t him, the filth ain’t stupid Dougie, just can’t see what they’re getting at, what’s their game?”
“They want them pair of cunts, the twins, that’s what I think.”
“And they think Al will turn them in.”
Dougie just shrugged as if to say maybe.
“Nah they know that ain’t our scene, they’re not that stupid to think Al will grass them up.”
“He’s looking at a lotta bird Tel, could be a 25 stretch if this sticks.”
Terry sighed loud.

“Laws putting it down to gang violence.” Dougie added.
“That’s what they done to Charlie and Eddie and they never killed anyone.” replied Terry referring to the Richardson gang who had just recently received 25 years for GBH and torture.
After a short silence Terry sighed loudly again as he grabbed for a cigarette.
“I don’t know what were gonna do yet Dougie but I’ll tell you this, our brother Alan ain’t fucking going down for this.”
“I wanna word with you Reg.” Violet said as her son entered the kitchen dressed in a dressing gown and looking rough after a heavy night out.
“Yeah morning to you too mum.” replied Reg.
“No seriously Reg, go start up the fire and I’ll make you a breakfast, I got something on my mind I want to say to you.”
“What?”
“Light the fire first son.”
Reg gave a long sigh, it was one of his pet hates lighting the coals but ever since a boy he always did it for his mum.
“Man’s work!” she used to cry out to him.
Once the fire was lit Reg pulled over a chair and sat warming himself just as violet walked in and handed him a bacon sandwich.
“What’s the matter then mum?”
“Now Reg.” Violet said sitting down next to her son.
“You know I never ask you or your brothers about business but I bumped into Shirley down the lane, and she said she is really worried about Sid, now I know you boys are always up to something but people calling her house at one and two in the morning isn’t right Reg.”
“What’s that got to do with me mum? I haven’t called him at that time, I can’t tell all the fella‘s to stop ringing Sid, if he‘s got problems with his Mum then it’s down to him to sort it out.”
“He works for you, don’t he Reg?”
“Yeah.”
“Then tell whoever it is calling to stop it, their scaring the life out of Shirley, by all accounts whoever’s calling is really rude to her, she asks him his name and he never gives it, just says he will call back and hangs up.”
“Mum I haven’t got a clue about it, but I will ask Sid who it is ok.”
Violet then hesitated before asking her son another question.
“I’m also hearing rumours that you and Ron are not so popular anymore.”
“What do you mean by that?”
“I Hear people are getting the needle with you two, they’re not happy about the way you’re behaving.”
“Argh it’s nothing mum, just the usual aggravation, it will sort itself out.”
“Make sure it does Reg, we don’t want our own turning on us.”
“Don’t worry mum, everything will be alright.”

“Thanks Reg.” replied Violet as she smiled and patted her son on the leg.
“Have you heard from Ron?” she then asked.
“Yeah he’s fine mum, told me he is going to Morocco soon”
“Morocca, where’s that?”
“It’s Morocco, I don’t know, somewhere near Spain, it’s near the sea though I know that, and do ya remember the Humphrey Bogart film Casablanca, that’s Morocco.”
Violet leaned back in the chair smiling.
“Who would have thought Reg; my boy’s going to Morocco.”
“Yeah, it’s nice for some ain’t it mum.”
“Don’t be like that Reg, if it was you going then Ron would be chuffed to bits for you.”
“Yeah I bet he would.” replied Reg sarcastically.
Slice em Sid sipped another swig from the bottle of whiskey he had been working on since eight o’clock in the morning, sitting in darkness his mother Shirley walked into the room.
“Now Sid I don’t know what’s bothering you son but you gotta snap out of this.”
“Mum you don’t know what your fucking talking about, just leave me the fuck alone will ya.”
“What’s the matter with you Sid, swearing at me?”
“Just fuck off will ya,”
“NO YOU FUCK OFF SID! I’m sick and tired of this, look at you, still morning and your pissed.”
Sid suddenly jumped up and kicked the coffee table in the air, his mother cowered scared that her son was out of control.
“SID!” she screamed.
“Just fucking leave me alone will ya, I’m fucked mum, I can’t get out of this fucking mess I’m in, I just want everyone to leave me alone.”
“Please son, son, tell me what’s the matter, if you’re in trouble I’ll speak to Reg, he’ll help you Sid.”
“No don’t talk to anyone.”
“Then go and see a doctor, talk to someone and sort yourself out this can’t go on.”
Tony Lambrianou and Eddie Brenner sat busily in the back room at the Carpenters Arms counting the days take, it was Friday which was pension list day, outside daylight had just given way to evening and both men were looking forward to a good drink
“That fucking Stevie Lester, always, every week shorts us Ed, I’d like to give the flash mug a slap.” Tony said.
“Ask Reg later Tone, the prick always does it, maybe a clump might liven him up a bit.”

“Would have hit him today Ed, but Reg don’t want any more rows at the moment.”
“Lester ain’t a row Tone, he’s a fucking toe-rag.”
“If he comes up short next week were take one of the cars off his front, did you see that rover he had, I’d like that.”
“Blue one.”
“Yeah, with the cream leather seats.”
“Saw it that used to be John West’s car.”
“John West from Clerkenwell?”
“Yeah.”
“Oh fuck that then, I’m not having that motor.”
“Why, what’s the matter?” Eddie asked amusingly.
“He’s a fucking slag! Fucking mug got nicked for immoral earnings.”
Eddie laughed at Tony’s comment, the sight of him with a cigarette in the corner of his mouth counting out a bag of cash and talking about immoral earnings made him laugh.
“What’d a call this lot then?” added Eddie pointing at the money.
“Pension list dosh.” replied Tony sternly without looking up.
“Yeah nice and clean living ay Tone.” replied Eddie sarcastically.
“Well I’m not sitting here counting money which some poor tart has earned lying on her back.”
“You don’t mind paying them Tone.”
“What! I’ve never fucking paid for it in my life, that’s your game, slipping off up Belgravia with Sid, don’t worry we know all about ya.” added Tony sternly at first then lightening his voice at the end.
“You telling me you’ve never paid for a tart!”
“Never!”
“Bollocks Tony, I don’t fucking believe ya.”
Tony suddenly pointed at his own face.
“Does this face look like it has to pay?” he answered.
Eddie smiled at first before taking a sip on his whiskey.
“Funny that.”
“what!”
“With a boat race like yours I’d have thought you’d always have your hand in ya pocket.”
“Fuck off!”
Reg with George and Billy Hayes walked into the Carpenters at 7.30pm, the pub was already busy but the owner stopped what he was doing and poured Reg and the boys a drink, just in time as they reached Tony and Eddie at the bar.
“How’d it go today Tone?” Reg asked referring to the collections.

“Good day Reg, everyone except Lester paid on time, that prick came up short again.”
“That’s the third time running he’s shorted us, give him a call and tell him I‘m coming to see him tomorrow.”
“Done!” replied Tony sternly.
Reg took a sip of his drink and looked around, It was payment night so all the Firm was there waiting for their wages everyone except Slice’em Sid.
“Where’s Sid?” Reg asked turning to Eddie.
“Fuck knows Reg, no one’s seen him.”
“Get him on the blower and get him down here, I’m getting sick and tired of his no shows”
Reg and the rest of the Firm couldn’t believe the state of Sid when he walked in at around nine o’clock, he was wearing a pair of trousers and shirt that were so creased it looked like he slept in them, he was unshaven and his hair was a mess, he was also blind stinking drunk.
“Sorry………… Reg.” he said nearly falling into Reg.
“Look at the fucking state of you!” Reg replied pushing him slightly away from him.
“What the fucking hells a matter with you.” added Reg with a look of disgust and disbelief
“g..g..give …..Us a minute …Reg and I’ll sort myself out.” replied Sid just before he belched really loudly by accident in Reg’s face.
Reg pulled his head away in disgust.
“Ah you filthy bastard, get him out of here Tone.” Reg added pushing Sid away.
“GET… GET ya fucking hands off me?” Sid shouted as Tony gently tried to usher him out
Angered by the outburst Reg stormed towards Sid,
“What ya gonna fucking hit me now, fucking put one in me?” Sid slurred.
Reg grabbed his neck and arm, then forcefully frogmarched him towards the door.
“Go home and get in the fucking bath!” Reg shouted as he pushed him out the pub doors.
When Reg returned to the bar there was a strange silence as the Firm couldn’t believe what they had just saw, Slice’em Sid had never been seen like this, he was always dressed sharp as a razor with a sharpened mind to match. A fearsome fighting man, some of the Firm thought he had aspirations to run his own Firm and if it wasn’t for the fact that he came out of Roman Road, Bethnal green which was Kray territory, he probably would have.
“I wasn’t out of order was I Tone?” asked Reg as he lifted his drink to his lips.
“Nah not a bit mate, what’s he expect turning up here like that.”
“Maybe we should have taken him upstairs and freshened him up.”

"We're not his fucking mother Reg."
"But we're his pals Tone, do me a favour, keep an eye on him for a few days will ya, and find out what all this is about."
"What quietly?"
"Yeah don't let him see ya, just follow him and keep ya eyes and ears open, something's not right, I've known Sid twenty years and never seen him like that."
"Sandown's on today son, while don't ya go down there?" Charlie Kray snr said as Reggie sat eating his breakfast in the living room with George Hayes.
"Love to Dad but I can't got a few things on."
"Leave em Reg, c'mon I'll come down there with ya."
"I want the rent money first Charlie Kray if you're going to the races! Violet snapped making Reg and George smile.
Charlie lowered the newspaper he was reading.
"where's all this cobblers come from woman, I'm getting sick and tired of these snidy remarks, have I ever not paid you the rent money if I have it."
"If you have it… that's the question."
"Yeah that's right, if I have it, times can sometimes be hard but I've always supplied for ya haven't I?"
Violet smiled but in a sarcastic way back at her husband.
"Yes you have, I'll give you that but once just once Charlie Kray… I would like to catch you before you slip down the pub or the spielers."
"Ah I can't fucking win can I."
"That's right Charlie Kray you're a lousy gambler, you never win, I would like just a share of all the money you lose down the pub."
"Can't a man go down the bleeding pub now?"
Reg suddenly rose to his feet grinning.
"C'mon George let's get out of here." he added grabbing his jacket and kissing his Mum on the cheek.
"I got more bacon in the pan Reg."
"No thanks Mum you two love birds have it." Reg replied as he patted his Dad on the arm and gave him a wink as if to say good luck.
"You're not leaving me on mi own with her are ya boys?" his Dad light-heartedly asked George.
Billy Hayes already had the car running as Reg jumped in the front followed by George in the back.
"Alright take me over to Stevie Lester's car site will ya Bill."
"No problem Reg." replied Billy.
"What'd ya wanna do with Lester Reg?" asked George as he lit up a cigarette and handed one to Reg.
"Smack him on the fucking jaw."
"I got a piece on me anyway; stick it up his fucking nose if you want."

“OI fuck off Billy we don’t need a fucking tool for this cunt.”
“Alright I’ll keep it in the motor.”
“Do you want me to chin him Reg?” asked George.
“No, I’ll do it, I don’t like the mug anyway.” added Reg taking a large drag on the cigarette.
Tony Lambrianou shivered as he huddled in a doorway down Bethnal Green high street, unknown to Slice’em Sid he had been following him at a distance all morning; Tony lit another cigarette as he waited for Sid to come out of another shop. Tony was cursing to himself as this job was beginning to get on his nerves and he was thinking about getting himself a gin and tonic from the nearest pub. For the last two hours everything looked normal as Sid went from one shop to another making Tony think he was just ‘doing the rounds’.
Then he noticed Sid come out of the shop with a flat cap on and his collar pulled up on his Macintosh, Tony immediately stiffened his posture.
“What the fucking hell is he doing now?” Tony whispered before following him towards Bethnal Green train station.
Charlie Adams was an old time bank robber, having spent almost half his life in prison he had now given up pavement work and worked solely as muscle for the Ryan family, Frank Ryan especially.
Adams was in his fifties but had a chiselled physique and eyes as cold as ice, during his last sentence he spent six years in solitary confinement where with nothing else to do he spent almost every hour awake doing sit-ups and push ups.
He walked with a limp from an old bullet wound and winced as he spoke which was an old wound from fighting the prison officers at Wandsworth prison where they kicked his face so violently he had suffered permanent facial nerve damage.
As Adams walked towards a terrace house in Hoxton he habitually checked over his shoulder to see if he was being followed or watched, he had visited this house three times before and each time he was given work where someone ended up getting badly hurt. Today was going to be the same and Charlie Adams was pleased that he got the call as he needed the money.
After one more glimpse over his shoulder he knocked the door.
After a minute or so the door opened and Frank Ryan quickly ushered him inside
“Frank.” Adams nodded as they walked into the room downstairs where another pal of Ryan’s was sitting, Joey Mullins.
“Hello Charlie been a long time mate.” said Joe holding out his hand.
Charlie Adams nodded but remained silent as he remembered seeing Mullins in Parkhurst prison a few years back, he shook Mullins hand and then removed his overcoat.
“So Charlie how you been?” asked Frank as he lit himself a cigarette.

"I'm alright frank, usual fucking problems, you know same old shit but I'm alright."
"I got some work for ya."
"Go on."
Frank glimpsed over at Joey Mullins who himself stiffened his posture and leaned forward, Frank then lowered his voice and continued.
"You heard about what happened to the Williams, Charlie?"
"Bits and bobs Frank, you know the rumours."
"Well it ain't fucking rumours! The twins done em, right on our doorstep."
Charlie just shrugged.
"On our fucking doorstep Chas, the fucking heat those cunt's are bringing is fucking us right over."
"What are your brothers saying about it? I thought John and Ronnie were pretty tight?"
"This ain't anything to do with John, Charlie this meeting is between us." Joey Mullins added.
Charlie rubbed his chin and glimpsed back at Frank.
"So what you saying Frank, I hear you're words but what is it you want here?"
"Get rid of the cunts…permanently!" snapped Frank.
Charlie opened his eyes wide in a gesture of surprise before reaching for a half bottle of scotch that was sitting on the table; Charlie took a gulp from the bottle and then replied.
"Just like that Frank, what you're asking mate ain't just a bit of work, who else knows about this meeting?"
"Just us Charlie." added Mullins.
"Good then make sure it fucking stays that way."
"You up for it Charlie?" asked Frank.
Charlie Adams took another sip of the scotch and took a few steps towards the living room window where he had a quick look outside.
"What's on the table." he said without looking back at Ryan or Mullins.
"Fucking plenty Chas, they got plenty of interests."
"Frank I ain't interested in fucking promises, if this thing happens then it's cold fucking cash that were talking about"
Frank smiled at Joey before replying.
"So you're interested then Charlie?" he said as Charlie turned back to face them.
"Course I'm fucking interested, if the wedge is right then I couldn't give a fuck who has to go."
"Sit down Chas and we're talk about it." Joey added as he handed Chas a cigarette.

“Fuck sake Billy get us out of this fucking traffic!” said Reg angry as they sat in the car stuck in the middle of the Commercial road. “Billy shrugged as if saying what can he do.”
“Go down the fucking back roads, or we’ll be here all fucking day.” added Reg.
“You alright Reg, you seem wound up mate.” said George Hayes.
Reg took out a cigarette before answering.
“Yeah I’m alright George, just so many fucking meetings; it just never ends, we’re meant to be living the good life mate, ha! Fat fucking chance of that. We got rows with the Andersons, the Maltese, the Ryan’s, and the fucking old bill.”
“Ah leave off Reg, it could be worse.” added Billy still trying to get out of the traffic.
“Yeah! Well give me a nudge when you think everything’s alright.” replied Reg with a sarcastic tone in his voice.
“Oh fuck me Reg I forgot to tell ya, when you left the Carpenters last night, a car turned up with a bottle of champagne.”
“what!” replied Reg turning in his chair towards George.
“Yeah it was from that music fella Don, had a note saying have a toast to our new partnership.”
“Donnie Harding?” Reg asked.
“I suppose mate, I know the Jones’s did that bit of work he wanted.”
Reg smiled.
“Well that’s some good news, I was worried about that.”
“All sounds good Reg, I know the boys did the business, well it looks like we’re in the music game now mate, Ron will be right fucking pleased.”
“Fuck Ron! Let him sun himself on some beach in Spain or Morocco while we sort out all this bollocks out.”
“Ronnie having a good time then Reg?” asked Billy turning to Reg which made Reg smirk.
“C’mon put ya fucking foot down” added Reg noticing that Billy had steered the car out of the traffic.
As the chill from the wind struck Tony Lambrianou’s neck he tugged at his collar trying to raise it and protect himself from the cold.
“What the fucking hell is he doing now?” he sighed to himself as he watched Slice’em Sid going down the stairs into Bethnal Green station, Tony waited for him to get out of sight then followed him being careful not to be seen.
Tony watched Sid buy a ticket then head for the platforms.
“Where’s that bloke going?” Tony asked the ticket attendant.
“What.” replied the attendant feeling intimidated.
“Look don’t fuck around, where did he buy a ticket for?”
“Marble Arch station.”

"Alright give me a ticket."
"Marble Arch?"
"No fucking Manchester you mug, c'mon lively." added Tony showing anger in his voice
"C'MON!" Tony added and trying to rush him up.
Slice'em Sid waited at the very end of the platform which was good for Tony as he could hide at the other end without being seen.
When the train pulled in Sid looked around and then got on it, Tony did the same and got into a carriage four carriages down from where Sid was.
Nine stops later the train pulled into Marble Arch station, Tony walked over to the door and waited until he saw Sid get off the train, he waited a moment till he felt safe he would not be seen then he jumped off and quickly walked to a nearby exit, luckily the way out was at the other end of the platform so Sid would not pass him.
The corridor Sid had gone down led into a small hall where elevators led to the outside, as Tony looked on he suddenly realised that Sid had not gone onto the elevators. Tony rushed back to the platform thinking that Sid may have doubled back and got onto the train but the train had now gone.
"Fuck it!" Tony said feeling he had been seen and tricked.
Then just as Tony was about to leave he saw out of the corner of his eye Sid sitting at the end of the platform , Tony stepped back out of sight and peered round a corner where he could see Sid now drinking a bottle, clearly alcohol.
"What the fucking hell is he doing?" Tony muttered.
Another train then pulled into the station and to Tony's surprise Sid did not get up from his seat then as the crowds of people who got off left the platform he saw a large built man walk over and sit down next to Sid.
Tony winced as he tried to get a better look.
"That's fucking LaSalle!" Tony mouthed in utter disbelief.
"What's he doing meeting that cunt!" added Tony trying to get a better look.
Sid and LaSalle spoke for around fifteen minutes in what was clearly a very heated conversation, LaSalle did a lot of pointing and gesturing, Tony positioned himself closer so he could try to hear what was going on.
"You have to come in NOW, if we don't nick em! Then we're lose the case against them." LaSalle said angrily at Sid.
"How many more fucking times do I have to say this, I'm not ready to come in, Ronnie's not even in the fucking country."
"Listen either you come in on your own, or we're force you to." added LaSalle.
Sid was clearly in despair now and took another long hard gulp of the whiskey bottle he was holding only for LaSalle to grab the bottle off him.
"That ain't going to fucking help you."

“Why the fuck did I get involved with you cunts?” Sid mouthed back at him now clearly drunk.
“You got twenty-four hours! And sober ya fucking self-up.” LaSalle snapped back at him before standing up.
“You got my statements; you got all the names, times and addresses why do you need me?” Sid added as he gazed at the floor looking almost distraught.
LaSalle grabbed him by the collar and lent forward.
“Twenty-four fucking hours, then that’s it.” he said before pushing him hard and walking off with an angry look on his face.
Tony stood froze to spot for a moment in sheer disbelief, at what he had just heard and seen, he knew full well what Sid was doing but the shock of it made him hesitate. He took a moment to compose himself and then walked over to Sid who was drinking his whiskey again.
“Sid what the fucking hell you doing?” snapped Tony as he grabbed the bottle.
“Tony!” Sid said as a look of horror came over him.
“Don’t fucking Tony me why are you meeting old bill?”
“What old bill, what you talking about/” replied Sid trying to excuse himself.
“I just fucking saw you, I just saw you talking to that cunt LaSalle.”
“Fuck off Tony; I’m just down here having a drink.”
Tony then grabbed him by his coat and lifted him up.
“What’s all this twenty-four hours about?”
Sid pushed Tony off as he began to get angry.
“Don’t fucking grab me!” he shouted.
“Grab ya, I should be fucking spitting on ya, what’s happening in twenty-four hours Sid?”
“Nothing, fuck off!” Sid shouted now nearly falling over from the drink.
Tony grabbed him again.
“Your fucking coming with me, let’s see what Reg says about all this.”
Sid tried to struggle but was too drunk to act sensible, Tony grabbed him with both hands and pinned him against the wall.
“You’re fucking grassing us up ain’t ya, you cunt!” Tony snarled into his face.
“Leave me alone Tony, I’m fucking warning you.”
“You’re not going anywhere Sid; you’re coming with me to see Reg.”
Sid smiled at Tony before kneeing him forcefully between the legs, Tony released his grip in agony as Sid pushed him away and ran to the far end of the platform, Tony got to his feet and ran after him.
Sid in his drunken state had ran past the exit and was now trapped at the end of the platform,
“You wanna try that again.” Tony said now ten feet away from him.
“C’mon Sid let’s get out of here and sort this out.”
Sid shook his head with a look like he was trying to fight back the tears.

“I’m sorry Tony.” he said as he saw that a train was pulling onto the platform. Tony looked and saw the train.
“Now Sid don’t be silly, c’mon we can sort this out.”
Sid looked at Tony in the eye where both men knew what was about to happen, Tony held out his hand.
“C’mon Sid, we can sort this.” said Tony now calm.
Sid walked closer to the platform and then smiled at Tony “Bollocks to it.” he said before jumping into the path of the oncoming train, there was an enormous thud and then Tony was splattered with blood as the train raced by, Tony jumped away shielding his face as he heard the screech of the brakes, a nearby women screamed which made the sound of the brakes seem much more sinister.
Stevie Lester owned a big car site on the Commercial road, he was commonly known as a ‘good earner’ and at the age of seventeen he owned his own business. At an early age Stevie had always shown promise and good enterprise, he drove fast cars and wore flash suits and hung around with lads from the Jewish communities in Hackney and Stamford hill. His only undoing was he liked to talk and act, like a tough guy, which frequently got him into trouble. Another vice of his was gambling where he squandered thousands, often where he had been cheated. He was a man who seemed to have the world at his feet yet he was always pushing the self-destruct button.
Reggie Kray was first out the car as Billy Hayes pulled into Lester’s car site, Georgie jumped out quickly behind Reg as he knew what kind of a mood Reg was in,
“I wanna word with you!” Reg snarled as he entered the office and saw Stevie Lester who was on the phone.
Reg then walked over and grabbed the phone out of his hand and hit him round the face with it causing Lester to raise his hands to protect himself, George put out a hand on Reg’s arm to stop him doing more damage.
“Please Reg what’s this about?” cried Steve Lester still shielding his face.
“You fucking shorted us again!” Reg growled as he threw a right hand which struck him on the temple and opened up a cut.
Reg then grabbed him by the scruff of the neck as Lester began pleading.
“Please Reg I had a few problems but I was going to pay George the rest today.”
“Fucking problems you slag, they didn’t stop you gambling last night did they, five hundred fucking quid you dropped at Downeys gaff last night.” added Reg as he grabbed his hair.
“Reg.” George said trying to calm Reg down as there was now blood all over the place including all over Reg’s sleeve and hands.

"What!" Reg snapped back at George who didn't answer but shrugged as if to say that he had got the message which did have an effect on Reg who released his grip and pushed Lester back into the chair.
"I want what's owed from last week and you pay next weeks as well, and I want it today, today or we come back and we clear all your fucking stock away."
"Ol bollocks!" Billy Hayes suddenly said as he noticed something out the office window.
"What?" George snapped back at him wondering what was wrong.
"Fuck it, old bill, Reg." Billy added as Reg and George walked over to the window and saw two uniformed coppers looking at Billy's car.
"What'd they fucking want?" Reg asked surprised.
"Go and see what they want." added Reg.
Billy Hayes opened the office door and walked out to the policeman.
"Can I help ya?"
"Whose car is this?" said one of the coppers.
"It's mine why?" answered Billy to the policeman who was now opening the car door.
"What's wrong?" asked Billy now getting agitated.
"Just calm down alright." replied the policeman as the second copper walked over and opened the passenger door.
"Well what's all this about then?" asked Billy.
"What's your name son?"
"Tom." answered Billy.
George who was inside the office looking out the window with Reg suddenly tugged Reg's arm.
"That tools under the passenger seat Reg." George said talking about the gun.
"What!" replied Reg suddenly realising that this could get fucking serious.
"I don't fucking believe this." he added as he saw the copper start to feel around the passenger side of the car.
"Reg what'd ya wanna do/" George asked.
"If he finds that shooter, Billy's fucked mate." George added.
Reg gave him a look before he opened the office door.
"Can I help ya, what's all this about?" Reg said as he walked menacingly over to the first policeman standing by Billy.
"What's your fucking game?" George said as he walked over to the copper who was nosing about in the car.
The first policeman recognised Reg immediately, in his mind he wondered what one of the Kray's it was.
"Now just back of sonny, you don't want to get yourself in trouble do ya?"
"That goes both ways son." answered Reg.

George had now reached the second copper and noticed him reach under the seat.
"Now you don't want to do that." George says sternly as he placed his hand on the copper, which made the first copper race across to aid his colleague.
"STOP RIGHT WHERE YOU ARE!" the first copper shouted as he pushed George away, George glimpsed at Reg as if to tell him what was going to happen next, Reg already knew and with a blink of an eye Reg punched the first copper on the jaw which sent him crashing to the ground, as soon as the punch was heard, George and Billy jumped the second copper and began to give him a beating, within moments both policeman were laid out battered and bruised.
"C'mon lets fucking go!" Reggie shouted.
The three men jumped in the car and within seconds the car screeched out the car site heading back into commercial road.
"BOLLOCKS!" Reg shouted.
"What's the fucking odds of that!" Billy replied.
Reg shook his head as he now knew the law would be after him again.
"Fucks sake!" he added through gritted teeth.
"Listen get me out of this fucking motor, drop me off over there, dump the car and get rid of that tool, I'll meet you at Gerard's in an hour."
Billy pulled the car over at the junction of Christian street where Reg jumped out and headed in the direction of Gerard's an illegal drinking den which was above a rag shop and was under the twin's protection.
Detective Lasalle was just about to start his lunch when a colleague of his burst into the café on Victoria road
"Guv, you're not going to like this."
What now?" LaSalle answered as he took a bite of his egg and bacon sandwich.
"Sid Wilson, he's dead."
LaSalle stopped chewing his food as his mouth dropped open and he spat it back onto the plate.
"If this a fucking wind-up."
"Guv he's dead, jumped in front of a fucking train!"
Suddenly LaSalle jumped up out of his chair and threw his plate onto the floor in anger.
"You sure it's him?" he yelled after knocking the chair he was sitting on flying.
"It's him guv, they got a witness, Tony Lambrianou was nicked at the scene."
"Where?"
"Marble Arch tube station."
"Then fucking get me there now!"

Toby Mazzer the old Jewish owner of Gerard's was busy wiping the bar when he saw Reg Kray enter the doors; he quickly put the cloth down, wiped his hands and ran over to shake his hand.
"Reg we have heard the news, I'm sorry. I'm sorry, it's terrible, is there anything we can do." said Mazzer trying to usher Reg to the bar.
Reg shook his hand and looked a bit confused as the fight with the cops was fresh in his mind and he thought how the fuck could Toby have heard so quickly, but the way Toby acted told Reg that what he was talking about was more serious.
"Toby, what you talking about?" asked Reg now thinking the worst, that it might be one of his family Toby was on about.
"You haven't heard?" replied Toby holding out his hands looking every part the East End yiddisher kid he was.
"Toby! What have you fucking heard?"
"Sid, slicem Sid, he's dead."
"Sid?"
"Reggie you don't know, everyone in the fucking bar is talking about this."
"Slicem Sid, Sid Wilson is dead, how!"
"It.. It's an accident; he fell in front of a train."
"He fell in front of a fucking train."
"This is what everyone is saying Reg."
"Who's saying?"
"Johnny Bremmer, he came into the club about an hour ago, came straight up said that Sid was dead."
"How does Johnny fucking Bremmer Know?"
"Reg I don't know, you're asking me things that I don't know."
"I need to use your phone."
"Of course, of course, you know where it is, I'll get you a drink, and do you want the usual Reggie."
"Yeah make it a fucking large one." replied Reg as he walked into Mazzer's office behind the bar.
"And get Johnny fucking Bremmer as well, I want to speak with him."
Reg sat down and picked up the phone and dialled Tony Lambrianou's number, the number rang about a dozen times before Reg hung up the phone, next he called home and spoke to his mum.
"Mum."
"Reg you okay?" Violet Kray answered noticing the urgency in her son's voice,
Reg paused a moment before answering.
"Sid Wilson dead mum." he uttered lowering his voice.
"Oh my good God no."
"Mum you there."

“Yeah I’m here son… are you okay?” she replied trying to hide the upset in her voice.
“It was an accident mum, he fell in front of a train or something I don’t know everything yet, I’ve just found out myself.”
“Does his mother know?”
“I don’t know mum, I’ll find everything out and let you know.”
“Okay son, I’ll get dressed just in case I have to go and see Shirley.” answered violet talking about Sid’s mother.
“Mum has anyone been round for me?”
“Eddie called about half hour ago; he said he would be in the woods if you needed him.”
“Oh and Manny Freedman phoned about fifteen minutes ago.”
“Thanks mum; I’ll give you a bell as soon as I find out what’s going on.”
“You coming home Reg?”
“Not at the moment mum. Let me sort all this out and I’ll see ya later.”
“Alright son, you keep safe.”
Reg hung up and looked up at Mazzer who had walked in the office with Reggie’s drink
“Is it true Reg?”
“Fuck knows, did you get hold of Bremmer?” replied Reg as he picked up the phone and started dialling the carpenters arms number after his Mum told him that Eddie left a message saying he was in the woods which was their phone code name for the Carpenters pub.
“Bremmers on his way Reg.”
After a couple of rings Rosie the barmaid at the Carpenter’s arms answered the phone.
“Alright love it’s me, put Eddie on the phone.” Reg asked.
A few moments later Reg heard Eddie’s deep voice.
“Reg.”
“Eddie I’ve just heard is it true?”
“Yeah it’s fucking true Reg, what the fucks happening today, the brothers just come in and told me what happened to you.”
“Fucking should have stayed in bed, what you heard about Sid?”
“Not much mate but he is dead, something about he went under a fucking train on the platform at Marble Arch tube station.”
“Fucking hell! Has anyone told his mum?”
“I don’t know Reg, we’ve only just heard mate.”
“Is Billy and George with you now?”
“Yeah there next to me.”
“Right listen I’m at Mazzers, get over here now and don’t park the fucking car anywhere near here.”
“Alright Reg, see ya in ten minutes mate.”

NOT GUILTY YOU'RE HONOUR
Chapter Eleven
'It's only business'

Since the turn of the century the American mob had always been interested in gambling, be it the numbers racket, back room card games, bookmaking, the swish carpet joints of Saratoga springs, Florida in the 30's and 40's where government officials were easily bribed to turn a blind eye up to Cuba and Las Vegas, wherever there was gambling in the Us you could bet somewhere along the line there was mob involvement.
The last few decades had seen the mobs from New York, Chicago and Cleveland along with other city bosses invest heavily into Las Vegas, this venture had been very lucrative and for years the mob had carte blanche to do as they wished in Nevada.
But with eccentric billionaire Howard Hughes buying up most of the casinos in Vegas and the FBI constantly arresting the mob bosses they found themselves in the position of being squeezed out of Las Vegas.
Mob gambling supremo Meyer lanky who was still seething at losing his interest in Cuba down to Castro and the revolution decided it was time to look

for new pastures, the mob spread their wings into country's all over the world, they branched into the Caribbean, Canada and some parts of Africa but to Lansky the real money was in Europe.
For Ronnie Kray the chance to get back into business with the mob was an opportunity too good to be true.
"6.30 Ronnie, we will meet them on my Father's boat" answered Mario after Ron had asked him what time the meet with the yanks was.
"How did they sound on the phone?" asked Ronnie eager to find out if the yanks had called New York to check him out.
"Very polite Ronnie."
"Nothing else?"
"Only that they are looking forward to sitting down with us and talking business, why! Do you think there will be trouble?"
Ronnie smiled and reached for a cigarette.
"Nah there won't be any bovver Mario."
"Good I would hate to get blood on my Father's boat." Mario added smiling.
"Yeah talking about the boat is it finished being done up?"
"Ronnie, wait till you see it, it is fucking beautiful, Franco himself could not own such a ship."
"It was nice before." added Ronnie.
"My Father and uncle have spent thousands on it, they have had marble from Italy laid on its floors and walls, oak panels from the forests of Bavaria and furniture from London."
Tony Lambrianou sat waiting for his solicitor in one of the holding cells at Marble Arch police station, he had been arrested under suspicion pending investigations for the murder of Sidney Wilson, Tony was still smothered in Sid's blood and he was outraged that the police had not let him wash.
He had told the police that Sid jumped, but because he was covered in blood the police had told him he would have to be detained until they had spoken to all the witness's. Tony asked for his solicitor Manny Freedman to be called and added that he would not be making any statements unless Freedman was present. When Manny arrived at the station he was immediately shown down to holding cells where Tony was.
"My GOD!" Freedman sighed seeing Tony smothered in blood as the desk sergeant unlocked the cell door.
"My God man can you not let him wash!" Freedman snapped looking back at the sergeant.
"We're get him cleaned up as soon as we can," answered the sergeant looking as if he couldn't care less before Freedman entered the cell and closed the door.
"Just knock when you want to be let out." he added just as the door slammed.

Manny waited a moment and then pulled out a packet of cigarettes which he handed to Tony.
“My god Tony, are you ok?”
Tony lit himself a cigarette and took a long drag.
“Can you get me out of here?”
“As far as I’m aware they are still interviewing witness’s Tony.”
“So it’s another fucking lay down!” Tony added spitting on the floor.
Manny sat down next to Tony and patted his arm.
“Okay Tony, now let’s just take a deep breath and tell me what happened.”
“I didn’t do it Manny, he fucking jumped, right in front of me, it.. It was like someone had thrown a tub of red paint at the front of the train. One second he is there, then smack! He was just smashed to fucking pieces and I got pieces of his head all fucking over me.”
“Were there any other people on the platform?”
“Yeah loads.”
“So what was doing on the platform, why were you standing so close to the edge?”
“We was aving a row.”
“With who?”
“Each other.”
“You and Sid were fighting?”
“We weren’t fighting we was rowing, having an argument.”
“People heard this, they heard you arguing?”
“Argh fuck knows Manny, I suppose so.” added Tony taking another long drag of the cigarette.
“Okay where was you when he jumped into the train?”
“I dunno. Ten, fifteen feet away from him.”
“Was you running or standing still?”
“Standing still, talking to him.” replied Tony.
“Okay that’s good.”
“Good?” asked Tony.
“It’s good that if you are fifteen feet away from him, then you could not have pushed him.”
“Manny I told you I never fucking pushed the cunt.” snapped Tony just before he got to his feet and walked to the cell door to see if anyone was outside listening.
“You spoke to Reg?” Tony added as came back to Manny and whispered.
“No I couldn’t contact him.”
Tony took another look over his shoulder before leaning closer to Manny.
“Listen you gotta get hold of Reg, Sid was a fucking grass Manny, five minutes before he died he was having a meeting with old bill.”
“He was there at the station having a secret meeting with that cunt LaSalle.”

"Sid was talking to LaSalle?" uttered Manny.
Tony winced and then nodded.
"That's why we were arguing, I caught him with LaSalle and fronted him about it, and LaSalle was telling him he has 24hrs then he would have to come in."
Manny looked at the floor in contemplation before leaning back towards Tony.
"Do not say a word about this to the police Tony, do you understand?"
"Alright I ain't saying fuck all to them anyway."
"Good now let me go and see what we can do for you here." Manny added getting to his feet and knocking on the door for the desk sergeant.
Reggie sat anxiously by the window in Mazzer.s office at Gerard's, he cursed as Eddie's ten minutes turned into twenty and he was just about to pick up the phone again when he saw out the corner of his eye Eddie, Billy and George crossing the road coming towards the club.
"Fucking bout time." Reggie snapped as the three men walked into the office.
"Jesus Reg what the fucks happening today?" sighed Eddie Brenner as he reached for a bottle of whiskey on the table.
"Have you heard anything more about Sid?"
"Nothing mate, just a phone call that he has been killed." answered Eddie.
"Who phoned ya Eddie?"
"Joey Pine phoned the Carpenters Reg."
"Joey? What'd he say?"
"He called about hour an half ago, asked for you, then said he had been given some information that Slice'em Sid had been killed by a train in central London, he said as soon as he finds out more he will get back to us."
"How the fuck does Joey know?" Reg replied.
Eddie shrugged his shoulders before taking a guess.
"Well we know his got a few old bill in his pocket, maybe one of them gave him the nod."
"Get Joey on the phone." Reg said as he passed the phone over to George Hayes.
George grabbed the phone and after a few moments handed it back to Reg.
"It's ringing Reg."
"Joe is that you?" asked Reg.
"Hello mate how are ya?" replied Joe recognising Reggie's voice.
"We're in the dark here Joe, no one knows much."
"It's true mate, and it gets worse, Tony's been nicked."
"What! Tony's nicked, what for?"
"Something to do with Sid, he is banged up at Marble Arch nick, speak to Manny I know he has been seen by a solicitor."
"What and he's asked for Manny?"

“Don’t know mate, all I know is what I told ya, but I should imagine if he asked for a solicitor then it would be Manny.”
“Alright Joe cheers mate, if you find out anything else let us know mate.”
“Course I will, listen look after ya self Reg and I’ll speak to ya later.”
The marina at Puerto Banus , Marbella was the dream of local entrepreneur don Jose Banus, his friends the Delgado family had supported him both morally and financially in creating what was fast becoming southern Spain’s premier destination for the rich and famous. The marina itself was far from finished but already it was attracting interest from some of the wealthiest people in the world.
The Columbus was the Delgado family yacht, over 100ft long it dwarfed most of the other boats moored at the marina.
“This is beautiful.” Ronnie said in awe, as he and Mario boarded the boat and a butler ushered them to the deck area where a large table had been laid out for an evening meal. Ronnie took a seat and poured himself a glass of water and then just sat back and took in the view. The climate and surroundings was having a great effect on Ronnie and looking at him you could easily be fooled into thinking he was a film star or part of the aristocratic society, he was dressed in silk tan trousers with fine Italian brown brogues, a white silk shirt with a brown paisley cravat, the hot Marbella sun had put colour into his face and with his slicked back black hair and dark ray ban glasses he looked and felt every bit the man he was.
When Americans Mark Ralindi and Tommy Spano arrived Ronnie noticed how impressed they were at the surroundings, Mario invited them to sit down as they shook Ronnie’s hand and Ronnie also noticed the difference in their attitude, gone was the brash and cocky persona and in its place seemed a much more humble and respectful demeanour.
“Jesus you guys sure are leading the good life over here.” Spano remarked sitting his bulk down and fiddling away as tried to get comfortable.
Ronnie gave him a slight smile and looked at Mario who took the hint and offered both men a glass of wine.
“You had a good day Ronnie?” asked Ralindi trying to break the ice, Ronnie hesitated in answering as he lit himself a cigarette before ignoring the question and replying with one of his own.
“So did you reach out?” Ronnie asked in a casual manner as he blew out a mouthful of smoke.
“Yeah! We spoke to our people; I think we can work things out.”
“Work things out.” replied Ronnie still acting casual but stern.
Ralindi reached across the table for Ronnie’s cigarettes then just as he was about to pick them up he remembered his manners.
“May I?” he asked holding his hand above the fags.

Ronnie nodded his head giving him permission where Ralindi then proceeded to take one and light one up before answering.
"Yeah we been told to work things out, the guys we work for, the guys you know, want to do business here in Spain. I know all about you Ronnie, good things, my people say good things about you. By the looks of things it looks like you already got yourself a great set up here, now we think it will be in all favour if we can all work together, you guys and our guys did some great things in London, things worked out well between yous, maybe we can do some great things here in Spain."
Ronnie hesitated in answering as he thought over what Ralindi had just said to him.
"We talking partnerships here." he asked.
"That's what were here to work out, partnerships to us Ronnie is like a marriage, it takes a lot of things to make it work, a guy walks in and hits us for a million bucks at the tables Ronnie, are you willing to pipe in with your half million bucks to cover the loss." added Ralindi showing his hand that their interest was as Ronnie presumed gambling.
"You wanna do gambling here then don't ya, that's what you want?"
"This town, this area this whole fucking country is ripe for gambling, you're at the tip of the Mediterranean here, this town could be bigger than Vegas but only if the right people are pushing it forward."
"There is no gambling here in Marbella." added Mario.
"Things change!" replied Spano which made Ralindi give him a look before turning back to Ronnie.
"Okay Ronnie let's put our cards on the table here, we ain't over here asking for permission, some way or another we gonna find someone who can help us over here. We got the money, we got the weight, and we got the balls and knowledge to do this thing here. We're here with you right now to see if we can work together, to see if you can help us do this thing of ours. If we can, then let's sit down and break bread, lets smoke a few fucking cigars, and lets spend the evening drinking and talking about how much fucking money we are all gonna make. But if there's gonna be a problem between us… then let's not sit here wasting each other's fucking time." Said Ralindi which definitely had an effect on Ronnie, who in turn stiffened his posture and removed his glasses, then looked coldly at Ralindi as if sizing him up.
"Well?" barked Ralindi sitting back into his chair and opening his hands for Ronnie to respond.
Ronnie nodded and gave a slight smile from the corner of his mouth before nodding towards Mario to fill him a glass of wine, Ronnie watched the glass being filled before returning his look towards Ralindi
"Okay let's talk." he replied before holding up his glass for Ralindi to toast him with his.

Manny Freedman was sat at the reception of Marble Arch police station waiting one of the Detectives who had arrested Tony Lambrianou to see him, he had been waiting for over an hour now and was fast losing his patience, just as he was about to ask one of the police officers at the desk what was happening he noticed the door opening.
"Mr Freedman."
"Yes! Who are you?"
"My name is Detective Knowles, you asked to see me."
"Yes Detective, I represent Mr Tony Lambrianou and I would like it if you could tell me what is going on with him?"
"We are still going through the witness statements."
"Could you explain why he is being held in the cell then?"
"The reason he is being held in the cells is we need to speak with him regarding what happened to Wilson."
"I understand it was a suicide." asked Freedman trying to get some kind of reaction from the Detective.
"That is what we are trying to determine Mr Freedman."
"Could you tell me then if you intend to interview my client anytime soon?"
"As soon as we have gathered all of our evidence we will be interviewing your client, until then I am sorry but he will just have to be patient."
"Maybe we should send someone over to Marble Arch, see if Manny is there?" Reg remarked as he bit into an apple.
"I'll see if I can get hold of little Sammy, Reg, send him over there." added Eddie.
"If Manny's inside the fucking nick, then how's Sammy gonna get to fucking see him." Billy Hayes barked.
"Well we gotta do fucking something, can't just sit in this fucking office all fucking day" snapped Reg now frustrated
"We gotta start thinking about what happened to us this morning Reg as well." added George Hayes which made Reg reach out for the phone and dial home.
"Hello Dad."
"Alright boy, the Laws been round ere, came knocking eight handed."
"Fucking didn't take them long."
"You alright son, listen don't come back here, there's still two of em sitting up the road." added Charlie Kray snr.
"Mum alright Dad?"
"She's fine son, she's gone over to Shirley's house, they want Shirley to go and identify the body."
"Fucking hell Dad, listen if Manny calls then tell him to leave a number where we can speak to him on."
"Alright will do, now listen keep ya eyes open these coppers looked like they mean business."

"Will do Dad, I'll see you later." Reggie said then quickly getting up and reaching for his coat.
"C'mon we're going let's fucking get out of here."
"Where we going Reg?" asked Eddie.
"We're going over to Marble Arch!"
Shirley Wilson was crying her eyes out as violet held her warmly in the back seat of the car as Sid's old girlfriend Jonie Harris drove them.
"Vi I can't do this, I can't go and see him." cried Shirley remarking about going to identify her son.
"I'll do it Shirley, if you want me, I'll go and see him." added Vi trying to sound strong even though the thought of seeing someone who had just been run over by a train was not something she would want to do.
The three women sat outside the police station for a further fifteen minutes until Shirley composed herself enough to get out of the car, as they walked into the police station Violet was surprised but pleased to see Manny Freedman sitting in the reception, the solicitor rose to his feet immediately and put an arm around both women.
"Is it true, is my boy dead?" Shirley asked Manny who didn't answer her not with his voice anyway.
Shirley once again broke down which forced Jonie to hold her and sit her down trying to console her, this gave Violet a slight reprieve where she noticed Manny giving her a sign to follow him outside.
"Violet I need to speak with Reg."
"What's going on here Manny?" asked Violet.
"I am not sure Violet but I think you need to speak with Reg about that, Tony Lambrianou is being held downstairs I am here for him."
"Why is Tony Here?"
"He was with Sid when it happened."
"Manny what are you saying, did he fall, did he jump or was he pushed?" asked Violet
"From what I have heard, Sid jumped in front of the train and Tony was with him, I don't know why Tony was with him, or what they was doing, all I know is the police want to interview Tony as he was a witness to what happened, anything else I don't know Violet."
"Have you seen Sid, Manny?"
"No I have not."
"But it's definitely him."
"It's definitely him."
"They want Shirley to identify him."
"Good god!" sighed Manny.
"What." asked Violet.

“Mrs Kray, from what I have been told there is not much left of him, I wouldn’t let Shirley see him.” replied Manny sounding very sincere, as through his years being involved as a solicitor he knew full well what a body looked like after it had been dragged under a train.
“I will see what I can do.” added Manny who suddenly looked up as he saw Detective LaSalle walking up the steps to the police station, LaSalle recognised Manny Freedman straight away as both men locked eyes.
“What are you doing here Freedman?” LaSalle sneered as he walked past.
“Detective.” answered Manny, as LaSalle showed the desk officer his warrant card and waited to be let into the interior of the police station.
When Tony Lambrianou cell door was unlocked he jumped with a feeling of relief that finally maybe he was going to be released or at least allowed to wash but when the door swung open and he saw detective Richard LaSalle standing there his relief soon disappeared.
“Hello Tony.” smiled LaSalle.
“What do you fucking want!” snapped Tony looking at LaSalle with disgust.
“Got ya self in a spot of bovver here son ain’t ya.”
“Just fuck off and leave me alone.”
“Don’t wanna hear what I got to say then?”
“Not in the fucking slightest.”
“So you don’t wanna know how I got you by the fucking bollocks then!”
“You got fuck all LaSalle.”
LaSalle smiled broadly as he took a step inside the cell.
“What I got, is you just about to be nicked for fucking murder, you ain’t walking out of this one Lambrianou, you’re going down, down for fucking life, now you can sit here acting all fucking brave or you can talk to me.”
“LaSalle you’re a piece of fucking shit.”
“Yeah well this piece of shit is your only fucking hope, give me Kray for the Fromer murder and I’ll make sure this gets knocked down to manslaughter, you’ll do four years.”
Tony sat back down and smiled, he looked at the floor as he tried to make himself laugh.
“You must think I was born yesterday you cunt, you got fuck all on me for Sid, he jumped in front of a train, you got no witnesses or nothing, so turn your fucking self-round and fuck off back to that cesspit you crawled out of.”
“Tony Lambrianou! The tough guy! Look, Do you think the twins will give a fuck about you, you’ll rot! You’re spending the rest of ya life behind bars.”
“What part of fuck off don’t you understand?”
“And what part of, I am all you got, don’t you understand?” replied LaSalle just before he heard footsteps and voices coming towards the cell.
“This is ya last chance.” he said quickly.

“Fuck off!” replied Tony just as he saw Manny Freedman come into view with two other policemen.
“Tony c’mon you’re being released.” Manny snapped as he forced himself past LaSalle.
Tony smiled as he rose to his feet.
“YOU CUNT!” he growled at LaSalle as it became clear what LaSalle had just tried to do,
LaSalle smiled at Tony with a sarcastic look on his face before turning on his heals to walk away.
“I’ll see ya soon.” LaSalle added still smiling as he walked off where after a couple of steps his face turned to anger.
“What did he want?” snapped Manny to Tony.
“Who let him in here with my client?” he added turning to the two policemen who in turn just shrugged.
“I’ll be reporting this to your superintendent.” added Manny before pulling Tony’s arm.
“This is disgraceful!”
Reg sat at a quiet end of a bar at the Cumberland hotel in Marble Arch with George and Billy Hayes, while he sent Eddie Brenner over to the police station to see what was going on, as luck would have it Eddies timing was perfect, as the moment he turned the corner he saw Tony Lambrianou now washed, and Manny Freedman along with violet Kray, on the steps of the police station.
“He was well drunk Vi.” he heard Tony say explaining what had happened as he approached them.
“Eddie!” Tony said surprised at seeing his friend.
“You alright Tone?” replied Eddie as he gave his pal a hug.
“Manny, Vi.” Eddie added acknowledging the solicitor and Violet.
“Where’s Reg?” asked Violet.
“He’s round the corner Vi, he’s alright.” Eddie replied to violet who in turn realised that the boys needed to talk so she excused herself.
“Listen boys I’d better get back in there with Shirley, tell Reg to call me later.”
“Will do Mrs Kray.” Eddie said before violet walked back into the police station.
“I need to see Reg, Eddie.” said Tony once violet was out of earshot.
“This food is fantastic!” Ralindi said complimenting Mario’s hospitality as he laid down his knife and fork and reached out to grab one of the Cuban cigars that the butler had just put on the table.
Ronnie watched Ralindi pick up the wooden cigar box and offer them around, first he offered one to Tommy Spano and who grabbed for it quickly with his fat stubby fingers, then bit off the end which showed his rough edges and lack

of class, Ronnie was next so he took two cigars out, and handed Mario one first before sitting back and lighting the thick end.
"So you have good information that the Spanish government will not oppose foreign investments in the casino business." asked Ronnie going back to a conversation they had been discussing over dinner.
"It's gonna happen, the government or shall we say some of the government officials can no longer turn up their noses, they're not fools Ronnie, they know the kind of money this business brings into the country." added Ralindi.
Ronnie then turned to Mario giving him the opportunity to add something to the conversation.
"I have spoken to my uncle about this and he agrees, there are and have been rumours in Madrid for some time now, Franco has almost disappeared from decision making, Spain is beginning to change and the people who are bringing in this change have commerce in mind."
"Your uncle the mayor." Remarked Spano.
"Will he help us?" Added Ralindi.
"Of course!"
"Then can he help us?" Ralindi asked.
"Let me just say that when you live in a country which has been under a military dictatorship for over thirty years, you learn how to get things done."
Tommy Spano let out a loud reassuring laugh at what Mario had just said, a laugh that had all the men smiling and then raising their glasses for a toast.
"Salute!" Spano cheered.
George Hayes was first to see Manny, Tony and Eddie enter the bar at the Cumberland hotel, noticing them he nudged Reg who in turn motioned the men to come over.
"You alright Tone!" Reggie remarked as he saw Tony wasn't wearing an overcoat or suit jacket and still had specks of blood around his collar.
"Don't Reg, the cunt jumped right in fucking front of me, just as the train pulled in, his fucking head exploded all over me."
"Cunt! What'd ya mean cunt you're talking about Sid." Billy Hayes snapped back.
"Yeah Sid, the cunt, he was fucking grassing us Reg!" Replied Tony with a real look of anger in his eyes.
"Grassing us, what are you talking about Tony?" Added Reg to Tony who then explained everything that had happened earlier.
"I don't fucking believe it Reg, not Sid." George Hayes sighed after Tony had finished.
"Fucking Sid, I would have trusted him with my life." George added still having trouble believing what he had just discovered.
"Fuuuucking hell." Sighed Reg as he rubbed his face.
"So you saw LaSalle at the nick?"

"That cunt came into my cell Reg and told me I was being charged for killing Sid, then get this he then tells me to roll over on you and Ron for Fromer and then he will make sure the charge gets knocked down to manslaughter."
"So what'd you say" Billy Hayes asked which had the effect of making everyone look at him as if he was an idiot.
"What'd ya think I fucking said!" Snapped Tony.
Reg then lit up a fag and took a large drag before blowing out the smoke from the corner of his mouth.
"So Sid was talking to LaSalle, I would like to know what he's been fucking telling him."
"I would take a guess by what he said to Tony that he has telling stories about Fromer." Added Manny Freedman.
"Sounds like it Manny, anyway how'd you get Tony out so quick today?"
"Weight of evidence Reg, everyone they interviewed gave the same statement, he jumped and if anything Tony was attempting to stop him, it wouldn't have made it past magistrate's court in the morning."
"Well thank fuck for that!" Added Reg sounding relieved.
"So did you push him Tony?"
"Fuck off Reg, I told you what happened."
Manny then intervened and made his apologies that he would have to leave, as he got to his feet he pulled Reggie to the side.
"If I was you Reg I would take a little holiday."
"What can they do Manny?"
"Until we find out what Wilson has been telling LaSalle we don't know do we."
"Yeah but without Sid he doesn't have a witness now does he, it don't matter what he's been telling him."
Manny then pulled Reg closer and lowered his voice.
"Reg take a holiday, he has turned one person in your organisation, how do you know he doesn't have another, this coppers out to get you, be smart! Take a break from the front line and see what happens when the smoke clears."
Reg listened hard at what Manny told him, he bit his lip and gave out a sigh as he nodded his head in agreement.
"Alright Manny, I'll disappear for a few days; anyway I think I'm in the shit again over something else."
"What is it Reg?"
"Had a fucking row this morning with two uniformed old bill, we gave them a kicking."
"Oh good god!" Sighed Manny "What are you crazy?" He added.
Reggie nodded and bit his lip again with a look that showed Manny he was disappointed with himself, Manny shook his head and patted Reg on the shoulder.

"You know where I am if you need me."
"Alright Manny, listen I'll get one of the boys to drop something off to ya tomorrow for today."
"Whenever! Listen look after yourself and don't be a Schmuck."
"So what's our next move?" Ronnie asked as he poured himself a glass of vintage brandy that Mario had fetched from the Columbus's wine cellar.
Mark Ralindi took a large drag of his cigar before and paused a moment before answering.
"Okay thirty percent on all action across the board, we set up the tables and we run the games." Answered Ralindi talking about Ron and Mario's night club Regines.
Mario looked across at Ron and saw that he was clearly uncomfortable with Ralindi's offer.
"Mark we been sitting here talking about partnerships all night, what you can do, and what we can do, then you want to give us thirty percent for the action in our club, what kind of partnership is this."
"We said we would buy the club off yous, we made you a good offer."
"We're not selling the club; we didn't buy the club to sell it."
"So how do you see this thing working, my guys back home have got partners, you want me to go back to the big guy back home, and tell him he is getting a share of fifty percent while you guys are keeping fifty percent all for yourself."
"But it's our club and we're going to get the licences pushed through, without that you have nothing."
"Ronnie I told you before that we will find someone for sale who will get the license's, all due respect Mario but the government in Spain is not the toughest place to clip, we got the money, we got plenty of money to throw around and there are other clubs in Marbella we can buy where we would own all the action."
"Look earlier on, you said let's put our cards on the table so here's our hand, we are supplying the club, we will get the local government to push through the gaming license and we will supply the security, plus we've already got a set up where these millionaires feel comfortable in our place." Added Ronnie.
"Mark when we say we will get my uncle to push for the gaming license this will not end there, once we are working together then we are working together, let's say that some rich playboy comes to our casino like what he sees and then wants to open his own casino just up the road, then we will have the power to refuse him the licenses. Or let's say a group of local gangsters want a piece of the action, what do we do there? Do we send in our own group of gangsters to fight them? Do you think my uncle the mayor will want wars in Marbella?"
"So what you gonna do with the local gangsters?" Added Tommy Spano.

“I make one phone-call and they are visited by the local Guardia civil.”
“The cops.” Asked Spano.
“So you’re telling me with you we got this town locked down.”
“Marbella will be ours to do with as we wish.” Replied Mario sounding very confident.
“Yeah I’ve heard that before.”
“Senor Tommy, Espanola is no like America, what you are forgetting is we have been living under a strict dictatorship for many years now, what matters most in our country is who we can trust, the people trust us, and families like mine, we have been their friends, and in this country our ways are based on what do for each other as friends.”

NOT GUILTY YOU'RE HONOUR

Chapter Twelve

'Ere we go Again'

The weather in London in late December was always freezing cold; tonight was no exception as the thermometer dropped below minus, there was a strong wind mixed with sleet which made the temperature feel even colder.
"Fuck me Eddie, put the heater on mate." Tony Lambrianou cried as he pulled the collars of his shirt up.
"Heaters broken Tony." Added Billy Hayes who was squashed between Tony and his brother George.
"Why are we in this fucking wreck anyway?" Added Tony.
"Ain't you told him yet Reg?" Laughed Eddie driving.
"We're on the run again Tony?"
"Fuck off!" Tony interrupted.
"We chinned two coppers this morning so they got their eyes out for all the other motors" added Billy.
"We chinned two fucking coppers"
"And stuck the boot in a few times tone" replied Reg

"Nah leave it out you ain't got me in a car full of wanted men have you!" Tony joked
"Where'd this happen then" Tony added.
"Stevie Lester's car-site, we went there to give him a dig for always coming up short then out of the fucking blue two cunt's in uniform start looking at the motor, then one thing led to another and we ended up giving them a slap." Said George.
"Did they recognise ya?"
"Yeah, slags already been round mums." Added Reg though not sounding too bothered.
"That's bird Reg." Commented Tony meaning its prison time for hitting policemen.
"Fuck them, listen we got more important things to worry about than two slags in uniform."
"Where we going anyway Reg?" Asked Eddie struggling to see out of the misted up window.
"Get us back on the manor Ed, drop me, Billy and George back at Mazzer's then take Tony to get changed, I'll sort something out while you're gone, when you get back we're slip away for a few days."
"What's in there?" Asked Charlie Adams as Joey Mullins walked into the dark alley just off Hoxton square where Charlie had been waiting, shielding himself from the wind and sleet.
"Two grand, it's just for starters, Frank said get on with it." Added Mullins as he pushed the envelope into Charlie's hand.
"No problem."
"Fuck me Charlie it's fucking freezing, couldn't we meet across the fucking road?" Added Joey nodding in the direction of the pub opposite.
"Too many eyes." Charlie replied as he thumbed through the money.
"Right you go back and tell Frank that this is on. And tell him that as soon as I find out where they are then this happen quick." He added as he stuffed the envelope into his pocket.
"Ronnie is still away from what I can gather." Replied Mullins.
"Alright then we're take Reg out." Replied Adams straightening his collar.
"And leave Ron?"
"For now yeah."
"Fuck me Charlie doing Reg and leaving Ron is taking a big fucking risk."
"We all know the fucking risks here, whatever way this goes down it ain't gonna be easy."
"As long as you know what you're doing." Added Mullins.
"Don't worry about that! Listen tell Frank if I need him, I will leave a message for him at the café."
"Will do Charlie."

Charlie then pulled the collar up on his overcoat and shook Mullins by the hand.
“Right lets go to fucking work.” He mouthed before disappearing into the wind and sleet.
As the chauffeur driving Mario and Ronnie pulled up outside their nightclub Regines in Puente Romano Mario noticed that a large crowd had gathered outside the entrance,
“What’s all this about?” He asked Gino the club head doorman as he opened the car door.
“It’s James Bond! Sean Connery has just gone inside.” Gino replied smiling.
“It’s James Bond.” Mario repeated as he turned to Ronnie who in turn smiled back at him.
Ronnie and Mario walked inside and went straight to their own private table where Mario called for the waiter.
“Get us a bottle of brandy and send two complimentary bottles of champagne over to Sean Connery’s table.”
“House champagne?” Asked the waiter.
“No give him the good stuff.” Mario added before turning back to Ronnie.
“Shall we say hello to him Ronnie?”
“You can Mario but I’m okay, let him enjoy his evening.” Added Ronnie before leaning in closer to speak above the music.
“Listen when you see the yanks tomorrow tell them that I have had to go away on business and that they should continue with you in my absence.”
“You’re not coming to the meeting Ronnie.”
“No, it's best this way, they heard my thoughts tonight, its best that I don’t become too familiar with them, oh and tell them that as soon as my brother Charlie is better then they’ll be seeing a lot of him as well.”
“Okay Ronnie I will do as you say.” Replied Mario just as Johnny Walsh walked over.
“Ronnie, Mario, how’d it go tonight?”
“Good we’re in business, the yanks are on board.” Replied Ronnie.
“James Bond’s over there.” Added Johnny smiling and nodding in the direction of Connery.
“Yeah license to fucking kill!” Replied Ronnie laughing as Johnny sat down and poured himself a brandy.
“The boats booked for midday tomorrow Ron.” Added Johnny.
“Good”
“What boat?” Asked Mario?
“We’re going to Morocco Mario.” Replied Ronnie reaching for his cigarettes.
“Morocco?”
“Yeah, fucking Casablanca!”
‘What we going out there for Ron?”

"We got some business to see to, then when we get back we're get Charlie out and start this thing with the yanks, Johnny, nothing is going to fucking stop us now, not the Firms back in London, the fucking Law, no one can fucking stop us now!"
The Horse and Hounds pub in Shoreditch at 6.00PM was packed to the rafters as eager workmen just finished work scrambled to get as much drink inside them before 'happy hour' ended at seven, sitting in the corner was a very sombre looking Charlie Adams, he had an empty scotch glass on the table before him and he sat looking at the merry workers, looking like at any moment he was about to jump up and smack someone around, Charlie raised his head as he saw Frank Adams and Joey Mullins push their way past the drinkers.
"You better take this back." Adams sighed throwing a large envelope on the table as the two men sat down next to him.
"What's that." Asked Frank though he knew it contained the upfront money.
"It's the fucking wonga, you've heard ain't ya?" Replied Adams sounding even more sombre and angry.
"Heard what?" Added Mullins looking aggravated.
"Reg, he's on his fucking toes, they bashed a couple of coppers up over Commercial road, there are fucking old bill everywhere looking for them."
"Ah for fucks sake." Frank Adams replied.
"So what does that mean?" Snapped Mullins.
"It means old bill is fucking all over em, jobs off." Replied Adams bluntly.
"Charlie there might still be a way, we could still find Reg."
"Joey are you fucking mad or what? What do you want me to do, go around asking all their mates where he is hiding, how the fuck am I going to find out where he is, look jobs off and that's that."
Frank sighed as he took a gulp of his scotch then looked over his shoulder before leaning in closer to Charlie.
"Alright Charlie, for now we'll take a back step but once all this has settled down take another look at it okay"
"Frank, you know I'll do them but it can't be done now, there's too much fucking heat mate."
"I know mate, look take a grand out that dosh and we're speak about this again once everything is back to normal."
"So what we doing now Guv?" Asked Sergeant Daniels as he sat next to Detective LaSalle who was just finishing his coffee they had just brought on Battersea bridge.
"We start again." Replied LaSalle.
"Fucking joke! We know everything about them, let's just nick em."

“We got no witnesses, I am not nicking them till I have everything in place, the next time I look at them across a court I want to see their faces when they go down for fucking life.”
“You don’t sound too pissed off guv.”
“Don’t you fucking believe that son, inside I am fucking seething, but I’ll wait, one way or another, those bastards are mine.”
Reggie Kray sat laughing as he cracked a joke with Tony Lambrianou which made Billy Hayes feel slightly uneasy, inside he wished he could share in Reggie’s care free attitude but silently he was shitting himself, Old bill was looking for them on two fronts, one for the assault and now having just found out Slice’em Sid was an informer the Law could know everything or anything about them.
“Fuck me Reg! You seem relaxed mate.” Billy uttered as he reached out for the bottle of scotch which was on the table. Reg suddenly stopped laughing as he heard what Billy had just said and he looked up at him.
“What’s the matter, how can you not laugh, stuck in this fucking caravan.” Replied Reg. Again smiling as he commented on his surroundings, a caravan on a travellers site deep out back roads of Cambridgeshire.
“Just have a fucking drink Bill and relax, everything will be alright.” Tony added but sounding more stern.
“So how fucking long we gotta stay out here for?” Georgie Hayes suddenly snapped which immediately sobered Reg up.
“You know the fucking game George, we’re stay here until things die down.”
“How do we know that things will die down Reg? Who knows what Sid has been telling the fucking Law, and that bollocks down at Stevie Lester’s car site has put us all in the shit, that’s a fucking lay down for chinning a copper, eighteen months to three stretch were looking at for that.”
“Don’t fucking say that cunt's name to me anymore, he’s a slag and he got what all fucking slags deserve, now listen, fuck what he has been saying to the filth! What fucking difference does it make, they suspect us of every fucking thing anyway but without that slag to go in the box they got fuck all, and don’t worry about what happened down the car site, if we got to go away for a year then so fucking be it.”
“That’s fucking great Reg!” Sighed Billy.
“Manny will sort it all out, leave it to him, we just gotta stay out of sight for a while till we get our story fixed, there was only two coppers, it is their word against ours, Manny will place us somewhere else at the time it took place, there will be a dozen fucking witnesses to say we were elsewhere at that time, so just have a drink and fucking relax, you’re starting to fucking make me feel on edge now.” Reg snapped.
“How did Ron sound today Reg?” Tony asked trying to change the subject as Reg reached for another cigarette.

"He's alright mate, he already heard about that slag grassing us."
"Typical, Ronnie hears about everything." Tony added with a smile.
"Nah he is out the way, just like we are, we both agree, let this fucking storm pass then we will appear again just like nothing ever happened."
"And we're be back on top of the fucking world again." Added Tony raising his glass in the air.
"No… We'll own the fucking world!" Reg answered.

The End.

Book 2
Not Guilty Your Honour…The 70's

Coming soon…

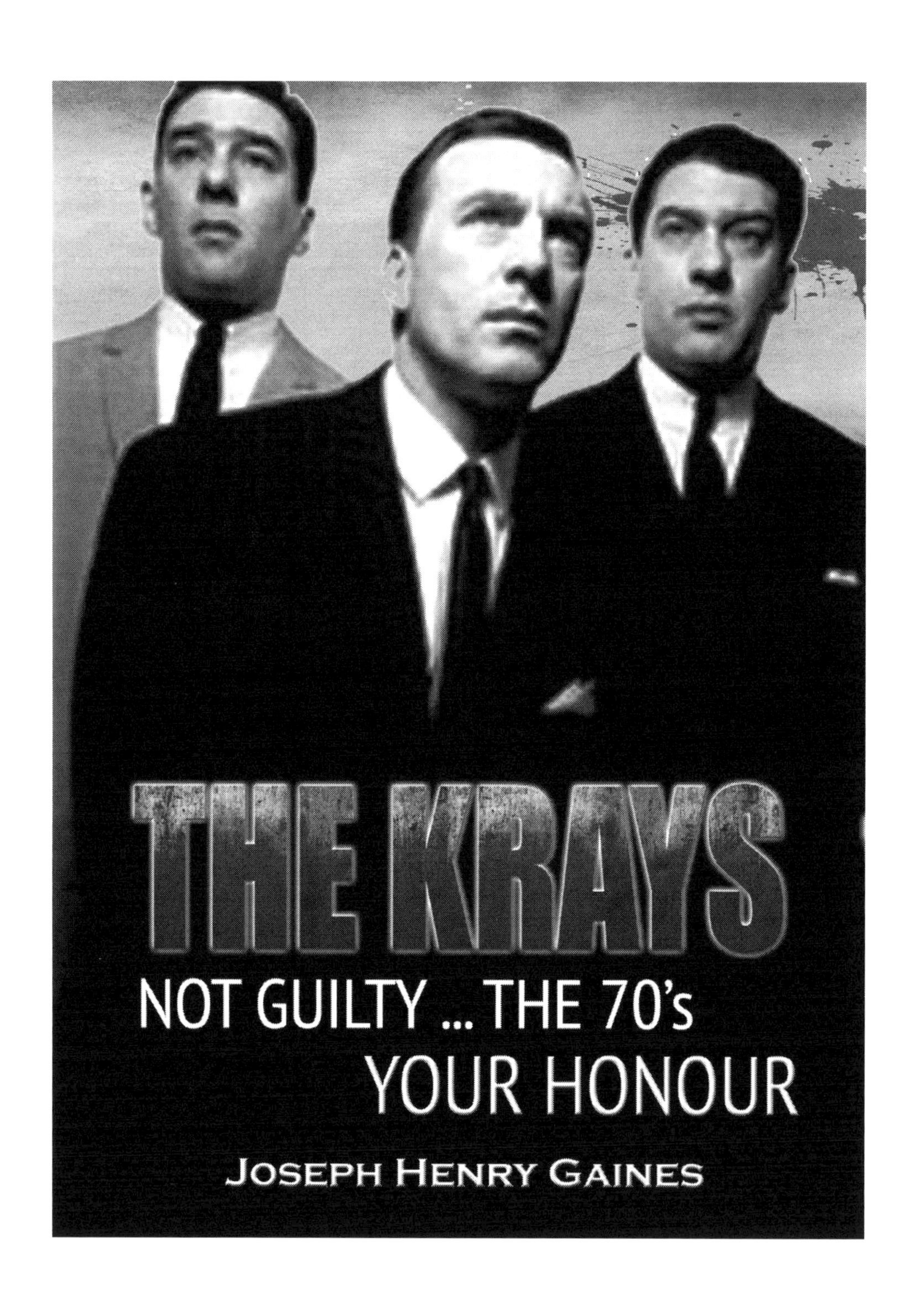
THE KRAYS
NOT GUILTY ... THE 70's
YOUR HONOUR
JOSEPH HENRY GAINES

Kray Slang Dictionary

Common words used in Kray's not Guilty and their meaning.

To some people reading this book it may seem like a 'school teacher's nightmare'. So we have added this last chapter to explain that many of the words are written as they are spoken on the streets of London and not spelling mistakes.

Londoners use a lazy kind of English where a lot of commonly used words are shortened. Sometimes I have misspelt a word to make it sound more as it is spoken so please have patience. The dialogue especially is written just as the characters speak.

Hers is a couple of examples;

When Ron Kray is talking about the prison Governor I have spelt it Guvnor, the guv part is spoken as it reads similar to dove or shove.

Another quick example is when the characters say 'we gotta go'. The correct pronunciation would be 'we got to go' but the characters in the book would not say that, instead they shorten the words Got to-Gotta.

Other words relevant to the story.

Manor (The area where someone comes from or lives) 'He's on our manor'. Means 'He is in our area'.

The Firm (a name for a London organised crime gang)

Dunno (Don't Know)

Karzee (toilet)

Shant (Alcoholic drink)

Bruv (Brother)

Mate (Friend)

Staunch (strongly reliable, man of his word) as in, he's staunch.

Straight goers (civilians, working people)

Knocker (someone who habitually rips people off for money)

On his toes (hiding from the police or other gangs)

Tooled up (to carry weapons)

Nicked (arrested)

Pavement work (Armed robbery)

A piece (A gun)

Choky (Solitary confinement in prison)

Snidy (Sneaky action or sneaky person)

Shrewdy (clever person)

Ya (You) as in I'm telling ya

Gotta (Got to) as in, he's gotta go.

Nah (No)

Em (Them) as in ' Just go and tell em'

Im (Him) as in, tell im.

Bigga (Bigger)

Names are also shortened frequently, in this book many of the characters names have been written down the same way that they would be spoken on the street.

Tone (Tony)

Ed (Eddie)

Vi (Violet)

For a more detailed look at some of the sayings and London slang check out the Official Krays Not Guilty Your Honour website.

www.krays.org

Joseph Henry Gaines

About the author

Joseph Henry Gaines (not his real name) was born into the criminal world. His father worked with the Kray's in various business matters. The world he was brought up in was a constant battle for survival. Times on the run, times visiting his father and uncles in prison, times where he and his mother lived on the breadline, times where they took holidays in Las Vegas, New York and Monte Carlo.

It was not what would be commonly known as a normal 'childhood'. "Some Dad's took their sons fishing at the week-end, my Dad got me in the Rolls Royce or Maserati and took me on the rounds to the pubs and spiels where he picked up money, sometimes he would bung me a fiver, sometimes I would see him chin someone, whatever it was, it was good fun".

When Gaines was a teenager in the eighties he began to carve out his own reputation, money was pouring in and he frequently travelled to places like New York, Johannesburg and Spain where he had numerous bits of business going on.

Gaines when in the UK would also visit Ronnie Kray as often as he could, Ronnie was being held in Broadmoor hospital which had different visiting guidelines than prisons, in fact he could have two visits a day, every day. So Gaines who now lived in surrey which was about thirty minutes' drive from Broadmoor often stuck his head in to see Uncle Ron, as he calls him.

Gaines also knew Tony Lambrianou very well, in fact when Tony finished his prison sentence he worked and socialised with Gaines. " I remember once where we was having some agro with the Africans who ran the illegal mini cabs outside the clubs in the west end, we put it on them really, sort of muscled in and told them they have to pay us, so one thing led to another and it started to get a bit heated, we sent Tony down there to see them one night and that was that, next week we picked up our money, then every Friday night it was payday!"

Gaines is now a successful businessman; he has had his wars with other Firms and done his bit of bird and still lives on the borders of south London where his house is usually like a clubhouse for all the boys on the manor.

It is with this first-hand knowledge and the understanding of how things were in London over the last few decades that he brings this story to life.

"To know Ron and Reg well, you have to have lived in their shoes a bit" Gaines says, it's okay writing fiction about them, but you need to have experienced the highs and lows and the colossal contradictions that living this kind of life brings you.

One minute you are fighting for your life, it could be the old bill looking to lock you up and throw away the key or it could be another gang who want you out the way.

Gaines has been asked a few times to write his own story but he has refused and replied that maybe when he ninety years old he might write a book.

It's the kray's idea that excites him now and with all his experience he says he is enjoying the writing and reliving some of the memories.

He has three more books in his mind and is also in conversations with a few producers about the possibility of turning the books into a film.

"But if this is going to be a film then it's got to be how the twins truly were, how they acted and how they felt, I want people to see exactly what they was all about, sure they were wicked bastards but that's the life we live in, doesn't matter if you live on the streets or the corridors of parliament, somewhere, someone is plotting to take everything you have.

It's a dog eat dog world, always has been and sadly, probably always will be."

Doubts and criticism can have two effects.
They can destroy you, or they can fuel you with determination.
If you want me beat then pat me on the head.
Slander me… and I turn into the North wind.
I never stop!
JH Gaines

For my three sons… you are the apple of my eye.
My past, present and future.
Whatever I do, it is all for you.

Printed in Poland
by Amazon Fulfillment
Poland Sp. z o.o., Wrocław